Gerhard Roth

Hell Is Empty —
And All the Devils Are Here!

A Novel

D1528109

Gerhard Roth

Hell Is Empty —
And All the Devils Are Here!

A Novel

Translated and with an Afterword
by Todd C. Hanlin

Ariadne Press
Riverside, CA

Hell Is Empty — And All the Devils Are Here!
By Gerhard Roth

Translated and with an Afterword by Todd C. Hanlin
reprinted with kind permission by the author
© 2022 Todd C. Hanlin

Gerhard Roth: *Die Hölle ist leer - die Teufel sind alle hier*
© S. Fischer Verlag GmbH, Frankfurt am Main, 2019.
All rights reserved by S. Fischer Verlag GmbH.
(ISBN 978-3-10-397213-9)

Front cover photo © Céline Colin 2015 CC BY-ND 2.0

Image credits, in order of appearance:
P. 125 *Voynich Manuscript*, 1404–1438 (probably), Yale University.
P. 135 Ustad Mansur, *Portrait of a Falcon*, 1619, Museum of Fine Arts,
Boston.
P. 136 Ustad Mansur, *Salt-water Fish*, 1621–1625, Red Fort Museum,
Delhi. From: Verma, S.P.: *Mughal Painter of Flora and Fauna Ustad
Mansur*, Abhinav Publications, Ed. 1, 1999.
P. 188 Giorgio de Chirico, *The Child's Brain*, 1914, Moderna Museet,
Stockholm.
P. 192 Joseph Klibansky, *Selfportrait of a Dreamer*. Photo: © Gerhard Roth.
P. 197 *Outline sketch*. Photo: © Gerhard Roth.
P. 250 Albrecht Dürer, *Melencolia I*, 1514, Metropolitan Museum of Art,
New York.

Publisher's Cataloging-in-Publication data

Names: Roth, Gerhard, 1942 June 24-2022, author. | Hanlin, Todd C.,
translator.
Title: Hell is empty — and all the devils are here : a novel / Gerhard Roth;
translated and with an afterword by Todd C. Hanlin.
Description: Riverside, CA: Ariadne Press, 2023.
Identifiers: LCCN: 2023920269 | ISBN: 978-1-57241-232-3 (paperback) |
978-1-57241-229-3 (ebook)
Subjects: LCSH Venice (Italy)--Fiction. | Murder--Fiction. | Paranormal
fiction. | BISAC FICTION / World Literature / Austria / 21st Century
Classification: LCC PT2678.O79615 H45 2023 | DDC 813.6--dc23

Hell is empty — And all the devils are here!

William Shakespeare
The Tempest

I

The Loneliness of the Beachcomber

Every morning Lanz went down to the beach and strolled from the abandoned Naval Hospital near his house up to the Hotel Excelsior and then back again. "I'm wasting my life," he thought as he walked. "I'm not living. I'm acting like some fish in an aquarium that just floats in the water, waiting for something to happen." But nothing ever happened since he was the only surviving fish in the tank. All the rest had been caught and eaten. The only things that connected him to the outside world were the sights and sounds from the unfamiliar beings that he saw through the transparent glass walls of the aquarium. And because one week resembled the next, he lived each day as if it were his last.

He was almost always on the lookout for flotsam and jetsam. He found different seashells and snail shells, a chunk of glass that had been polished by the sea, an abraded rock or small remnants of twigs and branches worn smooth by high and low tides and the saltwater. Sometimes he found animals, still living or already dead: crabs, but also fish, and occasionally even a dead seagull. But he couldn't ignore the odds and ends—of nylon bags, plastic bottles, crumpled drinking cups and cigarette butts. He was usually out so early in the morning that he rarely ever saw anyone else, except for men and women walking their dogs. They seldom had a conversation. In winter he had encountered a strange gaunt trumpeter who faced out to sea and made pathetic sounds on his instrument.

But a few weeks ago he had found a dead refugee child whose body had washed ashore. At first he thought it was a piece of luggage. And when he got closer, he thought it was a dead animal. But finally he saw that it was a small African girl. The child was lying on her side, slightly curled up, her face swollen, her mouth half-open, the index finger on one hand pointing back out to sea. But Lanz saw nothing out there, he only saw the coming and going of the waves that produced a gentle dull booming farther out and then a slapping sound as they came ashore. The girl was barefoot, wore a red T-shirt, a small silver earring, and what was left of her denim jeans. A clump of algae had collected beside her head and one knee. As he stood there, staring at the child, his mind was blank. He no longer heard the waves or the seagulls. His complete attention was now focused on the sight of the dead girl. Suddenly a dog was beside him, barking and sniffing the corpse while vigorously wagging its tail. Then it began to bark, and wouldn't stop even as its owner commanded the dog to heel. Lanz turned around, since the dog—a black-and-white-spotted border collie—had begun to bound in the corpse's direction. Still frantically barking, the dog hurried back to the girl, before it excitedly ran over to an elderly woman in a windbreaker, though it then turned and raced back to the dead girl. Lanz realized that the woman was as panicked as her border collie. She screamed at the dog, but it wouldn't calm down.

Just as Lanz was about to say something, a policeman appeared. After bending down to examine the girl, he told the woman to take her dog away and wait for him over by the public showers. Lanz had forgotten that he was the one who had called the police from his cell phone, but he suddenly realized that was the case. While the officer questioned him, other policemen and men in plain clothes rushed up to search the area for evidence and to photograph the dead girl. After half an hour, Lanz was allowed to leave, but the incident remained on his mind the whole time.

He found no articles in the next day's newspapers and nothing the day after that. It wasn't until a week had passed that he read about a dead girl being found "several days ago in the Lagoon" and that she probably belonged to the illegal Africans on the beach who sold washcloths and bath towels or offered imitation Rolex and IWC watches. After that, there were no further reports. Apparently they didn't want to harm the tourist trade, Lanz thought.

Several times he went for a walk along the beach at nightfall. It was already warm, and he saw a man and a woman on an air mattress, embracing in the semi-darkness. The woman was making gentle mournful sounds, the man was strenuously panting. The only things Lanz could make out were the movement of a white shirt and the woman's splayed legs. As he walked on, he thought he had also seen long blond hair and the man's jeans down around his ankles. Lanz quickly turned away toward the water.

Several evenings later by one of the beach cabanas he noticed a couple who seemed to be silently wrestling with each other. After that encounter, he didn't walk on the beach again till early the next morning. At one point upon his return home, he realized that his mail was being delivered by an African, not by the usual Serbian postman. When Lanz gazed at him questioningly, the man explained that from now on he would be bringing the letters and packages. Lanz offered the mailman a can of Coca-Cola that the man quickly and silently guzzled. Lanz learned that the man's name was Samuel Goodluck Oboabona. He spoke English and Italian, but he didn't want to talk about his native Nigeria nor about his migration—only about his immediate family at home. Lanz had the impression he had seen Oboabona before, and then remembered that it had been on the beach where the mailman, as a vendor, had sold fake brands of lady's handbags. The man had now died his hair blond, it was also cut differently, most noticeable were the absent sideburns.

Before the African left, Lanz thought about the dead girl on the beach and asked Oboabona if he knew anything about the incident. The mailman gulped, his gaze wandered, and he stammered that it was the daughter of a friend who had taken her to the beach that evening after dark. Tears came to his eyes and he abruptly turned away. Lanz hastily said goodbye, gazed out the window, and saw the mailman with his moped and mail cart, ringing the bell at the garden gate of the villa across the street.

Until evening Lanz translated more of *Gulliver's Travels* from English into Italian and then read his translation from the beginning to the part where the ship *Antilope*, on a voyage to the East Indies on 5 November 1699, struck a reef, the lifeboat capsized, and the only survivor, Gulliver, at last swam ashore where he fell asleep, exhausted. Since the young man's first name was Lemuel, it continually reminded Lanz of the mailman whose first name was Samuel and of the drowned girl. As a child, Lanz had read *Gulliver's Travels* in a condensed illustrated edition. As he translated, he could see the colorful drawings in his mind's eye, alternating with Granville's illustrations in the copy he had used while studying the English language. Lanz thought it was wonderful that Gulliver survived the ocean, was washed ashore, and—exhausted by the hot weather and a pint of brandy he had drunk before leaving the sinking ship—had fallen asleep. From that point on, the author Jonathan Swift had all the possibilities of a fantastic journey at his disposal. Had it only been a dream? Had Gulliver gone insane as a result of his extraordinary experiences? Had everything simply been a fabrication, constructed from some seaman's yarn? Or was it actually based on a true story, even if in some exaggerated sense?

Lanz closed his laptop and left the house. He took the river walk on the Lungomare Gabriele D'Annunzio with its benches between the trees, on down to the main road, the Gran Viale Santa Maria Elisabetta, sat down on one of the sidewalk chairs at a fast food outlet and received a glass of Merlot, a pizza Margherita, and a friendly greeting from the proprietor. They never spoke to each other because Lanz was always lost in thought when he took a break there. Only that first week, when he had eaten pizza, spaghetti, lasagna or a roll with creamed salt cod and drunk Merlot, the proprietor had gone out of his way to introduce himself, asking Lanz to call him

Giuseppe. And when Lanz replied that in Italian his first name was Emilio, his last name Lanz, Giuseppe had jokingly erupted: "Ah! Mario Lanza!" After that, Lanz had avoided the pizzeria for two whole weeks, and the next time he came in, Giuseppe conspicuously greeted him as "Signor Lanz" to show his respect. And that was the way it went on all subsequent visits, sometimes they only nodded to each other briefly.

This time Giuseppe had served him a second glass of Merlot, "on the house," as he put it. After the meal, Lanz went home, tired. The whole way back he imagined he was Gulliver, lying bound on the island of Lilliput off the northern coast of Australia. Stretched out on his couch, he drank several more glasses of Merlot until he became drunk and closed his eyes. As he was drifting off, he remembered the pistol he had stuck in an empty drawer of a cabinet. He had sworn not to take it out until it was his last resort. In the two years it had been stowed there, he had never looked at it and had considered tossing it into the ocean.

He woke at daybreak. For a time he just lay there, lethargic, and then corrected his translation of Gulliver's adventures with the giants in Brobdingnag, an episode that made him recall his own childhood fears and daydreams. At noon he strolled down to the ocean. He had barely reached the Lungomare named after Gabriele D'Annunzio when he noticed a woman in a black bikini, kneeling on the shore, photographing something. At first glance he felt attracted to her. He hurried to one of the beach cabanas that he had now rented for the past two summers, took off his sneakers, his T-shirt and jeans, and slipped into his swimming trunks. He remembered to take along some money.

The woman was still kneeling on the damp sandy beach. He approached her and discovered that she was leaning over a large transparent jellyfish. At the same time he saw in the water a smaller swarm of these marine animals. He studied the woman more closely: her blond hair, her long fingers and toes, and her trim body. When she put her camera down and briefly glanced up at him, he had the elated feeling of being someone spontaneously in love. She had large dark eyes, makeup on her lids, lashes, and eyebrows.

It was not a good idea to go out into the water, but she went without hesitation to get pictures of the small jellyfish swarm. She slowly approached them, raised her camera, looked through the viewfinder, and then quickly came ashore.

"Jellyfish?" he asked in Italian, "*Meduse?*"

"Yes, a million of them," she answered in English, and laughed.

He waited until she had walked off, and then followed her tentatively. Ever since he had been living on the Lido, he liked to follow people, both attractive and repulsive folks. On his pursuits he had also discovered many little alleys. More than anything else he loved the villas and green canals where motorboats docked and the shoreline was covered with grass and trees. Last year he had bought a bicycle that he used now and then and a boat with an outboard motor. Once, when he had followed a pretty woman undetected, he crisscrossed half the town until she finally disappeared in her sailboat on one of the canals. Another time he snuck around, following a man with grey hair, a straw hat and a cane. The man frequently sat down on various benches and spoke to himself. So Lanz was forced to find a bench that would allow him to keep an eye on the stranger. After an hour the old man took a seat at Giuseppe's Pizzeria Plaza, so Lanz asked the proprietor to introduce him to the stranger. To his surprise the man had been an archaeologist who had spent more than ten years working on the excavations in Pompeii. He was delighted by Lanz's interest and told him the latest about the frescos in the buildings that had been buried when Vesuvius erupted.

Meanwhile it had become so hot that Lanz scooped some water to cool his head while the woman got under one of the public showers along the beach. First she had handed her camera to one of the attendants in a white uniform, exchanged a few words with him, and afterwards he handed her a beach towel. She took back her camera, hurried over the hot sand to a small shop in a hut, and reappeared with a sun hat on her head and flip-flops on her feet. Lanz quickly bought a green baseball cap for himself and ran back down the beach, but couldn't find the woman. By now he could see small white clouds in the sky, and when he waded in shallow water, he could feel sharp crushed shells beneath his feet. If he escaped to the beach, the hot sand hurt his feet, so he went back in the water. Large bunches of green or pale grey seaweed made him think of paper streamers at the conclusion of Carnival. In addition, trash had washed ashore, a sight that always disgusted him on his walks. At that moment he felt that he had all the qualities of a misanthrope.

While keeping an eye out for the woman, he spotted a crumpled cigarette pack with the familiar camel trademark, a cap from an empty plastic bottle of Coca-Cola, an ice cream cup, a torn plastic bag, seashell fragments, a squid's oval white breastplate, crabs in the water at his feet, and a blue cigarette lighter that had washed ashore. He finally saw the black bikini and the woman's sun hat as she was kneeling again in the water. When he reached her, he was amazed to learn that she was photographing the same objects he had just seen. She stood up, took a couple of steps, and stopped to pick up the black shells of some sea mussels. He gradually realized that the woman was taking random snapshots of objects that had washed ashore, still-lives of dead matter, a lifeless dark-brown jellyfish floating in the receding waves, first showing its underside, but then being tossed on its side by the water's movement—at the mercy of the current—along with cigarette butts, a small red plastic airplane (the kind you find in surprise eggs), half a newspaper page, shoelaces, the grip from an old wooden cane.

The water at the shoreline was crystal clear, it foamed as it receded, and continuously emitted gurgling sounds of the waves that, as Lanz often said, began to speak when they reached the shore. Meanwhile the woman was photographing shells from other mussels and conchs, also a yellow plastic bottle of suntan lotion, flat stones, chips of tile that were worn smooth, bits of Styrofoam, and a gleaming wet pinecone. Seagulls silently floated overhead. He could hear people calling out, shouting, and snippets of conversation from the guests' beach chairs, the drone of a single-engine airplane, and the distant rumble of jets in the blue-and-white sky far above.

Lanz turned to study the woman's well-groomed feet, the shape of her toes and toenails, and secretly envied the man who lived with her. It was probably some stuffy rich American who needed her as a façade for his masculinity, he thought to himself. The woman had noticed Lanz some time ago, but didn't pay any attention to him. Schools of tiny fish zigged and zagged in the water, as if frightened by something, and he lost sight of them. Lanz thought that the woman photographer might be trying to document the consequences of the process of civilization. The destruction of beauty by greed that only focused on its own possessions. He felt his idea was both pretentious and accurate. The woman was aiming her camera at a small boulder beside a concrete jetty that went out into the sea when she suddenly turned and, without saying a word, took his picture. She laughed, waved him over, and showed him the display on her digital camera, featuring the image of Lanz in the green baseball cap with his usual gloomy expression. He smiled, unintentionally nodded, and kept walking without looking back. I'm an idiot, he told himself. Why don't you turn around and wave back at her? He now discovered a dead pigeon in the sand and some tracks of black-headed gulls with the indelible impression of the webs between their toes. Two men dressed in white were walking back and forth in front of the closed Grand Hotel des Bains, surveying everything with their attentive gazes. The row of cabanas with their straw roofs gave the beach the appearance of some native African village at the end of the 19th century. He again had misanthropic feelings and thought about turning around and going home—after all, he had seen these ugly sights before—but he paused.

The Grand Hotel des Bains felt abandoned. Some young American college students were gathered on the beach in front of the sacred literary edifice that plays a role in Thomas Mann's *Death in Venice*, collecting clams that probably symbolized death to them. As Lanz continued walking, he saw tourists on two white paddleboats just coming ashore and other bathers, scattered here and there, lying on towels in the midday heat. Small boulders near the concrete jetty that extended out into the sea were studded with seashells and covered in algae. Close rows of colorful beach umbrellas were positioned beside the hotel. Lanz couldn't understand why they suddenly attracted his attention. Just as he was debating if he should go back and look for the woman, he spotted her by yet another group of jellyfish in the water. He approached unobtrusively. The larger jellyfish looked like Mille-fiori paperweights, he thought, the smaller ones like little toy parachutes. The photographer was so preoccupied with the dead animals that he was able to move on, unnoticed.

He had thought about suicide several times over the past few months, he now recalled, even though there had been no specific reason to do so. He had then automatically found something else to occupy his time. He either dug into his translation work or turned on the TV, and sometimes, when the thought had become too intense, he went to Giuseppe's and stayed there until closing time. Only then would he go home drunk and fall asleep. Each time he wanted to commit suicide someplace where there would be no witnesses. But as soon as he began to feel better, he forgot these thoughts. This time he considered it only logical that, as soon as he got home, he would take the pistol from the cabinet and shoot himself in the heart. Or, he thought, maybe it would be better if he rode his bike to the lighthouse behind the small airport and put an end to his life there.

Before *Gulliver's Travels*, he had translated the early science-fiction novel *The Invisible Man* by H.G. Wells, where a scientist, Dr. Griffin, discovers a chemical formula that makes him invisible. Dr. Griffin experiments on himself and becomes invisible, but is unable to reverse the process. So he wraps himself in bandages and wears sunglasses when he leaves the university in hopes of hiding in a snowy village. While working on his translation, Lanz imagined that he was the invisible man, as he had done back when he had first read the story in high school. He had had a desire to be invisible throughout his childhood and this had nurtured his curiosity of learning more about people than anyone else had ever done. Even in high school he had thought that lies, conspiracies, cheating, and violence were apparently as common as breathing.

Since he was distracted, he didn't notice that the woman had passed him on the side of the cabanas. She greeted an older man with a kiss on the cheek. His hawk's nose was impressive, as was his black and grey beard. Judging from his hair and gestures, Lanz concluded that he was an American or an Italian—and an alpha male. Lanz turned back, since he was already at the Hotel Excelsior. His feet, his back and the backs of his legs were all sunburned; the sand was so hot by now that it was almost impossible to walk on it. So it was probably best to turn back. Two hours after he had taken off to follow the woman, he came to the Lungomare D'Annunzio and his cabana, took off the baseball cap, showered with cold water, and ran out into the ocean. He swam over to the white lifeguard station. The two young men, dressed entirely in red, sat on the beach not far away, between a motorboat and a rowboat that were also red and bore the same white inscription: "*Salvataggio*"—"Rescue."

The water was warm, mixed with a cooling undercurrent that he found invigorating. He let the current wash him ashore, but he didn't swim back out to the open water as he often did when he was younger. Lost in thought, he floated on his back. Even though he tried, he couldn't get his mind off the woman. He remembered he had reacted awkwardly when she showed him his picture on her camera's display. Shouldn't he have said something like: "Who is that man?" Or invited her to a drink and asked for a print of the picture? He could have said that now it was his turn to photograph her, or something else, anything else . . . Perhaps the encounter was an indication that he would remain alone, still be the lonely fish in the aquarium, the oddball who translates the books of writers into another language, and who has become one or more imaginary characters in an imaginary world.

One of the rooms in his small villa was chock-full of books, his drug of choice (in his own words) that made it possible for him to endure his daily existence. Now that he had finished the translation of *Gulliver's Travels*, he felt useless. Reading only became truly alive when he was translating novels, plays and poems, or when they swallowed him from the very first line. He felt that every reader was a Jonah, swallowed by a monster and captured deep under the surface of a sea of thought in his own strange inner world. For a time, that shielded him from the unpleasantness of the day and from the emptiness and apathy of his loneliness.

But that wasn't the real reason why he thought about the new woman, her lips, her hair, teeth, fingers and toes. It was the awareness that he hadn't been sociable. He was not a flop with women, but he did lose his eloquence whenever he fell in love. In the first phase of infatuation he rarely felt sexual stirrings, just a deep devotion that only gradually became desire. However, if he picked someone up just for sex, strangely enough he was a good lover from the outset.

As he lay there on the beach, blinking at the water and the waves, the woman photographer continued to haunt him.

Then he thought again about his pistol, about death and nonexistence. He would become a droplet in the ocean, he told himself. His death would change nothing—other people would live in his house, sunbathe on the beach and be happy or sad, contemplate their old age, their youth, and, not least of all, their death.

Later, a single-engine plane took off from the small Venezia-Lido airport and flew along the beach, turned out to sea, and then finally came back over the houses and returned to the airport. Each time it flew overhead, it made him think of death. Over and over again he thought about the jellyfish, the dove that had washed ashore, the seashells, and especially the dead child. Their perceptions and feelings had been extinguished.

On his morning stroll along the Lungomare D'Annunzio he noticed on a tree trunk the obituary and color photo of an old woman. He calculated from her birth and death dates that she had been 94 years old. He pondered how old he would be if his own mother died at 94. By then, would he be more or less indifferent to her passing? For example, especially if she had been suffering from Alzheimer's? Wasn't it great to lounge on the peaceful beautiful Lido beach and still be alive? Just then he realized how much his emotions and decisions fluctuated. On the one hand he loved life, but on the other it seemed as if he were leading an empty existence. If the woman photographer had spoken to him, he thought, he might be happy right now.

A seagull sat on the peak of one of the large tents at the beach bar. The young attendant seemed to be bored, stomping around, calmly yawning in his cabana, then scratching his head, whistling, yawning again, and moving off to check on the rows of lounge chairs and umbrellas. The man had barely disappeared when an older beach peddler with a white beard came over to Lanz and apparently wanted to sell him original Indian jewelry. Lanz saw that it was junk, but he felt sorry for the old man, so he listened to his spiel. But he didn't want to buy a ring or a bracelet supposedly made of silver and precious stones—in fact, they were plastic with colored glass. He finally made the fellow understand what he thought about the goods. Without hesitation, the man reached into his shirt pocket and offered Lanz bits of dried plants.

"Tea," he whispered, pleading: "You make tea and you dream to be in paradise."

When he noticed that Lanz was interested, he explained that these were dried parts of mushrooms that you use to make a tea that can transform your world.

"Only a pretty small piece"—he held a piece of mushroom in his fingers: "Not too much or you become crazy." He briefly bent double from laughing and then asked for 30 euros.

"Will you still be here tomorrow?" Lanz asked.

"Yes, tomorrow. And the day after. All week."

"If it's any good, I'll buy all you've got tomorrow. But I'm not going to pay you anything for it right now."

"Oh, no! You must pay thirty euros!"

"For a single piece?"

"No, for three."

"Fine, I'll take one."

The Indian was visibly disappointed. "I not know if I have something tomorrow," he responded stubbornly. Without another word he handed Lanz a little paper sack, stuck the 10-euro bill in his pocket, and walked off without saying goodbye.

That evening Lanz used the Montblanc ballpoint pen that his father had given him for graduation to correct the second part of *Gulliver's Travels* that is set on the peninsular kingdom of Brobdingnag on the coast of California—a place in the book that always reminded him of a certain similarity with Lewis Carroll's *Alice in Wonderland*, since Alice herself alternately becomes gigantic and teeny-tiny. Moreover he remembered that the piece of mushroom from the Indian was lying in a teacup on the kitchen counter. Of course he knew how to brew tea, but he wanted to finish correcting the manuscript first, so it made more sense to drink coffee now. He found an opened package of cookies and worked up to the episode where Gulliver is suddenly attacked by twenty giant wasps, each one as big as a partridge. They were "humming louder than the drones of as many bagpipes . . . However, I had the courage to rise and draw my hanger, and attack them in the air." –The wasps are my imaginary monsters, Lanz said. "I dispatched four of them, but the rest got away, and I presently shut my window," he continued reading. The people in the book were giants and up to 40 feet tall, corn stalks were 30 feet tall, hailstones 18 times bigger than "anywhere else." The rooms in the royal palace had a height of 230 feet, the temple tower was 3000 feet tall, its walls 100 feet thick. The mountains were 30 miles high and each book in the King's library stretched for 20 feet; Gulliver had to walk ten paces just to read a single line. Lanz still knew the approximate measurements from his childhood when he had read the English version for ten-year-olds. "One day the governess ordered our coachman to stop at several shops," Lanz had read, "where the beggars, watching their opportunity, crowded to the sides of the coach, and gave me the most horrible spectacle that ever a European eye beheld." Swift also described the execution of a murderer. "The malefactor was fixed in a chair upon a scaffold erected for that purpose, and his head cut off at one blow, with a sword of about forty feet long. The veins and arteries spouted up such a prodigious quantity of blood, and so high in the air, that the great jet d'eau at Versailles was not equal to it for the time it lasted: and the head, when it fell on the scaffold floor, gave such a bounce as made me start, although I was at least half an English mile distant."

It took Lanz until one in the morning to finish his corrections. He then lay down in bed and imagined he was Gulliver, living among the giants whose indifference far exceeded his own.

Around three a.m. a noise woke him, and he thought there was someone in the house. He was convinced he could hear the open window in his library striking the other one and the dull sound of a person jumping to the ground. As quietly as possible, he got out of bed and crept into the entrance hall, and from there to the second floor where he took the pistol out of the cabinet drawer. Since he had completed his military service, he knew how to use the gun. He loaded a full clip, went back downstairs in the dark, took the safety off, and waited for further sounds. Once again he heard the window banging . . . He silently opened the door and turned on the light-switch. He immediately realized that a storm was threatening outside. Even though he couldn't hear any thunder, he could see lightning flashes in the distance, wind gusts shook the windows. He put the pistol down on a chair, closed the shutters, and went back to the bedroom, taking the pistol with him and putting it on the nightstand beside the bed.

When he woke up, it was quiet, and the sky was just beginning to grow brighter. He looked outside and decided that the storm had apparently passed. Since everything was now calm and the sky was stunningly beautiful, he concluded that it was a good day to die. He took a shower, brushed his teeth and got dressed because he felt that he was now truly ready to take his own life. He glanced at the clock. It was eleven minutes after six, so it was easy just to jump into a vaporetto and sail off somewhere quiet. The Lido or the open sea would be too melodramatic for his passing. It should come off like the most natural thing in the world and not cause a sensation. Actually he just wanted to finally disappear from his own life. The best thing would be to simply dissolve in thin air like H.G. Wells' invisible man.

He put the loaded pistol in the pocket of his olive-green

windbreaker, didn't forget the wallet with his ID, credit cards, and enough cash. He left his bicycle at home and set out at a leisurely pace to the Santa Maria Elisabetta vaporetto station. He felt nothing but the usual loneliness and emptiness.

Where should he go? Actually he wanted to leave it to chance, but then he thought through all the possibilities and decided on the island of Torcello. Until now it hadn't been a favorite destination because he wasn't interested in churches. His father had been an atheist and his mother had always told him she didn't have time for religion, while up until the time she died, his wife Alma had always accused him of being apathetic. But what Lanz had never told anyone was that in the most difficult times of his life, he had silently spoken with his Maker. He had even perceived a voice in his head and followed its instructions. On the surface he was sometimes an atheist, sometimes an agnostic. He considered the major religions "assembly-line religions" and always refused to talk about faith, the afterlife, or reincarnation, because then one banality inevitably led to another. For him, religion was an internal language that found its expression only in music—in symphonies by Mahler and Bruckner, in Schubert's quartets and Webern's twelve-tone pieces, the Passions of Johann Sebastian Bach, or in the music of Arvo Pärt and Sofia Gubaidulinas. But in the last two years he hadn't listened to any music, it was only stored in fragments in his memory. In its place, his passion for books and paintings had greatly increased.

He didn't have to wait long at the Elisabetta station. Stepping from the shelter out onto the gangway, he could see the vaporetto approaching. As he boarded, he noticed migrants on the boat who were hoping to get illicit work somewhere. Just the sight of them embarrassed him—he was about to throw his life away, even though he had a good life compared to the refugees and immigrants. Some of them now disembarked and silently moved on; Lanz watched them go, as if they were the ones who were going to die, and not he. They had come to Europe to improve their lives, he thought, full of hopes and dreams, like Franz Kafka's Karl Rossmann in the novel *Amerika*. In that book the 16-year-old Karl leaves his homeland and arrives in

America, innocent, though accused of having gone astray. For Lanz the novel had always read like a slapstick movie with subtitles. He had picked up the book many times throughout his life and asked himself—as with Kafka's short stories and other novels—how the author had known all that, because every line seemed to him to be a patient's examination report from a psychiatrist who withheld any pertinent commentary. Rossmann skitters from one catastrophe to the next, until—lured by a help-wanted poster—he travels to the "Nature Theater of Oklahoma" where he is welcomed by angels with trumpets. In reality the angels are women in costumes in a huge traveling theater that will take him along on tour. Or else Karl has already died and gone to heaven.

Out of the blue it occurred to Lanz that on a trip to Hamburg he had also stopped in Bremerhaven and visited the famous German Emigration Center. He had first entered a lofty exhibition hall where he could see the huge side of the steamship *Lahn* in the water. Roughly thirty life-size mannequins of men, women, and children were standing in semi-darkness on the reconstructed wharf: the men with caps, hats, hoods or bareheaded, the women wearing scarves. You could tell the poverty of the emigrants from their clothing. Lanz had the impression he was back in the year 1888, among fugitives "from all regions of Europe," as the catalogue noted. He had heard over a loudspeaker harbor sounds, the voices of people as they waited, and seen luggage—suitcases, handbags, trunks. The visitors to the museum had mingled with the simulated figures, giving everything a dynamic impression. Just as the figures appeared about to climb the gangplank, he had joined them and looked down over the large dolls and the people beneath him.

Later he entered the *Gallery of the 7 Million Migrants*, an expansive room in twilight with blue bins full of drawers preserving letters, photographs, passenger lists, mementos and memorabilia from especially noteworthy expatriates, going back from 1880 to 1913. He pulled out some drawers and saw a comb, keys, a black-and-white photo of a couple with their child in a garden, an ashtray, a hairbrush, identification documents and foreign currency, but also a Bible and a broken pocket watch. It all seemed to him like evidence from a trial that was attempting to explain why the individuals in question had left Europe.

Riding along in the nearly empty vaporetto, Lanz recalled more about the emigrant vessel and its narrow white passageway to the cabins. The motion of the waves was recreated outside the portholes at the waterline and, in addition, the passageway swayed back and forth. The small low cabins were packed with bunk beds, human mannequins, and luggage—and with an equal mixture of fear, desperation, and hope. The emigrants came from Germany, Austria, Ireland, England, and most of the existing European countries of that time; it is estimated that, all in all, they totaled twenty million people. They had left everything behind, even their loved ones, and had preferred to flee into the unknown than continue living in the certainty of misery that threatened to consume them.

Sitting in the vaporetto, Lanz was amazed at what he was feeling and at the speed with which everything was racing through his mind. He now saw before him steerage on the ship in Bremerhaven's Migrant Museum, stacked with hundreds of the passengers' various colored suitcases and wooden chests, models of the steamships in glass showcases, and, last of all, the barred cells on Ellis Island off New York, the "human cages" as he called them back then. Eventually—as in Kafka's "Nature Theater of Oklahoma"—they entered the new world, though it only existed in their heads and, in most cases, their search was probably in vain.

All those thoughts occurred to him as he watched the nearby tired migrant workers leave the vaporetto. At the same time he became aware that he himself was on the verge of migrating . . . into death. The vaporetto resumed its journey, and he tried to calm his thoughts with remembrances of other trips, other museums, other encounters that completely confused him and, where possible, dissolved the inner emptiness he felt and, as a consequence, now made the decision to take his life uncertain.

The remaining passengers just sat there, silent and motionless, most gazed out at the Lagoon. A young man was reading an apparently lengthy article in a newspaper, a worker in a windbreaker and hood had fallen asleep, his head listing to one side, and his neighbor was staring off into the distance, distracted. Also among the passengers were housewives, overweight and tired, clutching shopping bags or shopping carts, two with baby buggies featuring sleeping babies. And old folks who seemed lost.

The sea was grey-green, gulls swam in the calm waters, and not far off he could see the cemetery island of San Michele he had previously visited many times. Near the brick wall that surrounded the island he saw in the water the black bronze sculpture of the *Barca della Morte*—a simple boat with the figures of two men with small heads, wearing coats. One of the two was pointing with outstretched arm at the cemetery. He suspected that they represented Vergil and Dante on their journey into Hell, through Purgatory, and finally into Paradise.

His fear of death had gradually subsided as he grew older. Only the sight of small children's graves reminded him that the confrontation with death—especially in grade school and the early years of high school in Bozen—had left him with somber and eerie thoughts. During puberty he had thought about suicide, and later considered it several times seriously. Of course he had also consulted literature on the subject, Goethe, Dostoyevsky or Camus. He soon determined that he would not kill himself out of desperation, but in a moment of apathy and emptiness. As much as people's indifference to the fate of others made him furious, it made him want even more for his death to be incidental so that he would be discovered only months later, like a mountain climber in a glacial crevice who had already been transformed into a part of the landscape.

Some time ago, as he now remembered, he had been reading on Wikipedia that the island of Sant'Ariano in the Laguna Morta, northeast of Torcello and Murano, had served the neighboring cemeteries until 1837 as an ossuary, a charnel house, "under the open sky," according to the website. A six-foot-tall wall surrounded an area the size of a soccer field. Even today, bones of the deceased are "piled three-feet-high" behind impenetrable brambles. But it wasn't his intention to shoot himself beside thousands of skulls and skeletons—as far as he was concerned, that was tasteless. He planned to simply disappear.

Lanz was distracted by a huge dredger with a suction nozzle that was excavating the floor of the Lagoon. He didn't see a single person anywhere, not a sign of life, not even on the dredge that appeared to be functioning on automatic pilot, he didn't spot a single bird in the sky. He realized that except for the droning of the vaporetto's engine and the dredger, you could envision you were on a watery cemetery. He actually thought the word "envision," because he knew his visions only too well. But his brain immediately surprised him with the mental image that all the current passengers were deceased, underway on their journey into the hereafter.

The vaporetto reached the "vegetable island" of Sant'Erasmo. Seen from the ship, it resembled a flat agricultural area with trees, bushes, fields, everything in earth tones and in all shades of green that, in passing, was transformed into monochrome monotony. The sight of the fort alternately made him think of prisons and huts. This early in the morning there was no sign of life, and Sant'Erasmo gave the impression that people had deserted it for all time, like some illusory coastline at sea.

Last summer he had taken his outboard motorboat from the Lido out to the island and then hiked on to Sant'Erasmo Chiesa, past scattered small villas with wash hung out to dry, greenhouses under transparent plastic sheeting, past friendly waving cyclists and small three-wheeled delivery vans—versions of the Piaggio Ape—past fig trees, pines, broom shrubs, and large market gardens. He had enjoyed the peace and quiet, and the seclusion had given him a feeling of security. Trees and bushes bordered the properties and provided shade. In the midst of his brief idyllic digressions a black-and-white image popped into his head as if from some documentary movie: for an instant he had defoliated and destroyed the island, and actually seen it uninhabited.

He often thought about a nuclear disaster, like Fukushima or Chernobyl, that would bring life to an end. The trip on the vaporetto—

that he truly loved—suddenly became arduous. The monotony of the usual impressions only served to strengthen the knowledge that he was on his way into eternity.

All the passengers disembarked at the Punta Sabbioni station and left the landing. He was the only one who remained behind, waiting for the vaporetto that would take him to Torcello. Actually he could have shot himself right here and then fallen into the water, but even that was too dramatic for him. The Lagoon spread out before him, only in the distance could he distinguish the outline of Sant'Erasmo, but it was so small, like a notation in tiny handwriting between heaven and earth on a color postcard of the Lagoon. Behind him, a mound of earth, and further on, the seaside resort of Jesolo.

Lanz read on a sign that the vaporetto to Torcello wouldn't dock for another 15 minutes, which also meant that he would probably remain alive for another 15 minutes. There were piers from the adjoining concrete building that led to two other landings. The concrete pilings that supported the piers, Lanz noticed, were encrusted with a thick layer of mussels beneath the waterline.

An old married couple had approached unnoticed, and as he was studying a rusted iron chain—also covered with mussels—the woman asked him in English what there was to see around here.

When Lanz answered "Nothing," the two of them stopped, still serious, and with an expression of boredom. The woman related that they had come to Venice with friends who slept all day. Apparently she loved to talk—her husband, however, was silent. When his wife wanted to consult Lanz, he grumpily insisted that he wanted "nothing more to do" with the Accademia, the museum with its Renaissance paintings. The Ca'Rezzonico with its insights into the 17th and 18th centuries was "terrible," he "didn't want to see" any more museums and palaces. He mentioned condescendingly that he had once gone with his wife from the train station, where their hotel was located, to St. Mark's Square: "Horrible." Yesterday they had been in Murano, also "dreadfully boring." Lanz listened to him, not saying a word, and with no intention of being dragged into the conversation. When the wife mentioned the cemetery of San Michele, her husband's face registered contempt, and with her remark about the "fascinating ghetto," he could only close his eyes, painfully affected, and blow air out through his bulging cheeks. "We've got a Henry James who wrote about Venice, and a Ruskin!" she challenged him. "What've you got?" The man turned to one side, spit in the water, and the conversation died.

Once in the vaporetto, the couple sat in the same row as Lanz, but neither of them spoke. Lanz gazed out intently. The Lagoon— he couldn't see any people, animals or equipment—was overgrown with yellow reeds. Small flat islands off to his right extended out to the horizon, leaving the impression that the swampy landscape was swallowing everything. When they encountered other vaporettos, he was blinded by the reflections of water and sun off their front windshields.

He now recognized the bell tower of San Francesco del Deserto off to his left. The convent on the tiny island—essentially lying "in the middle of the water"—had to be a strange place, he thought. Here you could lead the life of a seagull. Cypress trees had been planted all around the beach and reminded him of a bird's nest. Almost everywhere on the Lagoon there were green-covered sandbars in the calm waters that, seen from the ship's deck, produced the image of a three-dimensional map and made the observer feel that he was moving within a giant model of an oceanic landscape. They passed a small island with a large building, now in ruins; it no longer had a roof. He saw a series of square black holes where windows had been. Weeds grew over the brick ruins. The following island, even smaller, featured only the fragment of a wall, the next island only rubble, garbage, bushes, a wrecked rowboat, and the vestiges of a moss-covered building resembling a shed. It crossed his mind that these were good places to shoot himself.

They overtook six paddleboats propelled by men and woman. A moment later he recognized the leaning tower on the island of Burano that he had visited in the beginning of his relationship with Alma who would later become his wife.

Back then he had been impressed by the village on the sea, the blue, red, and yellow houses, and the lace-making trade—he still remembered them to this day. Lanz had studied English and French while he was still living in Vienna, he also spoke fluent German and Italian because his father Johann came from South Tyrol and was initially an assistant at the Institute for Applied Mathematics in Milan. Later, as a professor at the University of Bozen, his father had given lectures on Computer Science. Lanz's mother Elisa came from Padua where she had completed a degree in osteopathy and then opened her own practice in Bozen after their marriage. All day long patients with "lower back pain" packed her office hours, and almost all—she insisted—were people whose lives had gotten "out of hand." She could tell stories about their illnesses. When Emil Lanz was nineteen, his father was appointed to the University of Vienna; his mother rented another studio above their apartment Am Heumarkt 7 and opened her practice there. His father was extremely proud of having found a home in the former headquarters of the Austro-Hungarian monarchy. Emil continued the language studies he had begun in Bozen, having already satisfied his military service with the Italian navy.

For his fifteenth birthday his father had given him a Rubik's Cube—one of 400 million sold, he later discovered on Google. The Cube by the Hungarian architect Ernõ Rubik fascinated him, so much so that for a while it was the only thing he did. As he tried in vain to solve the puzzle, Emil had experienced the feeling of infinity, and from that point on, he wanted to experience it again and again— though each time he failed to solve the Cube. He knew that it had 43 trillion possible settings and that there was only one single correct solution—that ran through his head every time he had difficulties later in life. Each time you had to find the home position, with each of the six faces in its respective color. It took Lanz almost two years to work the puzzle, and then only with the help of his father who had let his son struggle alone that entire time. Even though he was still in puberty, Lanz knew he wouldn't fulfill his father's wish for him to study mathematics as his father had done. But since his father had gone out of his way to show him how he could solve the Cube, Emil had obediently continued to study math and let his father spend entire afternoons explaining chaos theory or the Koch snowflake, entropy, Einstein's theory of relativity and his parallel universe, the Leviathan number or the mathematical constant Pi, named after the 16th letter of the Greek alphabet that was also the first letter of the word "Perimetros"—"circumference"—, and with its value of 3.1415926535… you could calculate either the circumference or the area of a circle. He had heard that number so often that he could have recited it automatically, like a poem. As his father contended, it was an irrational transcendental number, though Emil had never understood this part of the explanation. But what he had heard, lingered on in his brain. Moreover he had not forgotten that in the meantime the number Pi had been calculated to the billionth part beyond the decimal point, and that it contained all the birth and death dates of all deceased, living, and future human beings.

He now saw the island of Burano in the distance, an intense reminder again of Alma. And feeling the pistol in his jacket pocket, he had something like an epiphany. Since he was convinced he was going to die soon and had tied up all of his life's loose ends, something must have taken place in his brain that couldn't be explained with logic. It had suddenly become clear to him that God was something like the mathematical constant Pi, and without it no one could comprehend his or her life.

When he met Alma, he put the Rubik's Cube down on his desk and never touched it again.

When he saw the sky, suddenly free of clouds this morning, the island of Burano seemed like a beautiful déjà-vu experience, though there was no sign of life as yet. And even the memory of Alma was affected, because he realized how much he had loved her at the beginning. He knew that when love collapsed, usually the knowledge of the original infatuation also dissolved. You often hated that it had been a part of your life, but now he was able to admit it.

At the landing, there were few passengers waiting for the return trip, and none of his fellow passenger headed for the second shelter for the continuation to Torcello; all were scurrying home or to work.

The interior of the other hut-like shelter gave the impression of a floating veranda with an open terrace and two large side windows looking out on the ocean. Here he could have put a bullet in his brain or in his heart undisturbed, he thought somewhat later. It would have even been best to begin his journey into nothingness from a shelter on the ocean shore, but again he was reminded of Alma whose parents had owned vineyards in Southern Styria, the reason why their daughter had studied at the viticulture school in Klosterneuburg. He had met her at the *Heuriger* in Nussdorf as he sat at a table in the open-air restaurant, alone after a Sunday stroll; a companion and classmate from her school had invited him to join them. He had immediately fallen in love with Alma, and the next evening she picked him up from his apartment Am Heumarkt. A week later, while his parents were traveling to Bozen, they had become lovers. As he gazed out the glass of the shelter, he now remembered they had looked out the third-floor window of the apartment onto the top of a plane tree, as if they themselves were floating on a cloud. This image appeared in his mind that was now waiting for a bullet from his pistol. In the same breath he decided to shoot himself in the heart, and that relieved him from his momentarily increasing fear. There was silence all around, he no longer heard the slapping sounds of the ocean, just the screeching of a seagull now and then. For a moment he saw himself reflected in the glass window . . . sitting on the empty bench in the shelter . . . as if an approaching tourist had just taken a snapshot of him.

A year after they had met and finished their studies, they were married at the registrar's office in Vienna and then, at the request of his new bride, in a church in Gamlitz. Soon they were spending most of the year in the St. Leonhard vineyards that, as far as he could tell, were extinct volcanoes overgrown with green vegetation. Thousands of years ago they were still active beneath the sea that had covered them at the time. But the wine growers never spoke about it. He recalled that from the beginning he hadn't taken part in the social festivities, they bored him. While he continued to collect more and more books in his study, Alma remained with her childhood

God, her childhood Jesus, her childhood Mary, Mother of God. She didn't rack her brains about the Creator—after all, He was beyond comprehension, she would say. Lanz had only accompanied her to church on Sunday on one occasion. And he also had no interest in becoming involved in winegrowing and the art of fermentation. So he rarely conversed with her friends and avoided wedding celebrations, funerals, or moving days. While translating, he secretly spoke with the dead poets, pondered each one of their written words, every punctuation mark, every expression, and in the evenings, when he had finished work, exhausted, he was unresponsive. Half of the year he would get drunk on the terrace, the other half in the tavern. When he had drunk too much, he would become talkative, but when that happened, no one else would engage him. Most of them worked from sunrise until sunset in the vineyards and in autumn in the cellars, they went to bed early. So he sat alone in the bar and—drinking all the while—watched whatever was on TV.

He remembered that Alma at first had begun to criticize him privately, then more openly, and eventually to hate him. She hated that his emotional life was so complicated, as she put it, and that there was nothing he could share with her. One day, after a chance encounter with a beekeeper, he began to raise bees in his spare time. He protected himself with a white coat and a beekeeper's helmet—through its netting he saw the world reduced to many individual entities as if through pinhole glasses—and work gloves that he no longer wore after a while; later, he also put aside the white coat. Once six bees stung him in the right cheek, and for a time it seemed as if a tumor would disfigure the affected side of his face. At about that time he and Alma had a heated quarrel. His wife accused him of provoking her family and their neighbors by openly showing that he wasn't interested in their work or their lives. She produced really fine wines, Sauvignon blanc, Pinot blanc, muscatel, and Welschriesling that were usually sold out before the following summer. As far as Alma was concerned, "everything had to be worked biologically," and she argued vehemently with her father Franz about it. Her mother Irmgard had died seven years before from an autoimmune disease.

His father-in-law Franz had gone hunting since childhood in the nearby woods. There was no indication in the house of his pastime, there were no antlers hanging from the walls. Irmgard and Alma had opposed this idea, the reason why the husband and father had mounted all his trophies from the rafters in an old wine press building. Franz also owned several rifles and two pistols. He was the kind of man whose words could hurt and even kill. And Lanz soon learned that as well, since they lived under the same roof. However, the father-in-law never dared to start an argument with Emil whose linguistic skills impressed him. And the beekeeping and the honey he ate each morning aroused his admiration, especially because his son-in-law had taught himself how to cultivate bees. Franz had a heart attack one Sunday and died at the front door on his way home from church. From then on, Alma was alone and had to rely on her friends and acquaintances to help out until she could hire a worker from Slovenia named Marco who went home on weekends and holidays but could also bring along his brother or one of his neighbors if needed.

Alma and Emil no longer went to Vienna, so he had a moving van bring his library from the Heumarkt to St. Leonhard. Ever since he had moved in with Alma, he had received books from various mail-order companies, a second reason for conflict with his wife since, before long, he had packed three rooms with his books. First he filled the bookshelves that he bought from IKEA, and when there was no more space, he stored books in shopping bags that he piled on the floor so that there was barely a path to the shelves. In no time he had piled books on his desk and all the chairs so that he had to find a new place to work. Meanwhile, he had become good friends with the mailman from St. Leonhard and invited him in for a glass of wine now and then when the man arrived around noon with the packages, envelopes, and boxes. The man admired Lanz and told the neighbors all about the staggering number of books he had delivered. He knew about everything that happened in the village, sometimes commented on events, and finally told Lanz that, due to a shortage of priests, the St. Leonhard parish would never get a new pastor; as a result, Lanz rented the top floor of the parsonage and spent more and more time in the three rooms and the kitchen of the former rectory. Although he and his books had now moved, books were still being delivered to Alma's house, so in the evening, usually when he was drunk, they always got in a fight. Nevertheless, at the end of every day when the bells at the church across the way struck six, he made his way home. On days when there were funerals, he would escape to his bees because there was a mortuary in the rectory annex where the bodies of deceased villagers lay in state for three days so everyone could come and pay their respects.

Soon the rectory had become a library, because Lanz continued to order books that he could no longer read due to their overwhelming numbers. Of course Alma also realized that, and she accused him of being a hoarder. What his wife didn't understand was that he was on a life-long expedition into his underworld. Before he began to live in the vineyards, he had signed a contract with an Italian publisher to translate a four-volume *Encyclopedia of World Literature* from the English. But the project was on the verge of floundering be-cause he and Alma were fighting openly and sometimes in the presence of Marco, the Slovenian worker, because the ever-increasing lava flow of books that poured into the house on a daily basis didn't stop at the bedroom door, forming smaller and larger towers, and one day the largest of them fell from the wardrobe on Alma as she was looking for a blouse. She didn't speak to him for two days, and, from then on, criticized him even more frequently. So, while he was translating a book, he would sleep overnight in the rectory more and more often. And when he returned home a day or two later, there were cartons of books, CDs or DVDs piled indiscriminately, like an admonition, on the large dining room table. Each time his wife greeted him with the question: "Where were you?"—though she knew that he had been at the rectory. Eventually he had called her every evening and morning that he spent in his "archives," as he called it (or "parsonage" as she called it), and apologized that he had translated all night long to meet the publisher's deadline. In retrospect he felt that was a mistake because it might leave the impression that he had a guilty conscience. Regardless, he never failed to take care of his bees. When he worked with the smoker or took out the heavy hive frame with its hundreds of six-sided honeycomb cells, his thoughts were in his inner world that, since his childhood, had always been an unknown planet. Sometimes Alma sobbed out of anger, despair and self-pity, and their infrequent mutual embraces eventually dwindled until they stopped altogether. In spite of that, he still loved her, but she had her own definite ideas about life that were, for him, a jumble of interest and disinterest, of attraction and revulsion. He told himself that, in contrast to her, he tried to form his life from within, while she took everything as it came and tackled it with terrific enthusiasm. He had a great deal of respect for her approach and frequently praised her "life intelligence," as he called her abilities for solving problems. But he totally lacked the desire to emulate her.

His black-and-white vaporetto slowly approached, and again Lanz felt the desire for an incidental death, an undramatic death, accompanied by indifference. He had spoken with Alma about it once, and she had remarked that there was a life after death, which had made him smile. "Some day no one will believe in fairy tales anymore," he had responded. "They are ultimately transformed into lies, like all ideologies," and she had disappeared into the kitchen and never spoke about it with him again. That all went through his head in the half-hour he waited for the vaporetto to Torcello—a daydream consisting of thoughts and memories, like some self-drawn comic book.

Before the waterbus arrived, another passenger had turned up in the shelter, and Lanz had ignored the stranger. Only now did he pay particular attention to him. He was tall, heavyset and bald, dressed entirely in black: black slacks, black sport coat, black shirt, and a black windbreaker. Lanz thought he looked like a bouncer at a discotheque or a pallbearer at some funeral home. Which, again, brought Lanz back to his topic of the moment.

A week before Alma died, he had discovered that all his bees were lying on the floor of the warehouse, dead. Instead of their humming and lively motion, he had found only heaps of insect bodies. The bee deaths had affected him more than he realized. They had been an omen, as he discovered only later . . .

After the vaporetto to Torcello had docked, Lanz followed the bald man across the gangplank and sat down on one of the seats inside the waterbus—with the dead bees still in the back of his mind. At first he had suspected that Alma had poisoned them. Or that it had been the Slovenian worker, Marco, acting on her instructions. However, judging from Alma's shock at the bee deaths and her concern about the grapevines, he had concluded she was innocent. The following day she informed him that she and a female friend had booked a charter flight to Hurghada in Egypt, to relax for a week on the Red Sea. That, too, had bothered him, because it was the first time that they hadn't travelled together. When he explained that he was working on his translation of the four-volume *Encyclopedia of World Literature*, she had responded that, apparently, he wanted to buy all the books mentioned in the *Encyclopedia* because more and more packages were arriving daily. The afternoon before her departure, she had hugged him and asked if he didn't want to fly off with her. She had sat down at her computer and communicated with the travel bureau, but found out that the flight was booked solid. At that point Lanz realized she really was going to leave. On the one hand, he wouldn't be able to complete his translation by the publisher's deadline, and, on the other, it made him furious that Alma had made her decision and implemented it without consulting him.

That night, after having had no physical contact for a long period of time, they slept together once again, and he asked her not to fly, even offered to reimburse her for the tickets, but she had insisted on taking the trip. The next morning they exchanged few words at her departure. At noon he received a call from the travel bureau that the charter flight had crashed over Bulgaria. He immediately set out to find the scene of the accident in the mountains. He had never imagined that he would experience something like this. He stopped at some distance from the ruins, without comprehending what had happened. When he returned, he read the list of passengers in a newspaper at the airport. The female friend Alma had mentioned wasn't on the list, though the son of a major wine grower in the neighborhood was, and Lanz then learned what everyone else apparently had known for some time—that she had been having an affair with him. Her lover had similarly told his family that he was flying to Egypt with a friend.

Since Lanz was the sole heir, he sold the vineyards and the spacious house to the largest and most respected vintner in the region, whereupon his mother, who had not attended Alma's funeral "due to the circumstances," had found a villa for him on the Lido where he has been living ever since. Shortly thereafter, at a class she was taking, his mother met and married an osteopath named Giorgio from Naples, and the thread that had connected them till now was severed. And after he gave his tomcat Johann to a neighbor, he has been on his own ever since . . . Most of his books were delivered to the villa on the Lido, and he donated the rest to the local library. Before he left the farmhouse in St. Leonhard for the last time, he pocketed his deceased father-in-law's pistols. Since then, he has kept one of them in the dresser on the second floor of his villa on the Lido. As he thought about it, he could feel it in the pocket of his windbreaker. After stripping down the second pistol, also a product of the weapons manufacturer Walther, he stowed it in a box up in the attic. While still in the house in St. Leonhard, he had filed off their serial numbers, as if he intended to use them to commit a crime.

II

Homicide and Suicide

It was going to be a hot day, he thought, as he left the vaporetto on Torcello and walked at a short distance behind the man in black who seemed to be in a hurry.

"Who's afraid of the Black Man?" he used to call out as a boy on the school playground. "Nobody!" answered his classmates and friends who had lined up on the other side of the playground . . . and they were off and running. He would run after them, and when he touched them they turned into "Black Men" who had to help him make all the other players into "Black Men." He had been a fast runner and from time to time had also taken part in little scuffles that were unavoidable in grade school.

The man who had been hurrying ahead of him suddenly disappeared—Lanz couldn't understand where he might have gone. He paused, glanced around, and it occurred to him that the children's game of "Black Man" had to do with the plague. At least that's what his mother had told him. Everyone who came in contact with the "black death" became a carrier of the virus and increased the army of sick people until all of them were dead.

Lanz walked along the canal with its green water, goats grazing on the other bank, and a tractor parked under a fruit tree. A little further on, in a dip of the meadow, he discovered a blue motorboat with its prow upturned, and a bit after that, a white boat between the trunks of tall trees. On his left was a wire fence, surrounding spring-green gardens with colorful beds of flowers, broadleaf and fruit trees, grass and beanstalks. Bricks were laid in a parquet pattern, forming a walkway, and up ahead a small motor yacht glided slowly and almost silently down the canal. On the opposite side, in the embankment of white-blossoming elderberry and acacia bushes, he discovered doors made of wooden planks and stone steps that led down to the canal. He smelled the sweet fragrance of the bushes, and it occurred to him that this was a good spot where he could slip away and shoot himself.

At the place where the man in black had disappeared, there was a two-story building. He noticed pilings in the water and a wooden boathouse with two cargo vessels behind it, stacked upside-down and reflected in the canal. But this time he interpreted the reflections differently than before, because they weren't simply reflections, but seemed to prove to him that the world was standing on its head.

He turned left at the tall building and saw that most of the *trattoria* and *alberghi* he passed were already open, their customers probably still asleep or arriving later on the vaporetto. That was advantageous for his mission, he thought, now he just had to find the right spot. He came to a field of vegetables with leaves growing out of the ground and debated whether it was a suitable place. He now noticed a man and a woman smoking cigarettes in front of two shacks. Lanz knew that only about twenty-five to thirty people lived permanently on the island.

Passing by houses, he could see inside through their windows, and behind the reflections he saw only furniture. He came to a smart restaurant, the Locanda Cipriani, according to the green sign with white letters. The dark-green window shutters were closed. Two seagulls perched on crooked pilings reminded him of the Holy Spirit in the center of the ceiling fresco in St. Leonhard's Catholic Church. A colony of seagulls that flew over the island were also reminiscent of Holy Spirits. They accompanied him on his way, he thought, and as some of them screeched up above, he felt as if they were trying to dissuade him from his intended purpose.

Lanz wandered alone over the seemingly deserted island. The colony of seagulls peeled off and, turning his head, he now recognized the bell tower behind the Santa Fosca Church that was, in his estimation, roughly 150 feet tall and loomed over everything. He decided he would climb it later and overlook the island and the Lagoon. There were also tall old trees and shrubs in front of the church, and he could hear water rippling in a circular basin enclosed by an iron fence and a low stone wall. He stopped, studied the column remnants, walked on, and came to the wall before the Museo Archeologico di Torcello with its discoveries from the island.

When he strolled back, the noisy seagulls had landed near the basin, and Lanz approached the church. The floor of the colonnade was paved with bricks that repeatedly formed a herringbone pattern, and through the half-open door he saw the altar of white marble, standing behind it a short elderly priest in a green-silk chasuble embellished with golden ornamentation and the sexton, he assumed, dressed in jeans and a windbreaker. Music was coming from somewhere, but Lanz couldn't detect anyone else in the Santa Fosca Church. Then, unexpectedly, two members of the choir appeared before the altar and, facing the entrance to the church, began to sing a religious song. The orchestra's music filled the echoing space, though Lanz still couldn't determine its location. He approached and at the same time was afraid he might interrupt, but no one paid any attention to him. It was as if he didn't exist. That made him think he could kill himself on the spot, but he also knew that he wouldn't do it.

He assumed this was probably a rehearsal. The priest turned, looked at the acolyte and whispered something to him while the two singers, accompanied by the invisible orchestra, continued singing. Lanz listened to the music for a while, then stepped into the colonnade, still without having seen anyone else in the church. Up till now, everything was going according to plan, he thought. The seagulls outside had quieted down and were foraging in the meadow or cleaning their feathers. He still didn't see any tourists. On the brick walls of the colonnade he discovered large blotches of black mold. Lanz took the blotches for a sign, first as actual letters of the alphabet, but when he took a step back, he realized that there must have been a cross at this specific spot, and, to the left and right, figures with halos. He also saw stucco remains that had apparently framed a picture, though today there was nothing left but the fragmentary outlines of three more figures. Or else it was moisture and a network of cracks that formed an asymmetrical spider's web. The large old baptismal font, originally whitish-grey, was made of stone and, like the nearby holy water font, had a darker tint; moreover they, too, were covered with yellow and green spots, as if they were being transformed back into nature. He looked at them for a long time and only turned away when the short elderly priest, now dressed completely in black and with a shopping bag in one hand, tip-toed over a connecting boardwalk and out into the open. The priest acknowledged Lanz and, in passing, asked his name. When Lanz didn't answer, the priest stopped and wanted to know where he was from.

"From Vienna," Lanz replied politely, and hurried to get away from the man since Lanz was determined not to be diverted from his mission. He headed off in the opposite direction, toward the Basilica Santa Maria Assunta. The closer he came to the edifice, the more it resembled a construction site, since here, too, plaster had fallen from the walls. Tools were lying around, a wheelbarrow was left nearby. Suddenly the seagulls took off, noisily flapping their wings as they flew away. Lanz glanced around but found no cause for their alarm other than himself.

He had to buy a ticket to get inside the Basilica. The face of the young unattractive woman at the window, he noticed, was puffy from sleep. The nave was in semi-darkness in spite of the many windows on one side. The first thing he observed was the old mosaic floor that resembled a carpet of stone: geometric shapes intertwined, squares, rhombuses. At one point it reminded him of the bed of a shallow clear stream, at another of the skin of some exotic poisonous snake, then again of the pattern of colorful seashells or a mathematical formula transformed into an image. It made him think of mosques in Istanbul that he had visited, their embellishments forming signposts to the invisible. He had only experienced something similar when, as a child, he heard music or picked up bird feathers from the ground without knowing to what species they belonged. While he was still living in the vineyard house in St. Leonhard, he had resumed collecting them and placing them on his desk in the rectory; of course in the meantime he had learned which specific bird the feathers came from, and even from what part of the plumage. To him the feathers seemed like short poems or fragments of verse, isolated lines or words, perhaps from one of Paul Celan's works: completely white feathers from a white swan that he had picked up during a visit to the Graz Stadtpark, lead-grey ones from the collared dove's secondary feathers, black-and-white feathers from the magpie's primaries, the oriole's basic black with bright-yellow tail-feathers, the black body of a great-spotted woodpecker, the light- and dark-brown striped plumage of a pheasant, the bright blue-and-black pattern of a jay's mantle, the radiant small blue feathers of a kingfisher . . . in his mind's eye he saw images of all the feathers. And once again he decided to climb the church tower and, with a bird's-eye view, gaze down on the island before he shot himself.

An enormous gold mosaic of The Last Judgment now decorated the wall behind the original door to the basilica. He would have preferred that it had been preserved in fragments because that seemed more appropriate to the mysterious invisible quality it suggested. Giant angels blew horns, and drowning victims surfaced from watery waves, along with fish that spit out human corpses. A woman sat upon a mythical creature with a horn on its head, and buried people with open eyes waited beneath the ground. While giant angels with brass instruments were hovering above, in the underworld lions, tigers, hyenas and other unfamiliar creatures— possibly mythical beasts—were spewing out parts of human bodies: he saw hands, feet, a head, and a torso. Lanz studied the mosaic on the wall like an archaeologist who had stumbled onto the evidence of some unknown religion. When he saw the black Lucifer with his "son" on his lap—the naked infant Antichrist that Satan had birthed as a demon—Lanz was again reminded of the children's game of "Who's afraid of the Black Man." And he had to abandon his intention of observing everything from the perspective of an uninformed archaeologist, because he was reminded of excerpts from Dante's *Divine Comedy* that he had recently translated for the 4-volume *Encyclopedia of World Literature*: the black Satan with horns and wings—in the sky high above him, a throng of martyrs, monks, nuns, and saints. In tiny chambers of Hell, however, the throng of the damned: naked hedonist in the process of eating their hands; naked hotheads dunked in icy water; jealous souls who saw 17 skulls—Lanz had counted them all—with snakes creeping out of their empty eye-sockets; misers represented by 11 seemingly decapitated heads in the eternal fire; and sullen figures, again depicted as heads, in this instance 10, with broken arms and legs.

He tried to view the mosaic again, as if he had been unable to interpret it. The result was a totally different perception. It now reminded him of when he saw Hieronymus Bosch's *Garden of Earthly Delights* for the first time in a book from his father's library, and his mother had laughed and tried to explain various details to him. Lanz didn't view the mosaic in the logical sequence, but let himself be guided by his curiosity, always fluctuating between knowledge and a feigned lack of comprehension: first, Hell in all its particulars, and then every detail of Heaven. Paradise with Adam and Eve, the praying Virgin Mary, the two good thieves, the pearly gates of Heaven guarded by a cherub, Peter, the archangels Gabriel and Michael, and the victorious Messiah—for Lanz they were now only the audience in a gigantic coliseum, while, at their feet, the mortals in the arena were being tortured and dismembered for the edification of the viewer.

He again gazed at the floor where he noticed worn but remarkably beautiful mosaic stones in their own distinct pattern that had evolved due to age and the footsteps of countless visitors. He didn't proceed to the altar. As if from a great distance he saw Mary in her blue garment with the baby Jesus, surrounded by the gold of the mosaic on the walls and at her feet the open arched windows with sunlight streaming in, giving the impression that the Mother of God was hovering on a beam of light between Heaven and Earth. As Lanz left the gold-embellished room, he felt that, for a moment, he had seen the universe from the inside.

Lanz went from the Basilica Santa Maria Assunta to a building housing an antique shop and gazed through the iron bars of an enclosure. A heavy-set farmer in blue workpants was intently checking the growth of the grapes while fingering the plants.

The vineyard was bordered by remnants of old columns, by stone vases and isolated statues. A bit further on he saw numerous garden figures that appeared to be from the 19th century. They made him think of a cemetery where the past was buried. Then he circled around the Santa Fosca Church, looking for the entrance to the bell tower. He didn't see anyone here either. This time it was the sexton himself who sold him the admission ticket.

Lanz knew that he wouldn't jump off the tower because he was afraid of the thoughts and sensations that would go through his head as he fell. He simply wanted to depart this life. The unplastered interior of the tower had a ramp instead of steps and made him think of a huge organ pipe. In his imagination he was floating upward, as if he were a musical note from a Mass by Bach, Mozart, or Messiaen. But a second later he was transformed into an organ tone that disappeared in mid-air.

The view from above overwhelmed him. The seagulls suddenly reappeared and he briefly felt that he himself was now a gull, the Lagoon spreading out beneath him. It occurred to him that if he were to be reborn, he would probably come back as a bird.

Depending on which tower window he looked out, the water had different colors,. On the ocean side, various shades of blue: indigo, cobalt hues, violet, midnight blue, cosmos blue, lavender, navy blue— on the landward side, however, greens: pale green, crocodile green, vitriol green, jasper green, lead green and cane grey. In the canals, between the shrubs and in the swampy part, it was clay-colored, umber, topaz, cabbage, iodine brown, field brown, and sand; but in the shade, jungle black, black orchid, sepia-colored. And, finally, at the horizon where the sky and the sea met, it was cloudy-white, soft white, clock-face white, albino, pigment white, yarrow white, and, lastly, golden and silvery from the reflected sunlight. Then he remembered that often in the vineyards in autumn he would watch starlings as they formed their flocks that wrote and drew in the sky. They clustered together to form a continuously distorting ghostly mass, a murmuration, scattering and dispersing into a termite-like swarm, joining up again, forming a huge giant mushroom, fingerprints in an imaginary dactyloscopic index, dispersing again and rejoining yet again, breathing, appearing as a shape in the sky, infiltrating their own formation, forming a chalice, blossoms, snakes, appearing to swallow each other and then regurgitating their companions, assuming the shape of sperm-clouds, showing that everything on earth consisted of atoms and molecules, of cells, of leukocytes and erythrocytes, of photons that created clouds of dust that, in turn, became flower pollen, shadowy creations, water drops, snowflakes, plankton, particles of light.

Voices from one of the lower floors of the tower distracted him, and the only thing he felt was a desire to flee, like animals in nature when they are discovered. He hurried down, gazed at the floor as people approached, and hurried off in a different direction in the hope of avoiding everyone. First he went back to the entrance of the Santa Fosca Church, and from a distance spotted a market stall on the opposite side of the street, hurried over to it, and discovered little paper-weights that were waste products from the glassblowers in Murano, along with postcards, a brochure about the two churches, T-shirts, baseball caps, and rosaries. Next door was the antique shop he had seen earlier. He noticed his reflection in its display window, and behind that mirror image, old furniture and lamps inside the shop. But in one sense he could see all that only as a collage inside the area that his shadow cast on the pane of glass, resulting in the impression that he was viewing the items as entrails within his body. The portion of the window in sunshine, however, reflected the two churches and the archaeological finds, as well as the three baptismal and holy water fonts at the front of the buildings.

At that point the antique dealer appeared in his shop as if on the stage of some puppet theater. He took various objects from the drawers of a storage cabinet and arranged them in the showcase up above: painted dinner plates, a chess set, an old model ship, candlesticks, two fruit bowls, books beside a vase with an iris, a globe.

Above the showcase Lanz saw black-and-white photographs of people from the second half of the 19th century. He was fascinated by the everyday life that he now saw as if for the first time. Perhaps, he thought, it's because it's for the last time. Just then he was startled by a group of tourists that had approached without his noticing them, and, without saying a word, he "skedaddled"—the expression flashing through his mind—as if he had just stolen something. He avoided encountering the additional arriving tourists and soon found himself at the edge of a broad flat field with no one in sight. It had grown warm, so he shed his olive-green windbreaker and tied it around his waist.

The path went behind the Locanda Cipriani and then along a five-foot tall brick wall that was covered with blossoming red, yellow, and white rosebushes. Through gaps in the foliage he could steal brief glances into the garden restaurant with its parasols; he assumed that the canal ran along right behind it. On the left, he could make out small bushes and the remnants of a stone wall. Right after the Locanda Cipriani's outdoor restaurant he came to a garden with well-tended flowerbeds. "I'm seeing everything as if for the first time," he told himself. Every detail leaped out at him, but in his innermost being he knew that he would never see all this again. Adjoining the garden was a yellow building with an unplastered second story and rusty iron gates that at one time had been painted dark-green, presumably a service building for garden tools and machines; beside it a huge elderberry bush in blossom that attracted his attention but was isolated behind a wall. He noticed that the wall was topped with round roofing tiles. Just then he heard the sound of a motor and saw a man cutting the grass with a lawnmower. He was wearing, a black shirt, jeans, and earmuffs to block out the noise. When he got closer, Lanz could see a lush and leafy path leading down to a boat dock. An expensive white motorboat was tied up. Another man, bald and in black like the man who travelled alongside Lanz to Torcello, was smoking a cigarette. Lanz himself didn't understand why he was "searching for wide open spaces," an expression that again flashed through his mind. Wasn't he really trying to find someplace secluded?

From this point on, the view expanded, and, off to his right, a narrow lateral canal appeared. He could now see isolated villas at a distance from the waterfront. First he strolled over to a red house, and as he came closer, discovered a shed with a rusty tin roof nestled in a thicket. Trimmed shrubbery bordered the waterfront. Lanz immediately thought: this was the place he was searching for to accomplish his mission. Building materials were stacked beside the shed, and farther back, in the tall grass, was a jacked-up motorboat, covered with tarps, inviting him to crawl inside. He glanced around. There was no one in sight. But how could he get across the narrow lateral canal unnoticed and take his life in the thicket? He heard laughter in the distance, turned in that direction and saw, further off, behind a tree and tended shrubbery, a white villa with a strikingly large red chimney. At the end of the property was a fence, and behind that, underneath a large tree, young people were sitting together, eating and drinking, lost in their own little world. He now discovered that the lateral canal was provided with wooden pilings along the banks, one or two stone stairways led down to the water, and a wind-blown beehive with space for several frames was standing there, abandoned.

Just then he remembered the plastic bag he was holding—he had actually forgotten that he had bought a chess set in the antique store. The dealer in his straw hat and reading glasses had happily sold him the expensive ivory merchandise, but the price was so high that Lanz had had to use his MasterCard. Afterward he considered giving it back, but the tourists had driven him away. It was strange that he didn't remember it till now, even stranger that he had even bought the chess board and pieces, since he couldn't play very well.

He put the bag down on the ground, took various pieces out of their packaging, studied them, then decided that he himself was a bishop who could only move diagonally over the black or white squares.

He packed up the game and walked along the row of shrubs until he came to a long one-story building that had a satellite dish and a window air-conditioner on the external wall. The tile roof was covered with a plastic tarp, the garden overgrown. He thought he had found the perfect place, but just then a blonde girl with long hair and wearing jeans appeared, an ice-cream cone in one hand, and focused her attention on him. He nervously kept walking toward a remote building with tall white-frame windows, four chimneys and a balcony, with pines and cypress trees enhancing its garden. He turned around, saw in the distance the Santa Fosca Church tower, poles bearing power lines alongside the path, and then the girl, who was still watching him. Further along the green lateral canal, he came to a dense thicket, then, suddenly, he found himself at a wooden bridge. He headed off toward the main canal, past cherry laurel and blooming acacia trees and two brick columns, each topped with a white lion statue gazing off into the distance. The path narrowed and seemed to lead through garden plots: lots of groundcover, vegetation, fields, and fruit trees without leaves.

All of a sudden he was standing at the famous Ponte del Diavolo, the "Devil's Bridge." He saw a procession of tourists filing from the vaporetto station to the cathedral. Motorboats were docked at a restaurant. He read a sign above the entrance to the "Osteria Al Ponte del Diavolo." He took the tourist path to the shelter at the Torcello station and on the way admired a garden with blue irises and white Madonna lilies. He passed a kind of crossing where more motorboats were docked and the canal went off in two different directions. He discovered an outdoor restaurant with umbrellas and a vacant table in the shade of an apple tree. Since it was self-service, he went to the counter and bought a bottle of red wine and fried calamari with home fries—the "prisoner's last meal," as he called it. A blue rowboat with a mast stood alongside children's gymnastic equipment in front of one of the lushly flowering elder bushes. He liked the fact that people came, ate and drank, and then left again.

After the second bottle of red wine, he set up the chessboard and began to play against himself. With the third bottle it gradually became nighttime and quiet, and, with the chess set in the plastic bag, he staggered off toward the Devil's Bridge. It didn't have a railing, was arched above the water, and accessible only over flat steps. With all that, it was like an invitation to jump off the bridge and drown. On this island, Heaven and Hell apparently were close together and even merged, he thought sarcastically. Perhaps that was the reason he had come to Torcello, he reflected. And the thought had barely occurred to him when it dissolved and reformed into his next thought, like a flock of starlings.

He had donned his windbreaker some time ago, now turned on the flashlight on his cellphone, and the light beam illuminated trees, grass, plants, and rocks. Cursing silently in the darkness, he came to an especially large elderberry bush that attracted him with its fragrance, and he laid down underneath it. Beside the bush was a wooden gate and, beyond that, stone steps down to the water. The canal was on one side, a field on the other. Everything was silent. The only thing he could see and hear were a few insects. Still somewhat out of breath, he took the pistol from his windbreaker, and suddenly everything seemed simple. There was nothing to it. He aimed the pistol where he thought his heart was, but suddenly heard the sound of a motor coming from the canal. A moment later he saw a white boat that was idling just a few feet from the bush where he was hiding. The motor growled for a few more seconds, then was shut off.

What happened next occurred so fast that at first he didn't understand it at all. Two men dressed in black dragged an unconscious person from the motorboat up the steps from the canal to the garden gate, opened it, and, once out in the field, beat the unconscious man. Meanwhile a man in a NY-baseball cap first watched it all from the boat and then turned off the spotlight before he cautiously left the vessel, holding the flashlight from his cellphone in one hand and a yellow plastic sack in the other. Lanz saw him approach, stop, listen carefully, and then step up to the unconscious man. The next thing Lanz heard was a dull thud, then a gasp, a moan, and a gurgling sound. When Lanz cautiously glanced through the leaves and branches in the general direction of the sounds, he saw in the beam of the flashlight the man in the NY-baseball cap drop the yellow plastic sack—one of the men slit the throat of the greying victim who was lying in the field in a dark-blue blazer. The stranger hadn't been able to defend himself and was now lying on the ground, lifeless. His death rattle was audible for a few breaths, then stopped altogether. Lanz stared at the black shoes of the man in the baseball cap and his black pants.

"What'll we do with him?" the figure with the knife in his hand asked.

"We wait," was the answer.

And suddenly Lanz knew who the man was. He had seen him under an umbrella at the Hotel Excelsior on the Lido, talking with the cute photographer who was apparently his mistress. He also recognized one of the other two men in black. It was the same guy who had come with him on the vaporetto from Burano to the island of Torcello. The man with the NY-baseball cap flicked off his cellphone flashlight and the men just stood around awhile in silence, smoking cigarettes, waiting. "Wash your hands, Manuel," the man with the NY-baseball cap ordered. Lanz glanced at the corpse lying before them in a pool of blood, smeared with blood from the chest down. Lanz still couldn't fathom what had happened.

"Put him in the sack!" the man in the baseball cap finally ordered, flicking his cigarette to the ground. He spit contemptuously.

Then he turned his cellphone light on again. Meanwhile the other two men in black suits put the dead man in the yellow plastic sack, hustled him down to the bank, tossed him in the boat, and leaped aboard themselves. In the light from the cellphone Lanz could see that the suit of the man who had slit the victim's throat was stained with blood. He slipped out of his sport coat and shirt, and, naked from the waist up, sat down on one of the benches. After intensely studying the canal and the thicket, the man in the baseball cap climbed aboard, the boat immediately cast off, turned, and sped away with beaming headlights.

The thought ran through Lanz's head that, once underway, they would have ample opportunities to get rid of the dead body, for example, on one of the deserted islands. It all seemed so unreal, because he could tell that he was still drunk. He was still lying there, motionless, the pistol in his hand. He put the gun away, activated the flashlight on his own cellphone, and crawled over to the spot where the man in the blazer had been killed. A large pool of blood and tattered leaves covered the grass. There was no one in sight. The thought of taking his life now seemed absurd to Lanz—that he had considered shooting himself filled him with shame. He "embarrassed" himself, as he formulated it, but this feeling soon dissipated. The first thing he would do, he thought, was go to the police. But how would he explain to the officers that he had been hiding in a thicket when he saw the murder? Because he was just about to kill himself?

As he tottered back to the road, he was baffled. It was like when he was trying to solve the riddle of Rubik's Cube. The plan to take his own life was now incomprehensible, as if it had never existed. At this moment his life simply went on, just as obvious and insignificant as his intention to die had been. He had no regrets, didn't blame himself, didn't have the impression that he was returning to life. He only decided that it would be better to get rid of his pistol before he went to the police. Why hadn't he shot the three men? Everything had happened too quickly, he told himself. By the time he realized that the men were going to kill the stranger, one of them had already murdered the unconscious man. And how would he testify to that? He didn't have an answer. He would admit he had been drunk and wanted to sleep it off under the elderberry bush when he was caught off guard by the incident. Of course that didn't make him look good, but sometimes the poorest excuses—the ones that made you look foolish—were the most effective.

He staggered over the Devil's Bridge, took the brick walkway to the vaporetto station, and turned off his cellphone flashlight since the path was lighted. There was no one on the deserted sidewalk. As he passed by the extended structure of the Locanda Cipriani that he had seen just that morning, he noticed a woman in the window of a room on the second floor, talking angrily on the telephone. He heard her ask three times in a furious tone "Perché?" and then shout "No!" ending the conversation. When he saw her face he realized to his astonishment that it was the woman photographer from the Lido. That realization made his chest hurt and instantly brought up images of the man in black, slitting the throat of his victim. Still, the incident, as brutal as it had been, was more like a scene from a movie that you would never forget. He automatically counted the oleander stems resting in large pots in the nook beside the front door—there were five. Without knowing why, he opened the door to the Locanda, stepped inside, and encountered the distraught woman photographer who was just sitting down at a table in the restaurant and was nervously asking for the check. The waiter asked politely, but nevertheless in a positive tone of voice, why she was leaving the hotel so hastily. She had booked for two nights, hadn't she? Lanz was so fascinated by the sight of her that he walked off with great reluctance. Outside, a group of inebriated tourists arrived who were going to take the vaporetto back to Venice, he assumed. Again the incident he had witnessed passed before his eyes: first, how the victim's throat was slashed, then he saw the photographer's lover studying the area like a sharpshooter, then the killer with the bloodstains on his jacket, and, finally, the boat turning and disappearing into the night. He remembered that he had smoked during his years at the university and suddenly felt the need for a cigarette . . . But he definitely had to have a glass of grappa . . . He sat down at one of the tables under the broad arbor and waited. In the next instant he had no idea what he was waiting for, then felt he had no choice but to wait and see what would happen. Just then the waiter came outside and the woman photographer left the Locanda with a small suitcase. She acted as if she hadn't seen him. Lanz leaped up, and—without a second thought—planted himself in front of her and stared at her.

Even though he was drunk, he realized that she must have found out about the murder, because her eyes shifted abruptly and erratically, and she seemed to be focused on something else.

"I want to talk with you," Lanz said, his speech slurred.

"I don't have time," she responded, confused, and tried to slip past him. When he didn't step aside, she obviously hoped to escape through the oleander bushes.

"I saw the man being murdered," Lanz said quietly, and since he was drunk, his voice sounded strange even to him.

She looked at him, shocked. "What do you want . . .?"

"It's not far from here. A motorboat tied up along the bank, and one of three men slit the throat of a fourth. I can show you the spot—"

"No—," she took a step back, as if she wanted to escape into the building.

"We should go to the police . . ." he said in a monotone.

"I don't know what you're talking about," she said, in an attempt to dismiss him.

"Just a moment ago you were telephoning from your balcony. Three times you asked "Why?" and then screamed "No!" You were talking with your lover. He ordered the killing."

"You're drunk!" she snapped.

Just as Lanz was about to urge her again to go with him to the police, he saw the man in black who had sailed with him from Burano to Torcello and who had participated in the killing of the stranger. He now knew that his name was Manuel. Manual had his back to them, standing in the semi-darkness not far from the Devil's Bridge, and must have known that they had noticed him, because even the woman photographer had discovered him and stared in his direction. Lanz asked her if she knew the man, and when she didn't answer, he told her that he had seen him during the murder. "I assume he's supposed to take you back to the Lido."

Drunk as he was, Lanz approached the man as if he were going to attack him. Manuel waited by the canal, then suddenly turned and rushed off.

Without exchanging a word, Lanz and the photographer hurried to the landing for the vaporetto to Burano, and as soon as they got there, they went on board.

From the stern they silently studied the surrounding area until the late-night vaporetto left, and only then did they take seats in the cabin. Lanz again felt the pistol in the pocket of his windbreaker, and the farther they got from the island, the less plausible everything became that had happened there. Everything had changed. The water was just water again, the black sky was black sky. Thoughts and perceptions that he had pondered just two hours ago, that had overwhelmed him, were now gone. Even the woman photographer was now a stranger to him. At first, on the Lido beach, she had been too close, and now she seemed too distant.

In the meantime she had turned her back to him and was staring out the window at the Lagoon.

"I could have gone back to the Lido with my bodyguard and left from there," she said, without turning around. He said nothing, and she continued: "I didn't see anything and I don't know anything."

"You can't force me to do anything," she added, after a pause.

She was probably trying to sound resolute, but she hadn't pulled it off, Lanz thought.

"No," he replied, "but I'm going to go to the police."

She turned to face him with a malicious expression, then stood up and hurried over to exit the vaporetto. In the meantime, at the front of the boat, the inebriated tourists he had seen by the Locanda Cipriani were giggling. Onshore, he searched for the shelter of the vaporetto line that would take him back to Venice, not worrying about what the woman photographer was going to do. He was almost glad to be rid of her.

A young couple and an old lady were sitting in the half-open shelter, the giggling passengers apparently had found their lodgings in Burano; another group of tourists, equally jolly, had taken their place. He briefly turned to cast a last glance at Burano when he realized that the woman photographer had followed him and had also taken a seat on one of the benches. Suddenly, an obese old man in pants too short, a torn vest and a crumpled straw hat, burst into the room and interrupted Lanz's thoughts. The old man closed the wide outside sliding door, turned to a few of the waiting individuals, and began to sing arias in a pitiful quaking voice. And when his vocal chords failed, he pathetically recited the words—all the while imitating the gestures of opera singers, his arms reaching out partway as if he were receiving a valuable gift. His face was marked by alcohol and he was visibly intoxicated. He sang, leaped over to a woman tourist with a camera as if he were worshipping her, then approached the young couple and the old lady who turned away in disgust, which only spurred the old man on more. In conclusion, he rendered "Nessun dorma" from Puccini's *Turandot*, fell silent, and then performed Verdi's "La donna è mobile." It occurred to Lanz that this was a former singer from some opera chorus. In the interim the man explained that he was eighty-years old; he sang and croaked, whined and recited until the vaporetto N—on its way to St. Mark's—finally docked. The opera singer stayed until the boat departed, standing in the illuminated shelter that seemingly floated on the water like a lake stage, and sang "Arrivederci Roma" until the vaporetto cast off its lines and sailed away.

Lanz kept watching through the window as the old man left the shelter and struggled up the gangway onto land.

Most of the vaporetto passengers now seemed to be drowsy, and Lanz, too, was so exhausted that he could barely keep his eyes open. In Venice he would get something to eat and drink and then go to the police, he decided. He didn't have to explain anything to the officers, and the excuse that he had wanted to sleep under the elderberry bush along the canal now seemed more plausible than before. The woman photographer unexpectedly sat down beside him, but without so much as a glance at him, just staring intently out the side window. After a short pause she suggested that they go to the police together. He didn't react, and she insisted that she wasn't going to return to the Lido, but would leave Venice and travel on to Berlin and eventually to America. She would leave all her "stuff," as she put it, in the Hotel Excelsior—she had her camera and lens with her.

Her name was Julia Ellis, she said after a pause. He only nodded, and she asked him his name. And his profession . . . Translator . . .

Could somebody live from that? . . . He didn't reply.

"I know you're mad at me, but everything was so unexpected . . . I still don't understand."

Lanz was too tired to carry on a conversation and, half-asleep, asked her if she trusted her boyfriend.

She didn't answer.

"Didn't you ever suspect that he was involved in shady dealings?" he blurted out.

Again she didn't answer.

She suddenly told him that the man was a big name in the gambling industry, with connections in Hong Kong, New York, Milan, and Paris. For several years now he'd been supporting her work and appreciating her art.

Lanz was out of questions, and she didn't expect him to talk to her. Still, it was obvious to him that she was upset: when he went to the police, she not only had her significant other on her hands, she would also have to disappear so she herself wouldn't be arrested.

"Where are you going to report to the police?" she asked.

"In Venice."

Lanz was so tired he didn't know what he was saying. Julia Ellis, however—he had remembered her name—calmly went on speaking. He learned that her friend's name was Will Mennea and that he had been extremely tense lately. In the end he had suggested she take a few days off and accompany him to Torcello. They had to leave early in the morning to be on time for a confidential meeting with a Serbian businessman named Borsakowsky, according to him. Then they would eat in the Locanda Cipriani restaurant and go on to explore the island of Torcello. So someone dropped her off at the Locanda, but all day long no one came to do anything with her.

From that point on, Lanz was no longer listening. It wasn't until the vaporetto's forceful impact with the pier jarred them that he came to and sat up, shaken. He didn't know how long they'd been traveling. The photographer—he had forgotten her name again— was still sitting beside him, and, driven by impatience, he gave in to his impulse to disembark. Ignoring the woman, he tottered off the boat. Obviously she must have followed him because she hurried along beside him and spoke to him incessantly.

"You can't go to the police in this condition . . . You're drunk . . . No one would believe you!"

He stopped, clumsily unzipped his pants and peed. He noticed that he was in a park connected to the Giardini by a bridge. So he had landed in Sant'Elena. He felt relieved.

"Come on!" he heard someone say, then Julia—he remembered her name again—led him out of the park to an unfamiliar building where a concierge asked him for his ID.

A large wide mirror was hanging opposite the front desk, and he saw himself standing on the floor with its chessboard pattern, and he instantly thought of the chess set in his shopping bag and the figure of the bishop that was he himself.

When he opened his eyes the next morning, it was already bright outside. His head hurt. He closed his eyes and thought he was dreaming, but his memory was conjuring up images that had overwhelmed his mind the day before. All at once he remembered what had happened. Disoriented, he wondered if he hadn't actually shot himself and awakened in some parallel universe? That seemed more plausible than his actual memories. He tried to persuade himself that he had indeed shot himself and had awakened in some chaotic afterlife that had greeted him with a murder and incoherent events. Further verification was provided by the fact that the woman photographer—named Julia Ellis—had embraced him last night and at some point had disappeared.

Just then he realized that he was naked, his clothes were scattered about on the floor. Dazed, he got dressed and after slipping on his windbreaker, noticed that his pistol was missing. He immediately searched the room with its elegant accommodations, its white walls and large white curtains, the king-size bed, two leather armchairs, and a television set. He even checked under the bed, but found only dust . . . Had Julia Ellis stolen the pistol? He wondered if he had told her he was going to commit suicide, but he couldn't remember what had happened from their arrival at the hotel until he had woken up . . . The only thing that haunted him was the impression that he and Julia had made love.

As he got up off the floor, he became dizzy and collapsed on the bed. It took an hour before he could think to some extent. His wallet was undisturbed, his MasterCard was still there, too. He also found his ID and his money—minus the amount he had spent for the ticket to the Basilica Santa Maria Assunta and for the fried calamari and wine. He even discovered the chess set in the shopping bag that he had put down on one of the armchairs. He scooped it all up and went outside. From the outside, the ground-level annex to the old building looked like a motel or a string of luxurious beach huts, each with a round ventilation window above its glass door. The meadow, divided by shrubs and flower beds into small islands with lounge chairs, meticulously created paths, English benches along the wall of the old building and tall trees that rose behind the annex—the totality conveyed a solid middle-class impression.

He went to the front desk and was greeted with "Good morning, Signor Ellis," but didn't respond. He just wanted to put this all behind him as quickly as possible. While the concierge totaled up his bill, Lanz glanced through an open door into the empty dining room and noticed a framed blurb about the history of the hotel that had formerly been a monastery. Beside that hung a detailed city map of Venice. As far as he could remember, police headquarters was located on the Campo San Lorenzo. He studied the colorful map in search of the site and found it just as he got his MasterCard back. Just then he noticed that the windows of the former monastery were barred.

At first he didn't know what he should do. Maybe going to the police could actually harm him . . . He had been a witness as Will Mennea—in spite of everything, he had memorized the name—had had a man killed, Lanz had seen the bodyguards in their black suits ruthlessly slit a stranger's throat as if they were simply shining their shoes or changing a light bulb. He knew the name of one of the killers, Manuel, had been tricked by Julia Ellia, and no longer had a weapon. Then he remembered the second pistol that was hidden in his attic and that he now had to assemble. He decided he shouldn't undertake anything without first considering all the possible consequences.

He impulsively hurried through the small park where he could see the Giardini and on down to the vaporetto station. When he saw the boat approaching the shelter, he decided not to go to the Lido, but in the direction of the Ospedale Santi Giovanni e Paolo which, according to the city map in the hotel, would enable him to reach police headquarters on the Campo San Lorenzo.

III

On the Run

The Line 4.1 vaporetto was half-full. He took a seat by the window, squeezed the shopping bag between his calves, and gazed out steadily without registering what was taking place before his eyes. Of course he had often taken this route, but now his thoughts were elsewhere. Again and again he saw the killing before him as one of Mennea's bodyguards slit the stranger's throat, but from then on, the images leaped out at him, jumbled and in no chronological order. He also saw the men smoking, casting off their boat, his own pistol, leaves from the elderberry bush, the Basilica mosaic, the afternoon in the garden restaurant, the bottles of red wine and, most of all, Julia at the Locanda Cipriani, and fragments of their lovemaking in the hotel room. He still felt the effects of the alcohol.

After the endless tall walls around the Arsenal complex, they reached the Ospedale SS Giovanni e Paolo. He was astonished to find that an attractive woman in oversized sunglasses had sat down beside him unnoticed, and that in the meantime the vaporetto had filled to the brim. In front of him a middle-aged man with a shoulder bag was just placing a cute little dog in his lap. It was orange-brown in color and had little black eyes like a toy puppy. As soon as Lanz stared at it, the little dog nestled closer to its owner who looked away each time Lanz looked at him. The dog didn't make a sound the entire trip. A young man in black with a backpack sat a bench away on the opposite side of the vaporetto and yawned.

Just before he got off, Lanz suddenly felt a cramp in his calf. It was so intense that he clenched his teeth in pain. First he tried to relieve it while seated, but in stretching the muscles he only made the contractions worse. It wasn't until Lanz took the shopping bag with the chess set in one hand, stood up and hobbled off the boat that the pain dissipated after several steps. The majority of the passengers from the waterbus were already entering the hospital, which was fine with him as he was reluctant to go through it alone simply because he wanted to take a shortcut to the Campo San Lorenzo. At that point he thought of the writer Philipp Artner, with whom he had once had a chance encounter Am Heumarkt in Vienna. The author, sitting on a bench in the courtyard under tall plane trees, had invited Lanz to join him. Apparently he was bored, because he gave a long lecture on Venice, how, as a child, he had been taken to the Ospedale, and from his room had watched seagulls above the sea and the San Michele cemetery.

Lanz gripped the railing of the gangway, turned, and now gazed at the walls of the cemetery in the distance and then at one lone gull as it flew from the roof of a building.

Two policemen were standing in front of the Ospedale Santi Giovanni e Paolo, scrutinizing the new arrivals. Initially Lanz was alarmed, but apparently they weren't interested in him. At that moment a prisoner in a white surgical mask, his hands shackled with an iron chain, was hustled into a building by two other policemen. Lanz immediately thought about the murder again and his intention to file a report. In his imagination Lanz saw himself in the prisoner's place, being led to prison.

As if he were some wind-up toy figure, Lanz just kept moving, but doubts that he was doing the right thing made him even more hesitant. He could tell from the scaffolding that the hospital was being renovated. New or already restored buildings were scattered among old ones, and in several courtyards he encountered patients, visitors, medical assistants in white scrubs, nurses and lab workers. Taking advantage of a large confusing signpost with the outlines of the buildings identified by abbreviations and single letters of the alphabet, he tried to find the exit to the piazza at the Chiesa Santi Giovanni e Paolo, but wandered into other larger or smaller courtyards. Some appeared rundown, old brick walls where someone had knocked off the plaster, and rusty gutters that looked like archaeological finds. This picture of desolation was reinforced with walls stained by blotches of dampness, broken flagstones on the ground, and cats that were lying on them, enjoying the warmth of the sunshine. At his wife's vineyards in St. Leonhard there were many cats, he remembered, but they had been so wary that they always ran away from people. He stopped and considered each individual animal, a red cat, a black one, a tabby, several with black-and-white patches, and even a calico cat. In one corner there was an old stone coach wheel, possibly the remnants of some tableau, along with podiums of metal and plastic, and a rusty locker that was sealed off with an iron chain. He again thought of the prisoner with the white surgical mask, but he suppressed the image so that it wouldn't elicit more visions. After some cul-de-sacs that forced Lanz to turn back, he finally came to the large inner courtyard of the former Scuola Grande di San Marco with its cloisters, a meadow, ancient deciduous trees and, beneath the arches of the colonnade, large pots full of red cyclamens.

He tried to think of nothing, to simply observe. Between the trees and a cherry laurel shrub the cats reappeared; he was certain they were the same ones he had seen earlier in the courtyard. But how had they gotten here undetected? So they had to be different cats. The greenery he saw was only this vivid in springtime, he thought. He found a glass waiting room, an aquarium where he instantly imagined himself, as a small fish, alone, as he so often had done. He sat down and tried to be an observer who could capture everything like a camera. But just the intention of trying to calm down defeated itself. He soon went to look for the exit from the hospital complex and ended up following a young man in black with a backpack whom he had noticed earlier on the vaporetto. A few feet further on, he entered a high-ceilinged room with two rows of columns and a broad red coconut runner. The word "runner" struck a chord—of course, since he had chosen the runner, the bishop, as his figure in the chess set that he carried around with him. Sunlight was streaming through the colored windows on the right side, shining on the stone floor and forming a bright pattern of blue, white, and beige squares. The coconut runner led to an exit where the young man in black was just leaving the building. On the piazza with its corroded statue of a *condottiere* were several cafés and ristorantes, and Lanz, whose doubts and fears had intensified, sat down at the nearest one so he could think in peace and quiet.

Someone had drawn a heart on the stone patio, and a group of young women were using a hand-held extension pole to take selfies of each other in front of the church. Tourist groups and couples continually appeared out of nowhere and took pictures with smartphones and large and small cameras.

Lanz ordered a cola and chips, quickly emptied the bottle without touching the chips, and put money on the table since he suddenly felt an urge to get away. Not long after, he got lost in a confusion of alleys that spread out and seemed endless, stone bridges on both sides with stair steps as well as open gates that he entered and suddenly no longer knew where he was. He asked passersby for bearings, and they always pointed their fingers in the same direction that he then took, past display windows with tourist kitsch, a black cat with white paws, walls, graffiti on walls and doors, small mounted posters and remains of placards, past a shop for hand-painted dishes, coffee pots and cups, past canals that mirrored the old buildings, and then into passageways so narrow that he couldn't sidestep oncoming pedestrians. So he retraced his steps to try again, finally sitting down on a small red fire hydrant and pondering how he could get to his destination.

But he came to no conclusion, so he "followed his nose" and, to his surprise, suddenly stood in front of the Campo San Lorenzo and its impressive old, brown-on-brown church in the shape of a masonry-colored cube with a prism-shaped roof, a tall main portal and two smaller entrances on either side; above that, in the middle of the front façade, two arcade windows that allow daylight to illuminate the nave. In addition, in the center of the roof construction, he noticed a small round window that struck him as a voyeuristic peephole—the eye of God, he said spontaneously. Since there were no other embellishments, the religious structure reminded him of a geometrically surreal temple. That impression was reinforced by the fact that on both sides of the piazza stood an equally geometric yellow and white, three- or four-story building complex with tall rectangular windows that led to the church. As he ascended the stone bridge over the green Rio di San Lorenzo, he had the feeling of entering a stage set created by de Chirico, the painter. The stage was enormous and perfectly suited to crowd scenes, but initially he found himself alone, as if he were required to sing an aria, like the eighty-year-old man in the Burano vaporetto shelter.

Curious, he turned and discovered that he was now on the other side of the Rio di San Lorenzo, in front of a dirty grey four-story building that had an oval white shield over the entrance that read "Commissariato San Marco." Beneath that was a blue rectangle with the inscription "Polizia di Stato." In one of the open windows, a man in a long-sleeved T-shirt was on the telephone, beside him on a flagpole hung an Italian flag that billowed in slow motion in a breeze that Lanz had scarcely noticed. Above and below the window ran separate rows of decorative railings, and in front of the entrance was a police boat moored to a blue-and-white-striped pole.

Once again he turned his back on the police building and walked over to the still vacant piazza before the church. He saw that its brickwork was permeated with countless ledges, and on each one there were nails to keep the pigeons from landing. The main door was barricaded. As far as he knew, Marco Polo's body was lying in the Gothic church. Lanz had read that the explorer disappeared during one of its renovations. Lanz was familiar with the book about Marco Polo's journey to China, his descriptions of Turkey, Mesopotamia and Afghanistan where he had supposedly encountered people with dogs' heads, viewed bizarre mirages, and even observed unicorns or witnessed marvels never seen before. Marco Polo and Gulliver ... now they had vanished into thin air, he thought, where just yesterday he himself had hoped to end up. Trees had been planted in front of both buildings, interspersed with benches, and in the center of the piazza was an old stone fountain. Seated at one of the benches, he now studied the *Questura*, the police station. The man in the long-sleeved T-shirt was still standing at the window, telephoning. Meanwhile two old folks came along, a man and a woman in wheelchairs, and approached one of the benches where their caregivers lifted them up and sat them down. Other old folks followed, leaning on canes or their nurses, and Lanz realized that the building they had exited was a nursing home. At the same time he again noticed the young man in black with the backpack who had just disappeared into the building. At the same time, a woman was struggling to push a baby carriage up the steps of the bridge over the Rio and then down to the square. High school and university students came from a side street and sat down on the stone steps in front of the church. Lanz still felt as if he were on a stage. Nevertheless, he tried to concentrate on what he would state for the record when he entered the police station and was asked about the sequence of events. Should he mention his intention to commit suicide? But what could he say if they ask him about his pistol? Would he have to tell them about Julia Ellis, or should he not bring up their relationship? He could also pretend to know nothing about Will Mennea and frame his story as if he didn't know any of the people involved. But now the desire to tell the truth was stronger than ever. There was no other option if he didn't want to become even more deeply involved in the incident. On the other hand, he didn't want to endanger Julia. Suddenly he was no longer certain that they had made love the night before, and wanted to see her again ... to see her again and spend time with her, he added to himself.

When he said the word "time," his gaze fell on the paving stones that covered the Campo and in particular on one inlayed white stone with the inscription "Anno 1747." It occurred to him that he might really be in the fourth dimension if he had shot himself the day before. But he then rejected that notion.

His pistol was yet another problem. Why had Julia Ellis stolen it from the pocket of his windbreaker?

He gazed at the church again and clung to the thought that the bones of Marco Polo were resting inside. The Venetian merchant had been travelling for 24 years, Lanz remembered, had reported on the enormous bird called Roc, on paper money and fantastic treasures, on strange religions, tropical islands and, last but not least, on his stay among Mongols at the court of Kublai Khan, the Emperor of China at the time. At one point on a Sunday stroll, Lanz had wandered past Marco Polo's residence near the Rialto Bridge and the Teatro Malibran, had identified with the world traveler, and also decided to translate the book with the title *Il Milione*. According to an earlier biographer, the people had given Marco Polo that name, since he had apparently spoken incessantly of Kublai Khan's millions and his wealth. Polo's contemporaries considered the account a collection of fairy-tales. In the last stage of his life the discoverer's relatives, friends, and even priests had encouraged him to disavow the "pack of lies." On his deathbed he refuted his challengers: "I haven't told half of what I've seen." And Lanz decided that he, too, was probably in a similar situation. They would analyze his statements, contradict them, and doubt him in the end. If his pistol didn't turn up, they wouldn't buy the story that he wanted to shoot himself. What other reason would he have had for lying under that elderberry bush? Because he was trying to sleep off those three bottles of wine? And what if Julia had turned the pistol in to the police some time ago? To mention in retrospect that he wanted to shoot himself would sound like an excuse and perhaps make *him* into a murder suspect. So it was necessary for him to see Julia Ellis first. As if hypnotized while he continued to brood, he glanced at the building housing the Commissariato San Marco and the officer who was still phoning at the window. As Lanz turned and again gazed at the San Lorenzo church, it occurred to him that Marco Polo had dictated his travels from China to a fellow inmate in a Genoa prison, because upon his return he had commanded a Venetian galley in the naval battle of Curzola and had been taken prisoner by the Genoans. Just the word "prison" conjured up the image of himself as a detainee.

Just then a younger man appeared on the Campo, possibly a student, and let a fat old bulldog off its leash. It was a dwarf combination of a rhinoceros and a pug and trotted, docile and sad, over to the stone fountain. None of the pigeons that were swarming and skipping about the piazza flew away. The dog was obviously struggling, it even limped a bit. Its muzzle was grey, the rest of its head was brown-and-white, the body brown, one of its paws was white. The high school students sitting in front of the church knew the dog, came over and petted it. The dog put up with the fuss, then climbed the two flat steps to the fountain, and from there surveyed the ground below.

Lanz took one last look at the church—it still seemed to him a gigantic grave for Marco Polo—and at the building housing the Polizia di San Marco, rushed over the bridge, looked up and confirmed that the officer beside the flag was still on the telephone. At that moment Lanz decided once and for all not to go to the police. He retraced his steps, pulled out the city map that he just remembered he'd put in the pocket of his windbreaker, unfolded it, and thought: "Places to meditate." And likewise, the point of this piece of paper was also to find a solution and establish a rationale. But like the future, it wasn't clear where he should go. And he still had doubts that he ought to go back to the police and explain everything; after all, it was Julia Ellis who had put him in this predicament. He also realized he didn't have a gun permit and that he had filed off the serial number in St. Leonhard. That alone was a criminal act and kept him from going to the police. That thought even settled him down as he walked back through the confusing little streets to the Ospedale Santi Giovanni e Paolo. At one point he stopped, startled, because he saw on a front door four miniature bronze heads with tassel caps. The faces had long noses and their mouths were open, at least indicating they had tongues. He realized they were an anti-

Semitic mockery. In the middle of the door was a black perforated iron plate, and behind that the intercom system. The nameplate indicated it was a law firm. Everything now related to his situation: the law office, like the bronze Jewish heads, seemed like a nightmare. He said to himself: no police, no lawyers, no trial!

He managed to wolf down a pizza somewhere, and to reduce the aftereffects of the alcohol, drank two cans of cola. This time he didn't go through the Ospedale to the vaporetto station, but walked beside the hospital building along the bank of the Rio dei Mendicanti. On the opposite bank he saw a boatyard and remembered that last spring he had seen lots of boats there—he thought: a "swarm" of boats—with men and women in casual clothes who were just coming in from the Lagoon. On a bus trip with his stepparents he had visited the Ospedale and the former Scuola Grandi di San Marco with its Biblioteca Medica, whose walls he was now passing. The tour guide had given a lecture, but Lanz now only remembered the auburn marble floor, the magnificently opulent coffered ceiling, the impressive frescos, the books in bookcases, the hall with the altar and, more than anything else, the old anatomical graphics displayed in showcases with illustrations that had upset him. And for a time he had not been able to take his mind off the old surgical instruments that were even more bizarre and had seemed to him like torture instruments. They had represented an alternate world. He even had a dream that as a child he was in a large richly-decorated gold container, that on the inside had looked like the halls in the Scuola Grande di San Marco. A stranger had tormented him, asking what he was doing there, until Lanz suddenly—as often in his dreams— had gotten up and floated to the gold ceiling where he looked down upon the mosaic of the floor and the small raging man, before he awoke.

Lanz turned and instantly noticed that a man was following him. He was bald, young, athletic, wore a backpack—and in that instant Lanz recalled seeing the man on the vaporetto, then in the Ospedale, and finally on the Campo San Lorenzo. To this point he hadn't appeared suspicious, but now, on the narrow Fondamenta

Mendicanti between the Scuola Grande di San Marco and the canal lying still beneath the flutter of a colony of gulls, Lanz thought immediately of fleeing. He was embarrassed to walk faster, so he slowed his pace. But no one overtook him. He nervously halted, glanced back, and saw that the young man with the backpack was pretending to gaze at the canal, as if he had seen something that had aroused his interest. Since Lanz couldn't come up with a plan, he hurried along, finally breaking into a run. However, the young man with the backpack must be chasing him, because Lanz could hear the sound of someone running and panting right behind him. As Lanz abruptly stopped and looked around, he was overtaken by a young woman jogger in a sweatsuit, while the young man was still standing back at the same spot and now seemed to be studying the gulls. Again, Lanz felt ashamed, but he ran behind the jogger all the way to the Fondmente Nuove and didn't stop until he had turned the corner. He was miserable and full of hate. That morning he had still wanted to commit suicide, and now he was prepared to run for his life. He resolved not to turn around anymore, and at the same time he was angry that he didn't have his pistol and that he had met Julia Ellis.

He could finally see the vaporetto station in the distance, the waterbus to the Lido was in the process of docking. So he took off running again, reached the landing, hurried into the shelter, and was pushed to one side by the surge of disembarking passengers. Only then could he make his way on deck where he hid in the back row of seats and resolved that, upon his arrival at the Lido, he would call the police from a blocked number and anonymously inform them that he had witnessed a crime. No, he decided, it was better if he did it now, on board the vaporetto. The waterbus was now leaving, and since there weren't many passengers, he set his smartphone on "anonymous," searched for the number on the Internet, and announced in a low and husky voice that he had witnessed a murder the previous evening. He gave the time, the place, and the name of Will Mennea.

"Will Mennea was found dead on his sailboat an hour ago. Who is this?" a voice responded in a suspicious tone.

Lanz immediately ended the call. He was sweating and, as the vaporetto stopped at the next station, he lowered his head so no one could recognize him. But as the waterbus sailed on, he saw he had no reason to be afraid. He just then realized that he must have gotten on the wrong vaporetto, because instead of sailing past the brick wall of the Arsenal, he saw off to the right the sculptures of Dante and Vergil. It was absurd. As if some form of punishment, he had gone from the hospital and the Commissariato di San Marco to the vaporetto that went to the cemetery. Now he had to remind himself once again how he had wanted to kill himself just the day before.

Then he noticed way up front in the waterbus the bald young man with the backpack who was apparently still following him. The bald guy didn't even try to hide the fact that he had been seen, because he nodded cynically to Lanz and made no attempt to look away. Lanz wasn't about to get involved in some "staring contest" as they used to do in school. He stood up and went to the front platform, determined either to get off if the young man remained sitting or to sail on if the guy got off.

With a loud growl, the vaporetto slowed, passing the brick wall of the cemetery. On the station platform ahead, a large crowd was gathering, perhaps coming from a funeral, Lanz thought. The waterbus had barely docked when he glanced over at the young man who smiled and nodded back at him, but didn't budge from his seat. Lanz quickly leaped off, flanked the waiting passengers who got out of his way, and ran as fast as he could through the walled gate on the right side. Overhead he heard the cawing of seagulls that were circling in the sky. But he didn't see any gulls between or on the gravestones. That was unusual.

It made him think of Alfred Hitchcock's movie *The Birds*, as he again discovered the young man with the backpack who had apparently disembarked only after the waiting passengers had first boarded the waterbus. Lanz now saw that his pursuer, squatting behind a gravestone in the meantime, had stopped and was warily surveying the area; he lifted his head, gazed at the gulls, and inspected sections of the cemetery. He then resolutely set out in Lanz's direction. But before the man reached him, he stopped, still intently scanning the area, and then disappeared on the long straightaway with the children's graves.

Lanz waited. It was crazy to run back to the vaporetto stop—he would be seen instantly and then there would be no chance to escape. But to Lanz's surprise the man came back, just as he himself was about to flee into the innards of the cemetery. His pursuer didn't head in Lanz's direction, but this time descended the stairs to the Camaldolese monastery where he studied the courtyard. Lanz took advantage of the opportunity and hurried down the path between the graves—scanning in all directions and suspicious that the stranger might still be following him. He had been to the cemetery many times before, to visit the graves of the poets Ezra Pound and Joseph Brodsky, as well as those of the composers Igor Stravinsky and Luigi Nono. But that didn't occur to him now. He only hoped to find a crowd of people, perhaps have a conversation with someone by asking for information which might discourage his pursuer from continuing to tail him. It wasn't difficult to imagine what the pursuer was feeling, his curiosity and desires. He himself had often followed strangers, but now he realized what it was like, what they might have felt when they thought he was stalking them. He knew that this athletic man could be lurking anywhere, behind a gravestone, a tree, or a bush.

The colony of seagulls high above was shrieking with outrage and anger, and Lanz associated the birds' warning cries with the man who was chasing him. On one grave there was a large rusty anchor in place of a tombstone.

A moment later he was relieved to see two men in yellow shirts and jeans, driving a small tractor with a trailer down one of the main paths. They stopped, jumped down, grabbed gardening tools, and, leaning on a shovel and a rake, began to talk with each other. Behind them and beneath the screeching seagulls, the vast cemetery spread out, bordered by pine and cypress trees and the brick wall. Every plot was furnished with a stone slab and a standing piece, reminding Lanz of lecterns with memorial plaques indicating names and dates attached at an angle. The next thing he thought about were laptops that weren't working, and then music stands that conjured up a symphony orchestra of the deceased, silently playing a requiem. In addition, cut flowers in vases were everywhere, as vestiges of a gradually fading ceremony.

The gravesite of the composer Luigi Nono was overgrown with bright-green ivy. A green lizard was lying in the sun atop the inscription "Luigi." And, at the front end, a large boulder—as if from a meteor strike—dominated the multitude of neighboring gravestones. The large rock had been refitted with a concrete slab and an iron chain bound it to a tree trunk. Lanz felt he was safe when a figure disappeared behind a chapel and didn't reappear. He hadn't seen if it really was the stranger, possibly it was only a visitor. Lanz stepped behind a tree and didn't take his eyes off the chapel, while the gulls kept up their screeching. Since his pursuer didn't reappear, he walked over to the two men by the tractor and asked about the grave of the onetime soccer manager Helenio Herrera that had to be around here somewhere.

"Over there," the first man replied.

"Behind the chapel," the other added. Lanz took a 5-euro bill from his wallet and asked the older man to show him the way.

"Sure," the younger fellow answered, took the money that Lanz was holding in his outstretched hand, and led him to the chapel where a tourist in clothing similar to that of his pursuer was just taking a picture of the lane with his smartphone. Above them the birds continued to make a commotion. Actually, Lanz should have been relieved that the bald young man was nowhere to be seen, but he was ashamed of his apprehension.

"Here," the cemetery gardener called out, stuck out his arm and pointed to a bricked gate that Lanz thought he recognized. As they were passing by, he immediately recalled that the final resting places for the American poet Ezra Pound and the Russian writer Joseph Brodsky were here. He hadn't found Helenio Herrera's grave yet.

The cemetery gardener had left. Several tourists were standing beside graves, and Lanz looked back to make certain that he wasn't being followed.

Wall lizards emerged from crevices where they had been hiding, then disappeared through seams and fissures in the graves or just lay motionless in the sunshine and let him observe them when he stood still. Up close, their feet seemed somewhat demonic, but from farther back they made an adorable impression. He was most attracted to the green and black patterns on their bodies. The whole time he kept looking up to see if anything had changed. But the tourists were still conversing at the graves and strolling around, the seagulls were still shrieking up above, though he still didn't see a single one of them on the ground.

A black tombstone had several large white spots that seemed to Lanz as if they were blotches of paint. Apparently they were lichens or a fungus, he thought. In an alcove he finally stumbled onto a stone replica of the World Cup that fans had adorned with various colored scarves, a baseball cap, and a jersey with the number 24, beneath it an almost illegible plaque with the name Helenio Herrera; the soccer manager had won the World Cup twice for Inter Milan. Lanz then noticed a massive stone container, presumably the legendary man's coffin. Or perhaps the World Cup replica held his ashes, Lanz reflected. He glanced down at a branch of ivy that was placed in a stone bowl with yellow hibiscus flowers.

The tourists looked up, some pointed to the sky and paused. Lanz, too, stopped between the stone crosses, the bare marble slabs, the cherry laurel branches and pines, and gazed at the noisy tiny insect creatures way up in the sky. He was amazed at what went through his mind: the fatal accident of his wife whose grave he hadn't visited since the funeral, the murder he had witnessed from behind the elderberry bush, the plan to end his life, his coupling with Julia, the vaporetto trip to Torcello, the view of the Lagoon from the church tower, the mosaic of The Last Judgment in the Basilica Santa Maria Assunta dedicated to "Our Lady of the Assumption," and the young athletic man who was pursuing him . . .

Lanz noticed that it had become quiet, and looked around: the tourists had left the grounds in the meantime, he was the only one left. Just as he was about to leave, he heard a gentle but definite buzzing and whistling sound in the air, then the dull thud of some object hitting the ground, and these sounds were repeated. He assumed they were coming from an empty space behind some shrubs, because through the leaves he could see blue and black splotches. High above, the gulls were now shrieking louder. On Torcello they had reminded him of the Holy Ghost, but now they seemed to be warning him of some imminent danger.

He cautiously approached and, after a few strides, encountered another young athletic man, bald, wearing a T-shirt. Using a lasso, he was just tossing some object into the top of a tall old tree. The object fell back on the ground with a thump. The man had on a white glove and was holding the end of a rope. At first Lanz thought the object was a small purse, but when he got closer, he could see that it was a mesh net pouch containing chunks of raw meat. The young man twirled the lasso with the pouch around and around like a windmill so that it made the buzzing and whistling sound that Lanz had heard. Suddenly there was a piercing noise coming from the foliage, as if a jagged knife were being held to a grinding wheel. Several times he heard the sound, "eechop-eechop," and with that, the seagulls again began to shriek with hate. One second later a bird of prey, a falcon, flew down from the top of the tree, landed on the man's other hand that was protected by a leather glove, and fluttered its wings.

Lanz came closer and, his curiosity aroused, asked what was going on. The young man—apparently a Bavarian—replied that he has been working at the San Michele cemetery for three weeks, scaring the gulls away. Surprisingly, his name was Richard Vogel, "Richard Bird," as he introduced himself, laughing. Of course it was a coincidence that his name was Vogel and was a falconer, but, he continued, it didn't bother him when people made fun of him. In the cemetery there were two thousand seagulls that paraded up and down between the graves. The gulls, the falconer went on, had recently become aggressive, they had even attacked children and old folks, that's why the city government had hired him. So now he was going to be hawking until the creatures were gone. That wouldn't take more than a week, because the raptor usually killed several gulls on each outing. Richard Vogel had had a chip implanted in the falcon, and a transmitter on his belt enabled him to locate the bird. Lanz learned that the falcon had come from Austria. It was beautiful, with black-and-white horizontal stripes on its breast, amber eyes with large black pupils. Its head was small, the beak sharply rounded, its back was brown, the talons yellow, and its long tail-feathers were black-and-brown striped. It had a stern expression, Lanz felt. The falcon was restless and several times attempted to fly off, making a loud "waiiik" cry. Then, with his left hand where the raptor still rested on the leather glove, Richard Vogel made a slight movement where he seemed to cast off the bird, but then caught it again. In addition, he calmed the falcon with noises that sounded like a gentle, barely audible "keteck," the falconer contorting his face as if he were purposely trying to scowl. Richard Vogel explained that since he had broken two fingers, the falcon was now perched on his left hand. The falconer had an elaborate tattoo of a falcon in flight on his pale forearm. It seemed to Lanz that the man wanted to be joined with the animal for his entire lifetime. Lanz was amazed to see the falcon now turn its head more than 180 degrees—because he had never seen a falcon up close. Instinctively he, too, turned around and saw to his horror that the young man with the backpack at the entrance was just pulling a dog mask over his head.

"I'm being followed," Lanz blurted out.

The man in the dog mask was already heading his way, but the quick-thinking Richard Vogel made a strange sound and the falcon flapped its wings, dove on the startled attacker, and took a powerful bite out of his bare head. The falcon then got a firm grip on the stranger's backpack, fluttered its wings, continued hacking away at the dogman's skull until his mask was spattered with blood and the color red was streaming down the side of his face. At the same time Richard Vogel had drawn a knife from his belt and raced over to the man. The stranger, flailing about with his hands, was trying to run off through the cemetery gate, but the falcon wouldn't let go. Just then Lanz realized that the seagulls up above were also panicking, as if *they* would swoop down and drive Richard Vogel and his falcon from the cemetery. It wasn't until the bald man fell and began to scream that the raptor eased its grip, and the bald man was able to escape. The falconer had quickly put the knife back in the sheath on his belt and commanded the bird to land on his arm, all without taking his eyes off the cemetery gate.

"I know that man. His name is Giorgio Fermi. Stay here," he said calmly. Lanz didn't budge. With the falcon on his arm, Richard Vogel then went cautiously over to the gate, disappeared from this section of the cemetery, and returned a few minutes later. The seagulls were still circling high above. Judging from Vogel's gait and his smile, Lanz assumed he that the danger had passed.

"Fermi's gone!" the falconer shouted, came over to Lanz and began packing up his things.

"And I know who you are, too," he then said.

Vogel went over to a bag that he had laid under a tree, pulled out a small leather hood with built-in protrusions to cover the eyes, and skillfully placed it on the falcon's head. Now the falcon looked like a huge dangerous insect. At first it still fluttered its wings and gave out insistent sounds that again set off the seagulls overhead. They made Lanz think of some drunken women's chorus where each one was crying out and thus creating a group cacophony. When the falcon had calmed down, they took the path that Lanz had chosen when he first arrived at the cemetery.

"You're Egon Blanc's neighbor, and I know the man in the dog mask with the backpack. As I said before, his name is Giorgio Fermi and is a member of Will Mennea's gang. They found Mennea on his sailboat today, shot and killed."

Lanz nodded and replied that he knew who Mennea was. He had also heard a great deal about his neighbor, Egon Blanc, but had never seen the man. People said he was over a hundred years old and a billionaire. The land where his enormous villa was located had supposedly been an amusement park in the old days.

"According to my information about the Mennea case," Richard Vogel went on, "they presume it was a suicide, based on the fingerprints on the weapon. But the pistol he shot himself with is more than forty years old. And, on top of that, the gun doesn't have a serial number. It had been filed off. Why would Mennea carry around precisely this gun and where did he get it?—Mennea's girlfriend, Julia Ellis, is being questioned by the police on the Lido as we speak, but apparently she has an alibi. She said that she had gone with Mennea around noon and gotten into his sailboat for an outing to Pellestrina. They had a fight and she told him she was leaving him, so she stayed in Pellestrina and one of Mennea's bodyguards, Manuel Saltesi, picked her up with the motorboat. The two of them were seen later at the Le Valli restaurant on Pellestrina, but in the meantime Saltesi has disappeared. Apparently Mennea was a big deal in the gambling business, that's what a friend told me who works for the police. I'll tell him about our previous little incident . . . But why did Giorgio Fermi attack you?"

"I don't know," Lanz nervously replied.

Meanwhile he was sure that Richard Vogel and his falcon wouldn't be allowed to ride back with him on the vaporetto, so the man must have a motorboat.

"How do you know about me?" Lanz asked.

"Your house used to be the staff quarters and guesthouse for Signor Blanc's villa. The cellar passageway to Signor Blanc's property must still be there . . ."

Lanz nodded. They had just reached the Camaldolese monastery and turned to go down the steps.

"The best thing would be to go to the police," Richard Vogel continued, "as soon as possible." He spoke in a casual tone, as if he actually wanted to stay out of the whole affair. The falcon was now calm, as if it were asleep.

At that moment a flower-laden wooden casket was carried out an exit to the sea and loaded on a blue funeral boat. A group of mourners dispersed, and only the closest relatives accompanied the corpse across the water to Mestre where they take the dead who can't be buried in San Michele because the island cemetery is at capacity.

With the falcon still on his arm and thus observed by the mourners with open curiosity, Richard Vogel showed Lanz the monastery's impressive cloisters. A monk in a brown habit and sandals with socks, a white cord tied about his waist, was just sweeping the steps at the entrance to the convent. The church was empty and smelled strongly of incense; perhaps the deceased in his coffin was blessed here a short time ago. Through an open door to the vestry they saw a second monk putting away a chasuble and performing other tasks so he didn't bother to look up and notice the two men enter with the raptor. The church was modestly furnished. Lanz noticed a fading fresco.

When they came back outside, the blue funeral boat had already left, and they spotted it through an open doorway at the end of the dark corridor as if through a telescope pointed at an insect in the sky. The closer they came to the exit, the more Lanz had the impression he was approaching a painting of a choppy blue sea with a motionless cloud overhead and a vaporetto just passing by. He also thought about the two monks: the one who was sweeping the steps in front of the convent and the other who had just folded the chasuble. He now imagined that it was his funeral he had just witnessed, because he again had the impression of not being in the here and now. He then asked himself how many burials the monks probably saw every day. What did they think, in case they had any thoughts about it at all? From the perspective of a person who lived in a cemetery and constantly saw mourners and burials, life must be an insignificant cloud of dust or a monk's habit that you fold up and put away in storage.

They were now "in the telescope," Lanz thought, as he continued to gaze out the doorway at the sea and the sky. He observed the mysteriously beautiful ocean with its moderate waves and the motionless high sky that receded, he knew from experience, as soon as you tried to get closer. Not until they stepped out of the corridor and Richard Vogel with his calmed falcon climbed into a covered motorboat did the magic disappear and left him with the conviction that he had, in fact, experienced his own death once again. By now he was so tired that he climbed into the boat without a word and thought only about the falcon with the hood over its head and an iron chain on its talon, calmly perching on a chrome bar behind the rear seat.

Lanz woke up when someone shook his shoulder.

"We're here," he heard Vogel call out.

They had just docked in one of the many canals on the Lagoon-side of the Lido, and the falconer, the raptor on his arm, was already standing before a slope that led up to the road. With his bag over his shoulder, he gave the impression of a biologist at work. Still half-conscious with sleep, Lanz followed the man to a VW Bus where Vogel first tucked the falcon away and then Lanz himself. Apparently he didn't want Lanz to fall back asleep during the drive so he talked non-stop about the falcon hood that was made of leather and then reinforced on the inside. It reminded Lanz of an Arabian knight's helmet, adorned with a faux plume made from strips of leather. Vogel went on, saying that you plunge the falcon into darkness so that it thinks it's nighttime. In the wild it would normally remain silent and motionless in its aerie until daybreak. The bird is actually blind at night and vulnerable to attack from a grey marten or an owl, for example, which are active after dark.

Once at home, Lanz could still see the head of the falcon with and without the hood, its beautiful plumage and talons, before he fell asleep . . .

It was the doorbell that woke him. He unlocked the door, stepped outside, and realized that it was a hot morning. He realized he couldn't remember how he had gotten home—perhaps he had only dreamed the episode with the falcon and Richard Vogel?

It was Samuel Oboabona, the mailman, who had brought him several packages of books that required Lanz's signature with a stylus on the display of some unwieldy device.

"How are you?" Lanz asked automatically.

The mailman fought back tears and shook his head. His forehead was covered with tiny beads of sweat.

"What's the matter?" Lanz wanted to know.

Again the mailman shook his head. He nodded to Lanz and left the apartment. The moment he had asked how Oboabona was doing, he thought of the dead child on the beach, his own intention to commit suicide, and the murder in Torcello. He felt shame and remorse for his thoughts and his behavior.

Later, however, he saw the peregrine falcon on Richard Vogel's arm, and he remembered what the man had told him about the house and his cellar and about his pursuer, Giorgio Fermi.

Lanz automatically went downstairs and turned on the neon light. The washing machine and the drier were in their appointed place, as was the table for dirty clothes and plastic bins, the shelf for detergent and other chemicals, and the old wooden cupboard with empty flowerpots, a pail, a watering can, and spare roof tiles, as well as a rack with two dozen bottles of wine. Meanwhile the face of the sobbing mailman Oboabona reappeared, and the vision paralyzed him. After a moment's contemplation, he pulled the cupboard out from the brick wall a bit and, to his surprise, discovered a locked steel door that was painted red. He thought for a second, then went back upstairs to the living area and searched for the old keys, though still unable to forget the mailman's teary eyes and the nightmarish events of the last couple of days. But ultimately the depressing memories gave way to curiosity about what was behind the steel door.

He had never touched the old keys. After examining the lock, he chose one that, to his amazement, fit. He opened the door that led to a bricked wall, like in the cellar, but he had no intention of giving up. He rushed up to the attic, put on a LED-headlamp, found the second Walther pistol disassembled in a box, and, finally, the pickax underneath a tarp.

On his way back, he put the case with the Walther in his desk, then used the pickax to smash a hole in the brick wall in the cellar. He put all his anxiety, his anger, and his feeling of helplessness into his blows until he stopped, gasping for air, and studied the opening and the darkness behind it. He was relieved to see that the hole was large enough for him to squeeze through. He switched on the LED-headlamp and slipped into the passage on the other side.

He quickly found a light-switch and, with a high-pitched ringing and a faint clicking sound, garish neon light flickered on and allowed him to see a tunnel that had a musty smell. The tunnel was about ten-feet high, roughly a hundred yards long, and reinforced with concrete. If he had to spend the rest of his life down here, he said to himself, he would go crazy. He saw himself trapped in a test tube, like some substance to be used in a medical experiment, perhaps because people were studying to see how insanity gradually took hold of him. He finally reached the steps to the door at the opposite end of the tunnel that, as it turned out, was also locked; as hard as he tried, he wasn't able to unlock it with any of his keys. So he turned around, crawled back through the hole into his own cellar, and fled to his study where he threw himself down on the couch and closed his eyes.

After several minutes of inactivity at the mercy of his memories, he got back up and gazed out the window. Cars were parked along the street, their windshields and chrome bumpers reflecting the sunlight. Young people with beach bags were heading to the seashore. Later he saw a young woman in sunglasses pushing a baby stroller with a little girl skipping alongside; her older brother was trying to rollerskate, but he soon lost his balance and had to grab hold of a telephone pole, a tree, or a parked car.

Lanz sat down at his desk and began to assemble the pistol. Once again he had to go up to the attic to get the small metal toolkit that he had also brought from the farm in St. Leonhard, meanwhile checking the bullets that he had saved in a carton. They were of different calibers. He still knew which ones fit the barrel of the pistol Julia had stolen from him, so he took the others. Also in the box was an owner's manual containing a description of the weapon with illustrations of the individually numbered parts.

When he sat back down at his desk, he saw the yellowed sketch titled "Exploded diagram" that itemized 38 individual parts. He first sorted them, cleaned them in the proper order according to the instructions, assembled them, and treated them with the gun oil that he found in the tool kit. He was very careful with the "precision instrument," as it was termed in the description. It had taken the entire afternoon to understand and implement everything, even though he had practiced the disassembly, oiling, and reassembly of a handgun while in the military. His brain was now full of terms such as "front sight," "lock pin," "firing pin unit," "breech catch lever," or "compression spring for the barrel bushing." That was fine with him because it distracted him from the thoughts that had preoccupied him for the past two days. Last of all, he loaded the gun according to the instruction manual, put the safety on, and went back down to the cellar.

When he turned on the light in the tunnel, he saw several rats scurry over the walkway and disappear several feet ahead in a crack he hadn't noticed before. Curious, he stepped over to the spot and stood before a small steel door in the wall that he was able to open with the same key that had fit the lock in the steel door behind the cupboard. To his surprise, he discovered a compartment with shelves holding tableware, ashtrays, silverware, vases, and a number of suitcases that he took out and opened. The first contained birth-, baptismal- and death certificates—presumably from the staff that had previously been lodged in his house. Now he understood why there were no windows facing the courtyard and the manor house—no one was to be able to spy on the activity in the manor. He also found old black-and-white photos of men and women on the staff, lined up in uniform, staring into the camera with serious expressions on their faces. Apparently a child had awkwardly drawn wings with blue ink on each and every staff member, including the kitchen personnel with their chef's hats and headscarves. Next Lanz found a picture of two chauffeurs in uniform, standing by two mature fashion models who, like the automobiles, were also sporting wings. Intrigued, he went through menus, old cookbooks, and an old illustrated edition of Hans Christian Andersen's fairy tales where, once again, all characters and animals were furnished wings drawn by a child. He then found a postcard-size picture of a man with a white beard who was roughly eighty years old. A leather glove protected his right hand where a small peregrine falcon was perched, apparently very young and yet already trained.

For the time being, Lanz took possession of the photographs and opened another suitcase where he saw children's toys. There was a goose that looked like Walt Disney's lucky duck, Gladstone Gander, sitting on a bicycle and wearing a straw boater with a large red plastic propeller. The figure still had a key in its back, and when Lanz wound it up and put the toy on the ground, Gladstone Gander with his propeller circled the floor of the connecting passageway. There was an old colorful tin spinning-top with a wood handle that you had to pump to make the toy spin amazingly fast and produce musical sounds like a pump organ. Even though Lanz had been a grown-up for many years now, he felt the magic from the dogs and cats, calves and children painted on the brightly-colored rainbow around the top, though they all became a blur in the gyrations of the madly spinning toy. In addition, he found a doll, a teddy bear, a remote-controlled Schuco auto with a long cord that was connected to a red child-size steering wheel so that you could control the marvelous toy. In addition, he discovered a wind-up tin solder, the model of a passenger ship, and a deck of "Old Maid" cards.

He carefully packed up the toys, put away the suitcase, took out the other one that had held the three photos, and put them back until everything was just the way he had found it, and then locked the door to the compartment. He just stood there for a while and thought, then went back to the hole in the wall, took the Walther pistol out of his pants pocket, cocked it, and giving in to a sudden urge, fired a trial shot into the back of the cupboard. The bang was so loud that at first he thought he had ruptured his eardrums. He sat down on the floor, waited until his head cleared, and then climbed back through the opening to see what damage the shot had caused. The projectile had gone through a wooden wall and the door of the cupboard, splintered two flowerpots that were in the bullet's path, and was probably embedded in the opposite wall. He looked for it and finally found the bullet hole. On the one hand he was satisfied with the gun, on the other he hoped that the loud noise hadn't attracted attention. He rushed back to his study, saw that the street was empty, closed the curtains, put the gun in one of the desk-drawers, and stretched out again on the couch.

By the time it was dark, he felt the urge to get out on the beach. He put the LED-headlamp in his summer sport coat, and as soon as he reached the ocean, decided not to walk to the Hotel Excelsior as usual, but in the opposite direction so that he could think things over. He had never set foot on the property of the abandoned hospital, the Ospedale al Mare. An unusual reluctance had kept him from it, because he suspected (and had already heard) that the homeless and illegal migrants were staying there. But now, he said to himself, now that he had tried to take his own life, there was no reason not to go. His plan was to ponder what he would say to the police during his interview the following day, and, while distracted, approach the unfamiliar terrain.

Of course he knew that it was reckless, but he was now so deep in these sinister complications that it no longer mattered what he actually did. Just the opposite—he felt liberated by the unaccustomed recklessness. Stepping out of the side street, he gazed warily up and down the Lungomare D'Annunzio, noticed that lights were still on at the tiny Chiosco Bahiano and that two Moroccans were smoking and drinking beer there. He waited as two cars drove past with their headlights on, then took a few steps out from under the streetlight and into the darkness to get a better look at Egon Blanc's house. He was very familiar with the tall yellow wall that also surrounded other buildings; it had always just been there. Behind that was the two-story mansion with its balconies and terraces, as well as palm and broad-leaf trees that towered over the yellow wall. On some days seagulls also perched on the pot-shaped brick chimney that resembled a large vase, or, screeching loudly, they flew out to sea. There was a light in just one window on the second floor. In order to observe the street-level windows he had to go down the Lungomare a few feet and peek through the bars of the iron gate. He hurried over to the entrance, crossed the road, and studied the building and the gravel walks—everything else was concealed. There was no light coming from the windows on the ground floor, he noticed, and he walked off in the opposite direction. He crossed the road once more and walked along, past the long row of beach huts and the arborvitae hedges and benches in front of them. Farther out, the ocean had almost disappeared in the darkness. Lanz could only hear the gentle clapping of the waves. Apparently it was high tide.

He didn't have to go far to reach the entrance to the Ospedale al Mare. He was also familiar with this sight. The entrance gate, connected to the yellow administration building with its windows shuttered by dirty-white louvers, was extensive; with porters' lodges on both sides, it seemed to him like a gas station without the pumps. When he came closer, he noticed the structure's rain gutters and a series of grey cables that left an impression of neglect. A yellow tin sign with a black arrow pointed out that the new hospital was nearby. The wide access and the silver-grey gateway with two wings had a sign announcing "Ospedale al Mare," the wall above it was painted white and someone had written in black unconventional letters: REALITY IS NOT WHAT YOU THINK IT'S AN ANCIND LYNK A. ♀ . . .

He had never looked at it closely before, but he now determined that the first part was in funny capital letters, while the second part had been added in cursive script. It was easy to translate the first, but the second half was more ambiguous: "It is an ancient central surveillance system."

The following overlapping circles represented a genogram, a concept from medical family therapy that depicted behavioral patterns. Lanz interpreted "A." as the first letter of someone's name. Finally, the Venus symbol indicated the author was a female.

Although the streetlights were dim, he had no trouble reading the sentences, but finally gave up trying to figure it all out. He put on his headlamp and activated it. The head of a giant rat, spray-painted on a wall, leaped out at him. Its open mouth, with sharp teeth that were almost completely filled with blue letters and a disproportionately large speech balloon containing the word ODIOTA in capital letters, expressed anger. ODIOTA was presumably a made-up word that might signify hate (*odio*) and idiot (*idiota*); later, on his laptop, he also found an Internet site, Odiota, with the picture of a dog. A large can of spray-paint was lying at the scene, an overturned steel-tube chair minus the seat and backrest, and, on the opposite side, piles of trash consisting of white, blue, and yellow plastic bags, of broken white-veneer planks like the ones used in kitchens, of pieces of tin, discarded file folders, and the blade of a ceiling fan. Tall grass and small shrubs were growing between the cobblestones and the large concrete slabs that formed the walkway, though it was more like a dilapidated street. Buildings to the left and to the right, as far as the eye could see. Closed blinds at the windows, partially torn down or open, presumably to make entrance to the rooms easier or to allow daylight in. Between the extensive patches of fallen plaster, he noticed numerous graffiti and slogans on and beneath a triangular blackboard in a red frame that displayed only a black exclamation mark on a white background. Grey railings were mounted on steps leading down to the underground floors with the laundry cellars, ironing rooms, pharmaceutical storerooms, and disregarded experimental trials and their results.

Just as Lanz was about to turn back, he caught sight of a male figure, smoking on the balcony of the next building. When the slender young man realized that Lanz was watching him, he silently disappeared. Lanz was certain that he had seen the man and was about to climb over the silver-grey entrance gate, but then couldn't imagine why he would do such a thing and what he expected to gain from it. The outer building formed one side of the walkway, of which he could see only a small part. The ground around the steel gate where he stood was littered with mounds of white plant seeds and fallen leaves, interspersed with cigarette packs, softdrink cans, and plastic bottles.

Lanz turned and went back to the road, noticing two more bricked-up entrances. One was captioned FUCK THE SYSTEM in red letters, the other with graffiti of the same color depicting the symbol of the ancient Egyptian god Horus—the sun eye. In mythology, Horus had adopted the form of a falcon or a human with a falcon head. Lanz immediately thought of the falcon at the San Michele cemetery. He didn't see any connection, but his brain continued its independent thought pattern as he took the path between the last huts on the public beach that were cordoned off by a chain-link fence. There was also a chain-link fence on the hospital side, part of it covered with a green tarp that was itself embellished with the sentence "fuck the police" in white paint. Beyond that, a possibly-inhabited concrete monstrosity. Several beach towels, bedspreads, and a blue swimsuit were hung on the fence to dry. He came closer and saw bicycles parked behind the tarp, but no people. Curious, he waited a few minutes without turning off his headlamp, but everything remained quiet. Rising up behind the cement apartment building were tall chestnut trees that had just begun to blossom. Lanz turned back toward the beach and walked on carefully because the path was constructed of sand and gravel. He almost stumbled over an elongated boulder painted white with the inscribed letters OAMTOPIA. Lanz figured out that it was a composite word, OAM = "Ospedale al Mare," and TOPIA = "utopia." Now he was convinced that the property was inhabited.

Lost in thought, he walked to the end of the path that, to judge from the gentle murmur of the sea, clearly led down to the beach. He crossed another field, where he almost fell again because a series of square cement blocks, intended as flower planters and filled with soil and trash, were right in his path. It was dark between the trees on both sides of the path, but it didn't take long for him to reach the neglected beach. He switched off the headlamp so that his eyes could become accustomed to the darkness. Countless stars in the Milky Way shone in the heavens above. Lanz sat on an old upside-down boat that was lying in the weeds and pondered whether he would really go to the police tomorrow. He had nothing to lose, he thought, and absurdly considered the dilapidated hospital as a place where he could hide out. But as he debated his ideas and thoughts, his body told him, by means of a brief attack of nausea and fear, that

that wasn't really a good idea . . . Besides, he still didn't know what had become of the pistol that Julia had taken from him. He didn't have a gun license. So if he testified that it belonged to him, he became afraid that it could mean a jail sentence for him and for her. So he could go to the police, but he mustn't mention the gun and his suicidal intentions . . . He would have to tell them that he took a trip to Torcello, had gotten drunk, and wanted to sleep it off under the elderberry bush.

He gazed up at the starry sky. That's what initially made him begin to question if there wasn't a creator after all. But the more closely he studied the question, the less comprehensible the physical and mathematical explanations he found in books became. For a long time his father had spoken with him about parallel universes and the fourth dimension, he recalled, and all of his father's explanations seemed only an expression of helplessness, considering the starry sky gleaming overhead. The natural sciences, too—beside religions, art, music, and literature—were languages with which you could gain an idea of something, understand it, and communicate it. The desire to understand encompassed every phenomenon, whether obvious or latent. Everything was part of an infinitely complicated enigma that, once you believed you had solved it, only produced further enigmas, and if you solved these and even more enigmas, you ran into contradictions whereupon someone questioned the hypotheses and theories you had found, and then replaced them with new ones. He now understood his experiences as an enigma, and even in the instant he thought this, he found himself to be an enigma within a virtually infinite enigma. He had been born in a labyrinth, he thought, and had spent his entire life trying to find a way out. The labyrinth was his own mind where he was forced to wander. Even the stars in the nighttime sky conveyed this image and left him so exhausted that he had to lie down in the sand. He briefly listened to the murmur of the ocean, closed his eyes, and then, caught in a sudden dizzy spell, fell into the star-struck heavens, realizing that he was a bird—a falcon, pursuing a flock of ducks in the sky—or a fish, trying to swallow the reflection of the stars on the surface of the ocean.

He woke up, shivering. The stars were still flickering in the night sky overhead. And the ocean murmured as before, and the waves, he saw, were retreating in the sand before him and washing up this or that seashell onto land. He turned the headlamp on again, shook the sand from his pants and jacket, and walked past the Ospedale al Mare back to the Lungomare Gabriele D'Annunzio where he reached the side road beneath the pine trees where his house stood. When he checked his watch, he realized it was 11:30 p.m. The Chiosco Bahiano had closed long ago, and under the streetlights everything looked empty and deserted, as if a leak in some nuclear power plant had released radiation and the public had been evacuated. He had read numerous books and seen documentary films about the catastrophes at Chernobyl and Fukushima, and they cropped up from time to time and on various occasions.

As he reached in his pocket for the key and unlocked the door, Lanz had the feeling that he was being watched. He turned around abruptly, but didn't see anything. Everything was dead, there were no lights in the other houses, there was no one on the street, nothing moved. He then noticed a parked car, a red Mitsubishi, and behind the windshield, someone sitting in the driver's seat. Out of curiosity he walked over to the car and bent down to peer in the side window. To his surprise, Julia Ellis was sitting behind the wheel, asleep. Her head had fallen back, her mouth was open as if she were dead. He knocked on the window and a second later she was staring at him, startled. She opened the door and got out, anxiously checked her surroundings, and told him they had to quickly go inside the house. He was suddenly wide-awake. He rushed ahead, let her in, and locked the door behind her. Only then did he turn on the ceiling light and see that she really was standing there before him. She was still half-asleep and her make-up was almost non-existent, but she was beautiful nonetheless.

He automatically put his arms around her and hugged her, and she hugged him. They stood there like that for a long time.

They spent the night in the guestroom on the second floor and fell asleep, exhausted, even before they had taken off their clothes, without having made love or even having spoken to each other.

At daybreak, Lanz opened his eyes, took a shower, made a breakfast of zwieback, crispbread, butter, honey, orange marmalade and tea—and found the dried plant parts he had bought from the Indian on the beach. So he made an extra pot of tea from them, put sugar and artificial sweetener on the saucer, and everything on a tray. He then stowed the Walther pistol in his windbreaker before he went back to the guestroom and placed their breakfast on a stool. Julia was still sleeping, so he climbed up to the attic, put the pistol in the bureau to make sure that Julia couldn't find it, and then lay down beside her on the bed. Startled, she lifted her head and then, when she recognized him, sank back down, relieved. She put her head on his shoulder, took one of his hands and kissed it. He quickly pulled his hand away.

"Did you shoot Mennea?" he asked and gazed up at the ceiling.

"No," she replied after a pause.

He waited before he posed his next question.

"Where is my pistol? And what did you do with it?"

"You're asking the same questions the police asked," she said, upset.

"And?"

"I'll tell you the same thing I told them at the police station," she answered stubbornly.

"Which is?"

"What do you want to hear? I'm not going to make something up just so someone will believe me," she responded indignantly.

"Do you want to tell me about the interrogation?" he asked.

She shook her head, but then began telling him that an Inspector Galli tried to trap her in contradictions. After all she'd been through, she wasn't able to concentrate and had requested a lawyer. But since she didn't know any attorneys in Venice, she desperately tried to find a way out, until she remembered Will Mennea's lawyer: Ignazio Capparoni. She didn't think he would be willing to help her, but he came to the station house in the Via Dardanelli right away. He refuted Galli's flimsy evidence until she was finally allowed to leave.

"What did you tell him?" Lanz asked next.

"The same thing I told them at the police station," she replied, "the truth."

"Who shot Mennea? And why was my gun beside the corpse in the sailboat?" Lanz continued.

"I have no idea — "

"You stole my pistol and went back to the Lido to kill Mennea."

She was silently thinking.

"I have to know what happened or else I can't help you."

"Does that mean you want me to leave?" she asked faintly.

"No," Lanz replied after a pause.

She thought some more.

"Why should I trust you?" she then asked.

"I haven't gone to the police because I didn't want to testify that you stole the pistol from me," Lanz answered.

She briefly looked him in the eye. "I know," she then said.

" ...but I don't know anything about you," he countered sharply.

When she stubbornly refused to speak, he began to pressure her. He just said whatever popped into his head. Whenever he and his wife Alma had a difference of opinion, it had been his habit to just improvise, and often that had been enough to get him out of some tight situations.

"So, you stole my gun . . . then persuaded Mennea to take a daytrip to Pellestrina. You raved about how lovely it would be to take the sailboat and go alone. He gave in. You found a ristorante in Pellestrina. Then you started an argument with him, telling him you were going to fly back to America. Finally, you phoned his bodyguard Manuel and told him to pick you up. And he did come with the car. You got behind the wheel and drove off alone. Meanwhile, Manuel shot Mennea, as planned, and put the gun he got from you into the dead man's hand. He set the steering rudder on Mennea's boat toward open waters and then swam ashore, to the spot where you were waiting for him. As a precaution, Manuel tossed his wet clothes in the trunk of the car and put on dry ones. At that point the two of you drove back to a bar and then to the Hotel Excelsior."

He was actually composing his theory as he spoke. He was amazed what all he had dreamed up.

"There's one question you haven't answered," he continued. "Is Manuel now Mennea's successor? Had all of this been planned in advance? And did you deliberately seduce him? Those are only suppositions, but they make sense."

"You're just making stuff up!" she exploded.

"So, you killed Mennea yourself? If that's the case, then Manuel must have been in a relationship with you long before that."

" . . . what makes you think of Manuel?" she shouted, outraged.

"What did you tell the police? Tell me, or else I'll have to . . ."

"Who said you have to go to the police?" she interrupted him.

"No one."

"Then why do you want to go? Do you want to identify your pistol? Mennea is dead and Manuel has disappeared, and I'm flying back to America as soon as I have clearance."

"Didn't they tell you not to leave the Lido until the investigation is over?"

"Of course."

"Are you still living in the Hotel Excelsior?"

"No, in the Hungaria, it's . . ."

"Why were you waiting for me at my front door last night?"

"I was afraid — "

"Of whom?"

"Of everyone . . . of his bodyguards, the police, the reporters. I left my smartphone in the hotel room so they couldn't trace me here."

"Do the police know about the murder in Torcello?"

"No. I don't think they'll ever find out about it. The man's name was Borsakowski and was Will's partner, a real bastard who wanted to take over the business."

"What business?"

"The gambling . . ."

"What else?"

"I don't know any more than that."

"What did you tell the police?"

"Just what I've told you—that I don't know anything. I can verify everything I've said."

"And after you called Manuel to come and pick you up, what did you do when you left Will Mennea?"

"Went looking for a gas station, filled up the car, and photographed the gas station and the attendant."

"What about Manuel?"

"I came back alone. I waited for him in the Excelsior until he finally showed up. Mennea had also had a fight with him and threw him off the boat at some breakwater halfway out in the ocean."

"Did anyone see them?"

She shrugged her shoulders and said nothing.

"How do you know about that?"

"Manuel told me."

"And you told that to the police?"

"No, I didn't tell them anything about Manuel."

"So, according to your account, it must have been Manuel who shot Mennea?"

"I don't know."

"Does that mean the police are out looking for him?"

She shrugged her shoulders, stood up, left her breakfast untouched, and walked out of the house. From the window Lanz watched her cross the street, get in the red Mitsubishi (presumably a rental car) and drive off.

I'm such an idiot, Lanz now thought to himself. Why had he interrogated her and not embraced her and offered her a place to hide. Because I'm an idiot, that same sentence echoing in his brain. Because I'm an idiot. He drank the tea with the dried leaves the Indian had given him and tasted nothing besides the bitterness in his mouth. So he put some sweetener in the tea and, suddenly thirsty, emptied almost the entire pot.

In any event he had now made himself a co-conspirator—and that was his own fault. On the other hand, he was surprised that his improvisations had apparently come close to the truth . . . Or Julia had led him to believe her story, while, in reality, something entirely different had happened. He again considered whether he should tell the police about the pistols and his suicidal plan or instead give out a variation of his intoxication and the wish to sleep under the elderberry bush. That would help Julia out, because his statement would place the blame on Manuel.

Suddenly Lanz realized why Giorgio Fermi, Mennea's other bodyguard, had been following him all day yesterday and eventually put on that dogmask: to warn him or even to kill him. He, Lanz, was the only witness to the crime in Torcello, and the perpetrators apparently knew it already. But how would they have found out? — There was only one possible answer: Manuel, who after the murder in Torcello had come ashore and seen Julia with him before they had gone back on the vaporetto. And Julia had had to reveal to him and to the others that he, Lanz, had been an eyewitness to the crime, because otherwise she would have had no explanation of why she left the Locanda Cipriani so suddenly and run off to the ferry. Now he was in danger of being killed so that no witness could tell the police about the crime.

He became dizzy and nauseous, ran to the toilet and threw up. A moment later his cellphone rang. He wiped his mouth with toilet paper, flushed the toilet, and searched his windbreaker for the phone, but he couldn't find it. He finally discovered it on his desk. He answered and could hear Julia crying.

"Are you still there?" she asked between sobs.

When he responded, she blurted out, whispering and sobbing, that she had been waiting at his house last night to warn him about Mennea's gang. Everything turned out differently than she had anticipated. She was calling from a trattoria so the police couldn't trace her call to him.

He heard her say: "I can't talk any more, I'll call you tonight—" and then the line went dead. The first thing that came to Lanz's mind was how she had gotten his phone number. Then it occurred to him that she could have gone through his things in the hotel in Sant'Elena, his wallet, his IDs, and his keys. She would have found his notebook where he had entered his name, address, and telephone number in the event that he had lost it and someone had found and wished to return it. He took it out of his windbreaker, quickly thumbed through it, found comments about some translations, and finally an entry titled "Marco Polo's Discovery of the World." Since he hadn't reached a final decision about going to the police, he decided to follow the bus line to Alberoni on his bike. He would make up his mind by the time he rode back. This wasn't a new route for him. In his first year here, he had often explored on his bike to learn more about the Lido. He also wanted to check out his boat, since he hadn't seen it in a long time.

But most of all, he decided, he had to watch out for Mennea's bodyguards.

He was still thirsty and emptied the pot with the tea he bought from the Indian. He then got on his bike, glad to be outdoors and active. As he set off on the Lungomare, it became more evident that going to the police was the only solution to get him out of this. Back at the San Michele cemetery, the falconer Richard Vogel had advised him not to do anything on his own.

From time to time he felt nauseous, so he waited on a bench until he felt better.

He rode from the Gran Viale Santa Maria Elisabetta to the Via Lepanto, down the Via Vettor Pisani to a part of the city that somewhat reminded him of Amsterdam with its cafés and stores, its red-and-white striped awnings, trees, green front lawns, and occasional new buildings, along with the silent mirror-smooth canals with their brick walls along the shore where motorboats and outboard motorboats were tied to pilings. All the boats were covered with blue tarps to protect them from the rain, and they all gave the impression of being abandoned. Along the narrow streets there were many conspicuous road and traffic signs, large trash cans under the trees and in front of the villas. The attractive old bridges with their tunnel-like thoroughfares gave the area a dreamy ambiance.

When the word "dreamy" popped into his head, he noticed that he was floating silently over the road like a falcon with outstretched wings, without really comprehending what was happening to him. Should he pull over and rest again? He again remembered the dried plant parts that he bought on the beach and put in his teapot. He had drunk the entire batch . . . He had briefly become nauseous . . . But his stomach was better now . . . And he was on his bike, sailing along . . . He still thought he was in another dimension of time. The plants by and in front of the houses, the trees, the reflections on the water, and his memories of the stars in the nighttime sky, a black wrought-iron gate with net-like bars of iron leaves, the semi-circular arches and narrow portico of an old house, hedges of privet, yews and hibiscus, hawthorn bushes, dozing motorboats, passing autos and occasional pedestrians were images that constantly changed and, in their variety, reminded him of Indian book illustrations like those he had seen at the Metropolitan Museum of Art in New York.

Time and again his loneliness blended his inner world with that outside. Having said that, it was the first time he had admitted his loneliness without anguish. But that wasn't important now, because he was floating up the canal where his motorboat was moored to one of the pilings, and he toyed with the idea on getting on board and sailing out into open waters. The idea undeniably distracted him, but he didn't give in to it. A pride of peacocks came flying over a yellow forsythia bush, then more and more and more. Lanz was now walking his bike, but in reality he was flying along the canals, to his death. The motorboat had blue feathers, and he slipped under its wings that gently folded over him. In the boat, everything was spinning. He had gotten caught in a maelstrom, and he surrendered to the force of nature without any resistance . . .

He gradually came to the realization that reality was BLUE. He slipped outside the blueness and squinted. When he looked at his watch he saw that it was already late afternoon. He was still woozy and disoriented . . . Still, he had the impression he was rational. He saw himself leave the boat and scramble onto land, re-secure the blue plastic tarp, push his bike out to the street and get back on. A butterfly fluttered by . . . He immediately recognized that it was a peacock butterfly ... Strange, he thought: first, peacocks flying over the forsythia bush, and now a peacock butterfly mesmerizing him.

He observed that he was floating down the Via Lepanto, alongside the canal and the brick wall containing other walls of arborvitae and privet, intermingled with blooming hibiscus and villas, houses, and, in the canal, more motorboats dozing beneath canvas ... It was beautiful ... And it went on and on. A little further along, he turned off on the Via Sandro Gallo where buses swayed down long boulevards and he felt safe in the bike lane. He stopped at a wire fence bordering a playing field. Teenagers wearing helmets and green-and-white uniforms were playing rugby. He noticed that it was a game with continuous interruptions . . . The young men clustered together like a flock of birds, froze in place, then dispersed, and then rushed together again. Lanz had the impression that he was seeing everything through a kaleidoscope. A component part, together with others, formed a merging, continually changing mosaic, a living artwork of everyday scenes that he had never seen in this way. Peering through the fence, he had the impression that the rugby players were behind bars. The grandstands were empty, a few figures were loitering by the clubhouse, and the sounds that came from the playing field seemed muffled. The strange part was that he believed he was seeing the world for the very first time. It consisted of microscopically small and macroscopically large particles of perception that were permanently in flux—apparent calm and solitude were fallacies, the results of a logical point of view. He thought of the trees in St. Leonhard, the sunlight that shone through the leaves of green, the growing plants, the flight of birds and insects, pollen, animals beneath the earth and in the forests. In the meantime he rode on, and at every large clearing to the Lagoon and in each small canal to the sea he saw smaller and larger motor- and sailboats, along with upturned rowboats in a field ... at one point a long row of parked white refrigerated trucks without commercial markings. He pulled over and suddenly felt the urge to memorize everything: he counted 9 refrigerated trucks, 23 motorboats, and 32 sailboats.

As he rode on, the canal disappeared (or at least this was the first time he noticed it was no longer there), but in the direction of the Lagoon he still saw small marinas, at one point a shipyard building in the water. The symbol of a bicyclist was painted in white on the pavement, "a signature that identifies the bike lane," he told himself. Then another field, a tall blue-coated steel structure, an industrial crane. Most of the ships were shrouded with green covers and made him think of coffins. He stopped again to commit everything to memory. He didn't know why—he just had to do it. He counted 12 coffins. He added to his catalog: a parked truck, various means of transportation on wheels, on the right an extended stone building with a corrugated tin roof, and back beyond that, on a high rig, a white sailing yacht with a tall mast.

He slowly floated on. A dog trotted alongside him and he suddenly understood what an animal was, because in its body he also saw birds and snails, fish, crabs, a pygmy elephant, a cobra, a vineyard snail, a doodlebug, chickens, an ox and a turtle. He had never seen or appreciated or comprehended reality this way, he rhapsodized, as he pedaled faster and faster. A rusted bicycle with a shopping basket was leaning against a gutted white boat that was full of junk. In the harbor basin he counted 21 motorized vessels, 3 cranes of various colors, and in a nearby field an impressively large motorboat under a black tarp that he silently christened CATAFALQUE, "ship's coffin," "ship's casket"—he didn't understand why these terms had never popped up in the books he had read or translated. Just then he noticed that he had overlooked the tall masts of the sailboats in the harbor basin, there were 4 of them. Opposite them, an old wrought-iron gate between 2 columns. He could see an ugly cube-shaped lump of a house—also rebar, boards, a ladder, and several red-and-white life preservers. He then noticed 2 large Donald Duck heads in an open garage. Or were they possibly white pedal cars for children? Or just plastic lawn chairs? To one side, a thicket, or was it a pile of rubbish? The best thing would be to just keep pedaling . . . He didn't stop till he reached Malamocco. He had turned off into a side street, but didn't know why. It suddenly looked like St.

Leonhard. Had he gone that far? A green canal—it made him think "creek"—blossoming hawthorn shrubs whose branches drooped down to the water, rocks along the bank that were green from algae, a brick wall with arrow slits on the other side, a low square tower with a barred window beside a wrought-iron gate, and on the canal side a second barred window. As he stepped onto the bridge with its steel handrail and a sign indicating pedestrian traffic only, he saw at ground level behind the gate several crates covered with metal plates, 2 cats sitting beside them. Their den? he wondered. Behind the walls he noticed bare white buildings with flat roofs. Spiraea branches with white panicles hung over the canal, "like tentacles of a sleeping albino polyp," his brain told him.

A rusty white camper was parked by the bridge, and on its windshield he read the word LAIKÁ in capital letters. He knew it advertised a company that rented mobile homes for trips in Italy. The vehicle was presumably just scrap metal at this point since it was affected by green lichens and looked like some moss-covered boulder; this comparison, too, came off the top of his head. From its hood, Lanz could see it was a Ford, and it even had a small license plate on the bumper. Lanz deciphered the white numerals on the black background and concentrated as if it were the number of a bank account that he was to forward money to: 73555CD. The lichens, it seemed to him, consisted of small, dense green islands and, between them, mostly green stains on white enamel that were by now barely recognizable. He tried to determine the number of dense green lichen islands, but he kept losing count. At one point he couldn't remember the number. Then he wasn't sure if he should count or ignore a smaller island. Or he had forgotten whether he had already counted certain islands or overlooked them. He wished he had a fishing pole—the German word "Angel" reminded him of the English word "angel"—so he could plop down on the bank and fish, but he couldn't find a suitable branch or a line or a safety pin that he could use as a fishhook . . . Besides, he didn't have a fishing license— an "angel license" went through his head, along with laughter. And he didn't even know if there were any fish in the water.

He remembered that LAIKÁ meant TIME in Lithuanian. He knew that because a publisher had once sent him a book with this title to translate, and he had asked what LAIKÁ meant in German. It was all a mix-up by some secretary who had sent a book intended for him to another translator and vice versa. Since a famous company that made cameras was called LEICA, he had remembered the word and its meaning. TIME stood still, that he understood. Nevertheless it had still undergone change. And he found himself in an afterlife where all possible memories lay around like rubble.

Twenty or thirty yards further on—as seen from the bridge—was a one-story apartment building and a wall with the canopy of a collapsed white umbrella peaking out. It made him think of the white inside a giant conch shell. He had this thought twice.

Meanwhile he pushed his bicycle through the gateway to the village of Malamocco. The large area beside the harbor—he counted the ships: 17 motorboats—was almost deserted. 3 young people approached him—2 men in jeans and inscribed T-shirts and a young woman in a thin blue-and-white-striped jacket and jeans with fashionable gashes and holes—all 3 wearing white sneakers. He hated those prefabricated holes and gashes in jeans. Rich kids dressed as poor people, he thought. Next, 2 cute little white Maltese dogs came along as he was putting his bicycle in one of the many bike stands. The homes were older, 2 or 3 stories with tall chimneys like you see in the paintings by Piero della Francesca, he thought. They left a romantic impression. Maybe he really had gone crazy, he pondered. Possibly because of the dried plant parts he had bought from the Indian and made into tea . . . But hadn't he already had those thoughts before he went to sleep in his motorboat? He was a world traveler, he thought to himself. He traveled from the external world to his inner world and from his inner world back to the external world.

He then found that the small streets were paved. One piazza was named "Delle Erbe," as he read on one of the buildings that bordered the area down to the sea. Under one window on the fourth floor, 4 pairs of children's sneakers hung out to dry on a clothesline, jeans and 2 orange T-shirts hung from another window, and from the next one a small bright-blue carpet. A broad street with concrete slabs led down to the ocean. He turned his bike around, sat down on a low wall, studied the wooden pier and the streaks of light beneath it that came through the gaps in the boards onto the water's surface, blades of grass and white blossoms floating on the murky green water, algae, and a few small mussels that he had seen before on pilings in the water. Just then he noticed the sign indicating that the city center was a pedestrian zone—nevertheless several Vespas and 2 motor-bikes were parked in front of the houses, and numerous cars were parked along the street. Why did it take him so long to comprehend everything? And on the other hand, why did he have a new understanding of so many things?

The dried plant parts that he had put in his tea came to mind over and over again. He strained to remember what the Indian had told him when he bought the nondescript merchandise on the beach ... He had indicated the intoxicating effects, at least that was what Lanz remembered. But there was also a word that had stoked his interest: "Chakra." No, but it was something like that ... "chacruna with yage" and "ayahuasca" came to mind. Right after he bought it he had read that it was a "shaman's brew," but had immediately forgotten it. He also recalled that "chakra" in Spanish meant "farmhouse," but also had something to do with yoga. Strange, he said to himself, that he should think of it at a time like this ... A roughly 12-year-old boy with a backward baseball cap rode past on a skateboard ... In any event, it sounded suspiciously like something esoteric, like Hinduism and Buddhism, he thought. All he knew was that it involved 7 energy centers in the human body or something like that ...

The water at his feet reeked. 2 elderly men in yellow jogging suits ran by, 2 middle-aged women strolled over the piazza, involved in conversation, and just then the boy with the skateboard leaped a ramp and slammed to the ground. Lanz ran over to him and helped him up. He had injured his hand, but it wasn't bleeding and the lad tried not to cry.

"You're hurt," Lanz said, worried.

The boy shook his head. "I've flown that ramp many times," he responded, defiantly.

"I believe you, but this time you're hurt . . . Let me take a look!"

The boy stuck out his arm and Lanz could see that the joint was swollen. And a tear ran down the boy's cheek.

"Where are your parents?"

The boy stuck his arm out again and pointed to a house on the broad street.

"Can you make it home alone?" Lanz asked.

The boy tugged at his baseball cap and nodded.

"Do you want me to carry your skateboard?"

"No, thanks."

Head down and looking at the ground, the boy hurried off, and after a few strides began to run.

The water and the streaks of light beneath the pier moved gently and silently. A large cat with white-and-brown spots was cleaning its fur on the steps to the harbor basin. The more closely Lanz looked, the more surprised he became that he had never paid any attention to the beauties of everyday life. But it was precisely things he had overlooked that now provided such wonders, he now realized: weeds that grew out of the ground between the concrete slabs, a cloud, a raindrop, the marks on a rock, dust motes flickering in the sunlight. It was as if his brain were trying to show him how the matter he had overlooked was actually a world unto itself. He watched a bus hurtling past with a young woman passenger, heard laughter without seeing any people, saw a Band-Aid on a child's lip, an overflowing trashcan, a partially burned newspaper, a dead butterfly. But those were only bits of broken glass under the refrigerator, meaning: something that will eventually see the light of day. But what did the broken vessel look like, and what did the hidden world actually look like? Dark matter, as theorized in physics? He knew that such matter accounts for 75% of the entire universe. It occurred to him that God was the darkness, the enigma, invisible, a secret—not the light. It was an explanation that apparently no one had come up with, and he decided to keep it to himself. Even in everyday life only a small fraction of what occurred was visible to each person. Most of it remained hidden—the countless comedies of the so-called OTHERS—behind the walls of their homes and in the hearts and minds of people.

Since he could tell how confused he was, he decided to go home as soon as it got dark. In the meantime he headed to a narrow alley—the Calle del Paradiso—he learned. Bicycles were leaning against the walls by the front doors of individual houses. Women were sitting at a table in front of a small *trattoria* and laughing. He was afraid they might be talking about him, so he hurried on. He then came to the end of the alley and saw a sign on the side of a house that identified the brick bridge as the Ponte del Paradiso. The counterpart to the Devil's Bridge, he thought. In order to remain in Paradise he turned around and noticed beneath the vault of a balcony a rustic Virgin Mary with the Baby Jesus in her arms. She was walking through a wooden doorway. She had a rosary on her arm, and there were several other rosaries draped over Jesus and his crown. To the front, vases and flower pots with daisies, roses, lilies, cyclamens, and forget-me-nots. This time he didn't mind making contact with the women. Since he didn't want to sit inside the dark trattoria, he asked one of them if he might sit down at their table and they cordially assented. And, as he often did on other occasions, he pretended not to understand Italian.

"Oh, I'll bet he can!" shouted one of the women and stared at him, while he simply smiled politely like a tourist without any knowledge of the language. He ordered garlic calamari, French fries, and a bottle of cola, and, before his meal was served, he went to the restroom. He had a powerful feeling that the world was spinning, not just the external world, but also his internal world. Once outside, he saw that the women were leaving in high spirits. He felt it was because of him, but dismissed the thought and then immediately forgot the whole thing.

It eventually became evening, and he could tell that he was gradually coming out of it. He didn't just feel better, once again he became aware of his basic situation: Julia Ellis, Mennea, the murder in Torcello, and the decision he must make, whether or not to go to the police. He was still torn, but he didn't have much more time to deliberate. The concept of "time" reminded him of the LAIKÁ company camper and dark matter. He wanted to develop his thoughts and then make his decision when he reached the Posto di Polizia. On his ride back along the Via Malamocco, he pedaled hard. Above him, the starry sky, and silence all around that was interrupted only by the few passing cars and a bus. As he approached the police station, he decided to report the murder, but with the modification that he hadn't had the pistol during this time. Just an excursion to Torcello, he thought ironically. And, against his will, a cloud of doubt obscured the sun of his inspiration, because he realized that in this version he would have to omit the encounter with Julia Ellis. But now he had to concentrate on riding his bike, because he was still woozy. It was definitely the tea—he no longer doubted its effect. With that thought, he stopped and peed on a pine tree before he rode on. He had already passed the two villa complexes of Ca'Bianca and Città Giardino, as well as the garden with sculptures of unusually fat people that the artist Fernando Botero had used as inspiration. The longer he sat on the saddle the more he was amazed at what had happened on his ride. In retrospect it seemed as if he were a child and had only dreamed it all. He also thought about his attempted suicide, about what had happened, and how he had gotten the impression that he had actually shot himself and was now in some afterlife. It still didn't seem unrealistic. Maybe he just had to get used to the idea, he wondered? Maybe he just had to accept what had happened to him? Since he had never been in a situation like this before, he didn't doubt his sanity as he turned off onto the Via delle Quattro Fontane and rode along the canal, past the hideous new buildings around the Casino Municipale and the Palazzo del Cinema, finally coming to the Via Dardanelli.

He followed a road sign to the police station and stopped before the villa with brick walls and arched windows. Two blue-and-white police cars were parked under large old trees. He didn't want to become lost in reality. Objectivity, he realized, unfolded at the moment only in his head and not in his senses. He took a couple more minutes to make up his mind, but he couldn't think calmly, ideas rained down on him until by chance (it seemed to him) he found a solution: when he entered the station-house, he had to tell the whole truth, he shouldn't deviate from that or else he would only harm himself. And furthermore: he had witnessed a murder and was thus compelled to go to the police. However, giving in to impulse, he got back on his bike and raced to get back to the main road and then on to his house. All the while he realized he was getting tired and his legs felt heavy.

Off to his left was the long yellow wall bordering Signor Egon Blanc's property. He glanced at it as he tried to pedal faster. Headlights approached from behind, presumably from a car that wanted to pass him, Lanz assumed. That was the last thing he remembered.

He woke with a headache and confused thoughts. He was alone in a small white room, in a steel tube bed, a triangle dangling in front of his face—a bed gallows, his grandparents called it. So he was in a hospital.

He slept for two days.

At one point Julia bent down and whispered in his ear that she loved him.

When he came to his senses, he was convinced that it hadn't been Julia who had visited him and confessed her love, but that he had only recalled the night in the Sant'Elena hotel. He was relieved to see how fortuitous his "accident" was for him. He could now claim to have forgotten everything. He could start all over again. But he kept coming back to Julia and her saying that she loved him. He loved her, too. He had thought she was wonderful from day one. Regardless of what she might have done, he didn't want to forget her.

During the doctor's rounds, he learned from the *professore* that he had been rear-ended by a car. An anonymous person, perhaps some pedestrian, had notified an ambulance and the police. In any event they had found him under a pine tree—someone must have dragged him across the asphalt to that location. It all didn't make any sense . . . If the driver left the scene of the accident, the *professore* continued, then who had tended to him? Lanz had been found some 45 feet from the scene of the accident, and expertly placed on his side so that he didn't choke. And if it had been a pedestrian, why had he fled before the ambulance had arrived?

"Where am I?" Lanz asked the doctor.

"In the Ospedale Psichiatrico e Neurologico."

"On the Lido?"

"Yes, on the Lido . . . just north of the closed Ospedale al Mare, if you know where that is."

That afternoon a Commissario Galli came to visit, and Lanz felt he had already heard that name before. His impression was that the detective was intelligent. He already knew Lanz's name, knew that he'd been living in his house on the Lido for two years now, and that he was a translator.

After the Commissario had asked how he was feeling and if he was well enough to talk, he wanted to know if someone was tailing him.

Lanz immediately thought of the bald young man with the backpack who had followed him and tried to attack him in the San Michele cemetery wearing a dog mask. But he was careful not to divulge anything, because he thought that might drag him even deeper into this mess that he himself didn't understand.

"What will you do all day when you're back in good health and at home?" the Commissario asked.

"I'll move from word to word." He was amazed at his answer.

The Commissario thought a moment and looked at Lanz as he posed the next question: "How's your head?"

"You'll have to ask the *professore*," Lanz responded faintly.

"Are you in pain?"

He has something like a migraine when he suddenly raises his head or turns to the side, Lanz thought, but that's none of the police's business.

"Yes."

"One more question: Did you, by chance, recognize the driver of the car that rear-ended you?"

"No," Lanz whispered.

"Or the other person who pulled you over to the side of the road and then notified the police?"

"No." Lanz closed his eyes and was silent.

"Fine," the Commissario said as if to himself, and placed his business card on the nightstand beside the bed.

"Speedy recovery!"

He had barely closed the door when Lanz thought he knew who had helped him after the accident. It was like a ray of light that suddenly falls into a darkened room and makes everything visible for an instant. It was the man named Richard Vogel. And he immediately suspected that his pursuer had been hoping to kill him but the falconer had prevented it. Hadn't Vogel encouraged him at the San Michele cemetery, as he now recalled, to report the man called Giorgio Fermi? But why hadn't Vogel waited for the ambulance after the accident? And now he also remembered that Richard Vogel, as he pulled Lanz out of the road, had recognized him. He had bent down and, furious, shouted "Shit!"

"But that's not my name," Lanz thought, before he fell asleep.

When he awoke, he found Commissario Galli's business card on the nightstand. It seemed to be a warning that he should be careful of what he might say.

His condition gradually improved. In reply to the attending physician's question, he claimed he only remembered riding his bike, but not where he was going or why.

"Is there anyone who can look after you?" the attending physician asked the morning of his discharge.

"Yes," Lanz lied. "I've notified my mother."

Late that evening Julia Ellis opened the door to his hospital room. The first thing she wanted to know was whether he was expecting any visitors. When he said no, she hugged him and again whispered in his ear that she loved him. He didn't say anything, but he believed her because he wanted to believe her.

IV

The Multiverse

It was late afternoon and Lanz was still lying in bed. For the past two days and nights Julia has been taking care of him. She has slept with him lovingly, brought warm carry-out from a pizzeria, gone food shopping, and discussed everything with him over and over again. In the end they agreed that he shouldn't go to the police because it wasn't clear what the ramifications would be for the two of them.

Julia also tried to convince him that she had not collaborated with Manuel Saltesi. She told Lanz she had warned Mennea many times that she was going to leave him. Each time he went crazy and beat her. Manuel Saltesi had witnessed the latest altercation and later assured her that he would stand by her if he were present at a similar incident. She then admitted that she had arranged with Manuel Saltesi to fly together to America.

"So you were having an affair with him?" he accused her.

"No. I promised him it would happen only after everything was over . . . because I didn't want to stay here any longer."

"Did you . . . sleep with him?"

"No."

"Tell me the truth."

"I'm telling you the truth."

She started to cry, and he hugged and kissed her until she hugged and kissed him. During the last two nights they had done nothing but make love to each other and talk about the two murders and the police. He still had doubts that she was telling him the truth. In addition, he was jealous, but he tried to hide it from her. And what was she hiding from him? he asked himself the whole time. There were contradictions and incompatible details, but Julia had insisted on her version.

When Lanz pressed her, she adamantly described the details of the incident, but each time other pieces of the puzzle didn't fit together, so she concentrated on the particular question and depicted yet again what had happened, then a few hours later it again occurred to him that something didn't jibe. This procedure was subsequently repeated until they made love or had a bite to eat to relieve their hunger and thirst, or fell asleep from exhaustion. As soon as they awoke, Lanz would again ask her to start all over again and tell him everything from the beginning, until she protested or began to cry. He felt he was almost at the point of learning the whole truth. She had presumably shot Mennea and then called Saltesi for help, he thought, but she denied it for the time being. While he was mulling it over, she came back from shopping and put the *Gazzettino* newspaper down in front of him. Lanz saw the photograph of Will Mennea on the front page and, beside it, a photo of Julia together with her lover in the sailboat where the dead man was found. To his amazement the article presumed that Mennea had likely committed suicide.

He heard the front doorbell ring and assumed that the mailman Oboabona had delivered a package, but a moment later Julia urgently called his name from the foyer. He leaped out of bed, slipped into the Japanese dressing gown with the dragon embroidered on the back that he had bought in London, and, as he entered the foyer, saw Julia with two policemen and the Commissario standing at the door. They looked at him without saying a word and were apparently waiting to see how he would react.

"Do you remember me?" the Commissario asked, and added:

"Commissario Galli."

"No," Lanz lied in a sullen tone.

"Don't you remember what we talked about?"

As he was speaking, Lanz had stepped behind Julia and put his arm on her shoulder.

"What's this all about?" he asked rudely.

"May we come in?"

Lanz removed his arm from Julia's shoulder and led the Commissario and the two policemen into the living room where he only went when he wanted to watch TV.

Since he hadn't aired out the room in quite a while, he opened the windows.

Two walls of the living room were filled by white bookshelves with hundreds of books, on the third wall hung a poster by the American painter Cy Twombly that looked like hasty scribbles and sketches from the notebook of an artist or a lunatic. Lanz loved this painting. For him it was the snapshot at a thousandth-of-a-second of the brain's activities, and it reflected his fantasies and anxieties. Commissario Galli briefly glanced at it before he sat down on the sofa and the two policemen occupied armchairs.

"I'm not surprised to see you here," Galli said to Julia. "You visited Signor Lanz in the hospital, at least that's what the night nurse who saw you told us. This morning she read the newspaper article, remembered you, and notified us. Are you two together?"

"Herr Lanz is a good friend of mine," Julia answered tersely.

"Really? How long have you known him?"

"Not very long."

"For the two days and two nights when you weren't in the Hotel Hungaria?"

"What's that supposed to mean?" Lanz interrupted.

"Am I under suspicion?" Julia asked, incensed.

"There have been some recent developments . . ." Galli turned to Julia and continued: "It's possible that Mennea's death had to do with revenge. Or maybe you shot him, Signora Ellis, so that you could be with you new friend in the future."

The Commissario seemed to be speaking to himself. He looked Julia in the eye and added: "Those are only considerations, theories, obviously. But I've got to consider all the possibilities if I'm going to get to the heart of the matter. Would you please answer my question?"

"We first met on the beach when Signora Ellis had noticed jellyfish in the water and was photographing them. I watched her at work and we struck up a conversation." Lanz was amazed that he could so easily tell such half-truths. "What's your point, Signor Commissario? Why are you here?"

Commissario Galli was still eyeing Julia and interrupted him: "So, you were with your companion and his friends and became acquainted with Signor Lanz," he continued his interrogation of Julia.

"So?" Julia asked. "Herr Lanz was interested in my photography and asked about the jellyfish photos ..."

"Are you also a photographer?" Galli now addressed Lanz.

"Why are you asking me?" He continued to pretend he was confused.

"Or were you just trying to start a conversation?"

"I can't remember exactly," Lanz rebuffed the question.

"As I can see," Galli glanced at Lanz's dressing gown, "you are still recuperating. The only thing I want to know is whether you are having an affair with Signora Ellis or not. Signora Ellis has referred to you as her good friend ..."

"As best I can remember," Lanz lied, "I made a date with her in Torcello. We got back together that evening ... She hinted at some of her problems. And I was trying to cheer her up ... In any event we rode as far as Sant'Elena ..."

"And then?"

"I can't remember," Lanz responded cynically. "The next day I went to the San Lorenzo church in Venice because Marco Polo is buried there and I had translated his book *Il Milione* into English." He lied, and had a great urge to keep lying.

"And then?"

"Then I went back to the Ospedale vaporetto station and rode to

San Michele."

"May I ask why?"

"I wanted to think."

"In the cemetery?"

"Yes, I was perplexed . . ."

"You don't say? How long were you there, and how long were you perplexed?"

"I have a witness, Herr Richard Vogel. He's a falconer working for Signor Blanc in the house across the street, commissioned by the city of Venice to drive seagulls out of the cemetery."

"We all know who Herr Vogel is. I will contact him . . . And so, what did you do then?"

"I don't know . . . Herr Vogel probably brought me to the Lido in his motorboat and taken me home from there."

"I understand. We'll check that out. You see, I don't consider you a suspect, even though Mennea had good reason to hate you . . ."

"He didn't know about it!" Julia interrupted. "If you consider me a suspect: I don't own a gun!"

"That's what you told us at the initial inquiry . . . But anybody can get a gun . . . That shouldn't be too difficult in Signor Mennea's crowd."

"Are you still trying to insinuate that I killed him? Why don't you go ask Mennea's associates?"

"We're doing that as we speak, Signora Ellis. Now I'll have to ask you to accompany us to the Questura."

She realized that it was futile to resist, took her shopping bag and her light jacket, quickly hugged Lanz, and left the house, followed by the Commissario and the two policemen.

Lanz closed the front door because he didn't want to see Julia climb into the police car. He still wasn't certain whether she'd shot Mennea, but, on the other hand, he didn't want to acknowledge that possibility. All of a sudden he felt as he did before his planned suicide. Except now he shouldn't drink any alcohol, he thought, the doctors had advised against it. And he didn't have any desire to go for a walk on the beach. He decided he would wait for Julia at home, so he went to the bathroom, resumed his morning routine, and once again heard the doorbell ring. This time it was Oboabona with a letter from a large Italian publishing house, asking if he would translate Shakespeare's works into Italian. The offer extended for a period of 25 years, with a monthly salary of 4,000 euros. At first Lanz thought it must be a joke, and when he burst out laughing, Oboabona turned back and just stood in the doorway.

"Everything okay?" he asked with concern.

"I'm not sure," Lanz said, took his wallet out of his windbreaker and gave the mailman some money that Oboabona refused to accept.

"You've brought me good luck, Samuel."

"What you talk about? I just have seen police here. And Commissario. That is reason why I deliver Signor Blanc's mail first."

"Come and sit down," Lanz offered. "And please take the money!"

The mailman slipped the bill into his pants pocket, and Lanz offered him something to drink, but Oboabona declined since he didn't have time, or so he said. Beads of perspiration had formed on his forehead. Lanz got a bottle of cola from the refrigerator and set it down in front of the man.

Oboabona obediently took a large gulp.

"Signor Blanc buy even more books than you . . ." he then said.

"How old is he?"

"Sometimes six, sometimes seventy, sometimes hundred, sometimes fourteen . . . whatever he want to be . . . His house full of books and paintings, like a museum. Mr. Ashby . . . he from England . . . tend to the garden and the greenhouse with the most beautiful plants! Signora Caecilia Sereno in charge of planetarium . . . There also a beekeeper, a blind priest from Slovenia, Signor Pedar Janca . . ." he added.

"And Herr Vogel?"

"He strange . . . has falcons . . . has owl . . . a young eagle . . . in old planetarium . . . the place used to be amusement park . . . and Signor Blanc had old planetarium fixed for birds . . . I see him four times, one time he scold the gardener because orchid in greenhouse die . . . Another time he sleep under an umbrella, he drunk too much . . . Some people say he lose his mind . . . I not know if he crazy . . ."

Oboabona took another swig from the bottle and got up.

Lanz also stood up. "Do you know the Commissario who came to my house with the two policemen?" he asked abruptly.

"The Commissario? He named Galli. He on my route . . ."

"And?"

"Very clever . . ."

Oboabona laughed. "Only one time, a murder in Venice, when he not crack case . . . People say five persons dead and later some man from Mafia—the Mafia man seriously injured. Someone beat his brains out with hammer . . . Signor Galli could not find wrongdoer . . . not enough evidence."

"I heard about that. By the way, do you know a lawyer named Capparoni?"

"Dottore Capparoni. Yes . . . very rich . . . but reputation not so good . . . He make question-mark deals, you understand? Help odd people in court . . . Very successful, very clever!"

"Where does he live? In Venice or on the Lido?"

"Has house everywhere! On Lido, in Città Giardino, Via Manin . . ."

Lanz walked the mailman to the door, locked it, took the letter from the Italian publisher and dialed the listed phone number. He was quickly transferred to Director Occhini who had signed the contract, and he was amazed that the man verified the letter.

"How do you know that I'm the right man for the job?"

"We've asked around and come up with your name. You will sign the contract, won't you?"

Lanz thought for a moment, and Director Occhini invited him to come to Umbria, in the region around Perugia where he was spending the summer. "We can discuss everything here at our leisure."

Lanz couldn't believe that everything was going so quickly and so smoothly, that he would be able to work for many years on a single project, and, on top of that, for an inordinately generous fee.

"Why didn't you just call me and tell me about this earlier?" he asked.

"Questions like that give me a guilty conscience . . . I simply wanted to surprise you with my offer. Does that make you uncomfortable?"

"No. But such a long-range and enormous project . . . I've got to get used to the idea."

"Signor Lanz, you are an honorable man. And you are a linguistic genius. I'm speaking as an experienced publisher, and I know what I'm talking about. Let's do something unusual: let's take a brilliant idea and undertake the immediate implementation of that idea. Do you agree?"

Lanz had a hard time containing a feeling of euphoria. He swallowed and replied: "Yes."

"Then it would be best if you send me the signed contract today."

"Where should I begin translating?" Lanz asked.

"How about *The Tempest*? Or *A Midsummer Night's Dream*?"

"May I think about it?"

"Of course. As soon as you've signed the contract, you may begin."

Occhini closed the conversation cordially, wished Lanz the best, and asked him to leave his bank account number with the secretary so that the first installment could be deposited.

And as Lanz conveyed his information to the cordial woman, he still couldn't believe that for years to come he would be "allowed to be with Shakespeare," as he formulated it. And what if they weren't satisfied with his work? In any event he had a contract.

He carefully read it through, didn't find any dubious footnotes, no ambiguities or other comments that made him suspicious, so he signed the document. He then got dressed, called a taxi, rode to the post office with the signed contracts, put the envelope in the mail, and pondered whether he should go straight to the Questura and ask to see Julia. But he had the taxi take him back home, since his presence (he assumed) could only cause trouble for her. The most important thing was that she had a lawyer. Of course he was upset that Ignazio Capparoni had been Mennea's lawyer. On the other hand it was probably to Julia's benefit, because Capparoni also knew the bodyguards, Mennea's business dealings, and Julia's relationship to his client.

Lanz paid the taxi driver and was about to enter his house when he noticed a new gift-wrapped road bike parked at his front door. He was perplexed . . . What's this all about? A small envelope, addressed in his name, was attached to the handlebars. He tore it off, opened it, and read: "Compliments of Richard Vogel," and the name of the shop that had sold the bike.

Upset, he parked the road bike in the foyer and tried to remain lucid. So it really was Richard Vogel who had caused the accident! He was determined to draw no connections so as not to come to the wrong conclusions. He first had to find out if Capparoni the lawyer was already with Julia. Then he'd phone Richard Vogel . . . or pay him a visit to hear his confession that he had been the one in the car that ran over Lanz . . . Of course the falconer could have sent him the road bike anonymously . . . Lanz saw Vogel's face looking down at him as Lanz briefly became conscious on the Lungomare. Then he thought of the falcon. No, Lanz thought, that didn't make sense. Of course there was no logical reason for Lanz's supposition, everything spoke against it, but he felt affection for the man.

After he had found the phone number, he called the Questura, and when a man's voice answered, he asked if Julia Ellis had already been questioned.

"Who's speaking?" the unfamiliar voice wanted to know.

Lanz explained that he was a friend of Julia Ellis and had spoken with Commissario Galli just a few hours ago.

"Commissario Galli isn't available right now."

"I understand," Lanz answered, and was about to hang up when he thought of Julia's defense lawyer.

"Could I possibly speak with Dr. Capparoni, Signora Ellis's lawyer?"

"I know Signor Dr. Capparoni."

"Is he presently at Signora Ellis's deposition?"

"No."

"No?"

"He's not in the building."

Lanz hung up and asked Information for the lawyer's phone number—but the only number available was that of his law firm. People at the firm reported they didn't know where he was, they had tried to reach him but had been unsuccessful.

"I'll take a chance," Lanz said to himself, "and try to find the lawyer by myself." He called a taxi, waited on the street until it arrived, and, as soon as he was seated, asked the driver for the lawyer's address in the Via Manin.

"I don't know the house number, but I'm familiar with the villa," the driver said.

They drove off, and in the meantime Lanz no longer cared that Richard Vogel had had a bike delivered to his door, and he no longer thought about the offer from Rome. He had agreed to it, of course, but he still didn't comprehend it. Of course he remembered full well that just a couple of days ago he wanted to take his life because everything just seemed so uneventful and monotonous. And since that time, everything had changed . . .

At that moment he could only think of Julia—her emotional state and whether Galli had cornered her. And suddenly his trip to the Via Manin seemed absurd . . . What was he going to do there? Presumably Dr. Capparoni wasn't even home. He was about to give the driver instructions to go back to his house when, seconds later, he decided just the opposite: to find the house and ask to see the lawyer. He would have the taxi wait at the garden gate until he came back out. Then he could go from the Via Manin directly to the police station and see about Julia.

They drove through a maze of streets, between villas and gardens, and even after having been here for two years, Lanz was totally disoriented. As they drove along he saw pansies in flower-boxes, colorful toys spread out on a lawn, an abandoned plastic swimming pool standing in the sun, sleeping cats, houses half-hidden by lush treetops, and rose-colored peonies—*peonia*, he thought, that's what the Italians called them.

The taxi pulled over in front of a forged garden gate with shrubs and drooping white wisteria on the other side. He got out, tried to open the gate, and found it unlocked. He stepped directly into a large garden. Walking under the wisteria made him think of an ice cave and stalactites. He loved wisteria . . . if it was a shade of blue, it was called "Blue Rain," he recalled. As he followed the garden path up to the house, the wisteria was transformed into a thousand eyes, all staring at him. He hesitated for a moment because he knew he could make a fool of himself, but it was crystal clear that he had to ask Dr. Capparoni why he wasn't backing up Julia at the police station. Had he declined to defend her? And if so, why? Was he ill? Didn't he have a proxy? Was he ultimately colluding with the two bodyguards, Manuel Saltesi and Giorgio Fermi? Had those two shot Mennea and then faked his suicide? But maybe it was Julia who had committed the murder? Or had Mennea actually committed suicide? It was also possible that the murdered man in Torcello had associates—Borsakowski or whatever his name was—who had picked up Mennea's trail and avenged their boss?

It was just an impulse that had made Lanz want to find the unfamiliar lawyer, the need to help Julia and, simultaneously, to obtain certainty for himself. With the hundreds of eye-blossoms behind him, Lanz tried to find the doorbell at the front door but had no luck. To his surprise, like the gate, the front door wasn't locked either. As he stepped inside, he saw off to his right a blue Alfa Romeo Mito with a cargo box . . . So Capparoni might be home after all . . .

There wasn't a sound inside the house. He didn't even hear noises from the kitchen, no murmured telephone conversation, no muffled voices from a TV or radio, no music, no toilet being flushed. Lanz called out the name of the lawyer—first, in a normal tone of voice, then louder, finally he shouted the name. But everything remained silent. He could see that the furnishing were expensive: modern furniture intermingled with Chinese and Indian pieces; paintings by various contemporary artists; chandeliers from Murano; Indian, Afghan, and Moroccan carpets, Asian rugs, parquet floors . . . Lanz opened the door to the elegant kitchen. Everything was spick and span and in its proper place, as if it were to be photographed. The same was true for the opulent bathroom and the living room with its leather trimmings, a TV set, and a library. He climbed the wooden staircase to the second floor and again called out the name of the lawyer before he opened a door and stepped into the bedroom. The blinds were lowered. At second glance in the dimly-lit room, he saw feet with black socks, and then a man hanging from the ceiling.

It immediately occurred to him that the dead man must be Dr. Capparoni. The man's eyes were closed, his face was peaceful, blood had run out his nose and left a large stain on his white shirt. A fly buzzed around and landed on Lanz's cheek until he shooed it away with one hand. Before he ran off, he noticed the chandelier lying shattered on the floor, and the open steel ladder behind the hanged man. In panic, Lanz raced down the stairs, through the lobby onto the garden path, and from there under the white wisteria blossoms that now seemed "stupid" due to their immobility and indifference and out onto the street where he tore open the passenger door to the taxi and told the driver to notify the police. The lawyer had taken his life inside the house.

"Dr. Capparoni?" the cabbie asked in shock.

"Yes—"

The taxi driver slammed the door shut, started the car, turned around with screeching tires, and headed back down the street in the direction of the Questura. Lanz cussed at the disappearing taxi, then decided to wait. After the trip to Torcello and his stopover at the San Michele cemetery, he had left his cellphone at home because he didn't want his calls traced. And he also hadn't opened his laptop, though beforehand he had checked his incoming email and read the headlines from online news sites. But since the trip to Torcello, his life had changed so drastically that he no longer thought about it.

He was glad he remembered the contract with the publisher

in Rome because it distracted him from his "dark thoughts," as he called them. Dark matter . . . the immense space in the universe that was dominated for the most part by dark matter—and at this point his head, too, he thought. Was it really Dr. Capparoni who had hanged himself or been hung? He didn't want to go back into the garden alone, but just stay where he was so he could keep an eye on the house. Perhaps someone was still hiding up in one of the upper floors or in the garden? He crossed the street, keeping the villa in sight the entire time. No cars drove past, no children called for their mothers, no dogs were barking, no birds could be heard.

In the distance he suddenly saw Oboabona with his moped and yellow mail cart appear at the intersection . . . He had just stopped, dismounted, taken mail from the cart and placed it in a mailbox. He then crossed the street and repeated the procedure at the building across the way.

Lanz wavered between hiding or calling to the man.

"Goodluck!" he shouted. "Samuel!"

Annoyed, Oboabona looked around, recognized Lanz, got on his moped and sped over to him. He pulled to a stop with an expression as if he were expecting something unpleasant or unsettling.

"Dr. Capparoni has hanged himself!" Lanz blurted out, swiping his index finger across his throat.

"Dead? Dottore Capparoni?"

"Yes . . . I was in his house . . . I wanted to see him . . . He didn't come to the police station." Then Lanz briefly related that he had come in a taxi and the driver, hearing the news, was horrified and disappeared in his cab.

"I call police, okay?"

Lanz nodded, and Oboabona pulled his cellphone from his pants pocket and dialed the number. But before he could be connected, two police cars with flashing lights were racing toward them.

"We stay," Oboabona said firmly. "Everything okay."

The two cars screeched to a stop in front of the villa. Four policemen sprinted through the garden to the house, while two more crossed the street. They put up roadblocks, Lanz noticed, and asked if he was the man who the taxi had dropped off here.

Lanz nodded.

"And you sent the driver to the police?"

"Yes."

"Your name?"

They asked him to sit in a police car and answer a series of questions before they took him home where he had to show his papers. They then took him to the station house.

Commissario Galli met him in his office and offered him a chair.

"Let's start at the beginning," he said. "Where, precisely, did you see Signora Ellis on Torcello?"

"I've already told you that."

"Nevertheless, I'd like to hear it again."

Lanz repeated, word for word, and reluctantly, his statement and, in conclusion, asked about Julia.

"We've let her go so she can find a new lawyer, but she's not allowed to leave Venice."

"And where is she now?"

"We don't know."

"Is she still registered in the Hotel Hungaria?"

"She didn't say she wasn't. And she must remain accessible!"

"She's innocent," Lanz said to his own surprise.

"We'll see. We'll also see what part you play in this entire case."

"I don't know what you're driving at."

"What do you have to do with Dr. Capparoni?"

"I called the police station and then his law firm, but no one knew where he was. So I went looking for him privately, to help Signora Ellis."

"So you didn't really know him? Did you at least ever see him in person?"

"No."

"And where did you get his address?"

Lanz didn't deliberate for very long, he wanted to avoid dragging Oboabona into this mess, so he responded that he got it from Signora Julia Ellis—since he assumed that she might have been there once or twice with Mennea.

"But she told me she had mentioned Dr. Capparoni to you incidentally just once."

"Yes."

"And that's when she told you the address that isn't listed in any telephone book?"

"Yes."

"And you memorized the address and the house number?"

"She said 'Via Manin,' and I know who Manin is."

"And how did you find his house?"

"The taxi driver knew Dr. Capparoni . . ."

Once again Lanz remembered that he had a signed 25-year contract with a publisher, and that was reassuring.

"Let's come back to your accident. How did it happen, exactly? Do you remember any more now?"

"No . . . after all, the car came from behind me," Lanz said insolently.

"Who?" The Commissario pretended not to notice Lanz's increasing resentment. "Were you able to make out anything? The driver? Or the license plate?"

"No, I lost consciousness, as you know."

"And who notified the ambulance and the police? We haven't been able to track them down."

Lanz could see the face of Richard Vogel, the falconer, as he bent down over Lanz, and he could see the new road bike at his front door. But he didn't want to divulge this knowledge before he could speak with Vogel personally. And if he were forced to reveal it, he could, of course, declare that he had just remembered it.

"My memories end with Malamocco," he answered tersely.

Lanz spent the rest of the day waiting for Julia to call. He had tried to reach her several times but was unsuccessful. The front desk at the Hotel Hungaria told him she wasn't answering her phone, and she wasn't at the police station, as Galli had already informed him. He decided to take his cellphone with him from now on and read the long list of emails on his laptop. He was restless. On the one hand he was tired, exhausted, and confused by everything that had happened; on the other hand, he suffered from inaction. Along with other crazy ideas, he thought he was being punished for his suicidal intentions. But by whom? Lanz did not want to admit to religious thoughts that were surfacing against his will. Hadn't things seemed too uneventful up till now? And now that he was up to his neck in something that he didn't understand, didn't he feel overwhelmed? His state of mind and his mood didn't improve, but the idea that he was being punished for his suicidal plans gradually disappeared.

The front door bell rang, interrupting his gloomy thoughts. He closed his laptop, hoping that it was Julia, afraid that it could be the Commissario, thought it might be Oboabona, but it was Richard Vogel. The road bike was still by the door in its packing—Vogel obviously saw it because he apologized immediately that he hadn't been in touch before now, but—

"Come in!" Lanz interrupted, and led him into the living room where they sat down.

"I'm in a hurry," Vogel began. "I can't stay long!"

"You're always in a hurry," Lanz remarked smugly.

"You're right to criticize me for that. I've been in a hurry my whole life long."

"If you don't have time, you don't feel time . . . You never look back," Lanz replied.

Vogel ignored this observation and changed the topic: "Signor Blanc is inviting you to come over."

"Really? Why?"

Vogel ignored his questions: "In an hour, but first I've got to check on the falcons. Want to come along?"

Lanz put on his shoes, slung his windbreaker over his arm, and followed Vogel.

"Thanks for the new road bike," he said, again in an ironic tone.

Vogel again ignored his remark and quickly walked ahead.

Vogel didn't speak again until they were in the botanical garden behind Signor Blanc's villa, sitting on a grey-weathered teakwood bench between iris, saffron- and royal lilies. Blooming all around them were gladioli, blue and red rhododendron, white lilacs, and dark and pale violet lilacs, sprouting yellow tulips, red and orange roses, yellow rapeseed, rose columbine, violet, rose, and white lupine, and red foxglove. And as Richard Vogel recited the names of the plants and pointed them out, Lanz smelled the sweet fragrance of the flowers and blossoms and heard the buzzing of the bees.

"I hope you can be patient. Signor Blanc is very impulsive," Richard Vogel continued. "Sometimes things move too slowly for him, other times too fast. As you may have heard, he is difficult and yet straightforward. He is a very wealthy man, he primarily owns stocks."

"Which stocks?"

"Stocks from watch companies, pharmaceutical firms, airlines, and also from gaming houses in Las Vegas, Monaco, or here on the Lido . . ."

"Casinos?" Lanz asked in amazement, and added: "He must be very rich."

"I don't like to use the word 'rich' because it has negative connotations, but Signor Blanc has acquired land in Africa, made it productive, and given it to the poor. He donates large sums for the victims of earthquakes and flooding, for refugees, and for animal welfare . . ."

"Does he have a profession? I mean, aside from bank speculation?"

"Signor Blanc doesn't speculate, he is a shrewd expert. He originally studied archaeology . . . He has financed digs and museums and has spent the past few decades studying cryptanalysis. At the moment he is deciphering the Voynich manuscript, a 500-year-old manuscript that had passed through the hands of John Dee, the alchemist, was acquired by the Habsburg Emperor Rudolf II in Prague, although Athanasius Kircher was then unable to decipher it. Lastly, it supposedly ended up in the library of the Jesuit Order in Rome when it was purchased by the American book collector and antiquarian bookdealer Wilfrid Michael Voynich. The script and language have not been identified to this day, so that no one knows whether the text has any meaning.

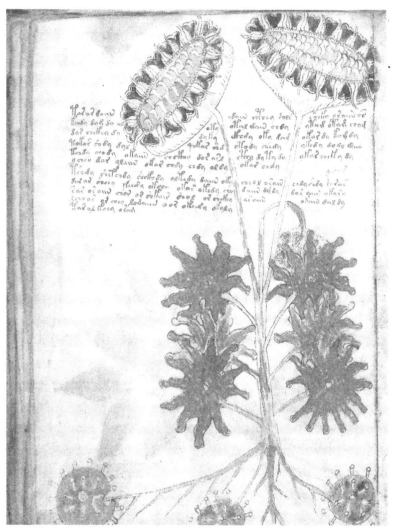

"I've heard about the Voynich manuscript," Lanz interrupted. "People say the whole thing is madness."

"You will be amazed, but Signor Blanc has not only deciphered the manuscript, he can even speak the language it's written in. He calls it 'Bacon'—after the monk, Roger Bacon, from whom John Dee acquired the manuscript. He has even taught me 'Bacon,' it's very complicated."

Lanz recalled that in the two years he has lived on the Lido, several times he had heard that Blanc made his fortune primarily in arms deals. So he returned to the question of stocks and casually asked: "Doesn't Signor Blanc have stock in weapons manufacturers?"

"I don't know about that," Vogel responded brusquely. "Just look at this botanical garden," he encouraged Lanz, and stood up.

The extended greenhouse couldn't be seen from the outside as it was located down in a basin surrounded by a sea of blossoms. Before they arrived at the basin, they walked through a garden with palm trees, and James Ashby, the gardener, a dedicated grey-haired elderly garden architect from London who apparently employed migrants and enjoyed working with them as Lanz deduced from his helpers' laughter and high spirits, joined Richard Vogel, exchanged words with him, and then accompanied Lanz into the greenhouse, while the falconer went off to his animals. A Chinese woman, Lanz assumed, caught up with Mr. Ashby and asked him something; Ashby, laughing, responded in her mother tongue.

The greenhouse, as Mr. Ashby explained to Lanz, was exclusively dedicated to plants mentioned in the Bible. It began with a bramble bush, "the burning bush where God appeared to Moses;" then came white umbels of the poison hemlock—Ashby then quoted the fifth Book of Moses: "Their grapes are grapes of gall, their clusters are bitter. Their wine is the poison of dragons, and the cruel venom of asps"—then mandrakes, and he now quoted from the *Song of Songs* 7:13: "The mandrakes give a smell, and at our gates are all manner of pleasant fruits, new and old, which I have laid up for thee, O my beloved." He seemed to enjoy his role as a guide through the plant labyrinth and no longer paid attention to Lanz who was too tired to follow Ashby's recitation; his mind simply floated along on the warm air. Ashby pointed out myrtle, coriander, pomegranates, and substantiated their presence with Biblical quotes from Nehemiah and Moses, continued walking on and on, disappeared in a cloud of butterflies. and waved at Lanz to follow him . . .

He led Lanz to the old abandoned planetarium of the former amusement park. It was a yellow building that Signor Blanc had renovated. As Mr. Ashby opened the door, Lanz saw inside large aviaries with birds of prey, attended by Arab caretakers. All the birds were wearing leather hoods over their heads and were calm. Just then, one of the caretakers appeared, carrying a frame with two horizontal bars where six falcons were perched in their leather hoods. The caretaker placed them back in the aviaries with the help of two other men who treated the birds with the utmost respect and, as Lanz noticed, were proud of the falcons.

Behind the old planetarium—imbedded in the ground—was a squat new planetarium with a round dome, a field ringed with trees in the background. Standing in the midst of all that green was Richard Vogel, swinging the rope with its game bag, a "feather lure" like the one Lanz had seen in the San Michele cemetery but with different bait. The feather lure consisted of a leather pillow with feathers and was tied to a long rope that Vogel swung over his head several times as a sign that the bird was to return to its Falconer, as Mr. Ashby explained before he left. Lanz just noticed that when the falcon was back sitting on Richard Vogel's arm, the bird was eating a piece of meat that had previously been fastened to the front end of the feather lure.

Lanz watched the exercise until Vogel introduced him to Caecilia Sereno, an astronomer who offered to show him the new planetarium. Actually, the beekeeper, Signor Janca, had been designated for her position, but he was away, visiting clients, and wouldn't be back until evening.

Lanz was relieved. There were no police to interrogate him, no one to pressure him. Besides, he liked Caecilia Sereno. She had long dark hair, a symmetrical face, white teeth, a slim figure, and wore red pumps.

"What would you like to see? A solar eclipse? The origin of the universe?"

"I don't know," Lanz said. "Maybe dark matter?"

"Then we'll be sitting in total darkness."

"That might be lovely," Lanz said.

She laughed.

"There is also an electron microscope in the planetarium . . . We don't just deal with the universe, but also with the microcosm."

Her fingers were long, like those of a pianist, and the red fingernail polish made them look like ten independent entities.

There were glass display cases in the lobby where you could view reproductions of celestial models.

"I know you must be tired, so I'll just give you an overview," she explained. "These are forerunners of planetariums that depict planetary orbits around the earth."

They then came to astronomical clocks. "The celestial models instantly adapted to each new revelation," she went on to explain, "for example, Kepler's discovery of the motion of the planets around the sun."

They were standing before a tall terrestrial globe where all the mountain ranges, rivers, oceans, cities and countries were projected in three dimensions. In a dark adjoining room a computer could enlarge any particular area to the point that every last detail could be viewed on a screen. At his request, Caecilia Sereno showed him the village of St. Leonhard, first as a three-dimensional geographic map, than as seen from an airplane cockpit. In the next instant Lanz could look right through all the walls, into the homes in St. Leonhard, into bedrooms and cellars, into restaurants and the church or the rectory. As he subsequently called up the city of Venice on the computer, gazed through the walls and could see people without clothes, naked and unsuspecting, who were going about their lives without worrying that someone was watching and therefore gave free rein to their desires, their animosity or their despair or simply pursued their daily routines, he was appalled.

He found earphones that would allow him to hear all the sounds, but the picture instantly disappeared, and a prompt for the "code" appeared on the display: Caecilia laughed and strolled ahead to show him the "accessible celestial globe." After Lanz entered, she closed the door and explained that "from here one can see the stars correctly, as they are in nature." They then sat down in the leather pilots' seats in a space capsule. In the meantime he had overcome his fatigue and also his doubts, his fears, his rage, and his misery. Time had transformed back into a succession of moments, each one demanding his attention.

Caecilia turned off the lights and a second later they were hurtling through space—at such speed that he initially had to shut his eyes. When he opened them, he was flying straight for the Butterfly Cluster in the Scorpius constellation, as Caecilia explained.

The cluster of stars at its core was the color of shimmering violet that gradually transitioned into a fiery orange on the outer edges; on closer inspection it seemed to Lanz like an enormous colorful frost pattern.

The entire planetarium above the space capsule next portrayed the origins of the universe, from an infinitely immense entity that, like an exploding bomb, disintegrated into particles of matter, shattered with and without streaking comets until, in a rain of sparks in configurations resembling fireworks, it was lost in space.

Then Caecilia steered toward the center of "our galaxy," as she called it, a gigantic black hole with a size of a billion light years and the mass of three million sons. It formed a boundary beyond which no light could escape.

Finally they climbed down an iron ladder to the microscope room. Using an electron microscope, Caecilia Sereno showed the astonished Lanz a tiny transparent proboscis from a water flea, yellow enlarged fleas with bodies of fish scales, as well as angel-shaped ones with four wings, mites with bodies like delicate filaments, and colorful collages of the strangest plant-, animal- and human cells.

Caecilia Sereno's cellphone rang quietly, so she headed in the direction of the big villa. On the way Lanz asked his companion if he could call her. She smiled warmly and handed him her business card—a good sign, he felt.

Richard Vogel was already waiting in the green vestibule that was actually a library. He led Lanz up a stone staircase to the top floor and asked him to have a seat in a waiting room. One of the walls in the large room consisted of perhaps a hundred glass beehives that were teeming with life. On the opposite wall was an equally large tropical aquarium with corals and fish. The third and fourth walls with doors slightly ajar belonged to a library. Lanz closed his eyes and only opened them again when Richard Vogel whispered in his ear that he could come in now.

The room was empty and white. White linen curtains in the evening light hung before the windows. A ceiling lamp cast a white light on a white desk, and Signor Egon Blanc, sitting on a white chair, was bent over his papers with his back to Lanz. The white stone floor gleamed and smelled of wax.

Blanc was wearing a brocade smoking jacket with ornamentation of alternating upright and inverted beehives that formed a heraldic design. He held a Mont Blanc fountain pen in his right hand with its white six-sided star and rounded edges that symbolized the snowcapped peak of Europe's tallest mountain—Lanz himself owned a ballpoint pen of that same brand.

"How are you?" Blanc inquired cordially without turning around. "Are you back on your feet again?"

"Yes."

"I want to apologize, and to thank you. Apologize for the pain I caused you, and thank you for not notifying the police," he continued. "I was the one who unintentionally rear-ended you with my car and my first reaction was just to get away. I then asked Herr Vogel to step in and look after you. Has Director Occhini from the publishing house already contacted you?"

"Yes."

"Did you agree to the terms?"

"Yes, of course—" At that moment Lanz realized what was going on.

"Starting today you will have your own room in my house that you can use at any time you wish. The best thing would be for Herr Vogel to give you the key for the door that seals off the connecting tunnel to your cellar. Then you would never have to ask permission when you wanted to use the room."

Lanz was speechless.

"I know that someone shot Will Mennea. My cook, Mr. Min

130

Chang, works in the Hotel Excelsior. He told me about it. And Herr Vogel has told me that Giorgio Fermi, wearing a dog mask, was about to attack you in the San Michele cemetery. Ms. Julia Ellis will be back with you soon, I have provided her with a lawyer, Dr. Amanda Falchi." He paused, apparently thinking. "And that Signor Ignazio Capparoni hanged himself," he continued, "will soon become evident. Manuel Saltesi, Will Mennea's second bodyguard, wants to take over," Blanc laughed briefly, rasping. "He threatened Capparoni that he would tell the media everything—and that must have been a lot—if he didn't leave Italy immediately. Mennea was a criminal—lately he earned most of his cash from prostituting refugees, along with human trafficking and smuggling. Many migrants paid large sums for him to bring them to Europe, but then drowned in the Mediterranean because the boats he provided were overcrowded. He surreptitiously brought survivors to the abandoned Ospedale al Mare where he kept reassuring them until they complied with his instructions. Lastly, Mennea had his competitor Borsakowski killed, because the man has been missing for a week now—Borsakowski intended to muscle in on the smuggling operation. The one thing that still puzzles me is the question of why you are involved in this matter to the point that someone wants to put you away."

Lanz was silent.

"Do you have an explanation?" Signor Blanc asked quietly.

Lanz shook his head.

"I understand," Blanc continued, without turning around.

"Maybe it is simply a case of jealousy, as most people assume. You hear all kinds of rumors."

Lanz remained silent. The silence was interrupted by Signor Blanc nodding his head and, in a language Lanz didn't recognize, directing Richard Vogel to do something. Vogel whispered: "We're leaving" and led Lanz out into another room. Vogel asked him to be patient, and disappeared.

Lanz was now in a huge "classroom," stuffed with globes, the walls and ceiling featuring glass and plastic eyes. Aside from Earth globes from various centuries he noticed celestial globes that were embellished with figures from the signs of the zodiac. On the Earth globes, however, he discovered animals, plants, and people painted in the individual countries. He could also recognize the seven planets—Mercury, Venus, Mars, Jupiter, Saturn, Uranus, and Neptune—and our moon among the gaudy assemblage, along with a complicated-looking formation of stars around a glass terrestrial globe. Some racks of globes were outfitted with a compass. There was even a black-and-white photograph of a factory, its walls lined with shelves of globes; women in the factory hall were at work gluing printed maps onto blank white spheres. There were white celestial globes with black dots on a brass frame that looked like lamps, there were black celestial globes with yellow dots, nautical celestial globes, geometrical and meteorological globes, traffic globes, and globes driven by a clock mechanism; and last but not least, completely black so-called induction globes with the following instructions: "Problems can be graphically solved in chalk on the black sphere with its shale surface, then erased when finished."

But the hundreds of glass eyes that seemed to be watching him on all sides—because even the floor, it turned out, was designed with a stone pattern of eyes—attracted his attention so that he stared at them as if hypnotized. There were completely white eyes with transparent pupils on the ceiling, the light filtering through them into the large "education gallery." Also on the walls were glassy human and animal eyes with various types of pupils, oval, round, squinted, some with red blood vessels or just the whites of the eyes. A large printed map at one of the windows displayed the various models with explanatory animal names. He read: "Birds' eyes—pheasant, goose, hawk, chicken, crane, partridge, sparrow hawk, mallard, ostrich"—and further below: "Fish eyes—perch, trout, pike, brook trout, catfish"—they shimmered on the walls, silvery and golden. Again, a paragraph further on: "Reptiles—frog, lizard, crocodile, turtle, rattlesnake"—and one last line below that: "Amphibians with various pupil forms," especially slit-eyes. There were also human eyes—green, blue, or brown. All these eyes seemed to be staring at him, and the fascination for Lanz that they exuded was gradually transformed into apprehension and ultimately fear. They reminded him of interrogations, hypnosis, and lies. He understood that silence could also be a form of lying. Nevertheless, he insisted that silence was a part of the universe—but just the thought made him feel helpless.

As he was deciding to leave, Richard Vogel appeared, noticed Lanz's insecurity, and explained that the room had previously been used to preserve and mount animals and then been converted into a room for hypnosis.

"For a time Signor Blanc performed as a hypnotist. Before he retired decades ago, he would put entire rooms of people into a trance. He also had the globe collection moved over here because he lost interest in it after he began working with computer programs in his planetarium. By the way, he asked me to give you the keys to your future guest room. We suggest you continue to use the passageway in your basement to reach our villa."

Vogel jogged to the first floor, opened the door to the guest room, and pointed out the double bed, TV, refrigerator, kitchenette with microwave, and, last of all, the desk. The bathroom was small but well lit and decorated with tile from Portugal—according to Vogel—featuring white and blue ornamentation.

"Your guest room is similar to those in hotels . . . You don't even need to clean up—our Frau Susanna comes by every day."

It had become dark by the time they returned to the garden, but it was the strangest darkness that Lanz had ever seen: everywhere he looked, fireflies were swarming, forming small clouds, drifting in slow-motion. Or were they glowing photons? Lanz didn't move, observing how they coalesced or drifted apart, how they seemed to hover in the air and then recombine.

"The star-spangled sky, garden version," Richard Vogel laughed.

Lanz said goodbye and tottered along the cellar passageway, back to his house. He cleaned up the plaster and bricks that were still lying on the floor, tossed them through the opening back into the passageway, then shoved the cabinet back in place and staggered upstairs where he flung himself on the bed, exhausted.

It was the doorbell that woke him the next morning. Images from the previous day appeared in his head and mingled with his perceptions. At first he couldn't decide what was just happening and what was memory.

When he opened the front door, Oboabona gave him three envelopes. Lanz automatically tore open the first one and found a picture postcard of a falcon. In the second envelope was a photograph of a dog—he instantly realized that it was a reference to his attacker's dog mask—and the third had a picture of a fish.

Lanz invited Samuel Goodluck Oboabona to come in.

"Shall we say *du* to each other?"

"Yes, Signor Lanz."

"Come in," Lanz repeated his invitation.

"I have little time. Much mail!" he called out, and hurried back to his moped.

Lanz closed the door and read the writing on the backs of the numbered postcards. On the first, in blue ballpoint pen and capital letters: "DO YOU REMEMBER?" On the second: "Your dog." And on the third: "Where you're going."

It was obviously a threat, a reminder of the encounter in the San Michele cemetery, and the swimming fish represented the bottom of the ocean. He was certain that the sender's name was . . . Giorgio Fermi . . . He figured that out right away, and studied the three picture postcards that he then put down on the table.

The falcon was a black-and-white illustration that filled out almost the entire postcard. With an unyielding gaze, it was perched on a stand. The white throat and the feather pattern, the fluffy belly and talons were depicted in impeccable detail. 1619 was given as the year of origination, and beside that, in delicate lettering: "Ustad Mansur, Museum of Fine Arts, Boston." It was an example of Indian "Mughal Painting," it said. He had always admired Muslim art.

The second picture of a black-and-white spotted dog was a photograph and vaguely resembled the mask that Fermi had worn. The third picture, again in black and white, portrayed a dead "saltwater fish," floating belly-up on the ocean floor, its eyes fixed

रारीबरीदमुइसोदाढोलीया ८६

in death. Underneath was written "Red Fort Museum, Delhi," and, again, "Ustad Mansur."

But Lanz couldn't concentrate. As soon as he saw the dead fish's eyes—the fish was shown from the side—he immediately thought

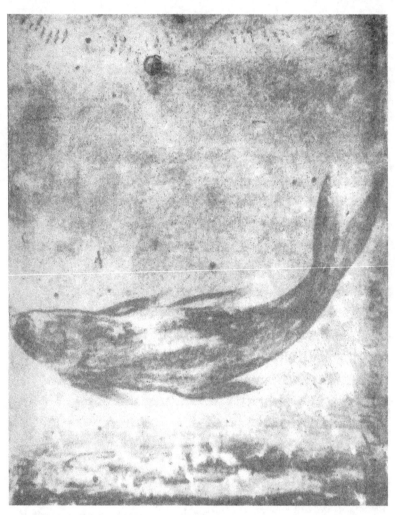

about Signor Blanc's room of glass eyes and about hypnosis.

The next thing he realized was that the postcard apparently came from Mennea's collection; according to Julia Ellis, the man had been interested in works of art, even if only as investments. In any event, Lanz eliminated the possibility that one of the bodyguards could have sent them . . . He gazed out the window and saw that the sun was shining and everything was as usual. He took a shower, got dressed, and tried to reach Julia in the Hotel Hungaria, but she didn't answer. Of course the receptionist couldn't divulge personal information, but he did learn in passing that Julia had spent the night in the hotel and had gone out this morning.

The doorbell rang again, someone punched him in the eye, and he felt a stinging pain that he thought signaled the end of his life.

When he opened his other eye, he thought about the dead fish on the postcard. Then the familiar dog mask was bending over him and a man's voice snarled: "Look down the barrel of this gun!"

The weapon came closer to his undamaged eye until all he could see was the muzzle.

"There's a bullet in there for your other eye, you bastard! It can't wait to get into your skull, right into your friggin' brain!"

The gun disappeared from sight, and the dog mask appeared in front of his good eye. "Get out of here! If you bring in the police, you're dead meat."

The sound of clothes rustling, footsteps . . . Lanz sensed the front door opening and closing. He struggled to get up, lost his balance and fell back down. When he finally made it to the window, there was no one on the street. His eye hurt. Half-dazed, he looked for the gun he had assembled, took off the safety, then put the safety back on. He then got a washcloth from the bathroom, held it under cold water, carefully wrung it out before placing it on his sore eye.

It took an hour before his head had cleared to some extent. The only thing he felt was emptiness. He wasn't depressed, wasn't desperate, wasn't dejected, he was just nobody.

Then he looked for the plastic bag where he kept his medications. After rummaging around he found the painkillers that a dentist had prescribed when he hadl an implant in Mestre, and took two with a glass of water. He hastily left the house, bought snacks and a cola at the Chiosco Bahiano, and took them back home. While he ate, he gradually recovered his composure. He wouldn't leave his home, nor the Lido, nor Venice, he decided. He had to be vigilant and could spend the night in the room that Signor Blanc had provided. But first he wanted to find Julia and, at some point, start translating Shakespeare's plays. He now clung to the contract so that he wouldn't lose all hope.

The pain in his eye wore off, and when he looked at himself in the bathroom mirror, he saw that the cornea was bloodshot and made him look like a thug. But that wasn't all bad. He took the Walther pistol, glanced at the two keys that Richard Vogel had given him, put on his light windbreaker, unpacked the new road bike in the foyer, stuffed the packaging in the paper recycling bin at the end of the alley, went back and, after locking the front door twice, rode the bike to the Hotel Hungaria.

The road bike was lightweight, and after pedaling only a short distance he had picked up quite a bit of speed. At the Hungaria he went to the front desk and asked the young lady to call Julia Ellis's room. The employee in her dark-blue uniform first cast a disparaging glance at his eye and then at the bike. She suddenly put down the phone and told him that Signora Ellis wasn't in her room. Moreover bringing bicycles into the lobby was not permitted, she added. She didn't even attempt to hide her misgivings.

At a newspaper kiosk on the ride back, he discovered a front page featuring a picture of the lawyer Capparoni. He braked, bought a paper and, after leaning his bike against the wall in the foyer, read the article in his living room. The three envelopes and the three postcards were still lying on the table beside the couch. He didn't look at them right away, but spent time reading the paper. Either the police had lied to the journalist, or the author had let his imagination run away with him. There was nothing about the murder of Borsakowski on Torcello, nothing about the migrants, smuggling, or the Ospedale al Mare. The paper had already reported on Mennea's murder, now covered his gaming enterprises and casinos and, as "breaking news," Capparoni's suicide. A photograph of the lawyer's dead German shepherd came with a caption announcing that Dr. Capparoni "took the dog along on his last journey." Lanz was especially upset that the article only spoke of "suicide" and didn't indicate any connection to Mennea's death. He also remembered that day on Torcello and how he had wanted to shoot himself beneath the elderberry bush. The only thing he had achieved, he thought, was that now he had to search through every square foot, every item of furniture, every object in an enormous building to find countless tiny puzzle pieces without knowing if they were even there. Besides, that crazy Giorgio Fermi with the dog mask was just waiting to overpower him. I can't make myself disappear, he thought, relieved himself in the bathroom, and afterward examined himself in the mirror as he was washing his hands. His eye was now almost completely closed, the cornea bloodshot, and his skin was revealing the first red blotches that would soon turn into a blue band.

It occurred to him that he should tell Richard Vogel about the threat and the attack, but the falconer, Lanz considered, would probably only advise him to notify the police right away. Besides, when he spoke to Vogel, he intended to tell him that he wasn't going to use the basement passageway but instead the iron garden gate out front. Clearly, that was silly. He opened the desk drawer and deposited the pistol and also the key for the gate at the end of the basement passageway, took his road bike (because it made him feel as if he had a means of escaping at any time) and decided to first visit the drug store in the Gran Viale Santa Maria Elisabetta to buy an eye patch.

As he rode past the entrance to Egon Blanc's garden and villa, he noticed that several yellow furniture vans were parked at the curb. Workers in overalls were carrying boxes, chairs, and other pieces of furniture out of the house and loading them into the cargo bays. The gardener, Mr. Ashby, was attending to two expensive painting that were wrapped in blankets. For a brief instant Lanz could see snatches of the paintings before they were loaded into a special white delivery van with "Arttrans" on the side. Lanz dismounted and pushed his bike through the entrance. When he finally reached Mr. Ashby, the man was at the point of closing the bay door of the "Arttrans" van.

"Is Signor Blanc moving out?" Lanz asked, and Ashby nodded.

"He left this morning."

"Where is he going?" Lanz asked, dumbfounded.

"He booked three flights, but hasn't used any of the tickets. That's just the way he does things. To tell the truth, we have since learned that he wanted to fly to Rio de Janeiro, then to Geneva, and, last of all, to Hong Kong because he has villas all over. Just an hour ago we learned that he bought a hotel in Damascus where the contents of his house on the Lido are to be delivered. Before he flies off, Herr Blanc always leaves precise instructions, but this time we haven't received any . . . What happened to your eye?"

"Nothing worth mentioning."

"Just don't tell me that you hit your head on a door knob."

"No," Lanz replied.

"It looks horrible."

"Yes, I'm just on my way to see a doctor."

The "Arttrans" van cautiously drove over the crunching gravel that struck the chassis and flew out from under the tires, and then it headed for the Lungomare Gabriele D'Annunzio, while the workers were still carrying out boxes containing the books from the library, as Mr. Ashby explained.

"What about the plants and animals?" Lanz asked in shock.

"The plants will be taken to the University of Padua, along with the greenhouse and the bees," Mr. Ashby said. "The planetarium will be disassembled and also taken to Padua."

"And you?"

"I'm going back to England."

"Why?" Lanz asked, astounded.

"Times change."

"I don't understand."

"Sometimes time sleeps, sometimes it's looking for something, then again, time may be on the run." He suddenly laughed, as if he'd told a joke, and then disappeared.

Lanz just stood in the garden, hoping to catch a glimpse of Richard Vogel, Caecilia Sereno, or Pedar Janca, the beekeeper, but not one of them appeared, just a small wiry Chinese man in jeans and a white T-shirt who had just stepped out of the house and seemed to be in a hurry.

"Are you Mr. Chang, the cook?" Lanz addressed him.

The man briefly looked him over and then said: "Lanz?"

"Yes."

"Signor Blanc sends his greetings. We have just received an e-mail from him that urges us to assist you however we can."

The Chinese man gave him a business card and hurried "back to the Hotel Excelsior," as he said. Since no one else appeared and the workers were still lugging boxes of books out of the villa, he decided to go back home, but then realized he had forgotten to buy an eye patch, so he set off for the drug store. In the store he tied the patch at the back of his head and then headed home. It was strange: first, the room of eyes, then the picture of the dead fish with only the one eye, and now he himself with his blue eye and a black eye patch. Giorgio Fermi, the bodyguard with the dog mask, had threatened to throw him to the fishes, and with one punch had fulfilled the first part of his threat. The next thing Giorgio Fermi would do is kill him.

Lanz rode slowly along the yellow wall up to the garden gate of Egon Blanc's villa. The yellow moving vans had gone and three new large ones were parked at the curb. Other movers were just carrying out the interior of the dining room, an extra-large-screen TV, beds, standing lamps, and kitchen appliances. Everything was done with great precision and without wasting any time.

Lanz remounted his bike and rode around the corner to his house.

He unlocked the door, briefly hesitated, since he thought it was possible that someone could have snuck into the house while he was gone and was waiting for him. But everything was quiet. He put the bike away in the foyer and listened once again. Then he quickly went into the living room, the kitchen, and his study before he stretched out on the bed. Time was like a living being, Mr. Ashby had told him, or words to that effect. It did with him whatever it wanted. Signor Blanc's eye room went through his head, and he had the impression that time had hypnotic powers. No one noticed how time controlled us, even though we continually encountered it because we didn't want to lose it. Just when we think we have triumphed over time, it pretends to stop, only to then tear itself away and charge off.

He stood up, untied the eye patch, got the pistol, and looked for another spot for the keys. He finally put them in the old porcelain soup tureen that he found in one of the kitchen cabinets and had never used. It belonged to the tableware from the house in St. Leonhard, and he had only brought it with him because it was part of the service. The blue flower pattern on the white porcelain had a calming effect. There still was such a thing as beauty, subtlety, the vessel stated.

He carefully closed the lid and remembered Alma's hands, especially her fingernails. In the beginning they had been so in love, and it was a mistake to move to the countryside, he thought. In the bathroom mirror he again noticed the red blotches around his eye were slowly beginning to turn blue. He decided that, from now on, he would keep the pistol in his windbreaker. He then called Julia's cellphone, but again heard only the ring tone. And she wasn't in the Hotel Hungaria. When he asked if she'd moved out, he got only a curt "No." He was so restless that he wasn't interested in reading, listening to music, or watching TV. He had to be patient, he told himself.

Lying on the bed, he closed his eyes and envisioned the face of the lawyer Capparoni as he hung from the ceiling. His last thought before falling asleep was that the whole thing was still far from over.

When he woke up, he briefly remembered dreaming about the furniture vans and the movers at Signor Blanc's house. "Crazy stuff," he said to himself. Outside it was nighttime. He put his phone in his pocket, put on the eye patch, pushed his bike out to the street, and carefully locked the front door. He then hurried off to Signor Blanc's villa to learn what was going on with the move.

Floodlights illuminated the garden, and the large globe from the planetarium was just being carried out, as Lanz deduced from the two semi-spherical shapes under green tarps that were then deposited in a moving van. Caecilia Sereno stood nearby and was closely following the operation.

"Why does everything have to happen so fast?" Lanz asked her.

"Only Signor Blanc knows," she answered with a smile. "The

microscopes and historical astrological instruments are already loaded, the computer is being disassembled . . . What happened to your eye?"

"Nothing," Lanz answered, and smiled.

He then noticed that the greenhouse had been dismantled and the plants had been carted off.

"Does that mean that Signor Blanc won't be coming back?"

Caecilia Sereno shrugged her shoulders and concentrated on the transport procedures, because in the meantime wooden containers of additional instruments from the planetarium were being loaded on a dolly.

"By the way, he's not in Damascus. At the airport he suddenly decided that everything should be sent to Spain, to a suburb of Madrid, Mejorada del Campo. That's where the former monk Martinez has been building his own cathedral for more than fifty years. He's around ninety years old and is still going strong . . . You can check on the Internet, under Justo Gallego Martinez. There are also films about him and his strange immense structure on YouTube."

"How big is it?" Lanz asked.

"It must be something special. For months Signor Blanc has been talking about nothing but the monk Martinez and his project. The church is supposed to be over fifty yards long, and the steel skeleton of the two towers, according to Signor Blanc, soars into the heavens."

"Will we see each other again?" Lanz asked, to his own amazement.

"Why not?" she responded, and immediately began giving instructions to the workers.

Back at home, Lanz again laid down on the bed. But he couldn't sleep because he kept trying without success to contact Julia. So he got back on his bike every two hours to see what the large number of workers had cleared out. The sun began to rise at 6 a.m., the lights on the property around Blanc's house were turned off, and, except for the garden and the falconry, everything was already on the way to the airport or already in Spain. Lanz was alternately amazed and shocked. It slowly dawned on him that he still hadn't comprehended what had happened.

The Chiosco Bahiano was closed and the Lungomare D'Annunzio deserted. There were only the sounds of the sea; indifferent, it continued to produce waves and rhythmically wash them ashore. The wall around the villa seemed horribly long to him, possibly due to his lack of sleep. At several locations he saw graffiti that seemed to be only signatures. He now realized that as a result of recent events he had become accustomed to repeatedly looking around, keeping the terrain on both sides of the street in sight. There was also no sign of life in the side street where his house was located.

He mechanically unlocked the front door and, after parking the bike in the foyer, immediately locked it again. Before he could get a yogurt out of the refrigerator and mix in some seedless dates as he usually did, the doorbell rang.

He wasn't especially eager to be attacked again, so he attached the security chain before he opened the door a crack.

It was Commissario Galli, he saw, but this time he was alone.

"Your eye! How did that happen?" he exclaimed.

Lanz ignored the question.

"Oh, the new road bike," Galli said after he had stepped inside and, without asking, had gone on ahead into the living room.

"What do you want?" Lanz protested. "You didn't tell me you were coming—"

"You'll be glad I came!" Galli replied, and sat down.

"What's that supposed to mean?"

"*You* tell me."

"I want to call a lawyer."

"Dr. Falchi? She was able to get Signora Ellis out. An amazing woman. But I'm the only one who can help you. You're in grave danger, Signor Lanz."

Lanz was silent. He suspected where Galli was going with all this, so he, too, sat down.

"Why didn't you tell me that you would have been attacked at the San Michele cemetery by a man, presumably Giorgio Fermi, one of Mennea's bodyguards in a dog mask, if Herr Vogel hadn't set his falcon on him?"

"Who told you that?" Lanz angrily snapped, and knew that it could only have been Richard Vogel himself.

"You act as if Herr Vogel is a snitch. He urged you to report the incident to the police because you are in danger. After all, you yourself were the one who gave Herr Vogel as a witness for the fact that you were at the San Michele cemetery. You've got to stop keeping things from me!"

"You yourself are trying to trick me and keep things from me."

"That's true to a certain extent, but it's part of my profession, unfortunately."

"As you probably know, I'm not under oath," Lanz said, and was completely dissatisfied with himself.

"I'll tell you what I know," Galli said, ignoring his objections. "You began an affair with Julia Ellis, and Mennea found out about it. He wanted to get you out of the way, but you were lucky enough to run into Herr Vogel with his falcon before Fermi could bump you off. Then Fermi tried to run you over with his car as you were riding home on your bike . . . You bought the new road bike and just acted as if the whole thing had nothing to do with you . . . I don't understand . . . Tell me why?"

"I wasn't able to see who really rear-ended me, and now I don't remember a thing."

"And who, other than Giorgio Fermi, gave you that black eye? He's a thug and presumably a killer! And now he's just waiting to kill you, because right this moment you've made contact with the police, with me!"

Lanz was silent, and since Galli said nothing, he turned around, gazed out the window, and tried to forget how much he hated the situation.

"He's going to kill you because you know too much. Julia Ellis could have told you things about his colleagues Fermi and Saltesi. I suspect that the two of them are now after Julia Ellis, and when they've gotten rid of Mennea's former lover, they'll be after you. Was it Fermi who first ran over you with his car and now attacked you? If it wasn't him and we arrest him, he'll have an alibi handy in no time at all!"

"I can only repeat that I don't remember," Lanz countered.

"How about that black eye? You also don't remember who gave that to you?"

"No, I do," Lanz replied after a pause and was silent.

"Who was it?" Galli pressed on.

"It was Giorgio Fermi," Lanz answered hesitantly. "I got three picture postcards in yesterday's mail. Not long after, the doorbell rang, and when I opened it, someone punched me in the eye."

"Are you sure it was Fermi?"

"He was wearing the dog mask."

"Does that mean it could also have been somebody else?"

"No . . . I recognized the way he moved."

"Tell me everything, from the beginning . . . I mean from the moment you were followed, to the attack in your home."

Lanz reported on his encounter with Fermi in the vaporetto, on the attempted attack at the cemetery, and, finally, on the successful attack at his home.

"He held the barrel of a pistol to my good eye and threatened to kill me if I go to the police. He left the postcards here," Lanz concluded his account.

"He could also deny everything, since you didn't see his face."

"I saw his face clearly in the vaporetto to San Michele and then recognized him again! He was wearing a backpack."

"A backpack?" Galli asked. "When he wasn't on duty guarding Mennea, Giorgio Fermi always wore a backpack. It can hold everything he might need—a knife, a dog mask, a pistol—"

Galli stood up and, after briefly hesitating and pausing to think, walked out without turning to face Lanz.

Lanz got up to lock the door behind him, but could hear that Galli was on his way back.

"I forgot to take the postcards . . ." he called out, before Lanz could lock the door.

Lanz went into the living room and was about to take the postcards to Galli, but the Commissario was standing right behind him: "Lock the door and stay at home . . . But, of course, you'll ignore my warning . . ."

Lanz handed Galli the three postcards, locked the door, as the Commissario had advised, and put the door chain back on. He then went to bed and fell asleep.

It was eleven o'clock when he got a phone call from Richard Vogel, asking if Lanz wanted to go along with him to the Jewish cemeteries on the Lido an hour from now. He had received a contract from the municipal government of Venice to frighten away the seagulls there as well; furthermore, Signor Blanc's deceased wife is buried in the New Jewish Cemetery—.

"Commissario Galli," Lanz interrupted, "has accused me of not notifying him of the attack in the San Michele cemetery—"

"You didn't go to the police?"

"No. You did it for me."

"I was sure you'd take my advice, and even if I'd known you weren't going to do it, I still would have informed the Commissario."

"It's nobody's business but mine, right?" Lanz angrily interrupted.

"You still don't understand what you've gotten yourself into—presumably you want to protect Signora Ellis."

Lanz considered hanging up, but then he remembered that he owed Vogel a great deal.

"I made a mistake," he gave in.

"And Commissario Galli advised you not to leave the house?"

"More or less."

"I'll straighten that out for you."

"What do you mean?"

"I'll call him and ask if you can accompany me—I mean, if you even want to go."

"Of course . . . Where is Signor Blanc?" he asked, hoping to change the subject.

"Signor Blanc, with all his treasures, has moved to Mejorada del

Campo. You're familiar with the story of Justo Gallego Martinez, the monk who is building a cathedral out of junk? Signor Blanc wants to help him."

"Why didn't you go with him?"

"I have to take the falcons to Damascus. All the other animals are already on their way there"

"And in Spain—I mean, who's looking after him in Mejorada del Campo?"

"Sanchez is there. A very good falconer . . ."

"But . . .?"

"I'm going to call Commissario Galli now."

The falcon, seemingly asleep in its leather hood, was sitting on its iron frame in the VW Bus, this time in the rear compartment.

"What happened to your eye?" Richard Vogel greeted him with alarm.

"Nothing. It's nothing."

"Who did that to you?"

"Fermi," Lanz said, and told him about the incident.

"Have you been to see a doctor?"

"No."

"But you have to. Do you want me to take you?"

"No." I've also got my pistol in my pocket, Lanz thought.

"Nothing can happen to us as long as we've got the falcon," Vogel said from behind the steering wheel.

"But the falcon . . . Fermi's got a gun."

"He won't be at the cemetery. The police are after him. The Commissario filled me in. He thinks they'll nab him—"

Although Lanz doubted it, he was relieved. "What about Caecilia Sereno? I mean, she's not going to Madrid, is she?" he changed the topic.

"She likes you," Vogel laughed. "Why don't you ask her what she's going to do," he blurted out, laughing.

As they drove up the Lungomare D'Annunzio, Lanz recalled his bike tour a year ago when he accidentally discovered the Nuovo

Cimitero Israelitico, the New Jewish Cemetery. First he had ridden past a brick wall and then come to a barred gate with buildings to the left and right, the entrance straight ahead. A sign announced that taking pictures was forbidden and no one could enter before 3:30 pm. He had kept going alongside the brick wall until he had come to another rusted gate that allowed him to see into the overgrown Cimitero. The crooked gravestones were over-grown with grass and dead leaves, among them a stone pillar like a broken tree stump. There was no traffic on the road, and he had thought to himself: a ghetto here, too—this time for the deceased.

When he again saw the brick walls, it occurred to him that not only the city's cemeteries were surrounded by walls, but also the former shipyard, the Arsenal, as well as the San Servolo insane asylum or the glass factories in Murano. Even Signor Blanc's villa was hidden from view by a yellow plaster wall.

"What will happen to Signor Blanc's villa?" Lanz asked.

"I don't know. He hasn't arrived in Madrid yet and hasn't called in . . . Some think he's lying in a hospital somewhere . . ."

"Is he sick?"

"He's very old . . . and, of course, he's . . . let's just say, a bit peculiar. You can't always understand what he's doing or thinking . . . People insist he's . . . well . . . peculiar."

"And you, what do you think about him?"

"He's my boss."

"Is he crazy?"

Richard Vogel was silent, decelerated, and asked in passing: "Beg pardon?" as if he didn't quite hear the question.

This time Lanz refrained from repeating the question. They were still going at a snail's pace alongside the brick wall and stopped at a workshop or a small factory. On the other side of the road, isolated by a wire mesh fence, he saw a decrepit hut with piles of crates. Parts of the fence were damaged and rusted, behind it an unfinished garage; the piled crates, he saw, were actually rabbit hutches—apparently unoccupied. Woven into the fence and nailed to the partly dilapidated wooden crates were strange children's toys. The small colorful and cheap stuffed animals and dolls had been exposed to the elements and looked weather-beaten. Lanz took a closer look at the toys in the wire fence: yellow painted suns and moons, teddy bears, clowns, cloth bunny rabbits, doll's faces, Jiminy Cricket from the Walt Disney movie *Pinocchio*, and many others things. Lanz had never seen toys in such condition. And the way they were arranged and hung seemed odd to him.

"These toys look as if dogs had played with them and chewed them up," Lanz said.

"This is where a migrant African girl and her father were hiding. During a raid they fled to the beach by the Ospedale al Mare and the father lost sight of the child. They found her on the beach two days later . . . drowned . . . No one knows how that could have happened—"

Lanz could see the dead child before him as he had stumbled upon her on one of his beach walks. He could still see the scene as if it had just happened. But he kept it to himself.

The car sped up again until it pulled over by the two buildings at the entrance that Lanz remembered. All along the wall the cemetery seemed like a jungle, overgrown with tall trees. For that reason he was especially curious of what to expect. At the Gothic portal gate with its iron bars stood a man in a faded blue-green patterned shirt hanging out over his jeans, with sleeves rolled up and its collar open, topped by a green-and-blue knit kippah. An unusual pretty silver snake chain hung around his neck. He smelled of alcohol, even from a distance.

Richard Vogel apparently knew him.

"Earlier the songbirds built their nests here, today there are only seagulls," the man greeted the falconer.

Vogel briefly introduced Lanz, but the cemetery caretaker took little notice of him. White seed fluff covered the fields and branches like snow. It was the same "snow" that Lanz had seen at the Ospedale al Mare. He bent down and grabbed a handful; it felt like cotton or a fluffy baby chick warmed by the sun.

"From the pine trees," Vogel explained.

"You can't take pictures," the cemetery caretaker said.

Lanz nodded, and the young man with the silver snake chain also gave Richard Vogel a kippah and then walked on without turning around.

"What's his name?" Lanz asked, indicating the falcon.

"Alien," Vogel replied. "Alpha in Italian, Ali in Damascus."

"Doesn't that confuse him?"

"No—The main thing is, he responds to *me*."

Lanz looked around, again briefly studied the white fluff on the paths and graves, and then said: "Like in winter."

Richard Vogel was too preoccupied with the falcon to respond, so Lanz went on a few feet to the first graves where he could look out over the entire next field with its new burial grounds. At this point there were no tall trees over there, no cypress, no acacia, no laurel bushes or box trees, no pine forest—just the field and the seed snow in the sunshine.

As he approached the first graves, he noticed they had small gravestones. As he came closer, he realized that they were for children.

Lizards darted out of their lairs, while scattered poppies gleamed in the midday light. He bent over and studied oval photographs that were inserted into the gravestones—in spite of the Jewish prohibition of photos. They had been scanned in black-and-white, at times so poorly that you could hardly recognize what was depicted: a boy in a sailor suit was floating up in the air in some type of flying saucer, a clearly distinguishable little girl was holding sheet music in one hand, while another photograph showed a child with long braids laughing at the viewer. The photo looked as if it had been scuffed, the white pixels and scratches gave the impression that the picture had been taken during a snowfall or a snowstorm. Many smaller gravestones had no images or names, just a date—which made him think of miscarriages. Once again Lanz was reminded of the dead black child on the sandy beach and, at the same time, the fence with the children's toys and the rabbit hutches behind that. There were numerous plaques without names, he realized.

Meanwhile the cemetery caretaker had ridden up on his bike and was observing him suspiciously, or so it seemed to Lanz.

Lanz smiled at him. "Got a lot to do?" he asked.

"I just make sure nobody's taking pictures," the caretaker responded. "Say, what happened to your eye?"

"Nothing," Lanz said.

The cemetery caretaker raised his eyebrows and shrugged his shoulders, but you could tell that he was irritated.

Embarrassed, Lanz asked about the organization of the cemetery and learned that the section toward the Lagoon—that is, the part facing Venice—was reserved for *Sephardim*, Jews who, as the caretaker explained, had originally settled on the Iberian Peninsula in Spain and Portugal, and after their expulsion during the Inquisition had fled to the Ottoman Empire or to France and Italy, but also escaped to Amsterdam or Hamburg. "Sephardic Jews," the caretaker continued, bending over the handlebars of his bike, "speak Ladino or Spaniol, a mixture of Spanish, Hebrew and Aramaic."

The other group, the *Ashkenazi* Jews, as Lanz then learned, spoke Yiddish or Yiddish-Daitsch and lived for the most part in Europe, at first primarily in Germany. "The Ashkenazi are buried, together with the Sephardim in the middle section of the cemetery. There is also a columbarium wall that a Venetian rabbi authorized in the 1920s. In general, this type of burial is forbidden . . . like the photographs on the gravestones . . . Off to the left"—the caretaker stretched out his arm and turned his head to face that same direction—"the lapidarium . . . where we preserve the old grave-stones. And in the third part, facing the Lido, Ashkenazi and Sephardim are buried side by side." The caretaker stopped talking, nodded, got back on his bike, and waved for Lanz to follow him as he rode off.

A few feet farther on, Lanz ran into Richard Vogel with the black kippah on his head and Alien on his left hand that was once again protected by a leather glove from his elbow to his fist. The falconer encouraged him to follow the caretaker since Vogel still needed some time to prepare his bird of prey for flight. The beautiful animal still had the leather hood on its head and looked like a caricature of its master in his kippah. Meanwhile a colony of seagulls, high above, had begun to squawk.

Just then Lanz realized that the cemetery caretaker was already waiting for him at the lapidarium.

An African worker with a broom was sweeping up large amounts of white pine seeds from the path to the exit, then absent-mindedly put the large shovel in a plastic trash can. Lanz had barely reached the caretaker when the man suddenly called out instructions to the African.

"He forgets everything . . ." the caretaker said, turning to Lanz. "His daughter was found on the beach, drowned."

Lanz nodded

"The man lives across from the cemetery in that unplastered garage behind the wire fence—illegally, that means without authorization. Did you see the toys in the wire fence and on the rabbit hutches? The dolls promised him that he'll see his daughter again."

As they entered the lapidarium, the man pulled a second kippah out of his pants pocket, handed it to Lanz, and waited for him to put it on before he began to explain the gravestones: an open book or a bunch of grapes stood for scholars; other tombstones, depicting two hands with fingers and thumbs paired together and almost touching, signified "praying hands" and were the sign for the Biblical name Cohen that indicated relatives of people with spiritual functions who would inevitably be priests; a pitcher and bowl on the gravestones of Levi stood for priests' helpers, for example in the washing of hands; the Star of David symbolized time, the six points representing the six working days and the center signifying the Sabbath . . .

Lanz felt as if the cemetery caretaker were explaining a book of spells. Furthermore, the names of the deceased were written on the tombstones in Hebrew. Some names were rectangular with half-rounded endings that represented the firmament, others had points that corresponded to a rooftop, and still others had simple horizontal forms with level closure. Then—pushing his bike along— the caretaker led Lanz into the pine forest where the white landscape gave the impression of a pond frozen in wintertime. He then stopped at a gravestone decorated with a chiseled pattern of lilies that belonged to "Signora Blanc." Instead of flowers, countless pebbles lay on the grave or on the ground in front of it. The caretaker pointed out a chiseled ladder on the back of the headstone, a reference to Jacob's dream in the Bible, as Lanz was aware. Up above, the seagulls screeched, belligerent but also alarmed, which meant that the falcon was already circling. Lanz stepped out from between two trees and immediately identified Alien up in the sky and the swarming flock of gulls in the distance like tiny ants.

He then became lightheaded. He lowered his head and focused on the large old rambling roots of a tree. The cemetery caretaker had disappeared with his bicycle. Lanz smelled laurel and juniper; little juniper berries were lying on the white pine seeds. A light breeze was blowing, and the shadows from the branches flitted over the graves. Everywhere Lanz looked, he saw faded snail shells, mostly on the backs of the gravestones. Fallen rose petals were lying on one marble grave that was adorned with a seven-armed menorah of black iron and a Hebrew inscription revealing who had been buried here.

Lanz now decided to look for Richard Vogel. It shouldn't be hard, he thought, because he and the falconer had been the only visitors thus far. But he saw only gardeners. The African father of the drowned girl was shoveling up pine seeds, the cemetery caretaker, standing beside him, briefly put his hand on the worker's shoulder before he spoke with him. Another gardener was coming down the path from the columbarium at the end of the cypress avenue, riding a motorized green three-wheeled bike with a cargo bed. As he approached, Lanz asked if he had seen the falconer. The man stopped, pointed back to the last section behind the entrance, and then rode on, as if half-asleep. As he walked, Lanz noticed that some gravestones were overgrown with orange, grey, and brown blotches, while a blackbird hopped over the pine seeds and sparse grass. With a deep droning noise a prop-driven military airplane from the Venice-Lido airport flew overhead. Meanwhile the seagulls and Alien had disappeared.

At first Lanz wanted to wait until he saw them back up in the sky, but then went to the columbarium where small stone coffins stood in a row, a flame representing final closure. The names and dates of birth and death of the cremated were indicated in Hebrew and Latin script. He didn't enter the columbarium, but took a shortcut back to the wide main road. Once again a military airplane flew just over the treetops, then over his head with a roar, and he hurried to reach the old overgrown part of the cemetery. The field wasn't mowed here, and there were few pine seeds—aside from the tiny cloud formations comprised of individual seeds that leisurely floated in the air or hung in the grass. Some gravestones had completely fallen over, others were crooked, still others were overgrown with shrubbery. The path was gently rolling, first leading uphill, then gradually back downhill. It looked as if this part of the cemetery had been forgotten, or as if no relatives had survived to care for the graves.

He finally found Richard Vogel standing in a clearing between acacia trees, gazing up at the sky. Lanz, too, stopped and looked up. The gulls seemed to have disappeared, but when he looked more closely he saw them far above, as small as a dancing cloud of mosquitoes in September. Then he tried to locate the falcon Alien, but couldn't. It wasn't until he spoke with Vogel that he learned the falconer could locate the bird at this point by radio waves. They sat down on a toppled gravestone and all at once Vogel began to speak: "Go to Herr Blanc's villa, hide out, and start your translation." And when Lanz didn't respond, Vogel asked him: "Do you own a weapon?"

That caught Lanz by surprise and he simply shook his head.

"If you don't have one, I'll give you my Glock that's in the glove compartment of my car. The best thing would be to conceal it."

"And why would I do that?"

"You have to assume that the police are going to search your house. It'd be best if you stash the gun in the connecting passage to the villa or take it along to your reserved room. Don't be startled when you unlock the door, we've stored a sculpture of an African boy in a turban and silk costume in your room since there wasn't any

155

room in the van."

"What about Julia? Do you know how she's doing?"

"The police are looking for her. The receptionist in the Hotel Hungaria hasn't seen her since yesterday."

They paused, and a bird's feather floated down and landed on the ground in front of them. It was orange-brown and had black horizontal stripes . . .

"Alien," Richard Vogel said, leaped up and scanned the sky. He then suddenly pointed to a black entity that was falling from the sky at tremendous speed like some heavy object.

As the thing got closer, Lanz realized that the falcon, in a power dive, was clutching a seagull in its talons, and as it landed on the ground, fluttering its wings—still gripping the white gull—Alien began to tear into it. Soon white feathers covered the grass. Lanz, who had meanwhile pocketed the falcon's feathers, also picked up a white one and stuck it in his windbreaker . . . This time, he thought, the falcon made a more aggressive impression—especially its gaze, when it looked up from its feasting, made Lanz sense a threat.

"We'll leave him in peace," Vogel said, and sat back on the toppled gravestone, keeping his eye on Alien the entire time.

"Are you Signor Blanc's confidant?" Lanz asked.

Richard Vogel didn't respond, still staring with fascination at the feasting falcon.

"You're a gull," he then said in jest.

"And what about you?" Lanz replied, after he had briefly pondered an answer.

"I'm Signor Blanc's falcon," he laughed. "No, I'm his adopted son. His marriage didn't produce any children."

"And Julia Ellis?"

"She would take photographs for him now and then."

"Really?" Lanz asked. "Of what?"

"Psychiatric wards, prisons, police stations, brothels . . ."

"Why?"

"Herr Blanc wants to know about everything. He would read something in the newspaper, for example, about animal rendering, an auto graveyard, a slaughterhouse, and he would have someone ask Signora Ellis if she could photograph it for him. If so, then he'd buy the pictures from her and send them on to his archives in California."

Lanz shook his head. After a pause he asked: "What do you think—did Julia kill her friend Mennea?"

The falconer considered the question.

"Do you think she could do it?" Lanz repeated.

"Yes, but that doesn't mean anything. Anyone can kill, it just has to make sense."

Before Richard Vogel left, he instructed Lanz one more time: "Hide out in the guest room. Start the Shakespeare translation and wait for things to cool down. The refrigerator is stocked—help yourself or get in touch with Min Chang. When he's there, he'll cook for you." He bent down over the passenger seat, took the pistol out of the glove compartment, and held it out to Lanz. "Take it," he said abruptly, slammed the door shut, and drove off.

Lanz went into his house with the pistol drawn. He checked all the rooms and when he didn't find anything suspicious, he traded the pistol in his hand for the one in his windbreaker. A friend who had worked for the police had told him how to use the Glock. Since he was too tired to hide it in the basement or in the passageway, he put it down beside the bed. He closed his eyes.

Startled, he suddenly realized that he was falling from the sky, he just didn't know how and why. He opened his eyes and saw that his arms were wings. They supported him, and he looked down at the Jewish Cimitero Nuovo. Where was Richard Vogel? Above him, seagulls were fleeing, shrieking. Amazed, he learned that his eyes were those of a raptor. Below him, the graves and the trees, tiny people going about their work, and the African whose dead daughter had been found on the beach. The man was just crossing the street to his dwelling. Lanz circled above him until the African had disappeared in the garage, and Lanz then landed by the entrance. There was no door to the garage, just a wall constructed from a plywood panel and slats. He hopped over to it, and since he didn't hear a sound, went into the open garage where he saw the African sitting on a crate at a dirty table, sobbing. Lanz wanted to say something, but he sensed that he could only make sounds, and the man's pitiful condition made him angry. He promptly found himself back in the sky above the Jewish cemetery and heard the radio wave signal. But where was Richard Vogel? Again the signal beeped in his head. With a jolt he came to, and understood that it was the smartphone in his pocket that was making the noise. It was dark inside the house and outside. He immediately recognized Julia's number. As he made the connection, he heard her scream: "Help me—"

Lanz was instantly awake. He grabbed his shoes and yanked the windbreaker out of the wardrobe before he raced out into the street. He realized that he had left the Glock lying beside his bed, dashed back and got the gun, ran back out and locked the front door.

Just then a red cargo delivery van came down the street, heading toward the beach. It braked in panic and started to skid. But Lanz had already run out into the middle of the street. Out of the corner of his eye he saw advertising for a laundry service on the Nissan, alertly yanked open the door and jumped into the vehicle.

"They're shooting at me!" Julia screamed in desperation and hit the gas. When they passed the Chiosco Bahiano, he glanced in the side mirror and saw two headlights closing fast.

"Head for the police station in the Via Dardanelli," he shouted.

"I don't want to go to the police," she almost screamed.

"Neither do I."

Just then several shots hit the delivery van with a loud bang. They were now on the Lungomare D'Annunzio. There was little traffic and Lanz reached for the Glock in the pocket of his windbreaker while Julia turned off onto the main road, the Gran Viale Elisabetta Santa Maria, that was well-lit and swarming with pedestrians and other vehicles. That had been a good decision, Lanz thought, but still their pursuers in the black Chrysler could easily keep up.

"We're going too fast," Julia said. "What if the police pull us over!"

She sped up, and the red delivery van raced up the Viale to the

Elisabetta vaporetto station, doubled back with squealing tires, and retraced their route. Meanwhile Lanz kept the Glock in his right hand, hidden between his knees. Again and again the van braked sharply to avoid hitting cars coming from the side streets or running over pedestrians who were crossing the road. The van jerked and jolted and seemed to leap, as if the engine were about to explode. Behind the Piazzale Bucintoro Lanz shouted: "Left!" and Julia abruptly turned into a narrow side street that was bordered on both sides by hedges, followed closely by the black Chrysler. In the side mirror Lanz saw that the car was so close that he was afraid that any second now it would force them off the road.

Following Lanz's shout, Julia braked hard at the police station and came to an abrupt stop beside the building's front garden.

They now saw that the Chrysler had also stopped. Slowly and almost silently it pulled back, stopped again at the entrance to the Via Dardanelli, and turned off its headlights.

"They're waiting," Julia said, still on edge.

"So are we," Lanz answered, and tried to act calm.

Nothing happened for a time, and Julia blurted out: "How much longer?"

Lanz cautiously opened the door, turned to face the Chrysler, and approached the police station. The gate was, of course, closed, so he had to ring the bell.

Just then Julia called to him from her open window: "They're leaving!" and he waited until she signaled that their pursuers were out of sight.

"Where did you get the van?" Lanz asked, as he got back inside.

"It was parked in front of the Hotel Hungaria. The driver left the keys in it."

"Put it in reverse, back to the Via Dardanelli," Lanz interrupted. "If they're trying to ambush us, I'll get help at the police station."

"I don't want you to!"

"Do you want me to drive?"

"No."

She put it in reverse and stepped on the gas. The van shot back to the entrance, as if she wanted to ram the Chrysler if it was still waiting for them in the darkness, and she didn't hit the brakes until they reached the corner.

They could see streetlights on the Via Dardanelli just up ahead.

Julia made sure there were no suspicious vehicles around before she turned left.

Recently, under the influence of drugs, Lanz had ridden his bicycle on this stretch to Malamocco, but tonight he could make out few of the boat docks or small marinas and harbors along the shore where they could hide out if necessary.

Right after Malamocco the Chrysler reappeared. Lanz had just seen a small bay with a long building when, between numerous moored and covered motorboats, he noticed a taxi just coming over a wooden bridge. At the same moment he pointed this out to Julia, he discovered the Chrysler by the side of the road, its headlights off, apparently without the two men who had been behind the windshield during the chase. Both of the front doors were open, and Lanz imagined that he had seen a leg in jeans on one side and an outstretched arm in a dark T-shirt sticking out the other side of the vehicle.

"What was that?" Julia called out, as she sped up.

"The Chrysler. Something happened to the men while we were at the police station—"

"It looks like they're dead!" she interrupted. "A taxi was coming toward us. Now it's behind us!"

Lanz glanced in the rearview mirror and spotted the car, an Audi with a TAXI sign on the roof.

Julia turned off onto the Strada Alberoni—a straight boulevard along the Lagoon-side of the Lido—and, as they raced past, he saw fishing nets and pilings where the gulls perched during the day, also maple trees and pines. A weakly-lit freighter momentarily appeared in their headlights like a ghost ship, and then the sign for Alberoni. The taxi closed in and tried to pass them, but Julia ruthlessly forced it off the road near a brick wall that bordered the large golf course and the Audi almost went into the canal—jetties and an attractive boathouse rushed by, the wooden bridge to a brick entrance gate, tall shrubs, motorboats with blue tarps lashed to pilings, and algae blooms on the water. The taxi was no longer behind them, and when they came to the bus barn and the fenced areas with gutted ships and replacement parts, Julia steered the van into a gap in the fencing, through a half-open gate behind an oil tank, then parked in front of a mountain of yellow buoys. She turned off the headlights, and both of them got out of the van amid junk, stacked wooden posts, a large broken scale with its big round pointer, scattered corrugated-iron shacks, and stacks of plastic crates. The area was bursting at the seams, as Lanz knew from his excursions. The new lighthouse towered behind it in the night sky, its light sending signals out to sea. Beyond that they could make out the old smaller lighthouse that had been decommissioned.

In the darkness, the Audi with the TAXI sign cautiously edged forward and stopped behind one of the orange buses parked by the fence. Lanz turned, glanced at the shoreline that briefly shone in the lighthouse light, and—the pistol in his right hand—with his left gave Julia a sign to follow him. Crouching down, they hurried over to one of the workboats with its crane and other mechanical equipment. It was hard to move about in the darkness. When they had almost reached the boat and turned around, they realized they were being followed by four men with flashlights who were searching the mounds of junk. Panicked, and acting almost spontaneously, Lanz raised his arm, aimed at one of the flashlights and fired. He shot two more times before dropping down behind several cable drums, just as shots went over his head. He could hear wood splintering. Once again he recalled that he had wanted to commit suicide just a few days ago, and it seemed simply absurd.

He concentrated on the anonymous pursuers and Julia who was crouching beside him. He leaped up again and fired at the flashlights—one disappeared from sight and he thought he heard someone cry out. So he shot some more until there were no more lights. Now, in the darkness, anything was possible. The men could turn off their flashlights, sneak up, and suddenly be behind them.

Or they could just charge, overwhelm Lanz and Julia, and execute them. He thought for a moment and suggested to Julia that they pull back to the dock. They were disappointed when they saw that the workboat anchored there had a long gangway, so Julia pointed to a wrecked white ship that had been beached and was full of scrap iron. Everything was quiet when they got to the ship and snuck into the wheelhouse. From this vantage point he could better overlook the junkyard and see if there were any moving lights. In fact he did see one, shifting back and forth in erratic movements, and without hesitation he fired at it. Their pursuers immediately shot back from out of the darkness, the bullets pinging against the side of the ship, shattering the wheelhouse windows, and forcing him to take cover in a corner of the bow. He saw that Julia was already there, crouching down and holding her ears. Then, all of a sudden, there were no more sounds. After a bit he cautiously raised his head. He glanced out at the piles of junk, but didn't see any lights.

Nevertheless Lanz went back into hiding before he checked the area again. Just then the taxi, hidden behind parked buses, went back out to the road, turned abruptly, and, its engine roaring, disappeared into the night. For a fraction of a second he thought about the prophet Jonah and the whale, his favorite story from the Bible. He climbed out of the shipwreck as if from the cockpit of a downed airplane and sought cover behind another pile of large buoys. From there he called out Julia's name and was amazed that she was beside him so quickly and silently. For the first time he was afraid. It was the uncertainty that came with every development, every noise, and every movement. It occurred to him that as he was hurrying off, he had left his smartphone by the bed, so he asked Julia to let him use the light on her phone. She concealed the phone as she activated it, handed it to him, and when nothing happened, he gradually stood up, shone the light on the ground and cautiously made his way back to the van, making sure that Julia was following him.

He thought he was safe, but the light suddenly revealed a man's body on the ground. He reflexively bent down and saw the blood-covered face of a man with glasses hanging from one ear over his nose and mouth, a bullet hole in his forehead. His glazed grey eyes were squinting into oblivion. Lanz noticed that the man was lying behind a rusty bicycle frame, a broken ship's propeller, and an oil-smeared diesel engine. The dead man's mouth was partly open. Lanz knew that he had shot the stranger, but it hadn't registered yet. He felt as if someone else had killed the man. He even tried to convince himself of that thought, but it didn't work. He felt neither pity nor guilt nor satisfaction nor hate.

"He would have done the same to us if you hadn't gotten him first," Julia said.

Lanz wasn't listening. His thoughts were all concentrated on the question of whether everything wasn't simply a consequence of having shot himself under the elderberry bush in Torcello—the demise of his energy, delusions, dreams, his memories and his fears. He knew it wasn't a dream, everything was too logical for that, he told himself without truly believing it.

He searched the dead man, reached into the breast pocket of his jacket, then into his pants pockets as well. Finally he checked the man's wrists, but the stranger had no ID, no money, no wristwatch. He was a dead nobody, Lanz thought.

They hurried over to the van.

"We can't drive far," Julia said. "We've got bullet holes in the loading doors."

Lanz had no idea what he would do next, but he didn't want to admit it.

"We can't leave any traces in the van, not even on the door handles, when we ditch it," he said, ignoring her earlier remark.

"It's a laundry truck, there's enough laundry in the back."

He got behind the wheel and drove off in the direction of the beach, but since the road at the lighthouse was closed, he turned around and chose the route they had taken earlier in the chase.

Julia kept looking around until Lanz took the fork that turned into the Lungomare Marconi on the other side.

"We can't go back!" she said, breaking the silence.

"I know," Lanz answered, still not knowing where they could

hide out.

"Not to your house or to the police," she insisted.

When he didn't respond, she added: "We'll leave the van somewhere . . . We'll get a hotel room. We can still go back to Venice on the vaporetto tomorrow, but it's just too dangerous tonight."

He didn't say anything, because he didn't agree with her. It wasn't until they turned off to the canals behind the Hotel Excelsior that he remembered his outboard motorboat that was on the bank of a canal not far away. They didn't detect any suspicious vehicles following them, no taxis, no police cars, so he pulled over in a poorly-lit side street.

"We're getting out, that's my boat over there," he said decisively.

She didn't ask questions, opened the sliding side door to the cargo area of the laundry van, pulled out a clean towel, and wiped down the handles, the steering wheel and dashboard, while Lanz pointed out directions to his boat. He didn't want to call attention to himself so he didn't run, just walked quickly. When he got to the boat, he untied the protective tarp, tossed it into the boat, and waited until Julia came aboard.

"We have to throw your smartphone away if you don't want to be traced," he reminded her.

She didn't say anything.

As he navigated down the canal that was lit by the windows of some neighboring houses, he finally had concocted a plan. Julia gazed silently through the windshield at the water.

"When I bought the house on the Lido, without knowing it I purchased a fisherman's shack on pilings off Pellestrina that belongs to the property. One time I spent two weeks there, working on a translation. It's not very comfortable. The toilet is a board over a bucket, you have to wash up in the ocean . . ."

". . . or not at all," she interrupted, and burst out laughing.

"We don't have any electricity, just the light from your smartphone, if you don't throw it in the ocean. But at least we'll be safe there."

He turned on the headlight, steered back to Alberoni, keeping the shoreline in sight while heading for the island of Pellestrina that, he thought, might be an unwelcome sight for Julia as a reminder of Mennea's death.

"And where is this shack located?"

"On the Lagoon-side of Pellestrina. Fishermen used to store their equipment there, and the previous owner used the shack to unwind."

She had closed her eyes and didn't answer.

"Nobody'll see us. Only a few people know about my boat . . . Tomorrow I'll pick up everything we need," he added.

Then, without any transition, he thought of Shakespeare—that he would be allowed to translate all the bard's works, that he was set for the next twenty years, and that he and Julia were together. While cold saltwater sprayed his face and the motor impartially did its job, he felt something resembling happiness in the midst of all the chaos of his life. More and more he was convinced that he had only imagined everything that had occurred.

He steered close to the shoreline, but in the darkness couldn't locate the fishing shack right away. At first he rode on past two other shacks that closely resembled his own. Only when he got closer did he realize that they weren't the right one. Julia dozed off or slept, and not even the restless rocking, the gentle rising and falling of the boat due to waves, or the cold water spray seemed to disturb her.

The shack wasn't far from shore. A long tall pier connected the port to land. But he could also tie the boat to one of the pilings and reach the front door by using a primitive wooden stairway. Lanz decided on the second option and woke Julia by hugging her and kissing her cheek. She woke with a start and impulsively resisted, but when she realized it was Lanz, she hugged him back. Everything went as planned, the key to the fishing shack was on the key chain that he always carried with him.

There was just one window onto the sea. In the dark interior he used Julia's smartphone to locate a flashlight and a petroleum lamp that he had purposefully left there on his last visit. They also found a ream of typewriter paper and a kitchen knife in a small carpentry chest, two beer glasses, an old bathrobe and two towels, as well as a bottle opener. He had always gotten his meals from a nearby pizzeria or a small store and used paper plates and plastic utensils that he then tossed in a trash bag near the door. When he left, he would take the bag, along with the yoghurt cups and empty wine and mineral water bottles, and place them in the containers behind the small store. There were also two air mattresses. The remaining furnishings consisted of a small table, a chair, and hooks on the wall and on the inside of the door to hang articles of clothing. Since the shack was simply constructed and had a tin roof that wasn't a tight fit to the walls, the place smelled of the sea, as if you were camping out on top of the water. When he would look out the lone window, he used to see only clouds and water and larger ships coming from Venice. He opened the skylight, got blankets from the carpentry chest, and began to pump up the air mattresses.

Meanwhile Julia sat by the window and looked out into the darkness.

"We would have been safer in a hotel," she said.

"You'd have had to show your identification. I don't have any ID with me."

"And no smartphone."

"Do you want to toss yours into the ocean?"

"No. It belongs to my lawyer, Amanda Falchi. She has several of them."

"And where is yours?"

"In my room at the Hotel Hungaria."

"Very clever."

When he had pumped up the first air mattress, he shook out the blankets at the door, then covered Julia and saw that she was already asleep. As he stroked her hair, he realized that he loved her.

Next morning Julia crawled under his blanket and kissed him. When she rolled onto her side to go back to sleep, he took off her panties and entered her. He could tell that she was awake and responding.

He liked being on his side since his face was on her breasts, his hands were free and he could fondle her. She moaned softly. A gull fluttered past and gave a call, and the rhythmic slapping sound of the waves beneath the fishing shack proclaimed that time would no longer proceed in its usual fashion.

At some point Lanz went to the small store.

"How are we going to get out of here?" Julia asked, just awaking as he returned with two full plastic bags.

"We'll see."

"Why not now?"

He unpacked the things he had bought and put white bread, butter, jam, two cups of yoghurt and a large plastic bottle of cola beside a bottle of wine and one of mineral water on the table. He then put the shopping bags, two toothbrushes, bodywash, soap, nail clippers and some deodorant in the chest with the towels and the bathrobe.

"I'm not hungry," she said stubbornly.

He took a drink of the cola, spread butter and orange jam on a slice of white bread, handed it down to her on the air mattress, but she waved it off.

"Why are we here and not in some hotel?"

He kept eating and, after taking another drink from the cola bottle, asked her: "When do you want to leave?"

"Not just now."

"This evening?"

"As soon as it gets dark . . ."

She turned on her smartphone and selected the app with news from the *Gazzettino*.

Her expression changed. She got up and insisted: "Here! Read this!"

"Murder in Mobster Milieu," he read and, benath the headline, found several black-and-white photos of the Chrysler with open doors, the Audi taxi, the junkyard near the Alberoni lighthouses, and headshots of Mennea and Dr. Capparoni.

The two dead men in the Chrysler that had chased them were

Mennea's bodyguards, Manuel Saltesi and Giorgio Fermi. The police had "recovered" Fermi's backpack and a dog mask, according to the article. The identity of the third dead man, from the junkyard, could not be determined, Lanz read. A seriously injured man with a stomach wound was found in the passenger seat of the abandoned stolen taxi. The police hadn't been able to interrogate him, it said. The police were working to identify the criminal organizations responsible, but to this point the only thing known for sure was that someone was out to eliminate Mennea's gang because they had been "interfering" in the gaming and casino business. The suicide of Dr. Capparoni, the lawyer, also supported this conclusion. Other than that, the police are out in force all throughout the Lido, the purpose being to "minimize" the unavoidable harm to tourism.

Julia turned off her smartphone and asked if he could recharge it somewhere.

"Sure, in the pizzeria."

"It'd be better if you found someplace else where they don't know you."

The seagulls that had recently had the roof of the fishing shack and the pier all to themselves now had to get used to the fact that they were no longer alone. Each time he opened the window or the door, they flew up, squawking, and acted aggressively, flying just past his head and scolding him from up above. But Lanz found that these were just preliminaries to an attack, just preliminaries to an insurgency, and not a real attack. He recalled the last time he was sitting outside the Caffè Florian on St. Mark's Square—a swarm of tourists were eating sandwiches when, suddenly, in a lightning attack, two seagulls snatched the morsels from their fingers and flew off, surrounded by other gulls that were trying to snatch away the plunder.

He had watched it with schadenfreude, because tourists with their selfie-sticks had taken over the Square, and the gulls had shown what they were capable of when someone tried to contest their territory. The thought was also an explanation for what had happened and the maelstrom that had drawn him in: Mennea, as head of a gang of smugglers that hauled refugees to Italy, and Borsakowski who had also gotten into the business and provided competition. After Borsakowski was murdered on Torcello (which he had witnessed), Borsakowski's men were now battling Mennea's thugs for dominance.

All that aside, the roof of the fishing shack and the long pier were full of bird droppings.

Lanz now felt he knew the basic facts of the matter and thought it was important to share them with Julia.

She was on her smartphone, reading articles from other news outlets about the events of the previous night.

"I'm going into Venice," she said, "to see Amanda Falchi . . . You know, the lawyer that Signor Blanc hired. I spoke with her earlier . . . She said I'm free and clear. Only Fermi and Saltesi could have testified against me, and they're both dead."

"But at least two of Borsakowski's men are still out there, the ones who chased us in the taxi," Lanz countered. "You're still in danger."

"They can also find us out here in the fishing shack . . . I'm safer in the city."

"Where are you hoping to hide?"

"In some hotel. The lawyer's arranging it for me as we speak. She also thinks it's better if I come to her place."

"When do you plan to leave?"

"Come over here," she said affectionately.

He undressed and laid down beside her. He knew that the tides changed every six hours, and the sound of the waves and the sound of seagulls and of gurgling water alternated to interrupt the silence. These perceptions disrupted the timelessness of which he was now a tiny atom that gradually dissolved in her.

At some point during the night he glanced at the clock. He noticed it was 2:46 a.m. And also that he was alone. He was so disconcerted that he got dressed, ran down the pier to the shore, and determined that his boat was also gone. He ran back to the shack, searched his windbreaker for the pistol—but in vain.

"Damn!" he blurted out. A mixture of anger, impotence, and emptiness coursed through him, and he fluctuated between rage, humiliation, and debilitating loneliness. She had taken off again, he thought, this time not just with his gun but also with his motorboat. Then, in a rage, he felt relief that the entire affair had now shifted. With this thought he fell asleep. He woke up around noon and didn't understand why it was so late. At first he didn't really believe Julia had disappeared, but then he realized that he had returned to a world of apathy. A new phase was beginning, his mind told him, but it wasn't easy to assimilate that fact. What could he do to fight it? he asked himself, and came to the conclusion that he had to find Julia. But that gave him the dismal feeling of chasing after her. The other possibility was to wait. Of course waiting meant putting off a decision; even so, he might better be able to see what he should do. He was suffering from restlessness, and it was restlessness that drove him to the decision to buy a bottle of wine. He checked his wallet and was surprised to find enough money to last him a week. He went back out over the wooden pier that was "covered with gull droppings," and thought of the phrase "to be on the wrong track."

In the small store he bought a daily paper, some olives, cheese, ham, mineral water, and two bottles of wine. Back at the fishing shack, he sat at the window and stared out. As he ate, he fed a seagull some white bread and allowed it to fly off with a piece of ham. Then he put the leftovers in the plastic bag and went back to staring out at the open sea. He was satisfied watching the waves and the clouds, the sun and, later, the stars. He had drunk a bottle of wine, and since he still couldn't sleep, he opened the second bottle. In a phase where he was internally dead and there was nothing but silence outside that was dominated by the sloshing of the waves, he stumbled out, stripped down, and slipped into the water beneath the pier. Since it was high tide, he could sit on the sandy bottom and let the waves wash over him. Why was he still breathing? He thought that if Julia hadn't taken the gun with her, he could just shoot himself right now. Or he could just wade far enough out into the water until he drowned. Next he thought about the falcon Alien and how Richard Vogel had laughingly responded to his question about Caecilia: "She likes you! Why don't you ask her what she's going to do?" The abandonment phase was replaced by a phase of rage, and he now hurried back to the shack.

Lying on the air mattress, he tried to think about Caecilia and to suppress any thoughts of Julia, but as soon as he set himself to the task, he saw only Julia.

Next morning he found the newspaper he had purchased, lying on the armchair. He pulled it over with his foot, sat up, grabbed the paper, and read on the front page that the severely injured man they had found in the taxi had died in the hospital before the police could question him. The man had had no papers, it said, no watch, no wallet, no keys. The police still thought it was a gang war over dominance of the gambling sector. There was nothing about smuggling operations. Incidentally, the criminals had stolen the taxi from right outside the house of its driver who was off duty at the time.

Lanz dropped the paper, sat down on the chair at the window and looked back out at the ocean, while confusion dominated his thoughts. Finally he told himself that he was 70% water, and that everything—pain, sadness, anger, love, and pity—was engulfing not only his body but also his mind. It later occurred to him that he had a contract to translate Shakespeare's plays, and his thoughts from this point on were in English, but it happened unintentionally. Of course he remembered his unsuccessful suicide attempt, Alma, Signor Blanc, the lawyer Capparoni hanging from the ceiling, the man he shot at the ship junkyard, and the cupboard in the basement that blocked the passageway to Signor Blanc's deserted villa. He then decided that when he got back he would occupy the room the old man had offered him and sleep there for the immediate future. He also thought about Oboabona, the mailman, about the Ospedale al Mare, the bodyguard with the dog mask, about Giorgio Fermi, Richard Vogel and his falcon Alien, and not least of all about Caecilia. Still, he focused most of all on Julia, believing that he loved her, but she had stolen not only his pistols but also his motorboat . . .

The fragments of memory gradually thawed the emptiness within him that had paralyzed his thoughts like an ice buildup in his head. Slowly his energy returned, and he deliberated whether he should spend the coming night in the fishing shack. He turned to face the entrance and in the sunlight saw tiny dust particles floating through the room; it seemed as if they represented a message for him. There were various possibilities for interpreting them: as a metaphor of life, as an analogy for his disorientation, or for the impartiality of events. He grew restless, but remained seated because he didn't have enough strength to get up and return to his life.

When evening came, he slipped into his windbreaker and went ashore. He instinctively kept an eye out so he wouldn't run into or be followed by anyone. He shouldn't start drinking, he told himself. But at the same time he craved a bottle of wine.

The small store was still open. He bought a bottle of cola and a newspaper, and in the brightly-lit shop read the headline: "Crime Riddle." This time he learned that there were bullet holes only in the cargo doors of the red laundry van, but none in the black Chrysler or the taxi. All of the gunshot evidence pointed to one or several Glock pistols, which only complicated the investigation. The two dead men in the Chrysler, Fermi and Saltesi, had been shot through a side window, the two others from head-on and from a greater distance. Moreover, any fingerprints in the red Nissan van had been meticulously removed, while a sufficient number had been found in the two other vehicles. They had also established bloodstains of the man who had been killed the day before and of the two victims in the Chrysler. In an interview, an expert had discussed all the possibilities of how the exchange of gunfire might have occurred.

Lanz tossed the paper in a trashcan and headed back to the fishing shack. On the way he decided to go to his house on the Lido the following morning. He could either go by bus, in which case he'd have to take the ferry and then the bus to the Lungomare D'Annunzio, or he could try to find someone here on Pellestrina who would take him by motorboat to the Elisabetta vaporetto station.

The shack was dark, he could barely make it out under the starry sky. Before he stepped onto the pier, he took off his clothes, laid them down on the shore as always, covered them with his windbreaker, and jumped into the cold water. This time it was low tide. He had made his way over to one of the front pilings that supported the shack when he thought he heard a car's engine and then voices. Apparently two men were talking, but from his vantage point he couldn't see them . . . They weren't speaking Italian and were in a hurry. The two men took the pier to his shack, picked the lock, and stormed inside. Lanz could hear each of their words and footsteps above him. At this point they were standing right over his head, discussing what they should do.

Lanz understood just enough Serbo-Croatian to figure out what was what.

"How much longer should we wait?" the one with the higher voice said. The other guy didn't answer.

"I'll call Miroslav!" the higher voice went on.

"Do it!" the other guy agreed.

Then Lanz heard him speaking softly, briefly coughing and whispering. Lanz overhead enough to tell that he gave the second man, standing beside him, instructions to stay, and then he left. So the other guy must still be in the shack, waiting for his buddy to return.

Fifteen minutes went by and nothing happened, other than that Lanz was freezing. He knew that he didn't have a chance without his gun, but at least he could try to peek through a crack in the shack and get a look at the man's face. But he immediately dismissed that idea. He knew his only chance was to go back to the shore, get dressed, and flee. He couldn't be seen from the window on the Lagoon, and his pursuer couldn't leave his spot in the shack since Lance could possibly ambush him.

"Didn't you want to die?" he challenged himself. "Yes," he admitted, "I could have avoided all this."—"But you weren't happy . . ." He interrupted his self-interrogation and listened, because he thought he heard something. He was then convinced that it must have been the short tone of an interrupted telephone call. He first heard whispering, then the voice of the stranger above became louder, he seemed to be wondering why he hadn't found Lanz. Seconds later he heard more footsteps above him, the door was opened, and, after several unsuccessful attempts, the man lit a cigarette with a lighter and blew out the smoke with a hissing sound.

Lanz knew that at high tide he would have had a much harder time understanding even fragments of conversation and any of the events that took place. Just then he saw three flashlights bobbing back and forth in the darkness. One of the men determined that *he* wasn't there, they'd looked everywhere. Then the guy who had ambushed him earlier said that someone had seen *him* in the small store, buying a newspaper. The man with the high voice interrupted and asked what they should do now. Then Lanz only understood the words: "Okay! Okay! Okay!" and deduced that they had a plan. He heard hurried footsteps on the pier and a sound as if some liquid was being poured on the ground above him. He also heard a gurgling and a splashing on the pier, then more running. It smelled of gasoline, followed by an explosion and the crackling of fire. Lanz dove underwater, closed his eyes, and swam to shore. He held his breath as long as possible and didn't surface until he ran out of air. No doubt about it, they had set the fishing shack on fire. Again he sought cover in the ocean water and held his breath in the cold darkness that was penetrated by flickering flashes of light until he surfaced once more, gasping for air. He was able to determine that the four flashlights were moving away, but above all else, he saw that the fishing hut was burning. Just then he heard car doors slamming and a car racing off without any headlights. While realizing that he would never forget the sight of the fire, he hurried cautiously to get ashore, because now he obviously had to disappear before the fire department or the police arrived. Nevertheless he didn't panic, located his clothes and shoes, got dressed, and ran to the small store, but it was already closed. On the way he kept glancing back at the shack that was still in flames.

He could see it from here, too. He waited for several minutes in

174

the darkness, not moving, and then ran in the direction of the road and the *murazzi*—the centuries' old stonewalls on the seaside—that had been constructed to combat frequent flooding conditions. The fact that cars were allowed in the villages made him even more cautious. He was afraid that his pursuers might be waiting somewhere nearby. But how had these men found his fishing shack—he himself had barely been able to recognize it in the dark . . . And how did they find out that, after many months' absence, he was staying there now? As he ran between new single-family homes and smaller apartment houses in the semi-darkness, he searched for answers. The most obvious was that his pursuers had at least one informant on the island. Moreover, since Lanz didn't know how to solve the problem of getting back to his house on the Lido and since he no longer had a gun, he felt that Julia had betrayed him twice now. She hadn't just disappeared, she had taken everything he needed to survive the dangerous situation she had left him in.

The longer he thought about it, the less he understood what he himself was doing. In spite of everything, why did he want to see Julia again? Then he considered going to the police, but dismissed the thought since he would then have to admit being an eyewitness to Borsakowski's murder. Julia was possibly already on her way back to America, he thought. One alternative, he felt, was that he could run to Santa Maria al Mare at the point of Pellestrina Island and from there take the Line 11 bus and then transfer to a ferry to the Lido. But that was as complicated as all the other possibilities.

He glanced back. The fishing shack was still burning, and, as always, colorful boats were docked at the wharf. He knew there was a landing for motorboats nearby, and if he wasn't mistaken, someone was there, smoking a cigarette in the dark. His desire to escape from the island was so strong that he ran back until he saw a man with a white captain's hat (the kind you could find in any souvenir shop), smoking a cigarette. Without a moment's hesitation, he approached the man and spoke to him. Strangely enough, the man wasn't surprised, but demanded a hundred euros for a trip to the Santa Maria Elisabetta vaporetto station. Lanz agreed, and the operator allowed him to take a seat in the cabin. As it turned out, it was, in fact, a water taxi.

"Did you see that, over there . . ." the man pointed his arm in the direction, ". . . a fishing hut is on fire?" And when Lanz didn't answer, the man went on: "Apparently that's all that happened—my brother had gone over there and phoned to tell me." Since Lanz only nodded, the man changed topics and asked how he hurt his eye.

"I fell on my bike," Lanz said.

"I hate bikes," the man in the captain's hat responded. "They come out of nowhere, without a sound, and when you're lying there on the ground and lift your head up to find out what happened, there's nobody around." He laughed.

Lanz was relieved when the water taxi set off, plunging him into the obscurity of the night, the ocean, and the sky. He felt that he had "dodged a bullet," even though he wasn't happy about it. At home he'd get the Walther pistol and his smartphone, pack a suitcase with his dopp kit, a volume of Shakespeare's works that contained *The Tempest*, his English-Italian dictionary, underwear and T-shirts, and take the cellar passageway to the room in Signor Blanc's villa for which he had the key. And first thing next morning he would meet with Richard Vogel and the falcon Alien that was now asleep under its tiny leather hood on its perch . . . What does a falcon dream about? he asked himself, and, from exhaustion and the monotonous droning of the motor, he closed his eyes.

He woke up as they came to the Elisabetta station, paid the operator, disembarked, and staggered to the taxi stand. There was the usual late-evening traffic on the Lungomare D'Annunzio.

At the well-lit Chiosco Bahiano he saw two police officers questioning the man behind the counter, their car parked on the other side of the street. Lanz walked the short distance to his house that now seemed strange. But the presence of the police at the Chiosco Bahiano and the occasional traffic on the shoreline was reassuring. Everything was normal. Besides, he couldn't keep his eyes open. So he postponed the move to Signor Blanc's villa and stowed the Walther pistol under his pillow. Even though Lanz realized he'd forgotten to lock the front door, he was too tired to get back up.

When he suddenly awoke, a dark face was bending over him. He sat up instantly and fumbled for the pistol in a daze. Then he realized that it was Oboabona who was himself so startled that he leaped back, mouth and eyes wide open, flailing about with his arms. "Scusi! Scusi!" he shouted as an apology.

It had been light for some time. Lanz had the impression that he had suffered something like a stroke. He went limp, sank down onto his pillow, and listlessly asked Oboabona what he wanted.

The mailman was in the process of fleeing the room and stuttered: "Niente, niente, Signor Lanz . . . I want to deliver mail . . . I ring doorbell . . . No one opens the door . . . I press against the door, door opens . . . I am thinking something wrong . . . I look around . . ."

Lanz, to his own amazement, was fully dressed, sneakers still on his feet. He propped himself up, apologized for still being asleep at this hour, and reminded Oboabona that they were saying *du* to each other.

"I bring mail . . . no one home," he repeated, "murders at Lido . . . murderers shoot murderers and burn down fishing hut on Pellestrina."

Oboabona reached for the mail that he had put down on the sofa table in the living room, pulled out the *Gazzettino*, and handed Lanz articles about the deaths from the shooting and the burned-down fishing shack. Lanz read that a man—whose description featured a black eye and thus clearly referred to him—had hidden out in the hut and presumably set it on fire.

"Thank you," Lanz said, acting as if he were still reading so that Oboabona wouldn't become suspicious, and then pensively closed the paper. He tried to clear his thoughts.

"Would you take me through the Ospedale al Mare?" he asked the mailman, because he now suspected he might find a solution to the riddle that has baffled him this whole time.

"Not good . . . not good for the people . . . and not good for you."

"Then I'll have to try it alone."

"Not alone—"

"I don't have anybody else who'll go along."

Oboabona thought for a moment.

"All say that criminals hiding in Ospedale . . . I say it, too. And many poor people . . . What did you do to the eye?"

"Nothing . . . Say *du* to me, as we agreed."

"Why you want to go there?"

"I want to know what's happening."

"Why?"

"Are you going to help me or not?"

Oboabona thought again.

"Is that your brother who lives in the garage by the Jewish Cemetery?" Lanz asked out of the blue.

To his surprise, Oboabona nodded. Lanz went into the kitchen, took orange juice and mineral water from the refrigerator, filled a glass, and placed it down in front of Oboabona.

"Brothers in our hearts . . . not real brothers . . ." Oboabona explained. "You have eye ache?"

Lanz shook his head.

"Good. I help," the mailman said, and emptied the glass.

"When?" Lanz wanted to know.

Oboabona didn't look at him, stood up, and went to the door. Then he glanced back with an indefinable expression and left. But before he closed the door, he poked his head back through the opening and answered, gazing at the floor: "Good. Tomorrow." He paused briefly. "You lock door. And you must believe—not good in Ospedale al Mare!"

Lanz locked the door, glanced through the mail, and found a package with a letter from Dr. Occhini that confirmed his contract, contained the first payment, and requested that Lanz phone him. A lavishly-illustrated hefty volume about Shakespeare and his works was enclosed.

Lanz dialed the number that was specified in the letter and asked the secretary to connect him with Dr. Occhini. She first wanted to know the subject of the conversation, and when he explained it to her, she replied that the publisher was in a meeting.

"Your contract is in order. Dr. Occhini will return your call," she said in a cordial tone.

On the one hand Lanz was delighted with the contract and the advance payment, but on the other hand he was irritated that he hadn't been able to speak with the publisher.

He took the suitcase from the walk-in closet and started packing his things for the move to the room in the neighboring house. Last of all he stuck the Walther pistol in the pocket of his windbreaker.

Early that afternoon—he had called Amanda Falchi about Julia, but learned that the lawyer was at a court case in Mestre—the doorbell rang. Lanz looked out the window and saw Commissario Galli, accompanied by a policeman.

His initial reaction was to not open the door, but then he did it anyway.

"Oh, you're home," the Commissario greeted him. "How is your eye?"

Lanz didn't answer, but strode ahead into the living room, inviting Galli to sit down with a wave of his hand.

"You know what's happened—I mean the shootout and the four dead men," Galli began.

"I read the paper."

"And the news that your fishing hut burned down?"

"I was there."

"In the hut?"

"I had gone for an evening walk and seen from a distance a man going down the pier and then, along with three others who had just shown up, pouring gasoline from a can."

"You watched?"

Lanz nodded.

"I mean, why didn't you call the police?"

"I didn't have a phone."

"Was it back in the hut?"

"No, I forgot and left it home."

"Not long ago you got run over on your bike. Aren't you concerned?"

"What do you want me to say?" Lanz asked, cynically.

"Do you want to argue? Would you prefer to make a statement at the station house?" the Commissario aggressively responded. "I came to see you because you didn't report the arson at your fishing hut. We had no idea if you even were aware of it. Let's cut to the chase: Who were those men, and is someone stalking you?"

"I didn't recognize any of them from a distance, and I don't know if I'm being followed."

"And you don't know why these men are after you?"

Suddenly Lanz was no longer able to say "No," so he just shook his head. "It must be a case of mistaken identity," he then said.

The Commissario flew into a rage, stared Lanz in the face and hissed at him: "Stop it! You're leading us on a wild goose chase. I just want to know why?"

"Why would I do that?" Lanz replied, decisively.

"You'd know that better than I."

"No, you tell me."

"I see we're not getting anywhere," Galli blurted out angrily, and switched into bureaucratic mode. Lanz was secretly amazed at the skill with which the man could put people under pressure.

"Tell me the sequence of events," the Commissario said, suddenly and sternly.

"After the men had poured out what I assumed was gasoline, they set it on fire."

"You're a translator: What language were the four men speaking?"

Lanz thought about the two men in the shack above his head whom he had overheard while he waded in the water. "I don't know . . . I was too far away . . . Possibly Serbo-Croatian . . . that's just my guess."

"What did they look like?"

"As I said, it was dark."

"You didn't see anything at all?"

"Four flashlights and four figures."

"And after they ran off, what did you do then?"

"I ran into the village."

"Why?"

"I panicked."

"And then what?"

"Then I came back and took a water taxi to the Elisabetta vaporetto station."

Galli kept up the questioning until he felt he had everything, but the entire time he became more and more suspicious. "You must remove everything that remains of your hut and the pier," he said unexpectedly and in a gruff tone of voice.

"I've already taken care of that," Lanz lied. He also failed to tell Galli about the wild chase and that Julia had been with him and had taken off in his boat—in other words, he didn't disclose the things he wanted to keep to himself.

"You're mixing truth with lies and hiding important information," Galli concluded, before he left the house with the policeman. He turned one last time in the foyer and asked: "Are you still together with Julia Ellis?"

"Ask Julia."

"I would like to, if I only knew where she is."

"I don't know either. And if I did know, I wouldn't tell you."

Galli gave him a contemptuous look but said nothing further. He and his companion climbed into the police car that was parked in front of the house. Lanz locked the front door and sat down at his desk. He later called the lawyer Amanda Falchi, but learned that she wouldn't be back in her office until tomorrow morning. The secretary made a note of his telephone number and his request to speak with Julia.

When it got dark, he put on his windbreaker, took the packed suitcase down to the basement, pushed the cabinet aside, turned on the lights, and discovered that someone had attached an aluminum rod to the back of the cupboard that allowed him to effortlessly pull the furniture piece back over the hole in the wall. In addition, the trash in the corridor had been cleaned up and a chair had even been placed against the wall halfway down the passageway.

He pulled out the key and unlocked the door at the other end of the passageway. He thought the doorway would lead to the basement of Signor Blanc's villa, but to his surprise he ended up in the man's garden. In place of the flowerbeds and the greenhouse, however, he saw only cultivated garden soil. There was a light in the old planetarium, though the villa looked deserted. He put down the suitcase and first went to look for the building with the falcons, where he found Richard Vogel on his cellphone. Each of the falcons in the aviary had a different leather hood on its head and was silently perched there; a large owl, perplexed, seemed to be studying Lanz between the bars of its cage. It seemed to him that he was in a school for raptors where the pupils were waiting for singing lessons or gym class.

Moments later Vogel came over and welcomed him warmly: "I've just received instructions that the damage from the fire at your fisherman's hut will be paid off in the next couple of days. It will be rebuilt from the ground up, and, by the way, your room in the villa is ready for you to move in. Will you come to dinner on the third floor?"

Lanz thought about Caecilia as he crossed the courtyard and entered the villa. The entire foyer was decorated with flowers that apparently had been cut during the closure of the garden and the greenhouse.

His room was much larger than he had remembered. In several different antique shops he had seen a statue like this one of an African boy in festive costume. When he looked at it, he had a guilty conscience and decided to ask Vogel to remove it. Beside it, in a Chinese vase, blue irises; he bent down to better be able to see the blossoms. The TV set was in one corner; he also saw two red leather armchairs, a queen-size bed, and bookshelves with coffee-table books. One door led to a bathroom that had a toilet. Blinds kept out the most glaring light, and an antique chandelier from Murano hung from the ceiling. He took a shower, found a large white bathrobe on a hook, opened his suitcase, and was surprised that he felt good for the first time in a long time. It was possibly also the certainty of being safe that was otherwise so natural that you took it for granted. He took out fresh underwear, got dressed, slipped on his sneakers, and glanced at his watch. It was now late enough that he could go to the third floor. On the way, he admired more of the sumptuous flowers that filled the house with their beauty and fragrance. In the hall he met the cook, Min Chang, wearing a black chef's outfit and looking like a karate warrior. The chef beamed at Lanz, greeted him, and led him into Richard Vogel's study that was furnished with older Venetian furniture. Before he could exchange a single word with Vogel, Lanz spotted a framed old painting depicting feathers of the falcon.

Vogel noticed Lanz staring at the painting, walked over to join him, and began to explain the picture in great detail. Lanz was too exhausted to be able to comprehend everything. As the falconer spoke, Lanz had a growing desire to be able to fly. He really could fly, but only in his dreams, though dreams were totally a part of his reality. After waking from dreams where he was flung into the abyss despite frantic resistance, he convinced himself that he could fly, and by the next nightmare of falling he had learned how to soar. Although he became dizzy, he had a marvelous feeling of wellbeing. But in the past two years after his wife Alma's airplane crash, he had only had nightmares from which he could awake after a brief period of agony, as he repeatedly reminded himself.

The female of the peregrine falcon species, Richard Vogel was saying, was one-third larger than the male, so they were preferred for hawking.

"Alien," he went on, "was originally named Alina, but the name wasn't appropriate for a raptor that killed other birds in flight. She is trained to respond to a certain signal that I produce with my lips, tongue, and a following short whistle, and then she attacks even larger living creatures, up to and including humans. Your pursuer in the San Michele cemetery, Giorgio Fermi, had the bad luck (that was, conversely, your good fortune!) to be wearing a dog mask and also that falcons can strike foxes and wolves. Mature falcons are dark on top, from brown to blue and grey, their chest is white and cross-striped like a zebra, the upper breast has dark spots, the iris of their eyes is amber, their legs yellow, and their talons black."

He reached into a desk drawer and pulled out a light- and dark-brown spotted feather, "from Alien's wing," he said, "to bring you luck."

"By the way," he continued, "your boat was released today. And I recommend you get a different make than a Glock so that they don't suspect that you had something to do with that gun battle where the four men were killed." And he took a black pistol, "a Beretta 92," as he described it, with the appropriate ammunition from a desk drawer. Richard Vogel paused and stared at Lanz. "You shouldn't believe that everything you see and experience is reality. It's only a tiny particle in the blackness of the universe, a minute detail. The most common mistake we humans make is to believe there is such a thing as an incontrovertible experience or perception. Each and every word instantly summons up the recollection of its opposite. As we are standing here, people are plotting against you, are betraying you and dragging you through the muck. People think you are ridiculous. People are laughing at you. People want to destroy you, to crush you like some pesky insect. Everyone you know has already lied to you, betrayed you, tricked you, belittled you in the eyes of others, or spit on you—and the entire time you haven't the faintest idea. However, the problem is that you're doing the exact same thing to others and are nevertheless indignant when you learn what's been happening behind your back. In a nutshell, don't get caught up in yourself. There's no worse mistake than insisting you can ostensibly be or live by yourself. You can only pretend that you're all by yourself. Just try to spend one single day by yourself, telling everybody the truth. Tell everyone just what you really think of them and what it is about them that bothers you. Then you end up in a turntable-world where the tables move asynchronously and no one understands you, and anyone who tries to emulate you will rub others the wrong way, will damage himself and, lastly, will languish in neutral gear. Only by deception, lies, by multiple personas, by the acceptance of one's own depravity can you find your way. Conventionality is the only language that helps humans understand one another and get along with each other. Don't put your faith in goodness, compassion, charity—hidden in all these concepts is deception, and, behind that, egotism, and even hate."

Vogel turned on the TV, and from a bookcase with hundreds, if not thousands of DVDs, took one from its white cardboard sleeve, put it in the player, and activated the remote control. Lanz was confused by what he saw. There were short colored movie snippets, totally out of context. He was patient, but no matter how hard he tried, he saw only optical fragments and duplications that kept repeating themselves: delicious foods and disgusting faces, sexual acts, brief argumentative scenes, assaults and fragments of dreams. Lanz was reminded of Luis Buñuel's film *An Andalusian Dog*, except that the content was trivial, superficial, even vulgar. Dream fragments were interspersed with bits of memory, resulting in a surreal event where the comprehensible was jumbled with the inexplicable: the sensation of a traffic accident, wrecks and injured people, together with the first day of school, children and large cones of treats, along with chalk messages on a classroom black-board. A bike ride through a burned-out forest—and a representation of the giant Ferris wheel in Vienna's Prater amusement park, with a view from one of the gondolas. A bee sting in a bare forearm—also a female swimmer with a bathing cap, and a birthday cake. A vague wedding scene that lasted less than ten seconds—and a woman's hand, writing numbers in a checkered notebook. The view of a scarred belly wound—and a child in a black wool cap on a sled. People crying in a room—and a white gallery with Monet's paintings of water lilies. A fist striking an adult in the face—and residents of an old-folks' home, licking popcicles.

The scenes had no obvious chronology, but appeared and disappeared spontaneously and with no apparent concept—Lanz had no idea what Richard Vogel had in mind. A moment later the falconer turned off the DVD player and the TV set and smiled.

"You're wondering about what I've just showed you. Signor Blanc has founded a new medical science at a California university, under the designation Cerebral Archaeology. We have just been watching memories from the brain of a deceased person. In other words, research has advanced to the point that we can visualize images from a person's memory stream after his death. A cohort of scientists is working on making the appropriate sounds audible; a different group is establishing a chronological sequence based on the coloration of the images and the age of the memories. With brain archaeology we will be able to refine the history of the human race down to the smallest detail. In the future each brain of a significant or powerful human being will be reconstructed and analyzed down to the smallest detail, in light of their physiological condition after death . . . Just imagine, we would have the opportunity to see and analyze the memories of Mozart, of Shakespeare or Hitler and Stalin, of every criminal or artist, but also those of the common man. I've given you this insight into our research to show that we are seriously dealing with the eternal question of what it means to be a human being. Signor Blanc and I will both make our brains available, and neither of us wishes that past injustices be found in our memories that we haven't tried to rectify. Signor Blanc again begs your pardon. By the way, Dr. Occhini, your future publisher, has informed us of your conversation and asks that after *The Tempest*, you translate *The Merchant of Venice* and *Othello*—in other words, the Venetian plays. Signor Blanc is especially interested in *The Merchant of Venice* and, after the Jewish Cemetery, we encourage you to also visit the world's first ghetto that is also located in Venice."

Richard Vogel explained to Lanz that the Venetian Ghetto is an island in the Sestiere di Cannaregio area of the city where the Jewish population has been living for more than four hundred years. Before that, a large foundry had been operating there, a "smelter." In Italian, "smelting" is called *gettare*, which originally gave the seven-acre island the name "ghetto." There the Jews were protected from the Spanish Inquisition and an arbitrarily administered legal system. The tiny island was originally intended to house seven hundred inhabitants, Richard Vogel continued, but less than one hundred years later there were over 5500 who were only able to find a place due to an increase in the number of floors in each house, though the upper stories were reduced in height until the occupants could barely stand upright. The tallest house had eight stories! Until Napoleon's conquest of Venice, only the poor part of the Jewish population lived in the Ghetto; the wealthy had moved out long before, and entire rows of homes had been torn down. In the National-Socialist era, the German occupation forces deported and murdered almost two hundred of the remaining three hundred dwellers. At this point, Vogel concluded, approximately three hundred residents were living on the small island in the middle of the city.

Lanz had translated a history of Venice into German and he could recall much of it. Still, as he followed Richard Vogel into the dining room, everything he had just heard continued to race through his head. He sat down beside Caecilia who greeted him with a smile. He remembered that on their trip to the Jewish Cemetery, Vogel had told him that she liked him, so he hugged her.

The beekeeper Pedar Janca was wearing sunglasses, as he always did. Nevertheless, Janca asked him how his black eye was doing, which somewhat irritated Lanz. Janca seemed visibly amused, because, after a brief pause, he added—his face now expressing mockery—that everybody knew all about Herr Lanz's bike accident. So he may be blind after all, Lanz said to himself.

The white dining room was furnished with a long light-brown table and matching chairs, a bookcase and, in one corner, a red leather bench seat and three wingback chairs. On one wall hung a painting by the artist de Chirico. Richard Vogel, following Lanz's gaze, explained that the portrait—painted when Blanc was still a child and had sat for de Chirico in 1914—represented Signor Blanc as the artist had brilliantly anticipated his adult features. He had depicted Blanc as a sixty-year-old and titled the painting *The Child's Brain*. Astonished, Lanz thought that Blanc must now be over a hundred years old.

"You see the face with a prominent black mustache and a small goatee. His eyes are closed. He has a receding hairline and, apart from that, is naked. As you know, Signor Blanc has never allowed

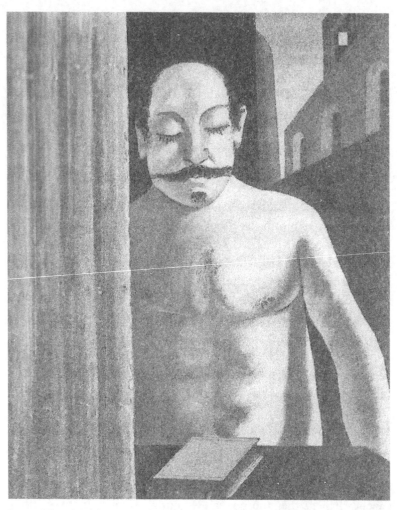

himself to be photographed or painted from the front. He doesn't want people to see his face. In the painting, he is shown from the navel up. On the table in front of him lies a book without a title or author—Signor Blanc told me it is the Revelation of the Apocalypse from the Bible. De Chirico had realized the child's calling at that early age. A third of the picture—seen through the window of an otherwise dark room where Signor Blanc is standing—depicts a segment of a fluted column on the left; on the right, the portion of a building with rectangular windows and the arches of an arcade. The artist had later painted the scene several times so that several versions exist, all very similar to each other. Signor Blanc's closed eyes allude to the blind prophet in Greek mythology, Tiresias, whose prophesies, according to tradition, were infallible. However, Tiresias formulated them as aphorisms that he only revealed with great reluctance."

As the meal was being served, Lanz felt a growing affection for Caecilia. The Japanese and Korean dishes were exquisitely pre-pared, served with sake and ice or with water. After dinner they asked Janca the beekeeper for a prophecy for the next few days, and at that point Lanz knew that the man was, in fact, blind. They all fell silent, but Janca was silent, too. Then, after a long drawn-out pause, he stood up and, without a word, left the dining room. As the guests moved over to the lounge area, Lanz and Caecilia remained at the table until Caecilia agreed with his suggestion that they take a walk, and they unobtrusively left the villa.

She stopped in the former front yard, called a taxi on her phone, and rode with him to the Santa Maria Elisabetta station where they waited for a vaporetto. Everything happened without discussion and almost incidentally. Although Lanz thought several times about the chase and about Julia, he felt as if he were someone who ended up in an insane asylum due to a case of mistaken identity and was finally let go after several days. The confusion about recent developments and the depressing days was still there, but he gradually found himself back in the freedom he had presumably lost.

"Herr Janca doesn't speak when he's asked for a prophesy," Caecilia said. "Generally it just makes him mad. Of course he knows what would happen if he did speak about it—the opposite would occur. Only when he foresees a catastrophe does he mention it out loud, so that it won't actually happen. We all know that—that's why we wait until he has left the room." She burst out laughing.

"Then today's our lucky day!" Lanz replied, ironically.

She looked up and gazed into his eyes, then looked away. He

took her hand as if it were the most natural thing in the world, squeezed it, and didn't let go. But he couldn't think of anything to say to her, every notion seemed mundane, and she seemed to feel the same.

In Venice they got off at the Salute stop, at the conspicuous basilica of the same name where the Grand Canal enters the Lagoon. When they came to a dark side street, they kissed and embraced. In his jacket pocket Lanz could feel the Baretta and the ammunition Vogel had given him. They hugged over and over again as soon as they were alone in one of the narrow alleys or on a stone bridge crossing a canal, until they reached the Fondamenta Bragadin where they stopped at a corner house and Caecilia unlocked the front door. In the dark they hurriedly climbed a steep stairway to the second floor, and when they entered the apartment, they quickly shed their clothes and slipped under the covers of a king-size bed in her bedroom.

Caecilia's smooth tongue reminded him of a little bird's tongue, her lips were sweet cherries, her hair was fragrant and fell onto his face, her eyes revealed that she was no longer in control of herself. Her expression was somewhat absent-minded, and she seemed to be suffering as they finally embraced and abandoned themselves to the moment. They didn't sleep all night—they made love, whispering to each other, turning on the light and laughing, drinking a glass of wine. The shame of their intimacy gone, they indulged their feelings until it gradually grew light.

They then began to tell each other about their respective lives. He learned that her mother was a Venetian Jewess, her father a jeweler and clock maker. While her mother's parents had a fabric store in Padua, Antonio's parents had had the jewelry- and clock-store for three generations. It had been the timepieces that had led Caecilia to astronomy, more specifically, a celestial clock she had seen while with her mother in Rome and a celestial map that she bought in a bookstore later that same day. At the age of 22, she married a fellow student, Giacomo Sereno, because she had gotten pregnant by him, but then lost the baby after a premature birth in her seventh month.

She battled depression for several months and lived separated from her husband at this time. Eventually she worked in one of the largest astronomical observatories in the world, the McDonald Observatory in Texas, and in the Palomar Observatory in California, and told Lanz about her observations and impressions. She didn't want to speak about any further relationships. On the other hand, she did want to know if he loved Julia Ellis. She assumed that he had slept with her, but didn't know whether they were still together.

This time it was Lanz who didn't want to answer. He observed her beautiful body, her toes, her hands, her hips and teeth, and he liked her speech and choice of words, her original way of talking— she always related the ending first and only then described how it came about.

Before he went to the bathroom, he glanced into her study. He noticed astrological maps, pencils and a notebook in an open drawer of a cabinet, photo albums filling a second drawer. He rushed back into the bedroom, secretly took the pistol and the bullets from his windbreaker and hid them in the second drawer. Only then did he go looking for the bathroom.

They ate yogurt with dates for breakfast before they made love again. At one point the room grew dark, and when he looked outside, Lanz saw the windows of several floors of a cruise ship that was just passing on the Canale della Giudecca, leaving the impression it was about to crush the building they were in.

Around noon, Caecilia told him she wanted to show him the Ghetto and the five synagogues; after all, she has been leading tours in the Museo Ebraico for years now. But first she would have to explain "some things," as she formulated it. Instead, however, they slept till early afternoon, then got dressed, went to a bar and ordered cod sandwiches, sardines, prosciutto, and mineral water.

"Where did you get the name Caecilia?" Lanz wanted to know.

"Actually, my name is Sara," she replied. "But since childhood, my grandparents have called me Caecilia due to their experiences during the Nazi years. I became so used to the name that I've kept it. And that won't change. But my official documents still list me as Sara."

When they had finished eating, they took the vaporetto to the train station so they could see the Ghetto from the outside. When they came to the Accademia Bridge and looked out through the smudged side-window to the yellow neo-Gothic Palazzo Franchetti where he had frequently seen sculptures on exhibit, he spotted a large white astronaut floating in the air. He and Caecilia got off so they could examine the sculpture up close. He read on a flyer that it was done by the Dutch artist Joseph Klibansky and was called *Self-portrait of a Dreamer*. The imposing completely-white figure had to be almost thirty feet high, with his left hand holding onto a huge white chair, as if he were going to vault over the backrest. In front of the neo-Gothic Palazzo, the astronaut looked even stranger than perhaps in some museum for modern art, and Lanz understood the astronaut represented a different way of thinking in our childhood. And something else registered in his brain: the feeling that he was no longer the suicide who wanted to take his life on Torcello . . . Suddenly that was all behind him, though it was clear that he hadn't yet escaped from the undertow of crime that threatened to engulf him.

On his right foot the large floating astronaut was balancing a white vase with a white bouquet the size of two soccer balls that only reinforced the playful display. He understood it as an unspoken suggestion not to lose sight of beauty. He then turned to the chair: it was one of those rustic bistro chairs, made of pine with a wicker seat that he recognized from pubcrawls. The tall chairback consisted of three flat slats, below the seat Lanz saw round slats: the way a small child would see a chair, he thought. The astronaut wasn't out for a spacewalk, wasn't transferring to a spaceship, no, he had just discovered the terra incognita within himself, his own fears, his doubts, and his dreams of a world he knew to be his home.

Lanz and Caecilia pensively strolled back to the vaporetto station, and it made him think about children in earlier times. For them the astronaut would probably have been an angel, Lanz thought, they would have considered his spacesuit a revelation. It now seemed as if all his impressions were going right through him and dissolving into nothingness.

Lanz kept his thoughts and ideas to himself. Instead, he spoke with Caecilia about the 1969 moon landing and Neil Armstrong. But he abruptly changed topics and asked Caecilia to tell him about the Ghetto.

"For centuries the Jews had had to pay higher taxes," she began, and described this story of hate. He now remembered how much veiled hatred he had noticed in the city: copper doorknobs that featured caricature heads of Jews and Negroes, also stone heads that peered out from a building. On one occasion he had entered an antique shop that had in its display window a Negro as a beast of burden. The store was furnished with mirrors in old Venetian gold frames, even the tables and the floor had been completely outfitted. He had asked the owner of the business—a restorer and gilder—if all these mirrors and figures were antiques, and the man had replied that they were, in fact, new; he had made them himself. The owner had been eager to start a conversation and, filled with pride, had brought out a framed photograph. It showed the antique dealer at the restoration of the archangel Gabriel on the peak of the St. Mark's Campanile. Since the copper shell had been damaged, he had repaired it in his workshop, he explained, and took a newspaper article about his artwork from a drawer and put it down on one of the tables. His imitation Negroes, mirrors, and also angels sold well, he then said, and smiled. Subsequently he showed Lanz a mirror, its remaining surface only isolated flat-silver islands, reflecting fragments of its milieu. It made Lanz think of congealed mercury that decomposed. The reflecting surface dissolved, got black spots and cracks and, with that, portrayed the second reality of the reflected objects. Finally, the mirror became completely unreflective, died, and lay in state in its frame-coffin until it became, Lanz thought at the time, a thing with no value whatsoever.

They got off near the train station and set off along the Canale di Cannaregio on the vaporetto line to the *Ghetto Vecchio*, the Old Ghetto, that, paradoxically, was built after the *Ghetto Nuovo*, the New Ghetto. From time to time he would see a Jewish resident with black hat, beard, long sidelocks, and a black suit. Caecilia glanced at her watch, then suggested they visit her friend, Riccardo Calimani, a writer who lived nearby in the Palazzo Fontana.

Lanz remembered the name Calimani, and it occurred to him that the man had written a photo brochure about the Ghetto and the Jewish Cemetery. When he told Caecilia about it, she explained that Riccardo was the author of the best book on the Venetian Ghetto, *The Merchants of Venice*.

Caecilia took out her smartphone, called a number, and joked with Calimani's wife over the phone as they were on their way to the

Palazzo Fontana. Everything was swimming around in Lanz's head about the astronaut and the dissolving layers of old mirrors. It wasn't until they walked through the front door of the Palazzo, saw the strikingly beautiful water well in the front yard, and rode the elevator to the third floor, that he focused on the actual visit.

A heavy-set gentle man with thinning hair and a shy smile opened the door. He was about seventy years old, wore a blue sport coat over a striped shirt which, along with a certain shyness, gave the impression that he was aristocratic but also otherworldly. Appearing beside him was his wife, the writer Anna-Vera Sullam, her hair dyed dark and wearing a black-orange blouse, also plump but dominating. She made it quite clear that she ruled the roost.

"Riccardo doesn't speak German or English. You'll have to go through me, and I'll translate," she said authoritatively.

"Emilio is a translator, he speaks perfect Italian," Caecilia responded.

Riccardo Calimani hurried ahead, while his wife and Caecilia disappeared into the kitchen. The rooms were impressively lofty and large. At first glance Lanz noticed only the Terrazzo floor, the few pieces of furniture, and the windows that overlooked the Grand Canal. He followed the scholar across a stone floor shimmering in the light of two chandeliers and stepped into his study. The walls of the small room were completely filled with bookshelves that reached to the ceiling. Back in the foyer the books had been piled 5 feet high, partially obscured by a large exercise bike. And in the study Lanz noticed another exercise machine that he assumed was for the treatment of back problems. An old Romantic-looking desk stood between two windows, and the view down to the Grand Canal held him spellbound. From the height of three stories, reality was different. He thought of the falcon Alien and Richard Vogel, the shrieking seagulls at his fishing cabin and on the island of Torcello when he had gazed down from the tall church tower, the cemeteries, and the owl in one of the aviaries in the old planetarium.

As he was still staring down at the Canal—imagining himself

a bird sailing unseen over the rooftops, the water, the vaporetti and the gondolas, then fluttering in mid-air, pausing and memorizing everything—Riccardo Calimani softly said to him that he understood German. In school he had read Heinrich Heine, Goethe, and Hofmannsthal . . . Lanz answered in Italian that they could also converse in German, but Calimani declined. His wife, who had telephoned with Caecilia Sereno, had told him that Lanz wanted to see the Ghetto. You can only understand the Ghetto, he was saying, if you understood its history. Lanz replied that he had already read the man's guidebook for tours of the museum and the five synagogues.

"*Scole* . . . we call a synagogue '*scola*,' that is, 'school' . . ."

"As you can see," Lanz interrupted him politely, "I really don't know much about it."

Riccardo Calimani continued in a soft voice while gazing out the window at the Canal, and Lanz, following his gaze, noticed the passing vaporetti and other boats while thinking about his future.

"Where shall I begin?" Calimani asked, and when Lanz said "at the beginning," the writer briefly paused.

"Approximately two-hundred to three-hundred people live in the New Ghetto today, covering roughly two-and-a-half acres," he began quietly, concentrating as he looked out the window, as if he were searching for words. "It is as long as a soccer field, but, though not visually obvious, in the shape of a pentagon. Since time immemorial there have been only two bridges across the three canals that make it an island. One of the bridges is over the Rio de San Girolamo-Ormesini, a second over the smaller Rio Gheto, the third canal is the widest, called the Rio del Battello. You could only reach the Ghetto through the gates at the two bridges that were guarded at night by soldiers, at the Jewish residents' expense, so that no one could get in or out. The only exceptions were Jewish doctors. But they had to report to the sentry the names of the patients to whom they were summoned." Calimani reached for a ballpoint pen and a piece of paper and drew an outline.

"There were already Jewish traders in Venice by the 5th and 6th

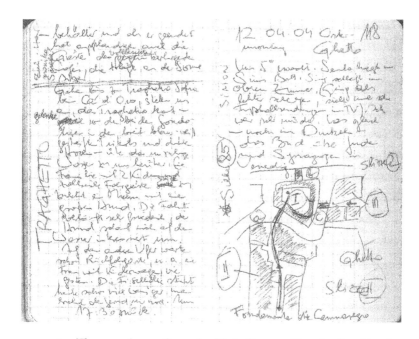

centuries. The merchants from the Holy Roman Empire lived in the Fondaco dei Tedeschi, those from Italy on the mainland. The first great influx of Jews took place in 1350, because people in Central Europe blamed them for the outbreak of the plague epidemic and persecuted them. From that point on, more and more Jewish immigrants came to Venice. At the beginning of the 17th century, on an island intended to house only 700 people, there were already 900 living here, and, by 1660, there were 5,500, because they sought shelter here, especially in the time of the Inquisition. Nevertheless, there was more and more harassment from city officials. In 1400 the order was given that their garments had to display a yellow identifier in the shape of a ring. A century later they were required to wear a yellow head cover or a black hat in public. At first, primarily Sephardic Jews arrived, those from the Mediterranean region, and then also Ashkenazi, mainly from the German-Polish-speaking area, joined at the time of the Inquisition by *conversos*, people from Iberia who were forced to convert to Christianity, along with Oriental Jews. Harassment increased, especially in regard to the taxes and fees that were drastically increased in comparison to those on the Venetian populace. Only in the fifty years after Napoleon conquered Venice were the bridge gates and sentries removed, and the Jews given equal justice with Venetians under the law. The defeat of Napolean, however, resulted in an economic setback for Venice."

Calimani rested a hand against his forehead and was silent as they continued to gaze down at the Grand Canal. When his wife Anna-Vera finally called to her husband, he raised his head and shyly remarked: "In any event, you know about the catastrophe in the 20th century," and looked Lanz right in the eye. He then hurried back to the living room, and Lanz followed. His wife had served warm pizza on a small table and, as they ate the crispy slices and drank red wine, the scholar conversed with Caecilia and his wife turned to Lanz. She first wanted to know why he was asking her husband about the Ghetto when there was a book and photo brochure. Then she wanted him to tell her if he intended to write about it or photograph it.

When Anna-Vera left the room to make a phone call, Calimani looked down and abruptly handed Lanz his business card.

"Call me, if you have any questions," he whispered in German. Lanz had already figured out that the man was the soloist and his wife was the conductor.

Their parting was cordial.

It was evening. They walked quickly, as if they were going to be late. On the Campo del Ghetto Nuovo boys and girls were playing with a soccer ball. This time Lanz noticed the three wells on the square that were sealed off with wrought-iron lids. An old man, smoking a cigarette, stood on the balcony of a house and watched the children. They then came to a building surrounded by scaffolding that housed the Jewish government, as Lanz read on a sign.

In the meantime a nervous elderly woman appeared. She wore a lightweight coat, had long hair, and was dressed in shabby clothes. Caecilia searched her purse for the key, while the woman knocked on the door with the brass ring. Caecilia finally located the key, unlocked the door, and let the woman go ahead. Lanz was still studying the bronze sign on the brick wall that depicted a scene from a concentration camp. A large wreath from the president of the Jewish community hung in front of it.

He learned from Caecilia that this part of the square was once one of the wealthiest Jewish residential areas in all of Italy. All day long the square echoed the cries of the garment dealers who sold used finery. Moreover the piazza was ringed by bakeries and by banks that loaned money. But even back then a ghetto wasn't simply a Jewish phenomenon—Venetian traders in the Orient also had to live in their own districts that were closed off at night for their own safety. There they could practice their religious customs undisturbed . . . In Europe in those days, however, there was scarcely any place where Jews could feel safe. They had to pay large sums as mandatory taxes and large amounts for festivities and events—for example, in the event of a state reception for high-ranking dignitaries who visited Venice—along with other forms of harassment.

"Most notably in the 16th century, Venice was a center of the Jewish printing industry," Caecilia continued. "Christian scholars worked with Jewish colleagues on translations of ancient and Arabic texts; in particular, educated Sephardic Jews were in close contact with Venetian families. There were Sephardic taverns with dancing and music that were also frequented by Christians. The *Ghetto Nuovissimo*, the Newest Ghetto, was established in 1633 and provided comfortable apartments and even halls. But discrimination continued to increase: for example, the "Jew runs" in Carneval were a staple of public entertainment, whereby fat sparsely-clothed Jews had to take part in a race. It was also customary that the races were punishment for supposed crimes of fraud, and were repeated many times to the delight of the Venetians. Documents attest that it was also an opportunity for spectators to throw stones at the Jewish participants."

For some time now they had been in the museum with its magnificent showpieces that Lanz remembered from Calimani's catalog: silver Torah pointers that are used to read the Torah—the five books of Moses—along with besamim boxes, artfully made spice containers, Hanukkah menorahs, and a silver dreidel (a spinning top for Hanukkah festivals), menorahs and wedding rings, a Judaica key with the star of David, polished Kiddush wineglasses for blessings, and much much more.

Afterward he could only vaguely recall fragments of Caecilia's guided tour, and when he did think back, it was primarily the images and not the explanations that had left an impression. But he wouldn't forget Caecilia's presence, he thought. They strolled through connecting doors and crossed the square, the Campo del Ghetto Nuovo, to view the Baroque Scola Spagnola, the synagogue of the Iberian Jews, the largest and most elaborate in the entire Ghetto. For Lanz it was an inauguration space, an opera, from a distance resembling a Masonic Temple that he had seen in photographs on the Internet. Candelabra provided light from the floor, chandeliers from the ceiling. The long benches in the reading room were on a marble floor, similar to an old university, the tall windows draped with red velvet curtains. A continuous gallery or *matroneum*, richly decorated with ornaments, was intended for the women. The Torah Shrine, the Aron, a type of altar where the Torah scroll is kept, was located on the front wall of the Scola, facing Jerusalem. No corrections or deletions are allowed on the handwritten Torah, which means any error requires that the entire transcription be redone. The Torah Shrine was covered with an embroidered yellow-gold curtain featuring a saying from the Hebrew Bible; before it, the Bimah, the richly-decorated gilded pulpit with a lectern and a table beneath a gold-tinted Heaven made of wood. The Torah scroll was read from this podium. Above the marble portal, Moses's Tablets of the Law were depicted, illuminated by divine rays of light.

Caecilia explained that Christian architects and artisans had built and furnished the Scola, because at the time it was built, the local Jews had neither architects nor specially trained craftsmen. She mentioned the Scola Canton, the French Synagogue that had dark walnut with gilded detailing and with a relief consisting of eight paintings of biblical scenes. Most significantly, one of Moses's arms is visible, a unique exception for a *scola*, because, as you know, the depiction of living beings is strictly forbidden in Judaism. The floor of the Scola was sloping, the Aron for the Torah scrolls open, and Lanz saw that it was lined with red velvet. They sat down on one of the modest wooden benches on the Campo del Ghetto Nuovo. From this perspective a normal Venetian wouldn't have noticed that—hidden within the surrounding apartment buildings which incidentally formed a wall—there were five synagogues: the Levantine for Greek, Israeli, and Oriental Jews; the Scola Grande Tedesca for German Jews; the Scola Canton for French, the Scola Italiana for Italian, and, in the Ghetto Vecchio, the Scola Spagnola for Iberian Jews. Each of these *scolas* had been a Noah's Ark for persecuted religious ideology, a microcosm and simultaneously confirmation of a reality that society had extinguished from real life and condemned as a fiction to the realm of fantasy and madness.

It was already dark outside, and Caecilia suggested they go eat near the Rialto Bridge.

They found seats outside an *osteria*, ordered spaghetti with clams and a bottle of Pinot Grigio, and enjoyed the simple meal. At first they spoke of the Ghetto, of Calimani and his wife, and of the life in their own families.

Caecilia said that she enjoys living with her family, perhaps because she's not home much. They only thing she hates are family quarrels. Of course, differences of opinion are inevitable, and family member lie, keep secrets, conceal . . . But as long as that doesn't provoke humiliation or insults, it's all part of everyday life. Reconciliation is often not possible for a variety of reasons, usually due to the stubbornness of one of the participants, and that can lead to bad blood . . . Lanz agreed. Laughing, he explained that he had always refused to translate family sagas. But conflicts within families belong to the history of mankind. Up to the end of the Second World War, humanity, in all cultures, had consisted of countless different family stories, from nobles to slaves, soldiers or outcasts who were violently separated from their relatives. Even Shakespeare had nothing but family tragedies: from *Hamlet* to *Romeo and Juliet*, from *The Tempest* to *King Lear* or *Macbeth*. Shakespeare had made universal poetry from these stories that were enigmatic like dreams, lovely like birdsong, loud and garish like bad weather, painful like a wound, and with humor like flames from burning toys. He could tell that it was the wine that made him talk like this.

They made love all night long and didn't fall asleep until it became light.

V

The Tempest

Disoriented, Lanz suddenly opened his eyes. The velvet curtains in Caecilia's bedroom were closed, and the doorbell wouldn't stop ringing.

He leaped out of bed, wondered where Caecilia was, found his jeans and slipped them on, and looked through the peephole out into the hallway. There was Commissario Galli with a uniformed policeman, motionless, gazing at the front door. Lanz, bare-chested, opened the door. The Commissario inspected him with disdain.

"Good morning," Galli said, sarcastically.

Lanz glanced at his watch, saw that it was almost noon, and, with a gesture, invited the Commissario to take a seat in the living room. The policeman also sat down on the couch, while Lanz rushed into the bedroom to put on his polo shirt.

"We saw Signora Sereno this morning in the Gran Viale Elisabetta, as she was returning from the vaporetto station. Since you weren't at home—we were just looking for you—and since you visited the Ghetto with her yesterday, as we were aware . . ."

"Who told you?" Lanz interrupted him.

" . . . we deduced that you might be staying at her residence," Galli ignored his question and continued: "I wanted to ask if, in the meantime, you had been able to remember this or that . . ."

Lanz considered whether he should give an answer to the Commissario's question or make an excuse about his memory loss. Without coming to a conclusion, he briefly remained silent.

"I was going to come see you today anyway," Lanz replied. "I'm not trying to hide from you. I went to Torcello to think about my translation of *Gulliver's Travels*. I had been drinking all day and in the dark crossed the Devil's Bridge to a road that was bordered on both side by gardens. Somewhere around there I climbed over a fence and crawled under an elderberry bush to sleep it off."

"Do you drink frequently?"

Lanz didn't respond. He paused briefly and then succinctly told what had happened. The Commissario listened skeptically, and asked him about specific details—in which bar did he get drunk, at what time did he buy the chess game in the antique store, at what time did he leave the Lido—and wrote everything down on a notepad.

"Why didn't you tell us about this earlier?"

"I had a memory lapse, and when I first thought I was remembering things, I assumed it was all just a nightmare."

"When did you remember?"

"Last night. Signora Sereno was taking me through the Ghetto."

"Have you told anyone about the incident on Torcello?" the Commissario asked.

"No, no one."

"Not even Signora Caecilia?"

"No."

"But you do trust her!" the Commissario insisted, wrinkling his eyebrows.

"But that's precisely why I haven't told her. That might have destroyed her trust in me."

Galli didn't follow up, reached in his coat pocket, and showed Lanz a photograph of the dead man. Lanz recognized him immediately.

"Do you know this man?"

Lanz was silent and asked himself if it was better for him to lie or to tell the truth.

"His name is Borsakowski. Does that tell you anything?" Galli insisted.

Lanz was still undecided and pretended to study the photograph.

"He was—like Will Mennea, the friend of Signora Julia Ellis—involved in the smuggling and trafficking racket," the Commissario continued. "For exorbitant prices, they brought refugees across the Mediterranean to Lampedusa. And they charged even more for different Italian cities . . . Since they had previously taken the refugees' remaining money and their papers, the ones who survived were at the mercy of the gang. They sell young women, even minors, to pimps or brothels. They also provide—naturally at a price—young men to businesses that deal in counterfeit watches, clothing, purses, or gold jewelry made of copper."

"I think I remember that face," Lanz said. "But it was nighttime and the man was bloody from the beating. That's why it's so hard for me to identify him . . ."

"Do you have a gun?" Galli interrupted.

"No."

"Have you ever had a gun?"

"No."

"Perhaps brought in through Austria?"

"No. Why do you ask?"

"We don't want to waste any time and are in a hurry, as you can imagine. You simply must answer me, that's all there is to it."

"But I'd like to know why you keep asking me that question?" Lanz protested.

"You're aware that Mennea was shot."

Lanz was silent. Finally he'd had all he could take.

"So what?" he asked.

"Presumably Borsakowski's men have something to do with it."

Lanz shrugged his shoulders to indicate his disgust and stood up. The Commissario acted as if he hadn't noticed, glanced over at him absent-mindedly, and then wanted to know if it was a coincidence that Lanz, of all people, had found the hanged lawyer, Ignazio

Capparoni.

"I've told you all about that at great length . . ."

At that moment Lanz got a phone call. He turned around without saying a word and went back into the bedroom where he closed the door. It was the publisher, Dr. Occhini, who apologized that he hadn't been available when Lanz last called. Furthermore, he wanted to discuss with Lanz the "true authors" of William Shakespeare's works. When Lanz let him know that at the moment he was involved in another conversation, Dr. Occhini terminated their chat, apologizing profusely, and signed off with the hope of getting to know Lanz soon.

When Lanz returned to the living room, Commissario Galli and the policeman had already gone. For a brief moment he thought he might have dreamt the whole thing, but then he finished dressing, got the Beretta from the cabinet drawer, loaded it, and put it in the pocket of his windbreaker. He also took the apartment key that Caecilia had put out for him.

Outside the building, he waited a moment to determine whether Commissario Galli was having him watched, and to gaze out at La Giudecca Island and the ocean. He suddenly remembered the astronaut and had a desire to see him once more. On the way he recalled how often he had seen refugees or migrants in recent years and how normal the sight of them had become. Oboabona, for example, his mailman, was increasingly becoming his trusted friend. He had always liked mailmen, perhaps because they brought Lanz packages of books or a distraction. The Chiosco Bahiano across from his house was also run by an African couple. Wherever he went, he encountered other foreigners: as roving vendors on the beach, as street peddlers of souvenirs, as waiters and waitresses in the hospitality industry, and as salesmen in mask shops or as illegal street hawkers between St. Mark's and the Rialto Bridge.

The telephone rang. It was Caecilia, wanting to know if she had woken him. As Lanz walked along the canal—past blue-and-white-striped pilings, gondolas, motorboats partially covered with tarps, and arched bridges—he reported what had taken place. Caecilia was frightened that he had witnessed Borsakowski's murder, so he didn't mention what all had happened since then. He also didn't bring up his suicidal intentions on Torcello. Meanwhile he had stopped walking and was leaning against a wall by the Rio di San Vio. Paddleboats were just passing on the water and two young women in T-shirts gaily waived to him, while he concealed most everything and lied to Caecilia. She had to finish the "paperwork"—in her own words—concerning Signor Blanc's intention to make an amusement park out of the property and the villa. Lanz was stunned. That meant for six months of the year he would be subjected to noise, and he was well aware that he could no longer stay in his own house.

"You've got two, maybe three years," Caecilia consoled him, "but, generally speaking, Signor Blanc doesn't consider objections. Once he's made a decision, he sticks to it. He can't be talked out of it."

Lanz felt the pistol in the pocket of his windbreaker and once again recalled that moment under the elderberry bush on Torcello as he prepared to shoot himself.

She said goodbye, "until this evening," she promised, and Lanz made an effort to think of something other than the amusement park.

There was a gentle breeze. The awnings of the small shops were already retracted, and a fox terrier-mix ran past, followed by two children. Maybe it was best after all, he thought, to find a new place to stay. And maybe Signor Blanc would buy Lanz's house before he built the amusement park? The thought gave him some relief. Maneuvering through a maze of alleys—still struggling with the thought of the amusement park and his house—he reached the Accademia Bridge, climbed it, and stopped to gaze over the wooden railing at the Grand Canal.

Without a thought as to why he should end up at the piazza in front of the Galleria dell'Accademia, the first thing he saw was the sculpture of the giant astronaut. He immediately realized that it was being disassembled. Two small cranes were lifting the astronaut in slow motion. He was carefully raised from the chair, and then slowly floated in mid-air as if he were weightless out in space. Lanz envied his weightlessness and remoteness, because his own problems again came to mind and he didn't want to think about them. He then noticed that the hand that held the astronaut to the chairback was missing; in its place was a piece of steel where it must have been attached. It looked like a prosthesis and the astronaut like a war veteran.

The vaporetti beneath Lanz wallowed past "like old whales," he thought, since he was watching the boat traffic from up on the bridge. When the waterbuses just passed under the bridge or came out the other side, he could only see their rooftops. The many gondolas were the jauntiest, often decorated with carpets in oriental patterns and mostly occupied by Japanese or Chinese tourists. They seemed like black toy birds that never flew in the air, but, like beasts of burden, carried people through the Grand Canal as if they were aristocrats or the deceased.

At the Palazzo Franchetti with its windows framed by ornaments that resembled the *Ca' d'Oro*, the Golden House, a mounted white poster with the image of a blue earth and the inscription "TOMORROW." At the bottom margin, in smaller type, "Joseph Klibansky"—he misread it as Kliban-Sky. The poster was a fitting tombstone for the astronaut, and the funeral for the "Dreamer" was just now taking place, he concluded.

In addition, the purple flag of the Republic of Venice with the winged St. Mark's lion was flying beside the next window. It all fit together in a remarkable way, it seemed, especially since the lion had wings that it could use if necessary to provide the astronaut a final escort. The "Dreamer" was slowly being lowered onto an elongated red cargo ship that was waiting in the Grand Canal. Workers in orange-colored anoraks were closely following the operation from the garden. Not one of them spoke a word during the silent ceremony.

A young woman with a sleeping baby on her arm came to stand next to Lanz and was just as fascinated with the fantasy burial as he was. When the baby was startled by the loud motor noises from a vaporetto and began to cry, the mother nevertheless remained standing beside him, so Lanz went to the other side of the bridge and watched the event from there, from a different perspective.

In the meantime several workers secured the giant astronaut (that Lanz now compared to Gulliver among the Lilliputians) to the cargo ship, which gave him the impression of bondage. The men had first spread out blue plastic tarps over the sculpture at the spots where ropes were wound around it, at the calves and shoulders. The crane still held the giant figure in the air. Next, the large chair and the flower vases were placed on the platform behind the prow and tied down.

As soon as Lanz realized that the two freighters would soon cast off with parts of the sculpture, he quickly ran to the other side of the Grand Canal where a Line 1 vaporetto for St. Mark's was just docking. In any event, the waterbus moved out before the two freighters. He thought he had lost sight of the astronaut, but then, at the next station, the two flat transport ships passed the vaporetto, but as it regained speed, they were now traveling behind the giant white figure like an actual funeral procession. First, they closed in on the cargo ship with the white chair and the astronaut's hand. The hand was lashed to the deck in such a way that it stood up vertically, seemingly waving at him. For an instant Lanz thought about his own funeral following his suicide on Torcello, but then the waterboat overtook the cargo ship with the astronaut who was turning his back to Lanz. He looked like some bizarre piece of furniture, perhaps a huge folded-up couch, Lanz thought.

The two freighters again passed the vaporetto at the Salute station, and since the waterbus sailed on a few moments later, he saw the astronaut one more time, as he was chugging up the Canale della Giudecca. The angle from which Lanz could observe the sculpture allowed him only a view from its boots to its shoulders. For the first time he noticed that the astronaut seemed to be raising his right leg in the air, like a dog pissing. The boat turned off to the right, and as the sculpture now was headed toward the train station in the opposite direction, Lanz could only catch a glimpse of the white boots and the raised leg.

He got off the vaporetto at St. Mark's. He could tell that the wind had picked up, and when he looked off in the direction of the Lido, as he always did on his visits to Venice, he noticed that rainclouds filled the sky. He had the impression that it had suddenly become oppressively hot. Beneath the arcade of the Doge's Palace a middle-aged man was sitting in the lotus position on a stack of flood footbridges. No one paid any attention to him. He wore jeans, sneakers, a red-and-black-checked plaid shirt, an unlined parka, and looked debonair with his stubble hair and aquiline nose. Lanz approached him and noticed that the man pretended to be painting, though there were no utensils, such as brushes, paint tubes or a palette in sight. All the while the man spoke quietly to himself, but Lanz couldn't understand a word. He was just pantomiming smearing paint with one hand while holding a paint tube in the other. He was gazing at the opposing white wall, studying it, as if he had just painted it; and, in fact, he continued working without a brush or canvas, would pause, then continue on another part of the imaginary painting, undisturbed by tourists gawking at or photographing him.

Lanz strolled past the Bridge of Sighs and the San Zaccaria vaporetto station on his way to the Riva degli Schiavoni, the broad beach road along the Canale di San Marco. He was suffering from the heat and the warm breezes, and realized that he hadn't had anything to eat or drink all day. He was just coming to the impressive bronze monument to Victor Emmanuel II. He approached the shoreline of the Canale di San Marco and was watching a brightly-flashing tiny school of young fish that darted through the water and disappeared in a seaweed thicket like microscopic comets in a dark-green sky— when he heard thunder in the distance. He walked to the bistro at the bridge over the Rio dei Greci, sat down outdoors under the awning, and ordered tramezzini and a glass of Pinot Grigio.

A group of Africans had assembled on the bridge and posted two of the young men as lookouts at both ends of the bridge. He observed that they yawned out of boredom and pretended to be watching something or other, but in reality they were intently scanning to see if a policeman was approaching. The others had counterfeit women's handbags and were trying to strike up a conversation with passing tourists. They all wore pullovers, in spite of the heat. An older couple stopped and, though skeptical, asked to see the wares. Next Lanz noticed a beverage cart on the beach, its chrome ice container dripping water onto the sidewalk. Pigeons played in the narrow gap between the container and the cobblestones, and meticulously cleaned their feathers. The birds that were already clean sat in the warm sun to dry off. The elderly couple was in the process of buying one of the purses when one of the Africans, a telephone in his hand, gave a sharp whistle—in a flash all the others left the bridge with their wares and ran off into side streets or in the direction of St. Mark's. A few moments later two policemen arrived, then two more from the other side of the bridge, and the four of them conferred. As soon as the policemen had moved on, the street vendors gradually reappeared on the bridge, as if some voodoo-spell had temporarily made them invisible. Meanwhile the pigeons under the ice container hadn't let the raid disturb their feather bath.

The police didn't reappear during the entire time that Lanz was eating.

He finally paid his bill and strolled along the Riva degli Schiavoni, wondering what Oboabona, the mailman, was probably doing at that moment . . . which brought up the Ospedale al Mare, the devastated buildings and the people who were hiding out there, the so-called "illegals" without papers. They had to stay out of sight or else they would be sent back, unopened, like improperly addressed packages. And, of course, he thought of the dead child that he had encountered on the beach—it was now more immediate than it had been during the horrible days since then. Apparently he had hoped to erase it from his memory because he felt he couldn't bear the thought of the girl, he told himself, and he now realized that the dead girl was the key that made it possible for him to understand what had happened since that time.

At that moment he saw Julia Ellis in a motorboat, along with a stranger and Richard Vogel who had his falcon Alien in its leather hood on his arm. Coming from a side canal, they were just merging into the Canale di San Marco. Lanz had recognized the motorboat immediately, because Richard Vogel and Alien had taken him from the San Michele cemetery to the Lido. He instantly remembered a remark that Vogel had made back then: that a veterinarian in a side street off the Riva degli Schiavoni provided medical care for his raptors. But what was Julia doing there? Lanz asked himself. Why hadn't she left Venice? And who was the third person, piloting the boat?

Just then, one of the huge cruise ships sailed past—he had grown to hate them. The wind had gotten stronger. Lanz ran ahead to the Arsenale station, and, as he was sitting in the vaporetto, in the distance he saw the motorboat behind the cruise ship, heading in the direction of the Lido.

The sky over the island had turned black, and Lanz knew it would soon start to rain. As the waterbus drew closer to the motorboat, the vaporetto stopped at the Giardini Pubblici station. Due to the approaching inclement weather, only a few passengers got on, and when they had resumed their journey, Lanz was relieved to see that he could still make out the motorboat with Richard Vogel, his falcon, and Julia Ellis, even if they were farther off. Meanwhile he wondered what he would say if he saw Julia again. Of course he wanted to know who she really was, but could that really be so important? Several times she had gotten him in trouble, she had stolen his boat and two pistols, and she hadn't called him on the phone.

The motorboat suddenly disappeared. The only thing he could think of was that it had stopped beyond the Sant'Elena station up ahead, because it didn't reappear on the route to the Lido. Following an announcement that all water transportation was temporarily suspended due to an incoming storm, he got off at the station like all the other passengers . . . The wind had suddenly become a storm that tore at his hair, shook the branches on the trees, scattered papers, and forced people to take shelter in their houses. He saw passengers scurrying to the two small bistros behind the park, and he, too, began to run. Without knowing why, he headed for the hotel where he had slept with Julia. Halfway there, he halted, leaning into the wind with his shoulders squeezed together, because he had gotten out of breath faster than he usually did. On top of that, his telephone rang, and when he saw on the display that it was Caecilia, he hastily answered.

"I'll call you back," he gasped, wanting to end the conversation, but she made him tell her where he was and encouraged him to take shelter in the nearest building. She warned him that a tornado was heading for Venice . . .

Lanz had run down the next cross street and come to the Calle del Carnaro that led directly to a canal with a wooden bridge. He had just decided to stop at any old house and press on any old doorbell to get shelter in the lobby when he saw Julia, Richard Vogel and his falcon, along with the pilot in a baseball cap, in the motorboat that was now protected by a rain cover; they were moving in the direction of the small island's yacht harbor. Without a second thought he ran to the bridge. When the rain began, he had pulled the hood of his windbreaker up over his head and now tied it firmly as he watched the motorboat being rocked to and fro in the storm's seething rain and waves. But then he lost sight of it. And the motorboats, tied to pilings on both banks of the canal and protected by waterproof covers, were also pitching wildly—they strained at their lines, swung out into the middle of the canal, were thrown back and threatened to capsize.

Lanz glanced in the direction from which the storm had come. To his horror he saw that a mighty black funnel-cloud had formed in the grey sky above the Lagoon, a rotor that spun terrifically fast and transformed the water into white foam. But it wasn't a machine, wasn't some gigantic vacuum cleaner. It was more like the trunk of a monster elephant that scanned the ocean, looking for food. He panicked at the sight of it and ran blindly between two brick walls on a boulevard of sycamore trees to the door of a building—the Sant'Elena Church, as it turned out—barely noticing the soccer stadium on the other side. The other side, he read on a warning sign, was a ZONA MILITARE. While the brick wall of the stadium was littered with graffiti and slogans, there was not a single mural on the other side.

Lanz's thoughts, perceptions, and deliberations collided inside his head, as if they were strong rains falling from the sky, whipped by the wind that instantly dissolved into nothing, and were more and more swallowed by a feeling of fear. Meanwhile the phone in his pocket had begun to ring again, but he was in the process of pulling open the heavy iron gate to the dim and secluded church in hopes of escaping from the roaring and the pounding, the overwhelming chaos. The first thing he noticed was the chess pattern of red and white floor tiles; next he saw the tall narrow lancet windows behind the altar, but then realized that his cellphone was still ringing. A children's choir in a side chapel was singing a reclusive song of the Virgin Mary as he pushed back the hood of his windbreaker and answered the phone call. Caecilia was still worried about him. She didn't calm down until Lanz reassured her that he had found shelter in the Sant'Elena Church.

In the meantime it had become darker in the nave, and the dull horrible roar had increased. It raged around the church, and at that moment three people—a man, a woman, and an old man with a cane—tumbled in and, distraught, took off their raingear. Lanz had instantly realized who they were and watched as Richard Vogel relieved his falcon of its plastic covering; the bird in its leather hood then sat calmly as usual on Vogel's forearm. The exhausted Julia had taken a seat on one of the chairs behind the church pews and began to look around. But before she could notice Lanz, he fled into the side chapel with the children's choir that was conducted by an elderly man with glasses and a necktie. When the thunder grew even louder and the chapel became darker and darker, the choir began the hymn *Gloria e Pace*: "Gloooooooria, gloooria. Gloooooooria, gloooria," the high children's voices sang out in the midst of the thunderous din, and the women—mostly grandmothers who had come to the rehearsal with their nephews and nieces—prayed with bowed heads in the pews.

Lanz hadn't seen the face of the old man with the cane. But he assumed it was the pilot of the motorboat, Egon Blanc, at least the man's hair and posture had led him to that conclusion. The old fellow must be in excellent health, Lanz thought, because he had handled the motorboat competently in the horrible weather conditions. Still, as they entered the church, they had had to support his upper arms on both sides, his chin had fallen to his chest as if he were sleeping deeply or had become unconscious.

Lanz then heard a rumbling from the roof above the church nave and then a crashing sound on the street outside, and alternating dull and sharp noises from the impact of objects, depending on whether the roof tiles (in Lanz's estimation) landed on grass or on asphalt. He knew the sound from his time at the winery courtyard in St. Leonhard when the roof had to be replaced and the old tiles were tossed off. But those days sounded like a piano concert in comparison to today. Commotion and weird whispering silence alternated like an ebb and flow, it became dark then dusky, a lightning bolt flickered harshly and penetrated the gloom. Finally the din fell silent.

At this point the children's choir was singing *Luce Siamo Noi*. The frightened, curious, and simultaneously relieved people that had earlier prayed and sought shelter, now rose from their seats and slowly left the church. Lanz discovered a statue of the Virgin Mary beside the altar. He knew that the altar was also the catafalque for a reclining sculpture clothed with relics of Saint Helena, mother of Emperor Constantine, though all Lanz could see through the glass were a silver facemask and a silver crown, along with a purple velvet gown embellished with gold braid, precious gems, pearls, and an embroidered golden cross on the breast, flanked by two cherubim with their four wings. In addition, a chain featuring a cross adorned the figure.

In the meantime, Lanz had left his pew in the side chapel and cautiously peered into the nave. Julia was just leading the old man out, while Richard Vogel was calmly talking to his falcon. Lanz waited until they were outside and the church gate had closed behind them. He opened it—surrounded by the children with their grandmothers—and glanced outside. Right beside the entrance he saw long conical roof tiles lying on the ground—a few undamaged, the majority broken and shattered. In addition, the asphalt walkway down the boulevard between the brick walls was strewn with branches, and it was still raining. He quickly pulled the hood up over his head. The tornado had apparently dissipated over the Giardini and the storm had moved on. The children began to chatter noisily, a smaller group marveling at the number of tiles and the damaged church roof, others picking up branches or standing by a tree that had fallen from the stadium side on top of the brick wall. The grandmothers with their umbrellas excitedly urged the children to move on. The priest, too, had left the church and was trying to estimate the damage to the roof of the building.

Lanz was in no hurry. At a safe distance and concealed by his hood, he observed how Richard Vogel and Julia had lifted the old man over the fallen tree while Richard held the falcon and its rain-covering on his forearm. A moment later he was surrounded by the children who wanted to see the raptor and touch it.

The three resumed walking in the direction of their boat, that is, if the tornado hadn't destroyed it. Lanz followed them, but stayed back so they wouldn't recognize him. The children ran over to the graffiti on the brick wall, joking and laughing, while the grandmothers looked anxiously skyward to make sure a large branch wasn't going to fall from one of the trees. From the bridge Lanz could see the tornado damage to the boats. Some were drifting in the canal, some were lying keel-up in the water or had been cast ashore, one was hanging from a piling, half-sunken. Richard Vogel, Julia, and the old man had already covered the distance along the shorter sidewall of the stadium and disappeared around the corner. Lanz now focused on the canal, where limbs, branches, and fallen leaves drifted. Quite a few windows on the rental apartments beyond were destroyed. There were still very few pedestrians on the street, and the children from the church began to run home, with their grandmothers behind them, occasionally calling out the names of their grandchildren.

Lanz now hurried to catch up to Vogel, Blanc, and especially Julia. In the yacht basin he realized the true extent of the damage:

several sailboats had capsized, the masts of others were broken off. Only Herr Vogel's red motorboat was apparently still intact behind the front corner of the long jetty—apart from the hundred and more sailboats with their masts jutting upward. The damaged yachts, floating in the yellowish water, would eventually sink, that much was obvious.

But where were Julia and her companions? Lanz realized that the red boat, too, was full of rainwater and threatened to sink. Just then he made out the old man with his cane on the cross-jetty, but he still couldn't see the man's face. From a distance Lanz tried again to comprehend what was going on. First he saw Richard Vogel with his falcon Alien climbing from a yacht onto land, then Julia signaled with raised thumbs that apparently everything was okay. Two men and a sobbing woman, wrapped in blankets, were crawling out of their sailboat; apparently they had survived the tornado below deck. Just then Lanz discovered a drowned man, floating face-down in the water, and before he could get a closer look, the first naval vessels arrived, followed by boatloads of police and firemen. Older folks and children gradually gathered in front of the rental apartments on the bank, advancing to the canal out of curiosity to get a better look. Since the yachts were anchored in several rows, Lanz could only get a limited overview, and his sight-line was also restricted by a long fence, overgrown with weeds, that ran from the stadium to the end of the jetty. As the yachts were lying helter-skelter, their masts made Lanz think of the jumbled straws in the game of Pick-Up Sticks. One by one the owners of the yachts arrived, and the confusion on the jetties was perfect cover, so Julia, Vogel, or the old man wouldn't discover him. It didn't take long for the divers to get to work. They recovered the dead, and two of the arriving cadets had begun to pump water out of Richard Vogel's red motorboat. That was the moment when the paramedics arrived, and he caught sight of Julia once again as she fought her way through the firemen and policemen to get to the landing. Lanz stepped behind a group of volunteers, let Julia pass by, and followed her at a safe distance.

The cadets were also at work in the canal. First of all they were concerned with the capsized, drifting, and beached boats. Julia was hurrying over the bridge in the direction of the vaporetto station and then disappeared behind the Hotel Sant'Elena where they had embraced. Lanz didn't want to let her get out of his sight and caught up with her at the park. An almost deserted waterbus was just casting off, and a full one was approaching from the Giardini. In the meantime he hid behind trees in the small park so she wouldn't see him. After Julia had boarded, he was just able to sneak onto the vaporetto. She was gazing out a side window, motionless, while he looked for cover on the front platform behind two young men. The vaporetto chugged on toward the Lido, steaming up to the Stazione Elisabetta, shuddering, clattering, and howling. To his amazement he realized that Julia stayed in her seat as the passenger cabin slowly emptied out.

During the trip he discovered no traces of the tornado, and the vaporetto station also appeared undamaged. The two young men ahead of him stayed on board, he could smell their overpowering aftershave. Lanz still had the hood of his windbreaker over his head, while the young men looked as if they were going to a party.

He studied the timetable on the sidewall and realized that he wasn't on the Line 1 vaporetto, as he assumed, but on the Line 4.2 heading for Fondamente Nuove. This was the second time he had gotten on the wrong vaporetto. Julia was still staring out the side window as the waterbus began to move and slowly took them toward the Ospedale. Lanz thought long and hard about why Julia would be sailing in this direction, as he already could see the walls of the Arsenal. To his good fortune, the two young men remained standing ahead of him, so that he could still watch Julia without being seen.

He asked himself if it wouldn't be better to just sit down beside her and start a conversation, but something held him back. He didn't even know why he was following her and what he expected to gain from it. Of course, for a time he had had a habit of shadowing people out of curiosity and boredom, but now everything was different.

He had conflicting impressions of Julia. She had presumably shot Mennea, she had gone into hiding, she had taken his boat and his pistols twice . . . She had loved him—at least he felt relatively certain that that had been the case. It was probably this contradiction that prompted him to speak with her one more time. They had spent many hours together in the fishing cabin—a day and a night—and yet he had never had the impression that they were "meant for each other," as people say in describing spontaneous love. He had never known what was really going on with her; instead, he had the feeling that one of them was insane and the other was involved in that insanity. For Lanz the naked reality, the naked specifics they spoke about—a luxury automobile in a display window or a shark in a huge aquarium—were things that you could definitely see, but from which you were separated by the glass windows. Maybe he had only imagined most of it, he concluded. But then he could also be imagining this trip on the vaporetto . . . On the other hand, there was no doubt that he wasn't dreaming. He could leave the vaporetto at any time. He could speak with Julia at any time. Why didn't he do it? He knew this route. Whenever he saw the walls of the Arsenal, he thought of a prison. But this time it seemed like the backside of a never-ending tombstone. Even before the vaporetto approached the San Pietro di Castello station, Julia came forward to the platform, causing Lanz to quickly turn away, take his phone from his pocket and pretend to be phoning. He wasn't sure if she was actually going to get off or if she had spotted him. He immediately realized that she was leaving the waterbus. He didn't want to follow her too closely because he was afraid that she might turn around, so he waited until three other passengers and finally the two young men who had concealed him went outside. He climbed to the pedestrian bridge that spanned the water. He could easily be detected on the piazza on the other side of the bridge, so he retreated into the shelter. It wasn't until all the passengers had passed by a shoulder-high wall in front of a two-story building that he followed them. The left side looked like a residential area; on the right he noticed a beach filthy with trash and two tall construction cranes—a third had apparently been toppled by the tornado; several men in uniforms were in the process of salvaging it. Normally, he would have stopped and watched them.

The narrow uninhabited flagstone alleys between the red and yellow houses, the exposed brick walls and masonry, and the chiseled street names in black letters, the fine rain and the grey skies all contributed to the atmosphere of a deserted district.

He finally spotted Julia hurrying along another long wall to a sidestreet, and he tried, as before, to follow her without being seen. He stopped over and over again, until she disappeared between the houses. She stopped only once, at the window of a basement apartment, and called out a name that Lanz didn't understand. Finally a woman answered in French. She said she was glad that "Madame Ellis" was back, and handed her a small key through the window up to the sidewalk. After Julia had rushed off, Lanz glanced through the security bars and window screen, down into the room. He saw a model cargo ship on the windowsill, metal staffs attached to a Chinese lamp above it, and toy fish hanging by string from the ceiling. No lights were on.

He hurried to catch up to Julia, and a few feet further on came to yet another walled alley that led to a bridge over the broad Canale de San Pietro. Here, too, there were countless motorboats moored on both banks, but these had been untouched by the tornado. A massive shipyard crane was standing abandoned, and there was also no one in sight near the motorboats that were covered in white tarps. The numerous empty pilings simply added to the impression that the island was deserted.

To his surprise, Lanz suddenly saw Julia with Richard Vogel on the St. Anna Bridge. They seemed to be in a heated conversation. Lanz's first question was: Where did Richard Vogel come from? Neither the red motorboat nor the falcon were anywhere in sight. Meanwhile the two of them had gone on a bit, and Lanz speculated that Vogel had left the yacht harbor, taken the old man and the falcon to the Lido, and—if it really was Signor Blanc—left him in the care of Caecilia or one of his other employees. At that point Richard Vogel must have taken the Line 1 vaporetto for St. Mark's Square, gotten off at the Arsenal station, and followed the Via Garibaldi to the other side to the St. Anna Bridge ahead of them . . . But why would Vogel have left the old man and come running over here?

Suddenly Lanz heard the screeching of the falcon overhead and saw Richard Vogel draw a pistol from his waistband at lightning speed, just as the two young men who were with Lanz on the vaporeto stepped out of a factory building on the other bank. They didn't hesitate for an instant, reached for their own guns and quickly fired off two shots. Julia escaped by leaping into the water. Vogel stayed put and shot back. The two men hastily ran to the bridge, and after a few strides, the first fell to the ground, the second, who had lost his orientation due to the unexpected volley, tried to flee. But Lanz, his Beretta pistol in hand, shot the man several times and he fell face-first onto the flagstones.

At first Lanz didn't know what had happened, he had acted automatically, as he had been trained to do in the military. For a moment the mostly old houses on both sides of the canal seemed like an idyll out of a children's picture book, and as he ran across the bridge, the pistol still in his hand, he saw Julia with wet hair as she swam between the boats on the walled bank. He stowed the pistol in his windbreaker and, using both hands, helped to pull her up to the sidewalk. Even before he could say anything to her, Vogel was beside him, helping Julia to her feet.

"We've got to get out of here!" Vogel shouted. Again, the falcon screeched high above, and an instant later something exploded in the factory the now-lifeless two men had just left. Julia, followed by Vogel and Lanz, ran to the burning building and gazed at the flames, aghast. She then turned suddenly to Lanz, put her head on his chest, and fell into his arms.

"They've destroyed everything!" she sobbed. "My archives . . ."

Meanwhile Richard Vogel yanked the pistol out of Lanz's windbreaker pocket, threw it into the water without further explanation, and screamed frantically: "Get out of here! Don't ask questions! Take off before the police get here!" Hearing this, Lanz now realized that he had shot yet another human being.

"Thank you . . . thank you," Julia sobbed. "You've got to go . . . Please!"

At first Lanz was confused, then, without thinking, he ran across the bridge and down the Fondamenta di Sant'Anna to the Via Giuseppe Garibadi, noticing out of the corner of his eye toppled trees and broken branches on the edge of the park. He kept running along the quay of the Canale di San Marco to the Ponte della Ca' di Dio, where he stopped, gasping for breath. He remembered that this was the canal where Richard Vogel, Julia, and the old man had taken the falcon to the veterinarian, and he asked himself once again whether everything he experienced in the aftermath had only been a figment of his imagination? Maybe his mind was playing tricks on him? Maybe it was just telling a stream of lies? . . . Maybe he's been dead for a long time now and is in some afterlife? Or maybe his mind is only deluding him with that thought?

The telephone in his pants pocket rang. He pulled it out, spoke while still out of breath, and saw thick black smoke rising from San Pietro Island, presumably from the burning factory.

"Did you have a tornado?" he asked Caecilia, to confirm that he hadn't dreamed the whole thing.

"Yes, but it wasn't as bad as on Sant'Elena. We've just taken Signor Blanc to safety . . ."

"Where is he staying?" Lanz asked.

"Are you on your way home?" Caecilia dodged his question.

This was a question he has been asked since childhood.

"I don't know," he replied, as he had always done as a child. "I'll be home by evening."

At this point he pulled down his hood since it had stopped raining.

"Great, see you then," he heard her say in an afffectionate tone, ending their conversation.

So, he could now assume that his mind hadn't been playing tricks on him. When he came to the bridge where the Africans had sold the counterfeit name-brand merchandise, he noticed that everything was proceeding just as it had a couple of hours ago. "A couple of hours ago?" he asked, amazed. He hadn't stopped to think how much time had passed, but he didn't have the impression that it had any special significance. Days and nights could have come and gone, or just a minute or two.

He sat back down at the restaurant where he had eaten lunch, ordered a glass of wine, and asked the bald waiter what impact the tornado had had.

"We had a storm with squalls, but no panic. Everyone ran inside the restaurant." He laughed. "Outside, chairs were overturned, but they didn't go flying through the air." He laughed again.

"What about the Africans with their purses?"

"They're still alive, as you can see," the waiter answered sarcastically, wiping off a table; he then disappeared inside the restaurant.

There were noticeably few tourists on the street, so the illicit trade on the bridge had come to a halt. But the Africans hadn't lost their sense of humor, they laughed and joked around until a potential customer approached, when they immediately became serious and pitched their merchandise. And, as usual, they would take off running, and, as usual, the police would appear, consult each other, and then withdraw, allowing the vendors to return, take up their posts, and unpack their wares. Even the imaginary painter in the arcade of the Doge's Palace was still painting or starting a new picture on his fantasy canvas, all the while staring at the wall with a serious expression.

To calm down, Lanz strolled across St. Mark's Square. All the chairs in front of the Florian and Quadri cafés had been cleared away, along with the podium for the orchestra. The birdseed peddlers had disappeared. Now and then a small group of tourists or a lone tourist with a selfie-wand would march by, tourists were taking pictures of each other, and Lanz had the feeling that everything had returned to normal.

He boarded a vaporetto, disembarked at the Salute station, got his bearings in the alleys, at long last locked the front door behind him, and then unlocked Caecilia's apartment.

He was awakened the next morning by Caecilia's caresses. She had learned about the incident on San Pietro and the burning factory, but only that it had to do with Julia's "archives" of photographs she had prepared for next year's Biennale. Of course Caecilia wanted to know more—she interrogated him about the smallest details and was astonished at his "bravery," as she called it.

They made love into the early afternoon until a phone call from the office of Amanda Falchi, the lawyer, forced him to return to the entanglements that dominated his life.

Someone or other must have arranged for the lawyer to help him. Lanz was irritated, but at Caecilia's urging he decided to meet Falchi in her law office behind the Rialto Bridge.

Amanda Falchi sat behind her oversize desk, looking like a child sitting in elementary school for the very first time, and she leaned as far forward as she could to shake his hand and offer him a seat. The black upholstered chair was a trap: when he sat down, he sank so low that his chin was level with the desktop, while the lawyer, as he noticed, had raised her chair to its maximum height. He was compelled to look up to her, as if to a goddess. Her earrings jangled with the slightest movement, her eyeglasses were too large and slid up and down the length of her nose, and it was obvious that behind her feigned cheerfulness was a belligerent personality.

"Are you doing alright?" she asked.

"Why do you want to know?"

"Events have gotten out of control . . . I don't know if you are aware that there was a firebomb attack on your house at the Lido last night? All I know is that the kitchen, your study, and the bedroom were destroyed. The fire department received a call around 1 a.m. and they were able to save the building, but it is now unlivable. Your neighbor—Signor Egon Blanc—is offering you a house on La Giudecca with a view of the Lagoon in exchange for the ruins— because, unfortunately, that is what the house is now—if you are not interested in renovating it." She made a cheerful grimace and smiled. "Furthermore, he is willing to replace your damaged furniture. What do you say?" Now she was laughing, as if at her own joke.

"Have they captured the culprit?" Lanz evaded her question

with a straight face.

"I forgot to mention that: he was fatally shot by the police around 8 o'clock this morning at the front gate of Blanc's villa; it was a 24-year-old Tunesian." She still had a playful smile.

"What was he doing there?" Lanz asked, and considered whether he should accept Blanc's offer so quickly.

"I must go back a bit," Amanda Falchi answered, now seriously involved. "At midnight the police had surrounded the Ospedale al Mare and searched the building. In the process, 41 persons— migrants from Iraq, Syria, and Nigeria—were liberated. Three of them fled, all of them, by the way, had entered the country illegally. After they were searched and registered by the police, Signor Blanc offered them shelter in his villa. He proposed to settle them on one of his estates near Padua. Until then, they could stay in his villa. But, as you can appreciate, the mayor wants everything to proceed as quickly as possible . . . You know, because of our tourism . . . It is no small matter . . . Five smugglers and traffickers were arrested . . ."

"How long has this been going on? And how was it possible?" Lanz asked, already intending to accept Blanc's offer.

"I ask myself that very same question, and I am certain that there will be further surprises in the future."

"And Julia Ellis . . . Her factory . . ." Lanz continued.

"The perpetrators were shot by unknown persons . . . The police are investigating. Oh, yes, Signora Ellis has asked me to give this to you." She reached for an envelope and handed it to him. "Be careful, it contains CDs or DVDs—I don't really know which."

"And where is Julia?"

"Signor Ellis flew off yesterday with Herr Vogel and his falcon, and I can't say where they are at this moment. Have you read the newspaper?"

"No."

She handed him the *Gazzettino*, and on the front page were pictures of the two corpses in San Pietro, covered with blankets in front of the burning factory. There was only a small photograph of the police raid in the Ospedale al Mare and a brief account ending with the sentence: ". . . in addition, a nearby house was severely damaged by arson."

"I almost forgot," Amanda Falchi continued: "Signor Blanc also wants to replace your fishing hut. In its place he is offering you a modest weekend cottage on San Erasmo. Are you familiar with San Erasmo?"

Lanz nodded.

"I ask myself what Signor Blanc has in store for you . . . I mean, he is very generous where you are concerned."

Lanz was silent.

She handed him several computer-generated forms.

"When you have thought it over, sign the prepared documents, and I will take care of everything else for you."

Lanz was secretly relieved, reached for his pen, and put his signature on all the contracts without even reading them.

"You can see that Signor Blanc has already signed everything. That means that the contracts are now in force."

When he was done, she put the documents in a briefcase and deposited them in her safe. She also took his copies, put them in an envelope, and handed it to him.

"I shall accompany you when you report to Commissario Galli and be present at the interrogation, if you wish," she went on. "Signor Blanc has instructed me to be your counsel."

She didn't wait for his response, but took a jacket from an old walnut wardrobe, informed one of the secretaries that she was going to the Lido, and left the office.

On the way to the vaporetto station they saw several policemen and people standing at a kiosk where a newspaper vendor from some Arab country, Lanz assumed, was selling a "special edition." The headline read: "Assassination in Rome, 49 dead and 112 wounded," and below that: "Assassination threat: 'We will destroy St. Mark's Square!'"

It was strangely quiet on the Line 1 vaporetto. The lawyer was just able to snag two seats and, like the other passengers, began to read the flyers that were lying on the seats. Passengers in all the rows were huddling together, studying the leaflets, or were sitting alone, immersed in the news. It looked like an orchestra rehearsal, with musical scores and musicians waiting for their instruments. There was no noticeable fear, and no one was agitated. The passengers were compliant, like patients in a waiting room.

The only sound was that of the vaporetto motor.

Lanz gazed out at the palazzi and the rain clouds, and thought about Caecilia. He then took his phone, switched it off, and put it back in his pants pocket. A flock of seagulls flew up in front of the Salute station.

And quite a few people were waiting by the huge church, reading the "special edition."

As they passed St. Mark's Square, a fat man with tangled hair, a grey pullover, jeans, and a large shoulder bag stood up at the sliding door. *"Non promsi santasco, soleilo,"* he began shyly, but abruptly became louder. It seemed as if he were engaging in a diatribe—but in reality he was speaking in tongues. None of the words had any meaning, but he was employing these imaginary words to express his feelings. Lanz secretly called him "The Preacher." No one could understand what he was saying. At first, people just listened to him, but then most of them went back to reading the newspaper or looking out the window. That just seemed to make The Preacher mad. He became louder, began to stomp on the floor dramatically and to make histrionic gestures. Suddenly he became silent and his facial expression was that of a child whose toy has been taken away. He grew hushed, spoke sadly, but it seemed possible that at any time he could start another tantrum. The entire time he focused on a girl and an old woman who sat two rows behind Lanz on the other side of the cabin. The woman wore glasses, had a crutch, and the girl beside her appeared to be her granddaughter. The girl followed the man's performance wide-eyed. Her lips formed the words that the man muttered. Suddenly, as the vaporetto slowed with a loud droning noise, The Preacher lost his balance for a second, let out a frightened cry, grasped a chrome railing, righted himself, and seemed to snap out of it. He picked up the bag that had fallen from his shoulder, hoisted the strap, and pantomimed a Bishop's miter on his head by forming a triangle above his head with his fingertips.

"Pace! Pace! Pace!" he mumbled, blessed the passengers by making the sign of the cross and, agitated, stumbled off the ship at the Sant'Elena station. Lanz saw that he immediately wanted to turn back, because three policemen were standing there and didn't board, until the crazy man rushed off in the direction of Giardini. A conductor also got on, and while the police asked to see IDs, everyone had to show their valid tickets to the conductor. The "special edition" had been cleared away, the vaporetto transformed itself back into a normal waterbus, and everything ran smoothly, as if it were a normal day. The passengers didn't look at each other during the ID and ticket checks, but gazed out the windows, spoke quietly with each other, or feigned dozing off. At the Elisabetta station, several uniformed policemen were also checking identification cards of the waiting passengers.

The lawyer waited for most of the passengers to disembark, then purposefully headed for the entrance to the glass hall where, as Lanz saw, Blanc's beekeeper and prophet Pedar Janca was already waiting. Although he stood in line inconspicuously, just the way he held his head revealed that he was truly blind, Lanz thought. Parked behind Janca was one of the taxis that he had previously hired. He climbed into the passenger seat as a matter of course, while Lanz slid over next to Dr. Falchi in the backseat.

"It's best if we go to the Questura first. Commissario Galli is waiting for you," Pedar Janca said softly.

"No, go to my house first. I want to see it," Lanz objected.

"I don't imagine Signora Dr. Falchi will enjoy that."

"I didn't say I was doing this for her enjoyment," Lanz responded rudely.

"I can take care of myself!" the lawyer chimed in, laughing.

Pedar Janca nodded, gave the driver the address, and fell silent. The lawyer also said nothing.

The Gran Viale Santa Maria Elisabetta and the Lungomare

D'Annunzio exhibited signs of the tornado: tattered canopies above restaurants, devastated front yards. As they rode past the gate to Signor Blanc's villa, Lanz glanced through the taxi's side window and saw on the sidewalk the chalk outline of the shot assassin and some pedestrians standing around, gossiping. A police patrol car passed them in the other lane, one of the officers checked them out.

As Lanz got out at his house, he first smelled the sharp odor of burnt materials and also saw his home's four black windows without windowpanes and, beyond them, blackened rooms. A yellow plastic tape closed off the entrance, but Lanz bent down and squeezed underneath it, took out his key and unlocked the front door. The stench of the burned-out building was overpowering and grew even stronger as he began to inspect the rooms. As he went on, he discovered that everything had, in fact, been destroyed by the fire and the firefighting efforts—the walls black from soot, the plaster crumbling, the charred doors lying on floors that were also black. But he didn't find any debris or remains of furniture, of books, or of kitchen utensils. And the refrigerator, the entire built-in kitchen with stove, sink, and dishwasher had disappeared, along with the bookshelves, the chess board, his TV, the living room furnishings, his bed . . . The worst part was that his books were gone.

He found nothing but black emptiness. For a brief instant he was convinced that he was wandering through a realm between life and death, that any moment the floor would collapse and he would fall into the totally black cellar where no one could hear his cries for help. But he didn't stay in the ruins for more than a minute, he estimated, because he realized that the place no longer belonged to him. With his contract, Signor Blanc had taken over everything, so it was no longer Lanz's concern. There was just one more thing he wanted to finish—to put an end to everything that had happened to him since his suicide attempt. The burned-out house and his lost books were just the beginning. He thought about the Walther pistol, and went to look for it, holding his breath the whole time, but he couldn't find it . . . Even if he checked all the rooms one more time, he probably still wouldn't find it. He finally gave up. But the loss of his books still remained in his memory as an echo of his pain.

As he left the house, he glanced up at the roof that was also severely damaged by the fire and then climbed back in the taxi.

"I'm sorry," Pedar Janca said.

The lawyer smiled and added: "But, in just a few days time you will have an incomparably more beautiful home in its place, and Signor Blanc will replace each and every one of your books. Just now he is having a list compiled from the remnants."

Lanz understood that Signor Blanc was trying to spare him the shock of the destroyed and missing possessions, but he didn't respond. Still, the entire time he asked himself whether he should inform the lawyer that he hadn't been able to locate his Walther pistol.

He was also thinking about his impending interrogation with Commissario Galli, but he couldn't concentrate on it because he could only envision the missing Walther pistol and the blackened rooms, the overturned charred doors and the emptiness.

"The firemen," Janca was saying, "took the furniture and everything that was on fire and tossed it out the windows, and when Signor Blanc informed the police that he was going to pay for all the damage, the next morning they threw everything into two trash trucks and carted it off. Signor Blanc, as I've said, will replace your books. As his agent, I will make sure that it happens as quickly as possible."

That allowed Lanz to hope that the pistol was possibly 'carted off' along with everything else.

"Where is Signor Blanc now?" Lanz asked. "And where are the others: Herr Vogel, Herr Ashby, Herr Chang?"

"Herr Vogel, together with Signora Ellis, was taken to the Marco Polo airport yesterday, and they flew to Spain early this morning. Our gardener, Herr Ashby, had the refugees brought to Signor Blanc's villa and is taking care of everything. Herr Chang is feeding them. In addition, Signor Blanc has hired your postman, Herr Samuel Goodluck Oboabona, as a translator and caretaker for the refugees. As soon as the screening is complete, he will accompany them on their transport to the locale near Padua."

Lanz definitely wanted to discuss that with the lawyer before the questioning began.

"And how about you, what are you going to do now?" he asked Janca.

"That is up to Signor Blanc. In any event I am going to stay with the bees."

Lanz had to process all the news, and then asked whether Signor Blanc was in Spain at the present time.

"He is here on the Lido, where he feels most comfortable."

"Really? They said he was in Spain!"

The lawyer made a sound that Lanz interpreted as a stifled laugh, but the beekeeper acted as if he hadn't heard it and explained that Signor Blanc was in the hospital.

"And how is he doing?" Lanz wanted to know.

"As well as can be expected. He wants to see you."

They pulled up to the Questura. Janca also got out, wished them all the best during the interrogation, and shook Lanz's hand, his head held high while gazing off into the distance. Because of the way the man held his head and rolled his eyes, Lanz thought he was casting a glance to the heavens to show Lanz the way into the afterlife.

Inside the fence in the inner courtyard the lawyer glanced around and whispered: "Signor Blanc is gradually losing his memory. He must go to the hospital from time to time for injection therapy. But when he is released, his mind functions the way it always has."

"I had hidden a Walther pistol in my house, and it's gone," Lanz said unexpectedly.

Dr. Falchi looked up. "You are just telling me that now?"

She looked directly at him.

"I could tell them that I got it for any eventuality from Herr Vogel before he left."

"Wait!"—The lawyer took a few steps aside and talked quietly but decisively on her phone. A few minutes passed, then she came back to Lanz and said: "Herr Vogel will corroborate your testimony."

As he entered the Posto di Polizia Lido, Lanz couldn't help thinking about his burned-out house, the pungent smell, the blackened rooms and their emptiness . . . He felt miserable and admitted to himself that he was afraid. What would happen if they took him into custody? Convicted him? Put him in prison for years?

"Keep a low profile if the discussion should get around to the pistol. Just say that Herr Vogel had given it to you for your safety," Dr. Falchi said, as if to herself.

Lanz nodded automatically, but he was secretly afraid.

Uniformed officers were on telephones or sitting at computers in each of the rooms. Only Commissario Galli's office was free of such activity. He hastily offered each of them a chair, and Dr. Falchi pretended to be amenable.

"A crazy day," she said.

Galli leaned back, focused on Lanz, and then turned to the lawyer with a cynical smile: "Which questions has Signor Blanc allowed the police to ask?"

To Lanz's amazement, Dr. Falchi asked if that was all the Commissario wanted to know? If so, then she and her client would be leaving the Posto di Polizia. "In any event, no arrest warrant has been issued."

Galli observed her like a biologist studying a certain type of snail, then gazed out the window and casually asked Lanz if anything had occurred to him since their last meeting.

Lanz bit his lower lip and shook his head.

"Does that mean 'no'?"

Lanz nodded.

"You don't intend to speak?"

"We are waiting for a substantive question!" Dr. Falchi interrupted. "Do not play mind games with us, Commissario."

"And don't you play defender games with me!" Galli aggressively replied.

"It would be better . . ." the lawyer interrupted, but was in turn immediately interrupted by the Commissario: "It would be better if you were silent!"

"You cannot muzzle me!"

Galli turned to Lanz in a hostile tone: "Do you know if Julia Ellis owned a pistol?"

"I didn't see one," he answered, and felt a chill run through him.

"And did she ever discuss Mennea's death with you?"

"No."

"I don't believe that! At that time you were in a relationship with her!"

"Sorry, I just don't remember."

"I know, the accident has damaged your memory," Galli smiled cynically.

"That has nothing to do with it," Lanz interjected.

"So, do you or don't you know whether she told you about it?"

The lawyer interrupted—"Please, get to the point, Commissario . . . What is the point of these questions?"

"Were you on San Pietro yesterday, after the typhoon?" the Commissario went on, unperturbed.

"No!" Lanz responded. "Why would I have gone there?"

"But someone saw you there!" Galli raised his eyebrows, triumphantly.

"Who?" Dr. Falchi asked in a combative tone.

"A woman who lives in a basement apartment near the Sant'-Anna Bridge."

"And where is this woman?" the lawyer wanted to know.

"I wasn't there," Lanz added abruptly.

"How could she recognize the face of a passing man from her basement apartment? When I was young, I lived for a time in a basement apartment . . ."

The Commissario interrupted her once again. "There was gunfire yesterday afternoon by the Sant'Anna Bridge. Two young men were killed."

"I told you I wasn't there," Lanz vehemently countered.

"Where were you that entire afternoon?"

"During the tornado I was in the Sant'Elena Church—"

"—the gun battle took place after the tornado," Galli intervened. "What did you do after the storm?"

"I went to the yacht harbor to see the destruction."

"And then?"

"Then I headed toward Giardini and on to St. Mark's. I was curious to see what the tornado had done."

"And then?"

"Took the vaporetto to the Salute station."

"Do you still have your ticket?"

"I have a five-year ticket and ten trips stored on the chip."

"Show me your five-year ticket and the chip!" the Commissario demanded.

Lanz complied with the request, but Galli left the ticket on the table, ignoring it.

"And then?"

"You can see where I was at the time . . ."

"And you are withholding more than you're telling me! Either you can't remember or you don't know anything!"

"Do not accuse my client of improper conduct!" Dr. Falchi interrupted.

"The Commissario can't help it, because he's ignorant," Lanz caustically butted in, and continued to provoke Galli: "In your incompetence you make up all kinds of things and don't know when to stop!" At this point he really wanted to put an end to the interrogation before Galli brought up the pistol again.

The Commissario slammed his fist on the desk and leaped up. "Don't say one more word!" he yelled at Lanz. "You're a suspect! I'll have you taken away!"

"There are laws that even you must obey," Dr. Falchi forcefully interjected. "Herr Lanz has an explanation for everything or else he simply does not know. If you have grounds for suspicion, then show us your evidence!"

"You're obviously overworked," Lanz added derisively, "or drunk."

"Silence!" Commissario Galli repeated, enraged, and turned to face Lanz. "You know exactly what happened to your house tonight!"

"My client," the lawyer contradicted, "had nothing to do with the incident. He had already sold the house—that has now burned down—to Signor Blanc. The offer from Signor Blanc came two days before the fire," she lied, and continued: "That means that perhaps someone intended it as an attack on Signor Blanc . . ."

"You think you can just feed me this crap and that I'll swallow it?" Galli shrieked furiously at the lawyer.

Lanz put it all on the line and provoked the man yet again: "And you're just feeding us crap, too!" he said calmly, almost as if to himself.

With that, Galli lost all composure. He grabbed the small paperweight lying on the desk beside several ballpoint pens and threw it in Lanz's face. Lanz tried to dodge, but lost his balance and fell to the floor.

"There will be consequences for that!" the lawyer screamed and leaped up, but Galli was so furious that he then threw pencils and ballpoints and even the papers on the desk at her. The papers briefly floated in the air and fluttered to the floor. As Galli ripped a ring binder from a shelf, intending to throw this at Dr. Falchi also, she quickly bent over Lanz and tugged at his shirtsleeve—he came to his senses and got up. She quickly snatched up his vaporetto ticket and chip from Galli's desk and called out: "I will inform Signor Blanc about this," and led Lanz out into the corridor. The heavy black binder just barely missed her.

They were able to escape out into the garden and then to the street. Agitated, Dr. Falchi pulled her phone out of her coat pocket to tell Pedar Janca that he should pick them up in the taxi. But Janca, who had apparently foreseen this scuffle, was already waiting in the taxi by the garden gate, ready to take Lanz to a doctor to treat the bleeding gash on his forehead.

The lawyer helped Lanz into the cab and, waving her phone, called out: "I have recorded everything that was said in the Commissario's office! I shall put an end to this!" She turned on her heels and resolutely stomped back inside the Posto di Polizia.

They drove back up the Lungomare D'Annunzio. Lanz had a headache and could feel blood running down his cheek.

" You haven't been blessed by good fortune lately," Janca said.

Lanz understood that the beekeeper was trying to say that he *was* lucky. Since Janca said the opposite of what was going to occur, he presumably influenced fate in this way. In any case, Lanz now knew that Commissario Galli could no longer harass him. But what if someone else tormented him instead?

A bus approached and several police cars were on the road, otherwise he didn't see anyone on the street. Meanwhile Janca was still phoning. As they stopped in front of Signor Blanc's villa, Oboabona was already waiting on the sidewalk. He hurried across the street and shouted as he opened the car door: "Signor Lanz! Happy to see you! Very much happiness . . . Your head, what is happening to your head?—You are bleeding!"

"Get in," Janca urged him.

In spite of his headache, Lanz looked Oboabona squarely in the eye. "We are friends, Samuel. And my name is Emilio," he said gently.

"Yes . . . Emilio . . . And your head? Accident?"

"Someone slammed a door in my face," Lanz deflected.

"Bad . . .! But, really . . . Someone threw stone!"

"You're right," Lanz attempted to calm him down.

"First the eye and then the head!" Oboabona patted him on the shoulder, as if Lanz were a young boy. "Oboabona watches out now!" he whispered. "Oboabona found Walther pistol in house—after fire and fire department—and give pistol to Mister Ashby. For always!"

They drove past the Ospedale al Mare, and Lanz noticed police cars parked outside and soldiers on guard duty. Their trip through the narrow street became extremely difficult because it was crowded with vehicles for photographers, reporters, and television crews, so that the taxi could only move at a snail's pace. Janca offered a half-empty pack of paper tissues, and while Lanz wiped the blood off his face, he now and then glanced over at the slowly decaying hospital complex behind the wall. The windowpanes in most of the buildings were broken, like those he had seen through the entrance gate. On an extension built of synthetic materials that was apparently added on later, Lanz discovered a large triangle with the Eye of Providence; beside it, in rough script, he could make out "Kill the Police." Lanz then returned to the smashed windowpanes and the outlines of the holes that reminded him of transparent maps with black islands in a transparent sea. Or his gaze came to rest on scraggly bushes fronting the wall of a building half-covered by ivy, its windows intact, almost all the Venetian blinds raised.

As Lanz pressed another tissue to his forehead, he was suddenly overcome by the conviction that the idea he was dead and in an afterlife had been correct. The paperweight the Commissario had thrown at him was the bullet that he had put through his head on Torcello. The time sequence of his death hadn't occurred chronologically. Everything he had experienced since he put the pistol to his head under that elderberry bush had already taken place in the fourth dimension. Thoughts flooded through his head while he stared at the gigantic complex of the Ospedale al Mare and concentrated even more on his perceptions. But the decaying buildings, slowly disintegrating into dust, suggested to him that they were only dice that determined the time dimension, depending on their position.

It suddenly occurred to him that he could be crazy . . . Was it possible that his hospital stay after the automobile accident was, in reality, treatment in an institution for the insane? And perhaps he was still there, just imagining everything? He now studied a kind of cloister where he noticed on a wall in the background a puzzling graffiti of violet, green, and white lilies that could represent water canals or tree trunks, a theater stage, the maw of a dragon . . . perhaps even parts of some other event in another time dimension. Several of the windows of the Ospedale reflected the wall of the Jewish Cemetery on the opposite side of the road and a row of tall cypress trees, their canopies damaged by the tornado. His last glance, before they resumed speed, was of a watchtower-like building with a lone window. The tower's plaster was flaking, lending the entire structure an aspect of something ruined, something destroyed, that was even more poignant due to one detail: a barely visible white porcelain insulator for an electric line that no longer existed, forlorn, sticking out of the wall like a blind eye.

"You are correct," Janca said at that moment, "time is not a straight line . . ."

Meanwhile the pain in Lanz's head had increased, and dabbing at the wound with the tissue hadn't stopped the bleeding. For several minutes trees, fields, elderberry bushes and more walls flew past on both sides of the car, then the taxi turned off to the right, to a large square and a long five-story building with a number of ambulances parked outside.

"Centro di Salute Mentale," The Center for Mental Health, Lanz read on a blue sign above one of the two main entrances.

There was no one in sight, not a sound could be heard.

Oboabona and Janca helped support Lanz and rode with him in the elevator to the fourth floor. The beekeeper checked him in, while Lanz and Samuel sat down on chairs—still without encountering anyone or hearing a sound. Lanz felt extremely dizzy and closed his eyes. Darkness enveloped him . . . Black matter, the burned-out room in his house, he thought.

When he opened his eyes, he was lying on an examination table. A likeable young doctor was just treating his head wound, and a nurse, holding a suture in her tweezers, handed it to the doctor. Lanz now could feel the doctor stitching up the wound on his forehead.

"He's coming around . . ." he heard a voice say. "Do you feel anything?" she asked him.

"No."

He blinked, saw, close-up, fingers in a rubber glove, and thought that he was now taking the last step into the fourth dimension, but then relapsed into semi-consciousness. He could see snow falling, points of light that reminded him of fireflies in Signor Blanc's garden, and he felt something akin to a gentle euphoria.

When he awoke, the face of the beekeeper Pedar Janca was

bending over him, asking how he felt.

"Fine," Lanz answered, and carefully sat up.

"Before long, Signor Blanc will be taken to his refuge on Mont Blanc," Janca explained, "initially by helicopter to the terminus on the tramway, the Eagle's Nest Lookout . . . and from there, on to the Goûter Hut. People call this mountain shelter, at almost 13,000-feet altitude, an oversized Easter egg." He laughed. "More than a hundred mountain climbers can overnight there. Presently the building is at Signor Blanc's disposal. Actually, the hut was closed some time ago because the ascent had to be blocked due to the threat of landslides. There have been more and more disasters in recent years. More than seventy people have died. Signor Blanc has since purchased the refuge and had a helicopter pad built on a nearby plot of land. Whenever Signor Blanc is there, a dozen doctors and nurses are on duty, with a number of cooks, waiters and waitresses. They all wear white, though Signor Blanc does not. He can't part with his bees, lilies, and celestial jackets. It is also white from the snow almost the entire time, and storms batter the mountain hut. You are welcome to fly on up with us, if you wish."

Lanz shook his head, felt pain, but smiled anyway. Janca, his head turned to the ceiling, laughed, too. "I haven't seen it myself, I'm just repeating what I've heard," he added mischievously.

Lanz learned that, in the meantime, Oboabona was accompanying Signor Blanc, who had been taken to the nearby Venice-Lido airport in a Red Cross ambulance—also owned by Signor Blanc.

"That's why I said Signor Blanc was at his favorite place. From there he can fly anywhere in the world. Flying is his passion. As long as it was possible, he himself sat at the cockpit controls. But I'm not certain if he allows himself to pilot anymore," Janca said, and accompanied Lanz—after a final check by the doctor—back to the taxi, and they drove the short distance to the airport.

He saw the sign "Aeroporto Nicelli" above the interlaced rectangular buildings. Janca and Lanz hurried through the lobby and, after the beekeeper had shown his credentials, arrived at the runway without any further screening where a twin-engine private plane was just slowly taxiing up. Oboabona was already waiting on the tarmac; he turned, laughing, and pointed to the white airplane: "Signor Blanc flies to his mountain!" he called out, and could barely contain his joy.

They stood there until the plane had lifted into the air and disappeared beyond the white clouds. Oboabona came back teary-eyed, wiping away his tears and mumbling with a sigh: "Good bye . . . always hard."

The taxi eventually brought Lanz back to Blanc's villa where Caecilia was waiting for him. Pedar Janca and Dr. Falchi had informed her of everything and she suggested that he call a doctor, but Lanz just wanted to sleep. He no longer knew what was reality and what was dream, what existed and what didn't exist, whether he was in the third, fourth, fifth, or in the sixth dimension, or whether he was still alive or had already died.

It took him an entire week to recover. Meanwhile Caeclia had been awarded an assistantship at the Astronomical Observatory at the University in Padua and would start work in late summer. The Rome assassins had been killed, there was no attack in Venice, and the refugees were already at their prearranged destination near Padua, awaiting further instructions. And the Lido also sank back into being the world that the tourists imagined. As a doctor was removing the last of Lanz's stitches, his lawyer, Dr. Falchi, called and excitedly reported that she had submitted the original taped conversation along with a new transcript of the interrogation she had drafted to Commissario Galli and he had reluctantly accepted them. Lanz's innocence was now documented. In passing, Lanz also learned that the house on La Giudecca would be habitable in fourteen days.

It was the day Caecilia had left to finalize her contract with the Astronomical Institute. Lanz took the vaporetto from the Elisabetta station to the Salute station, gazed out the window and wondered yet again whether he was alive or already in some afterlife. The removal of the stitches and the call from Dr. Falchi rather indicated that—in case he really had shot himself—he had returned to life. He almost fell asleep at the Arsenale station and noticed that not a single policeman was guarding the station or requesting to see anyone's papers. Even the passengers behaved as usual, and damage from the tornado—with the exception of the Giardini, the Sant'Elena church, and the harbor facilities—was limited. In a word, it was almost "the way it was."

In Caecilia's apartment he made some toast, picked up his jacket, took out the envelope the lawyer had given him before the interrogation and found two unlabeled DVDs. He put the first one in Caecilia's laptop. It turned out that it contained photographs—in fact it was a documentation of the individual buildings and rooms of the Ospedale al Mare. There were no people present, just the desolation of decay: empty damp rooms, the walls dark-grey from mildew . . . a white metal cabinet, blocked by two beams . . . wheelchairs of steel tubing . . . parts of a filthy stone floor in a checkerboard pattern . . . a rusted manhole cover . . . a wall where much of the plaster had fallen off so you could see the bricks underneath . . . numerous coat hooks . . . stair steps thick with fallen chunks of plaster . . . a decaying empty blue swimming pool in a hall that used to be painted with blue-and-white stripes. Lanz saw that the old blue-and-white striped radiator was also rusting. Furthermore, upended chairs and patient beds that looked like strange giant dead beetles, their legs frozen in mid-air . . . a run-down heating system: the huge brick oven without its doors . . . a round white surgery light with four purple circular spotlights . . . a stairwell with two automobile hubcaps in front of a floor-to-ceiling arched window . . . a decimated large building, completely covered with mold, its exterior plaster gone, except for a small yellow patch underneath the balcony . . . a hall with tall windows and countless white spherical lamps hanging over a shattered trash-littered floor . . . a long corridor inside one of the buildings, with numerous windows and broken doors once equipped with glass panes, now in ruins, piled along the wall near the entrance. Then, outside in the overgrown park, a rusty woman's bicycle without wheels that was tossed aside against a sycamore tree standing in a thicket . . . Remnants of an old exterior staircase and the hospital's operating theater with its colorful ceiling painting and pillars, in addition to a stage with a closed white curtain and a balcony for the audience. Finally, three executed human traffickers, resting in large pools of blood. They are lying on their stomachs in pseudo-military uniforms like lifeless mannequins.

Lanz put the DVD back in its sleeve and inserted the second one into the laptop. "My Archives," he read on the label. There were photographs of devastation: rusted locomotives and rusted cattle cars on a field in Bolivia . . . the rusty gutted pre-war model of a car in a deserted village in Poland . . . the ruins of a church, overgrown with weeds and bushes in the former GDR . . . a building in Chile, blown volcanic ash filling it to the roof . . . a church steeple, rising from a red lake near an abandoned copper mine in Romania . . . timber beams, the only reminder of a cavernous old factory in Italy . . . ghost towns, ghost hotels, ghost theaters, ghost skyscrapers in many countries around the globe . . . an enormous empty concert hall in Spain, its piano shrouded in spider webs . . . an empty prison with thousands of now useless iron bars in America . . . rusted shipwrecks in the sands of the dried-up Aral Sea in Kazakhstan . . . the abandoned industrial island of Hashima and the disabled Fukushima nuclear power plant in Japan . . . Chernobyl after the nuclear disaster in the Ukraine . . . the skull museum and victims of the Khmer Rouge in Cambodia . . . the Auschwitz extermination camp in former Nazi Germany . . . the museum and memorial in Hiroshima with pictures of the atomic bomb attacks in Japan . . . a decommissioned hydroelectric power station in England . . . a car-barn with plundered streetcars in Poland . . . snow-covered airplane wrecks in Iceland . . . a derelict roller coaster in the ocean along the coast of America . . . abandoned amusement parks with rusting Ferris wheels . . . castle ruins in Scotland and Austria . . . closed monasteries with forgotten libraries in the Czech Republic . . . the remnants of an off-shore drilling platform, destroyed by an explosion . . . dozens of wrecks of Russian tanks in Afghanistan . . . military cemeteries in Italy and France . . . one horrific image after another . . . Lanz studied them intently, with the thought that he was seeing the world following the extinction of mankind.

He later took the vaporetto to the island of La Giudecca, lingered on an extended wooden bridge, and for the first time saw his new house on the Fondamente San Angelo. Curious, he hurried down the small street and was soon standing in front of the building's scaffolding. Inside the house, workers were painting the rooms all in white. They wore dirty white coats and basically ignored him.

Lanz climbed the white staircase up to the second floor, stepped to the window and happily looked down on the Rio del Ponte Lungo and the docked motorboats and sailboats. The tornado hadn't caused any damage here. A white poodle barked on the sidewalk below. Even the clouds in the sky were white. An old white table was standing behind him in the middle of the room where he found a package with a note signed "Your Pedar Janca." He sat down on one of the kitchen chairs and opened the package. He first took out a colored layout, unfolded it, and saw that it was a game, based on a city map of Venice. *Start* was Lanz's house on the Lido, *Finish* was St. Mark's Square. All the locations that had played a role in recent events were highlighted in red and indicated that the game token could either be penalized by returning to *Start* or might advance several spots closer to the *Finish*. He found not only Torcello and Sant'Elena, but also the San Michele and Jewish Cemeteries on the Lido, the beach as well as the junkyard in Alberoni, the fishing cabin on Pellestrina or the square behind the San Pietro Bridge with the workshop for Julia's pictures, and finally, Caecilia's apartment. In another small box were tokens and two dice. He took out the tokens and had to laugh when he realized that their heads resembled people he had encountered. At the base of the figures were initials of the people they represented: RVA for Richard Vogel and Alien, P.J. for Pedar Janca, J.A. for James Ashby, and M.CH for Min Chang, G.O. for Goodluck Oboabona, J.E. for Julia Ellis, C.S. for Caecilia Sereno, and C.G. for Commissario Galli. There were also tokens for Mennea and his bodyguards—Giorgio Fermi in his dog mask and Manuel Saltesi, dressed all in black—and he recognized Borsakowski, Ignazio Capparoni, the lawyer who hung himself, and Dr. Amanda Falchi. The figure of Egon Blanc, which was larger than all the other tokens, had no face, only a head with the initials E.B.

Lanz knew that in the future he would play the game frequently, perhaps until the time when his token was the first to reach the St. Mark's Square *Finish* line. He packed everything back up, put the package under his arm, and left the house while the painters were still at work, painting the walls white. He discovered that the piled banana crates contained books, above all, a leather-bound edition of the works of William Shakespeare. He put the packet with the game on one of the scattered boxes with vases, dishes, glasses, silverware, lampshades and curtains, took the volume with Shakespeare's *Tempest* under his arm, and boarded the next vaporetto back to the Salute station. It gradually grew dark. Various lines from Shakespeare's plays went through his head. So, first he would translate *The Tempest*—that much he knew for certain. And he wasn't really worried about which one he would do after that. He was happy and thought about Caecilia. When he came to the building with her apartment, she came running to him. Even from a distance she began waving to him, laughing.

#

AFTERWORD
"Deaths in Venice"

Gerhard Roth was born in Graz, Austria, on June 24, 1942, the son of a physician and a nurse. He studied Medicine at the University of Graz to fulfill his parents' expectations, but quit to work in a data-processing and computing center in order to support his wife and three children. His first publication, at the age of 30, signaled a new trend in Austrian literature and allowed him to focus entirely on his literary craft. His resulting seven-volume cycle, *Die Archive des Schweigens* (The Archives of Silence) dealt with the development of fascism in Austria, and was followed by another seven-volume cycle entitled *Orkus* (Hades), that featured "foreign" crimes, based on his travels to four continents—to the USA, to numerous European countries, then to Israel, Egypt and Japan; in yet another cycle set abroad, *Hell is empty—And all the devils are here!* is the second novel in a projected trilogy set in Venice. Roth is the recipient of almost thirty literary prizes spanning four decades, thus confirming the enduring importance of his work. Along with his devotion to literature, he has frequently been praised (and loudly criticized!) for his political engagement, his outspoken support for social causes, and documentation of crimes against humanity. For the past thirty-five years he and his second wife, Senta, have been living in Vienna and in a small farmhouse in Styria.

STYLE

In his early works, Roth frequently employed extended complex sentences, packed with information and asides. But over the years, he has consciously worked to simplify his prose, beginning with the actual creation of text: he has developed a system by which he begins a new manuscript in longhand, dictates that text into a recording machine, and a typist enters that into a computer; printouts are then edited multiple times until Roth is satisfied with the result; the oral component contributes to his goal of keeping the style "simple."

He is simultaneously a visual artist, with his main character's intellectual interests and cultural education indicated by the inclusion of numerous illustrations. A talented photographer of seven published photo albums, Roth uses his photos to remind himself of the concrete reality he presents in his fiction. In addition, the many detailed descriptions of physical edifices and venues (vaporetto stops, museums, palaces, streets, colors) also provide an anchor, placing his character in recognizable and familiar sites and thus strengthening the novel's credibility.

Roth is a realist in the grand tradition. The entire novel is told in the third-person from the main character's perspective, based solely on his experiences and perceptions, his hopes and fears. To this end, Roth frequently employs run-on sentences, providing a stream-of-consciousness that reveals Lanz's momentary reactions to stimuli: changing conditions, encounters, thoughts and memories. Readers are limited to and thus dependent on Lanz's interpretation of events, since we experience them simultaneously with and through him; we can then judge his responses and the results. There are outside entities that provide a complement to his perception of reality, such as newspaper articles and information from others: Commissario

Galli, Oboabona, Julia, Vogel, et al. In addition, real-life events—for example, the tornado and the Klibansky sculpture—corroborate actual reality and thus counter Lanz's delusions of an afterlife or possible insanity.

A common thread in Roth's later novels is the extent and variety of life experiences. Lanz encounters a foreign city, its structures, history, ambiance, etc. In this novel, Lanz also comes under the influence of hallucinogenic drugs and moves about the city, seeing familiar surroundings as if for the first time, even if it is only the detritus of a modern society:

> The more closely Lanz looked, the more surprised he became that he had never paid any attention to the beauties of everyday life. But it was precisely things he had overlooked that now provided such wonders, he now realized . . . It was as if his brain were trying to show him how the matter he had overlooked was actually a world unto itself. (103)

Roth also expands his character's knowledge through interaction with various disciplines; for example, with viniculture, archaeology, astronomy, falconry, botany, and apiculture—a recurring feature in recent fiction by the autodidact, Roth.

Roth has also been engaging in literary experimentation of late, emphasizing numerous interpretive possibilities. In *Labyrinth*, five narrators cobble together a sequential tale. Or is one of them the author of four distinct heteronyms, à la Fernando Pessoa? To muddy the water, the Writer in *Labyrinth* states: "I'm beginning to think that a work of art is nothing less than the artist's monologue with his own madness (241)." In *Grundriss eines Rätsels*, the writer Philipp Artner has supposedly been killed in a gas explosion, but then reappears as an omniscient narrator and as a gorilla of the same name. Consequently, depending on which reality the reader believes, we encounter two possible readings, two possible novels, and it may be impossible to decide which view predominates. In his current novel similar doubts arise as to the reality of events, as will be discussed later.

Gerhard Roth's Venice novels form a provisional trilogy or triptych in and about the city. Like his literary heroes, Kleist and Kafka, Roth places normal unsuspecting characters into baffling situations that destroy their everyday routines with a life-and-death scenario; the characters' responses constitute the plot. One reviewer summarizes our current novel thusly:

> As is so often the case with Roth, a middle-aged man in a serious life-crisis is at the center. In this instance it is the literary translator Emil Lanz who had settled in the city of Thomas Mann's famous story *Death in Venice*. Lanz is searching for the same thing, that is, death by suicide.[1]

SHAKESPEARE'S *TEMPEST*

At first glance, the obvious references to Shakespeare—evident in the title and the introductory quote, as well as in Lanz's intended translation of the Bard's play of the same name—would seem a tantalizing hint as to the novel's intent. As one commentator notes:

> The tornado that destructively breaks over Venice and forces Lanz into a church, is, of course, an illusion to the tempest in Shakespeare's play of the same name. The spirit Ariel is represented by the falconer named Ricard Vogel. The archetypical Caliban stands for the African migrants whose sad fate is described by

---

1 "Was aber ist nun die Handlung dieses Romans? Wie so oft bei Roth steht im Mittelpunkt ein Mann mittleren Alters, der in einer schweren Lebenskrise steckt. In diesem Fall ist es der literarische Übersetzer Emil Lanz, der sich in jener Stadt niederlassen hat, von der es in Thomas Manns berühmter Erzählung heißt: "Tod in Venedig." Den sucht auch Lanz, genauer gesagt den Freitod, den Suizid." Autor SWB, interview "Venezianische Trugbilder," in *Onetz*, August 9, 2019.

Roth, while the mysterious multi-millionaire Egon Blanc (who directs the inscrutable events in Venice) can be no other than the magician Prospero. But simultaneously, the characters in *Hell is empty—And all the devils are here!* are not simply their literary antecedents. With his new novel, Gerhard Roth has created an independent narration that can be read on several levels.[2]

The parallels are certainly obvious: a cataclysmic event (both the actual gratuitous tornado and murders involving Lanz), magic (Blanc's unexpected generosity), and blossoming love affairs (with both Julia and Caecilia). Though the novel does not "end" per se— and thus makes it difficult to speak of a "happy ending"—, we definitely leave Lanz with prospects for a better future.

LONELINESS—CURSE OF THE AGES

While Gerhard Roth has typically included several illustrations in this latest novel, I take the liberty to insert yet another that informs his main character, Emil Lanz: Albrecht Dürer's *Melencolia I*, indicating the main character's loneliness and resulting depression.

At the outset, Lanz is alone. He wife has died and he has no family or friends, no apparent acquaintances, not even a household pet. His day-to-day existence is monotonous and boring. He is

---

2 "So ist der Wirbelsturm, der vernichterisch über Venedig hereinbricht und Lanz in eine Kirche flüchten lässt, natürlich ein Verweis auf den Sturm aus Shakespeares gleichnamigem Theaterstück. Hinter dem Falkner mit dem sprechenden Namen Richard Vogel verbirgt sich der Luftgeist Ariel. Hinter den afrikanischen Migranten wiederum, deren trauriges Los von Roth geschildert wird, steht archetypisch Caliban, während der mysteriöse Multimillionär Egon Blanc, der im Hintergrund der un-durchschaubaren Vorgänge in Venedig die Fäden zieht, niemand anderes sein kann als der Zauberer Prospero. Doch zugleich lässt sich das Hand-lungspersonal von Die Hölle ist leer, alle Teufel sind schon hier nie simplifizierend zurückrechnen auf die literarische Vorlage: Gerhard Roth hat mit seinem neuen Roman ein eigenständiges Erzählwerk geschaffen, das sich auf vielfältige Weise lesen lässt." Uwe Schütte, "Venezianische Stenogramme von Gerhard Roth," *Wiener Zeitung*, April 27, 2019.

drawn to the literary figure of Gulliver, whose initial shipwreck and later life among unfamiliar tribes mirrors Lanz's own exceptional status, as even his profession is a lonely endeavor. For a translator the task is, as with most professions, routine: he assembles his source materials, relevant dictionaries and thesauruses, encyclopedias and specialized reference works, and perhaps even interpretations, and then proceeds; only the text offers any variation. Otherwise, within the scope of his talents and preferences, one text is much like another. Lacking any other raison d'être, Lanz has decided to end this life.

DEATH AND TRANSFIGURATION?

Lanz is unexpectedly forced back into existence by the death, the murder, of a complete stranger, an anonymous man on the island of Torcello. Lanz realizes that his concept of reality—his daily existence and routine—has been challenged, and repeatedly questions whether this new reality is a consequence of his attempted (and successful?) suicide and if he is now residing in some form of afterlife. Was there really a murder right before his eyes? Or has he, in fact, committed suicide and is now experiencing a "fourth dimension" or some other unknown reality?

At the beginning of the novel, during his translation of *Gulliver's Travels,* Lanz anticipates just such possibilities:

> From that point on, the author Jonathan Swift had all the possibilities of a fantastic journey at his disposal. Had it only been a dream? Had Gulliver gone insane as a result of his extraordinary experiences? Had everything simply been a fabrication, constructed from some seaman's yarn? Or was it actually based on a true story, even if in some exaggerated sense? (12)

Yet another possibility arises during his rambling thoughts on Kafka's *Amerika,* as the main character attains a type of salvation when he is accepted into the Nature Theater of Oklahoma: "Or else Karl has already died and gone to heaven." (24)

Lanz's reality has been changed dramatically, seemingly in an instant and with unpredictable results: his boring lonely routine has been shattered, from his drug trip via the dried bits in his tea to threats, attacks, gun battles with gangsters, and ultimately killings; moreover, his fishing cabin and his home—especially his treasured library!—have been destroyed by arsonists.[3]

---

3 This is familiar territory for Gerhard Roth: "For as long as I can remember, I have been attracted by misfortune—death, suicide, crime, hate, madness (...) For me, misfortune is real life." Roth: "Solange ich denken kann, zog mich das Unglück an—der Tod, der Selbstmord,

Yet, almost unbelievably, Lanz the widower, the loner, the potential suicide soon has intimate relationships with two accomplished young women—coincidental sex can be seen as an indication of vitality. And, in yet another unexpected stroke of good fortune, a mysterious benefactor provides him with a new house and vacation home, an unrestricted budget to replace his library and furnishings, and an incredibly lucrative contract to translate the works of his revered Shakespeare over a twenty-five year period— for many translators a dream come true. In a matter of days he has a stimulating and rewarding new life. Has he indeed died and gone to Heaven?

But this type of "heaven" is hardly an attractive alternative: while Lanz suffers injury and loss (though apparently not death), he now faces a milieu of brutality and carnage: Borsakowsky executed, Mennea shot on his sailboat, the lawyer Capparoni hanged, five various mobsters gunned down—Lanz kills two of them himself! This life-and-death situation forces him to focus on his own survival, on killing or being killed.

Before his planned suicide attempt, Lanz visits the Basilica Santa Maria Assunta on Torcello, viewing the huge mosaic depicting the torture and suffering of sinners and unbelievers—like Lanz himself. Since Lanz is an avowed agnostic, he dismisses the possibility of an afterlife in the traditional Heaven:

> On the surface he was sometimes an atheist, sometimes an agnostic. He considered the major religions 'assembly-line religions' and always refused to talk about faith, the afterlife, or reincarnation, because then one banality inevitably led to another. (23)

In Lanz's case, this is regrettably no heaven, for his present and future are still unresolved. He is left with the possibility that he

das Verbrechen, der Hass, der Wahnsinn (…). Im Unglück sehe ich das eigentliche Leben." In: Hans Rauscher, "Schriftsteller Gerhard Roth: Unter dem Nussbaum," *Der Standard*, July 11, 2020.

has gone mad—like the "imaginary painter" at the Doge's Palace, "The Preacher" and the "opera singer" on the vaporettos—and is now dwelling in an insane asylum. But he clearly has freedom of movement on familiar terrain with familiar routines and has no restrictions in that regard. He acts differently in response to specific situations, but has no mental limitations or incapacity.

The inserted illustrations, the physical geography and weather relate to Lanz's actual reality and not to some fantasy world, madness, or reincarnation after his putative suicide. With the physical pain and injury he suffers—being assaulted, run-over on his bike, or bloodied from a paperweight strike by Galli—one would, of necessity, lean to the real life option. Aside from his various wounds, Roth offers three indications that support this as reality: the appearance of Joseph Klibansky's astronaut sculpture, "Self-portrait of a Dreamer," that was actually installed in Venice at the Palazzo Franchetti from March 24 to May 1, 2016, and the presence of a tornado that struck Venice that same year on June 4; another instance that supports a continuation of verifiable reality is Lanz's visit with the living Italian writer Riccardo Calimani, the author of works about Jewish history in Venice.

TIME AND MEMORY

In his confusion and inability to cope with present circumstances, Lanz questions whether he hasn't arrived in some fourth dimension, i.e., in another, unfamiliar "time." This is expanded in the examination of chronological vs. experienced time. Our life-"time" is a series of experiences in chronological order—as exemplified by the narration of Lanz's experiences in this novel. Memory, however, is not bound by chronology: our mind can dredge up random moments from any point in our past. In basic terms, historical reality is objective time, memory is subjective time. Objective time is a product of *Homo sapiens*, of thoughtful intelligence, while subjective time may be manipulated by *Homo ludens*—thus the mention of "games" in the novel, such as Rubik's Cube in Lanz's youth, chess, and the Venice "game" at the novel's conclusion. Like the Cube and its one possible solution, there is only one true chronological time, measured by clocks and calendars, one valid sequence of causes and effects. Yet our memory can "play" with isolated events or characters, recalling them and combining them into fanciful possibilities of "what might have been."

Since we already know the objective course of world history, Blanc's notion of Cerebral Archeology is intended to investigate the subjective memories of dead individuals and provide yet another interpretation of events—how they were experienced and evaluated by each individual, famous or humble, and thus serve as a chronicle of how each person "lived"—though we must note the caveat that memory is, of course, flawed and not necessarily a reliable marker of past events.

> The scenes had no obvious chronology, but appeared and disappeared spontaneously and with no apparent concept—Lanz had no idea what Richard Vogel had in mind . . . .
>
> "You're wondering about what I've just showed you. Signor Blanc has founded a new medical science at a California university, under the designation Cerebral Archaeology. We have just been watching memories from the brain of a deceased person. In other words, research has advanced to the point that we can visualize images from a person's memory stream after his death. A cohort of scientists is working on making the appropriate sounds audible; a different group is establishing a chronological sequence based on the coloration of the images and the age of the memories. With brain archaeology we will be able to refine the history of the human race down to the smallest detail. In the future each brain of a significant or powerful human being will be reconstructed and analyzed down to the smallest detail, in light of their

physiological condition after death . . . Just imagine, we would have the opportunity to see and analyze the memories of Mozart, of Shakespeare or Hitler and Stalin, of every criminal or artist, but also those of the common man" (188).

Yet another aspect of time and memory is interwoven into the Venice board game at the end. The "game" only pertains to the past, since the present is malleable, is being experienced in the moment, and the future is basically unpredictable (in spite of Pedar Janca's assumed prophecies). From the end of the novel forward, neither Lanz nor the author knows what will happen next—perhaps the character (or the author!) might die and nothing further would transpire. This gift from the prophet Janca changes nothing about the actual events in the novel: Lanz will still end up at Caecilia's apartment, as in the novel's final sentence. The "game" only confirms the reality of the events, dispelling notions of an afterlife or of insanity. However, the "game" supplants the actual chronology of events and thus encourages Lanz to speculate on the infinite number of possible ways the recent past might have been different—how and when the various personalities interacted, which would most certainly change the entire plot: had Lanz not witnessed the murder of Borsakowski, for example, everything that followed would be different; perhaps he would not have conquered his loneliness and depression and indeed have ended his life. Still, such speculation, such "play" as to "what might have been," could hardly have led to a more propitious result for Lanz.

CONCLUSION

Roth has said: "In spite of the Hubble telescope, we don't know enough about the universe, and despite electron microscopy not enough about the microcosm."[4] In the context of this novel, Venice is

---

4 "Wir wissen trotz Hubble-Teleskop nicht genügend über das Universum und trotz Elektronenmikroskopie nicht genügend über den Mikrokosmos." Sven Hanuschek, "In der

the macrocosm, while Lanz represents a microcosm. The development of Emil Lanz's character and his human potential for beauty as well as brutality!—the extremes of the main character's personality, from craftsman to killer—is magnified in the entity that is Venice.

Venice is not merely the backdrop for the events that occur, but an equally significant co-character, an aggregate of the individuals who have contributed to its makeup. Critics have observed that Roth's Venice triptych represents Hell, Purgatory, and Paradise. Roth concedes that to have been his organizational principle:

> Venice is timeless, the city is a revelation, it shows what mankind truly is. Not only history depicts who we really are, it is more evident in art. The true face of mankind becomes accessible, visible and tangible in literature, in architecture, music, the fine arts. I was aware of that when I began my Venice project.[5]

Venice features magnificent palaces, museums, and churches, and the reader is led, as if on a guided tour, through the wondrous city. However, Roth insists: "Paradise is, of course, a sham."[6] This striking paradox is embodied in the milieu, that Venice is indeed a different reality.[7] Beside the opulence, Venice also features poverty, oppression, intolerance, and brutality: two representative sites are the world's original Jewish ghetto and the ruins of the Ospedale al Mare where minority inhabitants such as migrants, refugees, and victims

---

Kunst wird das wahre Gesicht des Menschen nachlesbar," in: *Frankfurter Rundschau*, June 6, 2019.

5 "Venedig ist zeitlos, die Stadt ist eine Offenbarung, sie zeigt, was der Mensch wirklich ist. Nicht nur die Historie stellt dar, wer wir in Wahrheit sind, viel mehr noch die Kunst. In der Literatur, in der Architektur, der Musik, der Bildenden Kunst, wird das wahre Gesicht des Menschen nachlesbar, sichtbar und fühlbar. Das war mir bewusst, als ich mit dem Venedig-Projekt begonnen habe." In: "Das wahre Gesicht."

6 "Das Paradies ist natürlich eine Fälschung." In: Ute Baumhackl, Werner Krause, Bernd Melichar, "Gerhard Roth: 'Das Paradies ist eine Fälschung,'" *Kleine Zeitung*, June 23, 2017.

7 "In Venedig ist man in einer anderen Wirklichkeit." In: "Fälschung."

of human trafficking—today's version of the Jews—are segregated.

The piling of contrasts—Venice as a city of splendor and horror, and all shades and variations between the two extremes—emphasizes the variety and extremes of life itself. Roth has said: "You can see all of human culture there, the city of Venice reveals what man is. In his cruelty, his beauty, in food and drink."[8]

A precursor to the Venice exposé is Roth's *Eine Reise in das Innere von Wien* (A Journey into the Bowels of Vienna).[9] Vienna, one of the world's most beautiful cities, with an enviable tradition of fine arts, music, and literature has also been one of the world's most brutal venues, and not only during its infatuation with National Socialism. Roth investigates several centuries of barbarity by the Viennese. Like Vienna, Venice is a showcase for the most noble of human accomplishments. However, below the surface lurk the most despicable traits of our species. Venice is the product of the entire scale of human endeavor, like the individual humans that formed it. That said, we must focus on Emil Lanz and his contributions to the legacy of this city.

In a categorization of his Venetian novels, Roth has emphasized that he considers them "Verbrechensromane," crime novels, and not "Kriminalromane, criminal novels.[10] There are, of course, criminals galore from the mob, but the novel is not primarily about the Mafia's crimes, but those of Emil Lanz, an educated intellectual who participates in the creation of fine art as a translator of classic literature and is then forced from his self-constructed cocoon to confront his human boundaries. What are his capabilities, when life is reduced to kill or be killed? What potential depths lurk in his subconscious, what emotions will he tap: "Dream, shame, greed,

---

8 Roth: "Man sieht die gesamte Menschheitskultur dort, die Stadt [Venedig] zeigt dir, was der Mensch ist. In seiner Grausamkeit, seiner Schönheit, im Essen und Trinken." Hans Rauscher, "Schriftsteller Gerhard Roth: Unter dem Nussbaum," *Der Standard*, July 11, 2020.

9 Gerhard Roth, *Eine Reise in das Innere von Wien*. (Frankfurt am Main: S. Fischer, 1993).

10 "Simpel betrachtet könnte man die neuen Bücher als Kriminalromane bezeichnen, aber es sind Verbrechensromane." In: "Fälschung."

fear, joy, despair or sadness transform our perception."[11] Under the proper circumstances, like all human beings, he may be capable of every possible emotion, every possible deed. Yes, and he may even be capable of murder . . . several of them!

Richard Vogel provides further examples of the extremes of human behavior and capabilities:

> As we are standing here, people are plotting against you, are betraying you and dragging you through the muck. People think you are ridiculous. People are laughing at you. People want to destroy you, to crush you like some pesky insect. Everyone you know has already lied to you, betrayed you, tricked you, belittled you in the eyes of others, or spit on you—and the entire time you haven't the faintest idea. However, the problem is that you're doing the exact same thing to others and are nevertheless indignant when you learn what's been happening behind your back (186).

Thus our mild-mannered suicidal bookworm, Emil Lanz, witnesses a murder and his humanity requires immediate involvement. He is able to kill others in its wake, but ultimately to have hope, to love and live again. Lanz interprets Klibansky's sculpture *Self-portrait of a Dreamer* as a representation of these extremes—an astronaut who "had just discovered the terra incognita within himself, his own fears, his doubts, and his dreams of a world he knew to be his home." If Cerebral Archaeology hopes to answer "the eternal question of what it means to be a human being" (188), that, too, is precisely the question Gerhard Roth investigates with Emil Lanz in this novel.

#

---

11 "Ich versuche die inneren Vorgänge gleichwertig zu den äußeren Vorgängen darzustellen. Traum, Scham, Begierde, Angst, Freude, Verzweiflung oder Trauer verändern unsere Wahrnehmung." In: "Das wahre Gesicht."

The Author

Gerhard Roth (1942–2022) was born in Graz, the son of a medical doctor and a nurse. He originally intended to study medicine, but soon discontinued his studies. For ten years Roth worked as a computer programmer to support his growing family, but since the mid-1970s he was exclusively a writer. His major works consist of a cycle of seven novels, *Die Archive des Schweigens* (The Archives of Silence), and another novel cycle, *Orkus* (Hades). His work has earned extensive critical acclaim over the years, including the Döblin Prize (1983), the Kreisky Prize (2002), and the Grand Austrian State Prize (2016), among many others.

The Translator

Todd C. Hanlin (1941–2022) was Emeritus Professor of German at the University of Arkansas. He authored a book on Franz Kafka, edited Charles Sealsfield's *Austria as it is*, and a collection of essays entitled *Beyond Vienna: Contemporary Literature from the Austrian Provinces*; he wrote on numerous Austrian authors, translated a dozen novels and a similar number of plays, as well as a volume on *The Best of Austrian Science Fiction*. Hanlin translated six novels by Gerhard Roth, including the Venice trilogy, all for Ariadne Press.

www.ingramcontent.com/pod-product-compliance
Lightning Source LLC
Chambersburg PA
CBHW072231300425
26020CB00009B/304